IVORY TOWER

BOOK ONE IN THE MASTERMIND DUET

MORGAN ELIZABETH

Copyright © 2022 by Morgan Elizabeth

All rights reserved.

No part of this book may be reproduced in any form or by any electronic or mechanical means, including information storage and retrieval systems, without written permission from the author, except for the use of brief quotations in a book review.

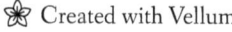 Created with Vellum

To all the girls who thought Tony Soprano was probably a hottie when he was younger.

A NOTE FROM MORGAN

Hey Reader!

Thank you so much for choosing to read Ivory Tower! As a born and bred Jersey girl, shows like the Sopranos and mafia influence has always intrigued me. Being able to bring my own spin to it has been a blast.

This is book one of two, meaning we're going to get two full novels of Dante and Lilah!

Ivory Tower contains mentions of cheating, verbal, physical, and financial abuse, assault, violence, gambling and addiction. Please always put yourself first when reading—it's meant to be our happy place.

I love you all with my whole being.

-Morgan Elizabeth.

PLAYLIST

Don't Blame Me - Taylor Swift
    Humble Quest - Maren Morris
    Fancy - Reba McEntire
    Growing Sideways - Noah Kahan
    To Hell and Back - Maren Morris
    Mastermind - Taylor Swift
    Misfits - Magnolia Park
    Anti-Hero - Taylor Swift
    Flowers in Your Hair - The Lumineers
    So It Goes... - Taylor Swift

GLOSSARY OF ITALIAN AMERICAN TERMS

fiorella - little flower
goumad - A mistress
strunzo - asshole
jamook - idiot
puttan' - whore
cazzo - balls
principessa - princess

PROLOGUE

My dearest Delilah,

You are the most beautiful thing I've ever been honored to lay my eyes on. I can't believe you're mine, that I had some hand in creating you.

Your mother wants me to write this letter—she says it will make a great addition to all those crazy journals she keeps. One day, you'll have questions, she says. One day, you'll wonder why you have a different father than Lola, wonder why your mother left what seemed safe and sat by my side.

So, I'm writing you partly at her request but partly because I want you to know who you are and will one day be.

You are Delilah Antonia Russo, the sole heir to the Russo family. If I can convince your mother, I'll give you a few brothers who will stare down the boys who fall for you like I did for her, or maybe some sisters you can boss around.

But no matter what, you are the first, and ruling is your right.

It might be hard, and you might be scared, but pressure turns coal into a diamond, just like it will do to you.

One day, I'll pass. I hope before that happens, I get the chance to show you the ropes, to teach you to be strong and powerful. How to be just and kind. How to better our community, to use the power you inherit and grow to help those who need it and hurt those who abuse their own.

One day, men will stare at you and tell you that you're in the wrong seat and that you don't belong at the table.

I want you to spit in their faces.

You will be a queen one day, my Delilah. You will have the power to take this family further, to help our community, to grow and to flourish.

Your grandfather, your mother's father, wanted to pair your mother with the Carluccios. He wanted power and greed and money, and he saw that the Russos weren't that. Your mother made choices that separated us, but in the end, we have our family.

In three weeks, your mother will leave Turner.

In three weeks, we will start our forever together.

But no matter what, I will love you forever and a day, mia principessa.

Love, your father, Arturo Russo.

ONE

-Lilah-

When I was a little girl, my favorite Disney princess wasn't Ariel or Cinderella or Sleeping Beauty.

I didn't like the idea of giving up everything I was for a stupid prince. I didn't want to sit around waiting for some fairy godmother to help me out or to be dumb enough to fall for the tricks of some bitch who was jealous of me.

No, I saw myself as Rapunzel.

Stuck in a tower, whisked away from danger, and meant to stay there. To be pretty and grateful I was even given the *opportunity* to serve those who watched over me.

As I got older, the parallels were even more apparent, and when I found the box of journals that blew my world apart, those fairy tales were the only thing keeping me together.

It wasn't even the promise of a happily ever after that saved me. It was the promise of *freedom*. The idea that those who hurt me, who used me, they would get what was due.

Just like Rapunzel, the person who locked me in the tower to use me for his own benefit was a man who called himself my parent. A man I would later find out wasn't that at all.

But of all the similarities, there was one I felt down to my soul. You see, Rapunzel looked out her window each day and dreamed of more.

She wanted to explore and live life and maybe, possibly, rule.

Before I even knew how much my life would one day reflect the story of the long-haired princess, I saw myself in her.

And now, I want revenge for both of us.

TWO

-Lilah-

This time five weeks ago, I would have been shutting down my fancy computer and calling a friend to see if they wanted to get a drink after a not-so-tiring day of working in a cubicle.

I'd probably head home first, pet my demon spawn of a cat, and then get dressed in something skimpy. Then, I'd go out and have fun, flirt with men until they paid for my drinks, and go home to start the whole day over again.

Five weeks ago, I lived a dream.

Well, at least one thing hasn't changed.

I'm still dressed in something skimpy and fun.

And I guess I still flirt with men until they pay me, so there's that.

But instead of dancing on a crowded dance floor of a max capacity bar in North Jersey, I'm dancing on a stage in a crowded gentlemen's club that smells like baby powder and Axe body spray.

Quite the change in circumstances, if I do say so myself.

Truly, if six weeks ago you told me that the virginal, sweet, press picture-perfect youngest daughter of Mayor Turner would be taking off her clothes at the mafia-owned club Jerzy Girls, I would have had you *committed*.

But one day, in a dark, luxurious office, my world of peace and parties and affluence changed forever.

-Five weeks earlier-

"How can I help you?" the man asks. He's my age, maybe a few years older, his hair cut short on the sides and combed back on the top, the color a dark dirty blonde. His face is serious, full of intentional aggression and intimidation, but he doesn't scare me.

I know his type.

Too much money, too much power, entitled since the day he was born.

The man who raised me is a well-loved mayor and has that same air: entitlement, greed, power.

And always, *always* stirring beneath the surface is the need to get more.

That's the weakness of men like this—greed. And if you use it just right, you can use it to control them.

But I was trained from the day I was born to combat that in public, to give the voters a balance. To smile pretty, to use my siren's eyes to win the vote, to get the donation, to distract from the unsavory side of politics. I mean, there is no way a man with a gambling addiction, who bet in underground games until he was so underwater he was emptying his oldest daughter's trust to keep his tabs balanced, could have raised such a picture-perfect specimen. He must be good, right? That's what my presence brings to the table. Stability. A reassurance that this is a good man worthy of your vote, your money, your trust.

"You know who I am, yes?" I ask, dragging my hand along the

back of the chair across from the man. My red-tipped nails have been filed into sharp points, the kind that makes a man wonder what they would feel like digging into his back.

Every part of my life has been about creating a trap for men. Now, I'm using that power for something else. Something new.

Right now, I am using it on Paulie Carluccio.

The grandson of the current boss of the Carluccio crime family.

Paulie's father was once destined to marry my mother before she refused to be tied to the rival of her secret love. Before she realized that if she got pregnant by her father's intern, she could avoid dragging her children through the seedy underbelly of politics, greed, and money of New Jersey.

Funny how that works, isn't it? How the best intentions can backfire so spectacularly?

"Delilah Turner," Paulie says then folds his fingers together like he's actually Michael Corleone in *The Godfather* instead of the near-powerless grandson of a true boss and just barely four years older than me.

Yes, I did my research.

Paulie Carluccio is four years my senior, and from what I understand, he just became a capo—or *captain*—of his grandfather's family last year.

It's clear the speck of power has gone to his head.

But that?

That I can handle.

A self-important man who forgets the power a woman has to destroy every hope and dream he's ever had if he looks at her wrong? I can handle that.

In fact, I *thrive* on that kind of underestimation.

"My father has a debt," I say, and he waves his hand at the seat across from him, indicating I should sit. But then again . . .

I know how the game is played. His desk chair is luxurious, dark, rich leather, and at least six inches higher than where the basic four-legged chair sits.

He'll stare down at me from that chair.

The intention is to put who sits there in their place, to remind them who has power and who does not.

I'll stay standing, keep my power, thank you very much.

He stares at me, waiting for me to obey, to be the sweet, innocent thing I'm sure he thinks I am.

I stare back.

"Yes. Tables and horses," Paulie says, breaking the silence, and I let a tiny, insignificant smile pop to the corners of my lips. *A win.* "He's racked up quite the bill, hasn't he. Unfortunately, it seems the man we originally had on the issue went a bit too far, to his own demise."

Johnny Vitale did just that, kidnapping my sister to use her as leverage against me. You see, Johnny knew who I am and the potential power that flows in my blood.

But with the way Paulie is staring at me like I'm insignificant and nothing more than a small-town mayor's daughter, I'm pretty sure he has *no idea* who I am. To him, I have no true purpose, no value.

How does he not know I have Russo blood running in my veins? That the right offer could make him a king in this underworld?

"I want to settle it." His eyebrow raises. "I want it settled, and I want him blacklisted." I tip my chin up just a hair with my words, words I practiced in the mirror of my high-rise apartment as I packed all my things up to move into the tiny apartment in Hudson City.

Paulie laughs.

The man laughs at me, and with that, I vow to make his version of retribution hurt just a bit more than I originally planned.

"Cute. You're cute, girl," he says, but I don't laugh. "You got a 100 large, sweetheart?"

I don't twitch.

I don't move.

I don't show any shock on my face.

Shock is weakness.

I am power.

I am strength.

I have a *plan*.

Instead, I let a small smile play on my lips.

"I think you know the answer to that, Paulie." My voice holds exhaustion, like I'm already over having to go through these hoops to get to the conversation we need to be having. If my father were here, he would gasp. He would give me a swift kick under a table, a glare, or a stern, "Lilah!" This man should be addressed as *Mr. Carluccio*. He should be *sir*. I should call him literally anything other than his first name.

His jaw ticks at the blatant disrespect.

Good.

"I'm happy to make a deal," I continue, looking around the room like I'm bored. Two men stand near the door, one looking annoyed, the other looking bored.

I would put money on the one who is bored being the one in charge and that his bored look isn't boredom at all. It's a carefully curated mask, put there to look inconspicuous. *Uninteresting.* You don't pay attention to the bored person in the room, and you don't watch your words in front of them.

It was my specialty, after all—staying quiet, looking pretty, and being bored. But always, *always* listening.

My father—the man who raised me—always says I'm his biggest asset because of it. That I need to be protected at all costs, that he needs me at every fundraiser, every gala as his secret weapon.

Smile and look pretty, my gorgeous Delilah. But keep those ears open.

And then I would be locked back up in my tower, unable to explore. Get the information, deliver it, and head back to my boring life in my fancy apartment.

My sister Lola got to explore, to stay in Ocean View, help with the negotiations and the planning. Lola got to start her own business, chase her dreams, and be fearless.

Of course, I don't hold that against her, not anymore. Not now that I know what it cost her.

But I'd be lying if I said there wasn't a time when I hated her for that, for having what I saw as freedom. It was really a prison of her own, though. Just a different version.

All created by Shane Turner and the Carluccios.

They'll pay, of course. Pay for putting us in our prisons.

"A deal?" Paulie says, knocking me from my thoughts.

"A deal. I want to make a deal with you."

THREE

-Lilah-

And that's how I got here, chatting with the dancers of Jerzy Girls on a random Tuesday afternoon, ready to start my eight-hour shift.

The deal we made was I pay off the debt my father collected by working at Jerzy Girls, dancing for the creepy men of Jersey City. Paulie gets my tips, and I get a measly allowance to live off of.

And my father is blacklisted.

No more betting.

No more gambling.

No more debts.

If he wants to rack up more, put his career and his family at risk, he'll have to do it in plain sight. Because when you're blacklisted by the Carluccios, word travels fast. Shane Turner will have to leave the entire tristate area to sit at a secret table. The addiction that once came easily will no longer be available to him.

And all it took was selling myself.

But, of course, that's not my only motivation for showing my tits to lonely men every night for nearly five weeks straight.

I'm here looking for dirt. Something to help me, something—anything—that I can use to take these fuckers down.

And hopefully, take Shane Turner down with them.

"Do you think he'll be here again today?" Tina asks when she sees me after walking through the door that leads from the dressing room to on stage.

I don't ask who "he" is.

I know.

"He" is the same man who has been coming in every Tuesday for the past five weeks. The same man who books a private room for six hours.

"We'll see," I say, brushing blush across the apple of my cheek once more before turning and standing. Today's outfit is outlandish and black with red piping, something I never would have worn in a past life even in private, but something about it makes me feel strong.

Powerful.

This whole journey—for lack of a better word—has been an exercise in power.

That power runs through my veins as I walk steadily in six-inch heels, heading toward the door that leads the dressing room.

I am power.

I am fierce.

I am revenge.

The words have become my mantra, the way I leave my own head when I need to focus. When I need to put up that wall between my subconscious that hates the idea of dancing for tips and the part of me that does it to advance my plan.

In my mind, that wall is constructed from the bricks of the tower I once was hidden away in.

But before I can step into the actual dressing area, I'm stopped by Marco.

Marco is a giant of a man, never looks happy, and always wears dark sunglasses. Once, I asked him why, and he told me because he has no eyes. At least I know he has some sense of humor, even if it's a very strange one.

He's also my absolute favorite person here at Jerzy Girls.

"Lilah," he says, his voice deep, and even though he doesn't speak loud, I can hear it over the sound of the thumping bass.

He's a bouncer at Jerzy Girls and, from the gossip in the back room, a high-up member of the Carluccio family. Possibly the right hand to Junior Carluccio, the next in line to head the family once Carmine passes. It was a fact I greedily took in and saved for later when the girls whispered it in the first few days after I started here.

I smile sweetly, continuing the friendship I've formed with the man.

"What's up, handsome?" He doesn't smile at my words.

Again, Marco never smiles. It's not his way.

"You have a request."

"Let me guess, six hours?"

"Mr. Romano is in room three. I'll walk you there."

"What a gentleman," I say with a smile, then I put my hand on the crook of his arm.

This has been going on for five weeks, nearly every Tuesday. The mysterious man hires me for six hours, the max allowed in a private room, taking up a good chunk of my eight-hour shift.

I'm thankful, of course—the break means less time shaking my ass on a stage while men whistle and shout and I risk breaking an ankle, but it's ... strange.

Strange in that I was only here for five days before the private sessions started.

Strange in that, from what the girls tell me, he only ever comes in on Tuesdays.

Strange in that the girls have never heard of this happening before.

Strange in that the expectations while I'm in the room aren't what you'd ... expect.

Marco leads me to the back of the club before unlocking the

unmarked door, the same one he always takes me to, then walking me in. Soft music is playing, and I smile at the man in a chair in the shadows before me.

Mr. Romano.

Mr. Dante Romano.

Strange how I know so much about this man, and yet I've found absolutely nothing when I've attempted to search his name.

It's like the man doesn't exist to the rest of the world.

It should surprise me, of course—you'd expect a man who is paying thousands of dollars a month at a strip club to use a fake name, to keep things quiet. But for some reason, it does all the same.

"Good evening, Mr. Romano," I say with a smile and a small, flirty wave of my fingers.

Strange that this exchange feels normal, almost friendly now.

"Six hours, yeah?" Marco asks in his gruff voice.

And then he's walking out. Despite being alone in a random room with a near stranger, I never feel uncomfortable here. Even on that first day, Marco explained all of the ways I would be protected and what to do in an emergency. For a strip club, Jerzy Girls treats the employees well, ensuring we're always protected and comfortable.

I got lucky in that sense.

The door won't be locked—another safety precaution the club has in addition to a small, hidden panic button that will send a silent alert if things go awry.

Still, the room is small and private, perfect for lap dances or more, as I've heard some girls whisper.

But Dante Romano doesn't ask for more, ever. He just sits in the shadows for hours and watches. And asks me questions.

"What are we having today?" I say, standing in front of the mysterious man who must have bottomless pockets. To spend at least a thousand dollars a night on a private room plus the generous tip he slips me—he has to have a good job. Or a healthy trust fund.

I could tell you that from his clothes alone: custom-made suits that I get glimpses of, the crisp white button-downs, and shoes that cost $400 to start. I could pass the man walking down the street and know he's loaded without him having to buy my time each week.

"Not sure, Marco's deciding," he says, his feet moving out and crossing at the ankle as he sits back.

"Got it," I say with a smile. I move around the room, moving my hips slowly to the beat of the music, moving my hands to my hair, fluffing it out.

"What are we chatting about tonight, sir?" I ask, because besides keeping my distance and dancing around in a skimpy outfit, this is what we do.

The first time I was brought back here was just five days after I started at Jerzy Girls. Just like tonight, the man sat in the shadows, a single lonely chair in the room, music playing low and sultry.

I was terrified, of course, the blood rushing in my ears, my mind on overdrive thinking about what would happen to me in this small, dark room. Terrified of what would be expected of me, what I would be forced to do. I'd heard stories from the women about men who request intricate lap dances, men who want to touch. Men who want ... more.

And in six hours, you could do quite a bit "more."

I'd sold my dignity to Paulie Carluccio and he owned me—he could tell me what to do, when to do it, and with who. But for some reason, when I made that deal, I didn't anticipate anything more than dancing on a stage with a fake name.

When I walked in this room for the first time, all the mysterious man said to me was, "Dance."

And I did that. It was easy. Dancing has always been something I love to do. I might be a shitty stripper, stumbling on stage at least once a shift and refusing to even look sideways at a pole because I know damn well I'll break something on it, but I love to move my body to music.

Of course, I assumed he would expect at the very least a semi-decent strip tease. After a few minutes of swaying my hips, playing with straps, flipping my hair, dropping it low and spreading my thighs, I started to move the strap of my bra down over my shoulder. Pushing it down, down, until—

"No."

I froze in panic.

What does "no" mean in the context of stripping at a strip club?

"No stripping," he said. "Not here."

Inevitably, the panic rose.

First off, *what in the fuck* could "not here" possibly mean? Because I was not leaving this room until Marco came to get me, and I sure as fuck wasn't going anywhere else.

And second: *no stripping?*

Who orders a six-hour-long private room with a dancer at a gentlemen's club and requests *no stripping?*

"I'm sorry?" I was sure I had misheard the man.

"Just move. Dance." I licked my lips, my teeth gnawing at the skin there before responding.

"But don't . . . undress?" I sounded confused because I was, but he just smiled and nodded.

I could see his white teeth on tanned skin even through the shadows of the room. "Exactly," he said.

His words made a chill run down my spine.

The good kind.

His voice was the kind you wanted to whisper sweet nothings in a dark room when you were dressed only in a sheet and a layer of sweat.

Still, I obeyed, moving my hips again, dancing around the room.

I kept it simple.

I didn't move closer to the man, just dancing in front, never entering the shadows he sat in, and that seemed to be enough for him.

"So, is Carmella a stage name?" he asked. I continued to dance.

"Why are you asking?"

"No reason. If you're not comfortable, you don't have to answer."

When I looked, his body had moved from sitting up straight to leaning back, his legs kicked out and ankles crossed, at ease.

And he wasn't making me strip.

Because of that small favor, that kindness, I answered his question and unintentionally started a routine.

"Yes. One of the girls gave it to me," I said, moving my hands through my long hair.

"Like *The Sopranos*? Fits you. Small, blonde. Italian?"

"Full-blooded," I said with a smile, the first time I'd said it. Until I found those journals, I thought I was a European mutt, my mother Italian and my father a mix of German, English, and Irish.

"Beautiful," he said, the words low, almost like they weren't meant for me. Another few minutes passed, the song changing before he spoke again. "Dante."

"What?" I said, moving to face him. The song was one of my favorites, and it added to my comfort level. Because despite everything, this felt a little weird, dancing in my bustier and tiny skirt for a man and knowing I would be doing it for a while still.

"My name. Dante."

"Like the inferno?" I said with a laugh, and he gave me one back. It felt like that, like he was giving me a gift with his laugh. It shook through the room, deep and intoxicating.

"You know, I don't know many people who have had the balls to say that to my face."

"Sorry, I—"

"No, not in a bad way. Yes, like the inferno." We were quiet as the song ended, as I danced and he watched, but when the music changed, I responded.

"Delilah," I said, my own words low.

"Hmm?"

"My name. It's Delilah. Lilah."

"Beautiful name for a gorgeous woman."

After that is when the questions started, and that's been the routine for five weeks. Six hours of dancing—eventually, Marco even let me play my own music during those hours—and a strange game of question and answer. I dance, stay dressed (to whatever degree I am—I work at a strip club, after all), and we . . . chat. Small talk. Silly things. *Favorite animal. Have you ever traveled? Do you read?* Small questions that, in the grand scheme, haven't taught me much about the mysterious man but have made him strangely feel like a friend.

It's actually kind of sad to think about how this total stranger knows more random facts about me than some of my best friends.

Then my own family.

"Let's go with childhood vacation. Favorite?" he asks today, and I cringe. Beyoncé sings her lungs out over the speakers as I work on an answer.

"Childhood vacation? That's all you've got?" I say, and he smiles in the shadows, white teeth catching dim lighting. In five weeks, I've still never seen his full face.

"Delilah, we've covered pretty much every like and dislike over the past few weeks. I think vacation is a very reasonable request."

"Yeah, why are you still coming here, Mr. Romano?" I say, trying to change the subject. Because for all the fancy dinners I've been to, the galas and fundraisers and talk shows I've been dragged to, I only remember one childhood vacation.

We drove there. I was six, Lola eleven, and Mom hadn't gotten sick yet.

It wasn't fancy, and it wasn't extravagant, but I loved it all the same.

Still, I want to be mysterious, gorgeous, cultured, and sophisticated in this room, even if I'm dancing for money.

"I'm bored."

"So bored you drop a couple grand a week at a strip club?" I ask, swaying my hips to the beat. "Sounds kind of depressing, Mr. Romano."

"Do you want me to stop?" he asks, and for some reason, my heart stutters. "Stop coming?"

Do I want him to stop?

The question might as well be, *Do you secretly pray that this man will stroll in and request a private room each shift? Do you hope to catch a look at him walking in from the parking lot when you start your shift? Oh, and the times he didn't come on a Tuesday but a Thursday, did you stress and worry that he was done with this strange routine?*

The truth is, I enjoy these hours with the mysterious Dante Romano. It started simply, as pure relief to have time off stage, away the dozens of eyes locked on my body. Relief from being semi-covered, from having an easy night.

It's somehow turned into liking this strange private time with him. It became answering his chaotic questions about everything and nothing, never asking anything personal or intrusive, and always, always returning the favor. Always giving back his own answers. Favorites and least favorites, firsts and never-have-I-evers. I know this man backward and forwards.

"I didn't say that," I reply, not telling the whole truth because that would be pathetic—telling a man who pays for your time that you actually like dancing for him.

He stares at me.

I smile, then I answer with a sigh.

"When I was a kid, we went to Lake George one fall. It was fun. My parents took my sister and me out of school for a few days, and they rented a little house on the lake, and we just . . . existed. It was fun. Rare, for my family." I move over to the chair Marco leaves me, sitting in it and taking off my towering shoes. "It was the only family vacation we took that I remember. My mom died a few years later."

He knows that part, the confession coming on the third Tuesday when he told me his mother died when he was five.

"Sounds nice." I don't reply, explain more, or justify my answer because I don't have to. It's not the way it works here with us.

The night goes on like this: silence and a few questions before more comfortable silence. It never feels like an interview or anything weird, more like how when you're on a long car ride and you have small talk to fill the silence.

Except today, he finally pushes the line in the fifth hour.

"Go out with me tonight." The words sound like they rush out, like he did everything in his power to hold them back but something in his subconscious won the battle.

"What?" I stop moving altogether.

"Dinner. Go out to dinner with me."

"I don't..."

"Give me the honor of eating with a pretty girl, yeah? A meal." He says it so naturally, I almost forget where we are, who I am.

There was a time when this was a compliment.

A wealthy man who wanted to take me to dinner, to learn more about me.

But my life has changed, and I'm not that person anymore.

"I'm a stripper."

"And?"

"And... you wear $400 shoes." Despite the dim light, I know his face is cloaked with confusion.

"What do my shoes have to do with going to dinner?" he asks, and I can't help but laugh at the absurdity of those ideas side by side.

My mind instantly moves to some obscure other world where both of our work shoes are sitting on an entryway mat at the front door—my tall stripper heels next to his fine Italian loafers.

God. It's insanity.

Because he's right. One has nothing to do with the other.

We shouldn't have anything to do with each other. I think that just now, I knocked myself out of the pretty little picture I had painted myself, stepping back until I could see reality better.

"Have a meal with me, Delilah," he says again.

I stare at him and give him a small, sad smile.

Part pity because I've heard of this—men coming in and becoming enamored with the girls, wanting the *idea* of them outside of the club.

And part sadness because one of the few things I don't hate about this job has to end.

"We can't, Dante. I work here. You . . . don't." In the shadows, I can almost see the confusion on his face.

God, I've never even really seen his face. This has gone too far.

"What does that have to do with anything?"

"Uh, everything? You pay me to dance for you."

"I pay you to spend time with me."

The world very well might stop spinning for a millisecond as mine rocks.

"What?"

"You're gorgeous. I like spending this time with you. I pay for your time."

"You pay for my time?"

"Of course," he says, like it's obvious.

"Of course?!" I'm pretty sure my voice ratchets up a notch.

"Think about it, Delilah. If I told you to come in this room on day one, sit in a chair, and just talk with me, would you have been comfortable?" I don't answer. "If I just came up to you after your shift, told you I wanted to take you out to dinner because you're fucking beautiful and for six weeks, you're all I can think about, would you agree?" Again, no response. "For one, I hope to fuck not, because that wouldn't be wise."

I raise an eyebrow and see his smile widen.

"I spent time with you. I got to know you. Realized I'm not just drawn by your looks, but by you—"

"Time's up," Marco says, opening the door.

I can't decide if I'm relieved or frustrated.

"I have another thirty minutes," Dante says, and from the clock over his head, I can see he's right.

"Got company," is all Marco says, and then Dante curses under his breath.

It makes no sense.

But almost everything in this place makes little to no sense.

I take the interruption as a sign from God that this has gone too far. That it's time to move on, move away from my Tuesday distraction of Dante Romano, and stick to my plan.

To *remember* the plan.

"It was nice to see you, Mr. Romano. Have a great night," I say, bending to pick up my shoes and ignoring the sharp intake of air from his side of the room as I realize my ass is pointed in his direction.

Then, standing quickly, I'm out the door, Marco escorting me to the backstage dressing room. I have two more hours on my shift, and I need to get ready to dance on stage.

But first . . .

"Hey, Marco? If Mr. Romano requests me again, can you tell him I'm unavailable? I know that I techni—"

"Something happen?" he asks, his face moving to look at me with concern, those sunglasses going to the top of his head so he can read my face better, I'm sure.

See? I told you. Marco is the best.

"Not really. I mean. Maybe?" I say, slowing my steps as we approach the door. "He asked me out."

Marco's eyes widen as a smile comes to his lips like he finds it entertaining.

"He asked you out?"

I slap his arm.

"Yes! Isn't that weird? He wants to take me to dinner."

"You spend hours chatting with him every time he's here, Lilah." I frown, not understanding if he's telling me I should have said yes. "I mean, you made the right call. He's a client and you shouldn't just go out with a client. Not safe. But he's a decent guy, as far as the men here go."

I think Marco is a good judge of character overall.

"Decent guy like, I should go on a date with him?"

"It's too complicated to boil it down to that and you know it as well as I do. Just saying. He's not a creep. He doesn't come here ever.

Came for a meeting, saw you dancing, requested a private." Marco confirms the story I was told. "Shocked me, to be honest."

"Hmm," I say, not sure what to do with this new info.

"Anyway. Next time he requests, I'll tell him you're unavailable. Now go. You're on in five," Marco says, tipping his chin toward the door.

And then I move on with my day. But the gnawing in my gut won't stop me from wondering if I made the wrong choice.

FOUR

A note from Libby Turner, found on top of her box of journals.

Delilah,

I hope you never find this letter.

I hope you never read these journals, at least not without me there to hold your hand, to explain.

But I'm sick and it's not looking great, and you're way too young to understand. Your sister will protect you, keep you safe, but there is so much you need to know. Things that Lola can only scrape the surface of when she explains everything one day. Even she doesn't know the secrets that lie in these boxes.

One day, you will have to take matters into your own hands. I just know it.

One day, they will come for you.

One day, you'll need to rule.

You've been a secret for so long. Your entire life, your true nature has been hidden. I promise I did it to protect you. If you hold that against me, I'll understand, but I beg you to see it from my side.

You are the sole heir to the Russo family. Your father was an only child, and you are his only child. There will be battles and arguments for who will move that family forward, who will rule.

But eventually, just like your father wanted, you will rise.

I know it in my bones. I know one day you'll wake up, sense your fate, and know where you belong.

In order to do it, you'll need to find the proof, Lilah. Someone who hates your family did it. Someone with more power than just a capo.

Prove you're the gorgeous ruler your father knew you would be, and it will all be yours.

FIVE

-Lilah-

On Tuesday, I am both relieved and miserable with the fact that I do not have a request for a private room with Mr. Romano. Instead, I dance on stage in thirty-minute cycles for the full eight-hour shift.

Either Marco kept his word or Dante refused to see me again after I turned him down.

Either way, it's for the best, I tell myself.

"Carmella!" Candy, the dancer who took on the role of mom for everyone, calls later that afternoon as I'm getting back into my street clothes. "You doing anything fun tonight?"

Candy is the one who gave me my name—Carmella, as in *Soprano*—because I'm blonde, Italian, and small. A cliché, for sure, but one I can tolerate because Carmella took no shit in that show, and I'm done taking shit.

I laugh at her question, pulling a pair of sweats over my ass and throwing my ridiculously high-heeled shoes in my bag. "I wish. I'm going home and passing out."

"A hot thing like you?" Gina, another dancer, asks. "You don't have a man at home?"

"Men are trouble," I say, thinking of the journals my mother left behind sitting at my apartment, waiting for me to reread them for the millionth time. Journals detailing just how much trouble men can be.

"I hear that," another dancer says, though I'm not sure who because the five or six other girls in the room all start laughing and agreeing. The back room is where we all change, eat, and get ready for stage time. It always smells like a cacophony of perfumes, hair spray, and sweat, but the women who work here are all *golden*. All of them are open and kind and willing to help.

Never in my life have I been surrounded by such genuine women. Women who aren't looking at this potential friendship as a stepping stone or bragging rights, but because somehow, we're all on the same path in life. We're all on even footing.

Sometimes, when I'm delicately weaving in stories through conversation to get information, I feel guilty about it, about the deception. Because these women are *good*. Good women who mean well and have opened their arms wide to me.

It's a contrast to the socialite friends I've had my whole life, the friends who, when I moved out of my fancy apartment and sold off my expensive things to keep my head above water, all abandoned me.

I don't have time to mull over that depressing thought before there's a distraction.

The bright side of this place is there is *always* a distraction.

"Where the fuck have you been, chica?" Fancy, a Latina dancer who calls everyone chica, shouts. Every head moves to her as we try to decide if she's talking to one of us or someone else, but her eyes are on the entrance to the break room where Sammi is walking in, a shit-eating grin on her face and a very pretty necklace around her neck.

She saunters in, tossing a bag to the bench, and sits, crossing her legs.

I should leave. I'm dead tired, so drained that I can barely focus on just why I should stay. I am terribly behind on sleep; late nights and way too much on my mind keep me awake even when I'm not working a night shift.

I desperately need the sleep an early night is promising.

But then I remember who Sammi left with last night.

"I win," she says, and a dozen girls groan.

"No fucking way!"

"How was he!?"

"I need proof!"

There was an ongoing bet in the back room, a battle for Tino Bucceri, the newest member in the Carluccio family. Rumor is he was made less than a month ago after four years of doing his duty with the family. And, of course, all of the girls want a piece of the hot guy whose eyes always stray to the stages.

Sammi sits on the bench, leaning back on her hands with a cat who got the canary smile as she prepares to tell her tale.

"So you know what he told me?" she asks, and all eyes widen in a *bitch, you know we want to know* kind of way. "So, you know Big Boss?" Everyone nods, and I do too, even though for the life of me, I have not been able to figure out just who Big Boss is. Asking too many questions raises too many red flags. "So apparently, he and Paulie are neck and neck in deciding who will, you know, be in charge when Carmine passes."

It clicks. Big Boss is Junior Carluccio, the youngest son of Carmine Carluccio, the current head of the family. The next in line to take over now that Tony Carluccio was put away from some kind of Ponzi scheme.

And Paulie is his nephew.

"You're shitting me," Gina says, a gasp in her voice. "But Paulie's just the grandson!"

"Seems that they can't all agree on the, uh, direction the family should go in. Tino wouldn't tell me who, but one of them wants to go back to how things were before: safer, easier. Helping the community. The other wants to go . . ." Her eyes move from left to right with major dramatic effect before she whispers, "Darker."

"Well, I can almost guarantee it's not Paulie who wants to play it safe," Tia says, snapping her gum and doing the last buckle on her shoes. "So what does this mean?"

"Nothing. It means nothing," Candy says, clapping her hands. "Tino's got a big fuckin' mouth. You think they're sharing the important shit with him?"

"Dunno, Candy. He seemed pretty worried about it when he was tellin' me about it this morning."

"This *morning!?*" Gina shouts. "He stayed overnight!?" Fancy smiles like she was waiting to drop the bomb.

"Oh yeah. And when he was sober, he was really nervous when he remembered what he told me and all. Made me promise not to spill to a soul."

"So you came in here and spilled instantly?" I ask with a smile. "What about the cameras?"

"Oh, he told me they're fake in here," Sammi says. "Big Boss isn't *too* bad. Apparently, he wants to give us privacy when we're dressing."

"And we're supposed to believe that?" Tina asks in disbelief.

"I mean, none of the guys *ever* come back here," I say with a shrug. "They always knock or send a girl in if they need something." Everyone nods, agreeing, before there's a knock on the door and a deep voice booms.

"Girls! Two minutes till stage time!" Instantly, women flutter around, fluffing hair and spritzing body spray in a familiar tornado of chaos. As it happens, I continue to pack my stuff up, categorizing the new information in the files of my mind.

My whole life, I've been taught to smile pretty and keep my ears open, to be someone people are comfortable talking around. It's a skill I've put to use here at the club. I silently track which politicians come in shitty disguises, which powerful married men get back-room lap dances, and who disappears into the offices where, I'm sure, deals and plans are made.

Oh, to be a fly on the wall in those rooms, to have that kind of access. Some part of me is sure that I need to be back there in order to get the information I need to bring to the Russos and take down the Carluccios.

To be honest, I thought the men here would give me the most, give me the ammunition I need to take to my blood family and earn my way to the top—and my revenge.

It turns out the women are the true gatekeepers of information.

I should have known, really.

It's always the women who hold all the secrets, and with those secrets, they hold the power.

"Alright, ladies, see you tomorrow!" I shout, grabbing my big duffel bag and waving to the girls, all in a mix of stages of dress.

"Bye, Carm!"

"See ya, blondie!"

"Don't forget to bring in that body spray tomorrow, Lilah!"

I wave, walking out the door and smiling at Marco.

"See ya, princess," he says with a warm smile.

And then I'm free.

SIX

-Lilah-

Of course, I didn't just jump to working at a strip club to get dirt on a mob family that ruined what my life could have been as soon as I left the hospital.

No, my dumb ass did something even stupider.

I instantly tried to find my grandfather.

Now, you'd think that would be easy, that pinpointing the Don of a big family in his home city wouldn't be too difficult.

You'd be wrong.

Unlike the Carluccios, who own a state-wide disposal company, clubs throughout northern New Jersey, and just about a third of Hudson City's own version of Little Italy, the Russos aren't as obvious. Their biggest business is Russo Contracting, which handles many of the big developments in the state but also has a multitude of offices.

I went with the option of Hudson City—where my father was born and raised.

Walking into the big office building, I was in awe instantly. The building was huge, with a giant first level showcasing tile and flooring options as well as paint swatches and carpet squares. Towards the back were what look like model rooms —a kid's option with bunk beds and a stunning all-white kitchen.

But in the front was a receptionist's desk where a woman was sitting when I first walked in, but when I glanced there again, she had stood and walked around to the front.

She was gorgeous.

Long dark hair sprinkled with silver, a tight dark green dress hugging curves but still work-appropriate with long sleeves and a high neck, and a pair of over-the-knee boots rounded out the outfit.

She was also *glaring* at me.

In fact, she didn't bother to greet me at all, just crossed her arms over her chest and leaned back against the desk.

Something told me this was *not* how she typically greets potential customers.

"Hi, I, uhm. I'm-"

"I know who you are," she said, her voice low and menacing. "My god. The fuckin' rumors are true, aren't they? He fucked the Bianchi girl."

I chewed the inside of my lip but smiled my sweet, politician's daughter smile.

Appeasing.

Sweet.

That's how you act when you meet your long-lost family for the first time, right?

"I would love to-"

"No."

"No?"

"No." We stood there, staring at one another for long, excruciating moments while I tried to figure out what to say.

Before I was able to make a decision, she spoke again. Somehow, it still didn't feel like I won the standoff.

"Why are you here?"

"I really would love to speak with-"

"Things are finally quieting down after fuckin' years of shit, and now this? What are you here for, little girl?" That grates. I ran my tongue between my teeth and my lip, irritation brewing, my perfectly curated sugary sweetness melting off.

"That's none of your business."

"I've been in this family for almost thirty years, married in when I was 19." *Married in* to the family definitely did *not* just mean she married a man with the last name Russo. "Been workin' for Russo Contracting for just as long. I keep the books in line. I think it's my business, honey." I didn't respond, trying to decide what to say, how to say it.

"And I know who your mother was," she said. "God rest her soul." Her hands moved to make the sign of the cross like a good, sweet Catholic girl would, but her eyes said differently. Her eyes said *mean girl*.

I still didn't respond.

"Look, tell me why you're here, or get out. I've got clients coming in any minute."

What do I have to lose? I thought.

"Fine. Yes. I'm here to speak with Alfredo Russo because I believe he is my grandfather. If he is, then I have a right to get to know this family. More of a right than you do, I'm sure." I realized that last part was probably a bit too far when her bitchy smile falls off her red lips.

"That's cute," she said, deadpan. "Cute that you think they'd take some random bastard child in like a *true* Russo. Like you belong here. What do you know about family? About loyalty?"

I thought about how I let my sister take on the drama for years without questioning it.

I thought about how I'm now diligently planning the downfall of Shane Turner, the man who raised me.

Not very loyal of me.

"It's not like the movies, honey. You..." She looked me up and down. Her face changed just a bit—pity. "You're cute. I'll give you that. But they will eat you up and spit you out. You need *grit* to make it out here." Her eyes roved my outfit up and down, and her face changed just a bit, her top lip moving in distaste. I wore a little cardigan and skirt set Shane picked for some gala, if I recall. I thought it looked cute and put together, but in that moment I thought maybe it's just giving. . . innocent idiot. "You'd get eaten up here, honey. And truly - they don't want you here."

I didn't get a chance to speak before the bell rang at the door, and a tall Italian man walked in, moving straight to the woman. He wrapped an arm around her waist, kissing her hair.

"Who's this?" he asked, looking at me, but speaking to the woman. His face had the look like he was trying to figure out a puzzle, like he recognized me from somewhere but couldn't figure out where.

"Oh, you know. Just another little thing trying to take a walk on the wild side," she said and the man sighed.

"Not smart. Not for a girl like you."

A girl like you.

God, I'm so *tired* of that. Of everyone thinking I'm some precious, breakable thing that can't know or do *anything*.

"I'm not-"

"I'm sure you're sweet as can be. But I'll be honest with you. You don't have the grit. I can tell from here." He gave me a small, pitying smile.

That was it.

I was done.

I decided then and there that I'd just do this the hard way.

"And, can I ask—who are you?" I asked, crossing my arms on my chest.

"Me?" he asked. I raises an eyebrow in an *are you dumb?* way. He smiled. "Sal. Sal Conte. Why?"

"Because I want to make sure I catch your face in a few months when I'm sitting at the top," I said, then turned around and walked away.

If no one would take me seriously, if everyone was so sure I'm too soft, that I lack *grit*, I'll just have to prove myself.

Easy as that.

SEVEN

-Lilah-

That's where my mind is when my phone rings as I'm walking out of Jerzy Girls. I know who it is despite her not having a special ringtone and me not looking at the screen.

I just know it's Lola. She's the only one who calls me these days unless it's one of the girls needing me to sub in for them.

I also know if I ignore the call, Lola will most likely *freak the fuck out*.

I've ignored three calls this week alone. Not because I don't want to talk to my big sister—that's not the issue at all. The issue is my sister owns a thriving bakery, so she keeps semi-normal hours.

She's baking by seven and clocking out by six, and, gosh, isn't that just the *perfect* time to call her sweet baby sister?

Of course, that would have been fine *six weeks ago*. It would have been the perfect time to call and chat, because five weeks ago, I worked a nine-to-five. A normal job where I was home or heading there when my sister would call to check in and decompress, complain about her neighbor, or tell me about some gala.

But now when Lola calls, I'm dancing on a pole and undoing the ties of a bikini top or just walking off stage, the background noise earsplitting. And calling my overprotective sister with *Thong Song* blaring in the background isn't necessarily ideal when you're trying to prove to her that you are *totally fine.* Nothing to worry about here.

So even though I'm too tired to have any kind of human interaction, I force myself to answer.

"Hello, favorite sister of mine," I say as I tap the green button to accept the call.

"Oh, good, you're alive," she says, and I can almost hear the eye roll down the line. "God, where the hell have you been?"

"Uh, busy?" I wave at Roddy as I walk out the back door. He's one of the few bouncers who looks at my face when he talks to me instead of my tits, and he loves a good smoke break behind the club. "I texted you!"

"Lilah, a text sent an hour *after* I call you that just says, 'I'm alive, love you,' does nothing to ease my all-consuming anxiety that's telling me you are not, in fact, alive." That's a fair point. But I've also been avoiding her calls because . . . "How are you? How's the city?"

Because she knows too much about me. Or, my old life. "How's Adrianna? Any fun new escapades?"

Adrianna was my closest friend five weeks ago, the friend who, when I confessed I had quit my job and work at Jerzy Girls to help with some family shit, stopped talking to me all together.

In truth, two great things came from the chaos that is my life right now.

One, I realized who the real ones were. Lola, the woman who sacrificed everything for me? She's real. Her boyfriend, Ben, who risked getting shot in order to save her ass? The realest. My dad? The fucking worst. My friends? Nearly as bad. It's crazy how you can put blinders on for so long and ignore the shitty personalities of people if you want.

And two, I finally understood why I always felt suffocated my whole life. Like no matter where I went, I couldn't get a lung full of fresh, clean air. Because I was constantly protected, a doll taken out to play then carefully returned to her box for safekeeping.

I've been locked in my protected little life since the day I was born.

Protected from my identity.

Protected from the boogeymen my mom and sister feared.

Protected from tainting my image, ruining the illusion my father had created.

"Sorry, sissy. I've been busy."

"At the firm?" she asks, her words . . . suspicious.

Goddammit.

"Uh, no. I actually . . . I, uh, I got a new job. At a start-up."

"A new job?" she asks. "Why didn't you say anything?"

"I told you, I've been busy."

"What kind of start-up?"

"E . . . Entertainment," I say, looking at the buzzing neon sign above my head that reads "Jersey's Finest Girls" in bright red letters.

"Entertainment?"

"Yup. It's a blast but crazy hours." An ambulance passes, lights and siren blaring and cutting out whatever Lola wants to say. "Sorry, I'm downtown, leaving work now."

"Hmm." Speculation is clear in her voice. My mom died when I was ten, which means for the most formative years of my life, Lola was my mother figure. Sometimes I think she forgets to hop out of that role and into "big sister." "Listen, have you . . . Have you heard from Dad?" she asks, and I can tell the words don't come easy. That in reality, she doesn't want to say them but has to.

We haven't talked about what happened in that hospital room, the secrets that were revealed or how life changed in the blink of an eye. We haven't talked about how she protected me for so long or how I let her make that sacrifice for me, whether I knew how deep it was or not.

I sigh.

"No, I haven't," I say.

"He hasn't reached out since the hospital." Her voice is low, and I wish I were there so I could read her face, see if it's irritation or concern or . . . sadness there.

"Same," I say. Though, that's not the full truth.

But it's the truth I'll give her, because my new purpose is to make my sister's life carefree and easy. It's my turn to pick up the mess.

"It's . . . weird, you know?"

"Yeah. I know," I say, though I think for me it's different. For Lola, it's probably strange to feel free, not to feel like she's in constant battle mode, ready to pick up the pieces. Instead, she's settling into an easy, predictable life, the one she always was supposed to live.

For me, I've begun preparing for battle, getting the tools and gear and insight needed to attack.

"Yeah?" she yells through the phone, but I know it's not directed at me. "Oh, shut it. I'm talking to my sister, you ass." There's a deep laugh and then a giggle on her end. "Yeah, yeah. Alright, Lilah. Gotta go. Ben says hi, but he's being an ass because I forgot to bring him back a cupcake when I closed." More rumbling, and then she sighs. "No, you *are* being a big baby." She's talking to her hot, tattooed boyfriend, and god, hearing her so happy and free fills my soul.

It also drags me down, knowing I didn't even realize she was missing that brightness for years.

"Okay, Lol, no worries. Tell the big guy I said hi and that I'm making an appointment soon."

"A tattoo?!" she asks in a panic.

"I'm not ten anymore, babe. Yes, a tattoo. Gotta go. Love you!" I say.

"Love you too, sissy. You tell me if he calls, yeah?"

"Will do," I say before hanging up, knowing damn well I will be doing no such thing.

EIGHT

-Lilah-

As I'm driving home, my mind moves over the fact that my father *has* reached out to me since the hospital incident. I just never told Lola about it, and I never plan to.

That whole conversation is a festering reminder of why I'm doing what I'm doing, and why Shane Turner is on my list of people who will fall when the time comes. It was four days after Lola's attempted kidnapping and two days before I would change my life forever.

"I need you to come down on Friday," he'd said casually. My heart had stuttered, and I thought the worst.

"Lola?" I asked, worried. "Are they taking that asshole to court? Does she have to testify? Does she need support?"

"What?" he'd asked, clearly confused. "No. There's a gala. Robert Kline asked if you would attend with him."

My word spun on its axis.

I don't think I realized that in the next minute, it would crash down.

"Robert Kline?"

"Yes. Son to Kurt Kline. He got caught up in a scandal, and he needs a date for the gala. Some pretty thing to get the people talking in the right way."

"He . . . needs a date to the gala." I said the words slowly, unsure if I heard correctly.

"God, Lilah, yes. He needs a date." He sighed like I was an idiot, and I realized then that I'd heard that sigh from him a lot. More than any daughter should from a man who allegedly loved her. Cherished her.

"The last time I heard from you was in Lola's hospital room." After we left, I drove home and started planning, contacting people to get some kind of insight, doing research—anything I could to find more about who I was and how I could get my revenge.

For my sister.

For my mother.

For my father—my real father.

Everything I had found in those journals . . . Now that I had a fuller picture, everything made so much sense. The whole situation, what I once thought was just my mother's guilt spilled onto paper, was so much more. So much *worse*. My mother and father were real-life Romeo and Juliet, and I was their doomed love child.

While they were no longer here to make things right, to make people pay, I knew that I could. I could do that for them. Just like Arturo's letter to me stated, I could take my rightful spot at the head of the Russo table. And if I played my cards right, I could take down the Carluccios in the process. Make them pay for what they did to my family.

"I don't have time for this, Delilah. Gala is at five. I need you here at three."

There was a time when I would drop everything and go. When I would think of my mother's last few words to me and do as my father asked.

Words whispered to an impressionable 10-year-old girl by her dying mother.

Listen to your father, Lilah. And your sister. They have your best interest in mind. Don't make waves; lie low. You'll be safe, I promise.

Lie low.

Be safe.

Don't make waves.

Shane Turner knew about my sister's promise to our dying mother—to help keep our father out of trouble and me safe—and he used it against her to get what he wanted. He manipulated everything and everyone.

Did he also know what words she whispered to me in those final days? Had he been using them against me all this time as well?

Possibly.

Probably.

"I'm not going."

The line had gone so quiet, you could hear a pin drop. I remember that part the most: the thick silence in the air. I'd pulled the phone from my face to make sure he was still there on the line, that it hadn't disconnected.

The time kept going up with each passing second.

"Hello?" I asked, putting the phone back to my ear.

"What do you mean you're not going?" The words were low and ominous, a storm cloud waiting to ruin everything.

"After everything that happened, you think I would want to help you with this?" That backbone I had been hiding started to stiffen, and I felt my chin lift. As if, even though he couldn't see me, every part of my body had to be a part of this rebellion.

"I spent *years* protecting your ass, Delilah. It's the very least—"

"I'm sorry, what? You protected me for *your* benefit." My words were cold, sure, and measured. Not violent or angry. Just . . . facts. "I couldn't be a shiny prize in your campaigns if I was a bastard child, could I? The pretty daughter, a spitting image of your dead wife that you could show off, convince the people of Ocean View you were just a sweet, loving widower. But really, what would have happened if it came out that you were so verbally abusive, so addicted to greed and power, that your wife tried to leave you for a *mob boss?*"

"Protecting you was mutually beneficial, Delilah. Get over yourself. Now, I made a deal with Kline. You can't just—"

"A deal?" My mind went silent, the word blaring with new clarity. A new understanding of what that word meant. But my father sighed like I was a petulant child and he was tired of explaining things.

"Yes, Lilah. That's what happens in my line of work."

"Like the kind of deals you made with Paulie Carluccio? With Johnny Vitale?"

Silence.

At that moment, it clicked.

It all made sense.

Lola was shaken down for money.

Lola was in control of keeping shit under wraps, of paying the debts with her trust fund, of figuring shit out.

"I'm right, aren't I?" I asked, staring out the window of my highrise, the puzzle pieces coming together. "We thought you kept me out of it because of Mom. But you didn't, did you? You didn't keep me out of your dirty shit at all. You were just . . . quieter about it."

"Delilah—"

"You whored me out." The words felt disgusting in my mouth, leaving a shameful coating I'd never be able to brush out.

"That's—"

"Dates with politician's son's that always wound up being crashed by the press."

"I—"

"Designer gowns to galas."

"Those—"

"The time Senator Farber kissed me, I told you about it." This time he didn't try to interrupt, and I wondered if it was because I had hit the nail on the head. "You said it happened, but to be quiet about it. That you'd speak with him." More silence.

"How much did he pay you?" I asked, my voice near silent as nausea churned up my throat.

"The fuck, Delilah. Who cares? I need you—"

Who cares.

Not a denial.

Not even an *attempt* at denial.

"So I'm right. He paid you off so you wouldn't tell the world that a state senator kissed an 18-year-old girl against her will." Silence.

It's funny how much you can hear in silence. How much is spoken in words unsaid, how much is revealed.

"And the dates? How much did those cost?"

Silence.

"Were they cash or favors? Votes?" I licked my lips as it all began to make sense, the blood rushing in my veins with a vengeance. "What—"

"God fucking dammit, Delilah. Fine. I did it. The dates, the galas. You have a good image, squeaky clean. Made sure of that myself." He said it with pride, and instantly, my mind went to all the boyfriends who would ghost me or dump me after a few dates.

Jesus.

No fucking way.

"My boyfriends. You made them dump me?"

"You were no good to me tainted. I need you pure, Delilah."

"Pure." I repeated the ironically filthy word under my breath. Funny how one word could make you sick.

"I figured if my wife was a whore and made me live with her mistake, I was going to get what I could from her." A silent gag came to my throat. "Never were very bright. You didn't figure it out. I was shocked it lasted so long, that you and Lola didn't talk, but I guess she was trying to protect you, and you were trying to help me, so it all somehow bypassed you two gossiping."

"You sold dates with me."

"Believe it or not, you've had a few wedding proposals in the past few years. But I did the math, and it wasn't worth it. I knew your sister's trust was running low, knew that would be a bust soon."

Four days before, I had thought my father was simply a gambler driven to madness with grief and addiction. Then, I thought he meant well, that he got too tangled up in debt and his addiction and things fell apart from there.

That his marriage to my mother was bad, not a great fit, but I held on to the chance that my mother had exaggerated, stricken by the loss of her fairy-tale love and venting to the lined pages.

But I was wrong.

I should have listened to the journals.

"I deserve this, at the least." There was a clinking of glass in the background, a sound I recognized as a rocks glass on his marble countertop. A nice, relaxing drink as he confessed his sins after a long day in the office. "I had to raise you, and you weren't even mine. Some gangster's bastard child. At least Lola was mine. She was loyal. Your mother had promise, but at the end, her death was all the good she gave me—a platform to use."

No. Absolutely not.

Because despite the marriage not being perfect, despite it being a last-chance, panicked thing, I know that for a time, my mother convinced herself she loved this man. After Lola was born, she had dreams of making things work, of being a beautiful family.

He had no right to destroy her memory like that.

No right to take advantage of *yet another person.*

"You do not contact me," I said, my voice stern, cutting him off before he could spew any more venom. "You do not contact me. You do not contact Lola."

"Delilah—"

"I have her journals." The phone went silent. "Everything is in them. How you met, how you tricked her into getting pregnant with Lola by saying she wouldn't have to marry Carluccio. The verbal abuse. How she wanted to leave. How you threatened to take Lola." I haven't shared this with my sister, knowing it will destroy her.

It destroyed me two years ago, in a way, when I realized it wasn't all rainbows and butterflies and perfect families torn apart by illness alone. I think part of me prayed and hoped it was an exaggeration, an emotional brain dump.

But now, I know for certain it was anything but.

"No one will believ—"

"Do you really think that? That no one will believe the stories that fall from the lips of your sweet, innocent daughter?" I felt something new taking over, or maybe breaking out. Any hint of obedience, any semblance of propriety evaporated. "You made me the weapon of your own demise."

Any loyalty I once felt toward him blew away as everything became clear.

I read it in my mother's beautifully scrawled handwriting, after all. Now it all made sense.

"No one would believe you, Shane," I said.

And I think with my words, he believed me.

Knew I didn't give a shit about him and his image and his campaigns and his, for lack of a better word, prostitution of his youngest daughter.

But it didn't matter if he did or not because I hung up before he could get in another word.

That day, my plans changed.

Or, they morphed.

Originally, my plan was to use the debts I was sure my father still had with the Carluccios to get an in. An excuse to enter the muck without raising suspicions.

You can't take down a family from the outside, can you?

My plan was revenge. For my sister. For my mother. For Arturo, the father who loved me beyond comparison but who I never truly met.

And once that revenge was gotten, I would head the Russo family, as my father always wanted. I'd come with the proof of my valor, of how far I would go for my family, and lead with integrity.

But now, I was adding another name to my plan of retribution.

Shane Turner.

I was going to take him down too, and I was going to make it fucking hurt.

My mind is lost in this world, in the place where my past and my present and my future meet, when I hear a thunk, feel the tire veer off, and then start clunking.

Just my *fucking* luck.

NINE

-Lilah-

Six weeks ago, I sold my beloved cherry red Audi and bought a 1992 Saturn.

Six weeks ago, I quit my job in an email, giving zero notice to the employers who hired me right out of college and nurtured my passion.

Six weeks ago, I left a hospital room in Ocean View, and my phone rang for the entire 76-minute drive north to my apartment. I packed up, subleased the apartment I loved, and used the balance from the sale of my car to pay for five months in my new, dingy apartment, plus a small cushion for living.

Six weeks ago, I put on my hottest red dress and my tallest black heels, curled my long blonde hair until it fell down my back in a perfect cascade, and walked into Jerzy Girls with a mission.

That mission being to finally take the chaos, burden, and stress of my father's debt away from my sister, who sacrificed for too long, and make a deal with the Carluccio family.

That is because six weeks ago, I got a call from my sister, and a man answered.

"This Lilah?" he asked, his voice deep and gruff. "Lola Turner's younger sister?"

I'd found the journals two years before and started to slowly put the pieces together, but not fast enough, it seemed.

"Yes?" I'd said, cold filling my stomach.

"This is Ben, your sister's man. She got into some trouble. She's hurt, but she's going to be okay. She's at the hospital in Ocean View."

I don't remember the rest of his words, just grabbing my keys and bag and running down the stairs, skipping the glass elevator I always loved riding in. I remember asking him to text me the room number and that I'd have my father handled.

I also remember the dull tone in my father's voice when I called to tell him my sister was in the hospital. Something had happened. I didn't have much information, but I was headed there.

I remember him telling me he'd wait for me to get down to Ocean View and we'd just go in together.

I found that odd, at the time.

I didn't 90 minutes later when I left the hospital.

It's funny how someone who once called you regularly to schedule meetings, to check in, to see if you could attend X gala or Y party with him can just . . . disappear from your life if you let him. How if you threaten a small, weak man who has used everyone in his life until the well runs dry, he'll run the other way.

It's been six weeks since I last spoke with the man who raised me, and not for the first time in those weeks, I wish things had been different.

Though, this time, it's not because the one who raised me is a gambling addict who would throw his own blood under the bus in order to manipulate and maintain his power.

But because the one who raised me didn't teach me how to change a goddamned tire.

Six weeks ago, I bought an old, shitty Saturn—a company that's so shitty and old, it doesn't even exist anymore—and the skeevy man from Facebook Marketplace told me the tires were nearly bald and would need to be replaced soon.

Of course, I didn't listen to him, instead driving through construction sites and sketchy parts of town for six weeks and, apparently, picking up a nail along the way.

I don't know how to change a tire, and I just spent the last hour of my shift pretending to slide around on a pole that I have no place being on. I barely have the energy to even lift my phone and google *how to change a tire*.

But, of course, the best part is that once I do that, once I hype myself up and decide that it *looks easy enough*, I realize I don't have the spare this car allegedly came with.

I have a big empty space instead.

Just my fucking luck.

Is this what I get for spending my life with my head in the clouds, ignoring the red fucking flags of my family? Letting Lola take over and handle everything while I went off to school and chased my dreams? It has to be, right? It has to be some kind of penance.

I get it, universe. I've been a little shit, so caught up in my own life, I ignored vital signs. No need to keep a girl down when she's trying to make it right.

Now all I can do is google how much a tow and new tires cost and mentally deduct that from my meager savings because the allowance that Paulie gives me barely covers food for the week, much less an emergency fund.

You know, once my sister told me this cute story about this girl she knows who had a flat tire and got totally stranded with no service, but she didn't leave with more debt and a crippling panic attack. No, a hot tow-truck driver came and changed the tire for her, and then she *married* that hot tow-truck driver.

I look in my rearview and side mirrors, hoping to see the bright lights of a big truck, but no luck.

I was born out of bad luck and shit timing and left a trail of it in my wake, so it truly is just time that it caught up with me, I guess. As I sit back, my head hitting the seat, my eyes linger on the loose spots where the lining is coming apart from the roof, and I try not to throw myself a pity party.

My life was magical seven weeks ago, everything I thought I had worked to get.

And now I'm a stripper in a car with a flat tire.

Funny how life works that way, I think to myself, closing my eyes for just a moment to try and recenter.

Then something knocks at my window, and I scream.

TEN

-Lilah-

When I open my eyes, a man is standing with his face inches from mine, a single pane of glass between us, and I think, *This is it*.

These are my final moments.

I'm going to die in a fucking 1992 *Saturn* on the side of the road wearing stripper makeup and a sweat suit.

As I continue to hyperventilate, I try to weigh my options. How far can I make it with a flat? Should I turn the key and floor it, or should I just accept that this is the last leg of my bad luck? But then the man smiles big and backs up, hands in the air like he's trying to say he's cool, he's safe.

His full lips are moving, too, saying something, but I can't hear him between the pounding of blood in my ears and the ringing from my scream that I think is still ricocheting in the small space.

"Jesus, Lilah, get it the fuck together," I tell myself aloud before slowly—so very slowly—unrolling the manual crank window. I also double-check my locks to make sure that those are in place. Once there's a one-inch gap, I speak.

"Can I help you?"

"I was going to ask you the same," he says, giving me a charming smile.

He's . . . cute. Tall. Very tall. Tanned skin, a bright white smile, dark, slicked-back hair with just a hint of silver at the temples. Adrianna would call him a silver fox, but I always thought that should be reserved for men with a full head of gray.

But his smile . . . very fox-like.

Despite the October chill, he's in a white button-down, sleeves rolled up to his elbows, the very edge of a tattoo creeping out under the white of the shirt, and a few buttons on top undone.

He's hot.

He's hot, and I'm pretty sure he knows it.

"Me?" I ask,

"You've got a flat."

Oh. Right. I've got a flat. I'm stranded on the side of the road, having a crisis of bad luck and shit timing.

"Yeah."

"You have anyone coming?" he asks, moving to look at the front driver's side tire, the one that's gone flat. I sigh, cracking my door open as I do and stepping out of the car.

"No. I was about to call a tow company," I say.

"No spare?" he asks, a small smile on his lips.

"Nope."

"Tow's gonna cost a shit ton, babe."

Now, most people in the world would find that offensive, a random person calling them babe, a stranger they've never seen before in their life . . . but he's the type. I can see it. I've been working around and with men like him for weeks. It's not meant to come off as belittling, but just . . . another way to address a woman.

Welcome to Italian-American men in the tristate area.

I just sigh at his words.

"I've got a buddy, can pick it up, get it fixed," he says as I stand beside him, staring at the flat. I swear, it seems like it happened in no time at all.

"I can't believe this," I say, ignoring him. "It was totally fine when I left work."

"A flat can happen in just a few minutes if a nail hits it just right." He moves his head to look for the culprit before pointing. "Right there," he says. "Shit luck that it hit where it did. Only takes one hit and a few miles and you're done."

"Sounds about right. I have the shittiest luck," I say with a shiver, staring at the tire. I should be thinking of the bottle of wine I was going to buy today that is so not in the budget now.

But that's not what has me looking up at the man, forgetting the drama of my tire.

It's the voice.

I recognize it.

I step back and look up before speaking.

"Do I . . . Do I know you?" I ask and squint a bit as I look him over, trying to figure out where I know him from. A fundraiser? Politics? My old job? My . . .

He smiles sheepishly then moves his hand to the back of his neck like he's embarrassed.

It doesn't look natural on this man who clearly has confidence for days.

His eyes are on his feet, and I follow the gaze, stopping at his shoes.

$400 shoes.

I know those shoes.

"Dante?" I say, stepping back once more with a hint of panic, bumping into the car because *what the fuck is happening?*

He steps back as well, raising his hands in a surrender pose.

Fuck, he's handsome, I think to myself as I get a better look at him. A break in his eyebrow from a scar is the only imperfection I can see. I've gotten glimpses through the dark, in the shadows, but never saw his full face.

I'm kind of glad I didn't. If I knew this was what I was dealing with all those weeks, I probably would have been a lot more nervous.

"I swear, I didn't plan this or anything creepy," he says with a laugh. "Just saw your flashers and—"

"I've never shown you my flashers," I blurt because apparently, I'm a five-year-old boy and *Jesus Christ, help me.*

He laughs.

I think if he had laughed as soon as I got out of the car, I would have known who he was based on that and the way my body reacts to it alone.

"Valid, I guess. But I swear I'm not a stalker. I'm just in the right place at the right time."

I blink at him a few times, biting the inside of my lip.

"Let me help you. It's cold, it's getting late, and you're on the side of the road."

Every common-sense alarm in my body flares to life because this is a man who, once a week, hires me for six hours to . . . chat.

"I've got a buddy. I'll call him up. He'll give you a tow, put on a new tire for you, and I'll cover it. Just go to dinner with me."

"God, that's . . . That's so kind, truly, but I can't. I don't even know you. That's not right."

"Got a lot of favors, babe. I can afford it." I look at him and then behind my car. A sleek black Corvette is parked there, sparkling like it gets waxed every day.

The man can afford it.

His shoes alone cost $400, after all.

"I don't even know you."

"The fuck you don't," he says, and I can't help but laugh. "You know my first pet was a dog, and I know your favorite food is the chocolate chip cookies your sister makes at her bakery." I did tell him that, didn't I? "You know my mom died when I was five, and I know yours died when you were ten."

"Well, we're both members of the dead-mom club, so that must mean you're safe, right? Serial killers never have a dead mom." He smiles at my words, and I see it now, the smile I've been dying to see in full view when I could hear it in his words through the shadows. His handsomeness overtakes the space, making air freeze in my lungs. His smile is big, laugh lines carving his cheeks, and I have to wonder if maybe—just maybe—my luck has changed.

This could be my moment where it all turns for the better.

"Let me take you to dinner. I'll tell you more reasons I'm definitely not a serial killer," he says, and I smile. He's good at this: flirting, smiling, getting a woman to do his bidding.

"Do women tell you no often?"

"No. They don't." *Of course they don't.*

"Ahh, a Casanova." I cross my arms over my chest, and he laughs. It sounds good. So fucking good. Deep and sexy, like I can feel it moving along my skin. "A Casanova who spends his days at a strip club?"

He takes a step, entering my personal space but not touching me.

I don't feel panic like common sense tells me I should.

I feel *heat*, despite the chill in the air.

"Had business at the club, a meeting." *Of course you did,* I think. "Never spent money there in my life. Saw you on the stage, knew you were something special, needed to know more about you." The breath freezes in my lungs. "Haven't heard a single thing yet telling me I'm wrong, that you aren't something exquisite. Except, maybe, that you don't like cilantro."

"It tastes like soap. It's a genetic thing."

His smile widens, and it feels like it lights up the space between us.

"Give me a shot. Text a friend, tell them you're going to Trattoria Seven with a stranger you met on the side of the road, then text her when we get there. Or tell them I'm Dante Romano, that Marco knows who I am, that I've been a customer. Best-case scenario, you make a new friend. Worst-case, you get out of the cold, eat a free meal, and get a free tire."

I stare at him.

He smiles at me.

A breeze comes, biting into my thin sweatpants.

"Trattoria Seven?" I ask of the fancy Italian restaurant owned by the family I work for. He smiles.

"They have good ravioli."

I do not like ravioli.

That's a sign, right? A sign from some higher being telling me this is a bad idea?

"Look, I appreciate this. Truly, I do. But I'll wait for a tow. I look like a sewer rat dressed in slum clothes, and—"

"You're gorgeous. Come, text a friend, and I'll call mine." His hand moves to his pocket and he grabs a phone, tapping a few times. "Joey. Yeah, Dante. Gotta car on the side of 98. Can you take it to your place, get it a new tire? Add it to my tab."

"Oh, I couldn't—" His eyes flit to mine, and something in them makes me shut up.

"Perfect." He taps the phone again without even saying goodbye, sliding it into his pocket before staring at me. "Handled. Text your friend, *fiorella*."

I chew my lip, a habit I formed when my mother was dying and I thought crying was inappropriate because my dad wasn't crying, and Lola wasn't crying, so I shouldn't either. I'd chew that lip raw until Lola had to make me swish salt water to help ease the ache.

"Now," he says, the word stern, a thick eyebrow lifting.

Marco trusts him, I think to myself. I'm pretty sure Marco is a good judge of character.

And because, really, how much worse can my life get, and because something about this man has the blood in my veins turning into electricity, I nod. I shoot a text to Candy, telling her I got a flat, that a guy that Marco knows gave me a ride, and we're eating at Trattoria Seven.

Any of my old friends would panic. Fuck, if I text Lola, she will lose her mind and drive up with Ben in tow to kick my ass.

But the girls of Jerzy Girls? Nah.

> Got it, babes. Share your location with me and be safe. Call if you need me.

ELEVEN

-Lilah-

The restaurant we pull up to minutes later is owned by the Carluccios. There are rumors about what happens in the connected butcher shop, about how they get the finest imports of cheese and dried meats, and how on earth they turn a profit when the price of the luxury meal barely covers the cost of ingredients.

Money laundering, some say.

Greasing palms at customs, others insist.

Tax evasion, even more whisper.

But I've always liked the version that isn't spread as often—that way back when, the Carluccio family saw that there were no authentic Italian restaurants in the area. That in a community of Italian immigrants, they deserved a hub. The story goes that the family built the restaurant and the butcher shop and the small Italian grocer with the idea of it being an asset to the community.

Years and years of being delusional and optimistic will do that to you—make you see the best in a literal mafia family.

Dante parks in the lot, walking around to open my door, letting in the cold night air.

"I'm sorry, but this . . . I . . . I am so not dressed for this," I say, biting my lip.

I feel small, and not in the way a tall man makes you feel small enough for him to protect.

Small in the way someone who is way out of their league feels.

"You're perfect," he says, his hand grabbing mine and tugging until I'm forced to step out of the car. He doesn't back up, though, instead pulling me up and into him until we're just inches apart, my breasts in the thick sweatshirt brushing against the white button-down he's wearing under the black suit jacket.

It's strange because this man feels like both a familiar friend and a complete stranger, and the way that heated electricity rolls over my skin when he touches me is like a long-lost lover.

"This place is . . . fancy."

"It's really not. It's just a restaurant."

"I'm serious, Dante." My voice is breathy, both from the nerves and him being so damned close to me. "Everyone walking in there is dressed nice, and I'm—"

"And you are perfect," he says.

"People will stare," I whisper. He looks into my eyes, and that strange mix of comfort and electricity runs through me.

Comfort and electricity and something so fucking *familiar*.

"They'll stare because some scum bag is walking into the restaurant with the most gorgeous woman on his arm." A blush burns my cheeks.

"I look like a slob."

"It's just dinner," he says. I don't respond, and finally, he steps back, giving me room to breathe.

Instantly, I'm cold, and it has nothing to do with the October air.

"Come. Let me feed you," he says. He puts out his hand once more, asking me to take it but still giving me the option.

And really, what are you supposed to do when a hot older man rescues you from the side of the road and then insists on feeding you?

So when he raises his eyebrows, waiting for a response, I put my hand in his and follow him into the restaurant.

"Menus?" the waitress, who is staring at my . . . date in a rather familiar way, asks. She smiles warmly at Dante and then moves her eyes to me, giving me a top to toe, and then another smile crosses her face—smugness.

This gorgeous woman knows I am no fit for the man across from me.

No fit for this fancy restaurant.

It's a strange realization.

I wanted out of my protective force field more than anything in the world. I wanted to live my own life, not let it be dictated by the wills and wants of other people. To have adventure and mystery. Now I'm here, but it doesn't feel as sexy and exciting as I thought it would be.

I went from galas, late nights in expensive VIP lounges, and the newest designer clothes to stripping in a mafia-owned bar. A nice one, but still—a strip club. There was once a time when a woman like this would look over my outfit and my date and know she was the one who didn't measure up. She'd ask me where I bought my dress or compliment my shoes.

Now I'm at a five-star restaurant in sweats and a messy bun.

Strange how the world works.

"No, we're good, Janine. Please tell Gino to send us the tasting menu, yes?" She nods, her charming smile returning to her lips as her face moves to him. "Drinks?"

"Whiskey for me and whatever Lilah wants," he says, tipping his chin to me. The waitress reluctantly moves her face from Dante to me, holding a pen to paper.

"I'll just have a Coke, please. Thank you." For a flash, her brow furrows and her eyes shift to Dante. He looks at her like he's annoyed that she's even questioning me before he nods.

"Go. Get it, Janine."

"Yes, of course," she says, running off.

Silence takes over the table.

God, this is a terrible idea.

"This is a terrible idea," I say out loud, looking around at the romantic, dim lighting, the exquisitely-dressed guests, and the looks we're getting. "I should go." I start to move, to stand, to do literally anything to get myself out of this situation. "Thank you for everything, seriously, but I can—"

"You can thank me by sitting your ass down and enjoying a meal with me."

"Isn't this weird? I mean, you found me on the side of the road after I spent hours sitting across from you in my underwear." He smiles, and I wonder why on earth I said that out loud. Why would I remind him of that?

"Yes. A sign, don't you think? That I stumbled across you in your time of need?"

"Or maybe you're just a creepy stalker following me and right place, right timed your way into a date I already turned you down for." With that, he laughs, full and deep, his head tipping back and a hand with small scars around the fingers going to his chest.

It's a good freaking laugh.

So good, every face in the vicinity stops what they're doing to look at the man seated across from me. The faces range from intrigued to out-and-out *shocked*.

Strange.

So very strange.

"If I were a stalker and we hadn't met the way we did, would you have said no? If I was just enamored with you, waiting it out, trying to get up the nerve, and I asked you out when we bumped into each other at the grocery store, do you think you would have turned me down?" He's asking in a way that I find both irritating and endearing. Because the point he's getting at—that if he had asked me out in a normal setting, I probably would have said yes, so what's the point of being a creepy stalker—is valid.

I scrunch my nose, not wanting to admit as much, and he laughs, loud and deep once again.

"Stop doing that," I say in an annoyed whisper. "Jesus, everyone is looking!"

"Doing what?" His laugh is dying down, but the smile is still in place.

"Laughing like that! It's loud. Everyone is looking at you like you've lost your mind."

"They would."

"They would?"

"They would think I've lost my mind. I come here a lot." I raise an eyebrow. "Not on dates. I'm very much single. I just live in the area, and I hate cooking."

"Okay . . . ?" I say, still not getting why anyone would think he's lost his mind.

"Lilah, look at me. Do I look like a man who bursts out laughing at random?" Again, I scrunch my nose, and he cracks a smile, but I continue to look him over. He has a handsome face—a wide Italian nose, thick eyebrows, one with that tiny break in it, full pink lips on tan skin. Cheekbones that makeup artists spend days trying to cut into people's faces.

He's handsome.

But the lines on his face don't scream "laughs a lot." Instead, the deep line between his brows and the ones around his mouth say something else entirely.

"You look like you frown a lot," I say then use a hand to cover my mouth, eyes wide, because *why the fuck would I say that out loud?*

What is wrong with me today?

His head tips back again, that deep laugh filling the room.

Okay, so, good sign: he's not annoyed.

Bad sign: he might be insane, and apparently, he never laughs.

Enough so that a place he frequents often is heavily confused when he finally does.

"Yeah, you can call it a con to my job. I'm the one always telling people they've done things wrong."

I want to ask what the job is. The nice car, the nice clothes, the fancy restaurant, the money to blow on private rooms for hours on end—they all steer toward something expensive and high-powered or something devious.

But I don't because questions like that are reciprocal. If I ask, he might ask how I got started at Jerzy Girls, and *I'm paying off my father's debts while I try to figure out how to take down one mafia family and earn my place in another* isn't really a great first-date conversation.

Is this a first date?

*Janin*e brings our drinks before I can ask, clunking a thick glass filled with Coke in front of me then gently placing a glass with dark liquid and a single giant ice cube in front of Dante.

God, could this woman be any more obvious?

"What else can I get you?" she asks, her back to me.

"That's all, Janine. We won't be needing your help anymore tonight. Just bring the dishes out, yes?" Now her face turns to me as if to say, *This is all your fault*, but she nods, walking away.

"She seems like a pleasant person." The doors to the kitchen swing angrily as she walks through them.

"She's fine."

"Is she an ex?" I ask, because apparently, the filter between my mouth and brain is no longer operating.

"No. Why, are you jealous?" He's not annoyed by the question. Instead, he's smiling.

Goddamit.

"No, not at all," I say, straightening my shoulders and letting the woman I was just a few weeks ago seep into my veins again. Chin high, smile light, power on full blast. It's like putting on your favorite sweatshirt—comfortable and familiar. Who cares if I look like a slob?

I am Delilah Antonia Turner.

Or Russo, depending on who you ask.

I am power.

I am fierce.

I am revenge.

I repeat my mantra in my head before speaking again.

"I just find it interesting that you would frequent a place where the waitress clearly wants you and then choose to bring a woman to that restaurant as your date."

"Does Janine want me?" he asks, and I raise an eyebrow.

He smiles.

"You're not a stupid man from what I can see, Dante Romano."

"So what does a woman who wants me do? What does she act like? Does she fight me at every turn when I try to take her out? Does she notice if other women are interested in me?" I stare at him, irritated, as I realize where I went wrong. "Inquiring minds want to know, Delilah."

That smile looks damned good on his face.

Even more, that smile looks good in better lighting, not hidden behind dim lights and shadows.

Thankfully, I'm saved from answering when the chef comes before us, dropping an intricate appetizer.

I smile at the man graciously, as I was trained to do, while he rattles off any number of ingredients in the salad, and I cringe internally.

The thing is, despite being raised with fine dining and frequenting five-star restaurants, there are few things that I hate eating more than *fine dining*.

When Lola and I were teens, we read an article about supertasters, people who genetically have more tastebuds and thus can taste more of what they eat. It makes them unintentionally picky eaters. Lola ordered some silly test with paper strips that you place on your tongue, and while she only tasted paper, I tasted the chemicals.

Just another fun thing my parents gave me. You know, anxiety, the need for revenge, tenure at a strip club, and the weird ability to taste things.

On the bright side, the women at the events I go to aren't necessarily graded on how well they eat. In fact, the more you eat at those parties, the more you're judged. So, I've learned to pick at what I don't hate and then push things around until the rest of the plates get taken away.

It works like a charm and has never let me down.

But I should have known that nothing gets past this man. My trick works through course one, but by two, Dante has questions.

Goddammit.

"What is it?" he asks, putting his fork to the side and looking at me. I straighten my back and smile wide.

"What?"

"Drop the look. What's wrong?"

"I don't know what you mean. Nothing's wrong."

"Nothing's wrong?"

"Nope."

"Then why are you pushing your food around like it might attack you?"

"I'm doing no such thing," I say, dropping my fork but also freaked the fuck out that he noticed.

"Delilah, don't play games with me. Other men you've been out with, they're fools. I'll tell you that now. I am not a fool. I don't fall for a pretty smile on a mouth I want to fuck." The air seizes in my lungs. "What's wrong with the food?"

My tongue comes out, tasting my lips, my mind still stuck on the sentence prior.

His lips turn up in a slight smile that is absolutely *devious*.

"Yeah, you heard me. But right now, we're talking about food, *fiorella*."

"Food," I say, the word a mere whisper out of my throat.

"What's wrong with it?" he asks, his eyes locked on mine, and something about it has me confessing. Something about the way his eyes lock to mine, the genuine caring in his voice despite the firm tone —I can't resist.

"It's great, I'm sure . . . I just . . ." I sigh, embarrassed. "I'm the world's pickiest eater. I can't help it. I taste things that people just . . . don't."

I expect the eyeroll.

I expect the huff.

I expect him to say something like, *Just give it a try! Maybe you'll like it!*

Or maybe, *You never grew out of that?*

Instead, he surprises yet again.

"What do you eat when you're out?" he asks, taking the napkin in his lap and moving it to the table. Again, despite the pounding embarrassment and panic in my chest, he looks at me, and I have to answer.

"I don't."

"You don't?"

"I mean, if I'm somewhere I like, I eat. But if it's a place like this —" I wave my hand around. "I just . . ." *Oh god, why am I telling this man this?!* "I make it look like I eat and then eat when I get home."

"Where do you like to eat?" he asks, again, not angry but demanding all the same.

"This is fine, seriously, Dante. I'm good—"

"What do you eat, Delilah?"

"Normal stuff," I blurt. "Burgers. Chicken fingers. Fries. I like salads, but nothing . . . fancy. Sandwiches? I don't know. Not all sandwiches. Pizza without all the toppings." I look up at the ceiling, where a gorgeous chandelier twinkles in the low lighting. "Why am I telling you that I essentially eat like a child?"

"Because I told you to," he says, then he starts to move, scooting out of his chair and standing.

"Dante, what—"

"Two minutes, I'll be right back," he says, but his eyes aren't even on me. Instead, they're somewhere in the back of the restaurant looking at someone. Something?

Less than those two minutes later, he's back, a smile on his face as he sits, grabs his napkin, and places it on his lap once more. "Okay, perfect. So, do you drink?"

"I'm sorry, what?"

"Drink liquor. Or do you abstain? You got a soda."

"I . . . I drink. I just don't drink when I'm out to dinner with a random man who picked me up on the side of the road." A server comes over, clearing plates silently. "What does that have to do with anything? Where did you go?"

"I went to speak with a friend," he says, lifting his drink and taking a sip before sitting back. "That's smart, not drinking around strangers."

"Yeah, I'm a genius, getting into cars with a random man who buys my time at a strip club and hoping for the best." His eyes widen, and that smile grows.

"Fair, not the smartest. But next time you're stuck on the side of the road, you'll call me, correct?" he asks, and I stare at him like he's insane.

"I don't know you. I don't have your number or—"

"That's fine. Next time you're in a jam, I'll find you myself," he says, and I don't even have time to question it, to ask how on earth he would do that, *why* he would do that, because he's already changing the subject and moving on with our pleasant conversation.

The next course comes, and I dread seeing what it might be. A plate is placed in front of both of us, a silver top on each, and Janine lifts the lids with very little ceremony before walking away.

I would laugh at how annoyed she clearly is, but I can't. I can't even speak. That's because in front of me is a pile of freaking *French fries*.

"Are you good with breaking it up into courses? Or do you insist on eating everything together."

"What?" I ask, confused, staring at the elegantly cut thin fries that I just know are going to be freaking amazing.

"Chicken tenders are next. I told Gino that he can send things out as they're done, but—"

"You did this?"

"I didn't cook them, no."

"You had a five-star chef make me *French fries?*"

"Well, French fries and chicken tenders aren't exactly on the menu, Lilah." He says it like it's obvious, but that I didn't know that fact.

I just blink at him.

He's so damned handsome, so damned elegant.

And he's lifting a French fry from a plate with those fingers that I could imagine doing other things to me, eyes locked on mine.

"You didn't have to do this," I whisper.

"You have to eat."

"I was fine with what we had. It was lovely." *If not too extravagant for my incredibly unrefined palate.*

How embarrassing is this? The man in front of me is a freaking god. And I am a peasant who likes to eat chicken nuggets and blue-box mac and cheese like I'm eight because it's safe and comfortable.

I put my face down to my plate and fight the urge to fidget, to bite my lip, to look around the room and see if anyone is looking at me, judging.

Delilah, hands in your lap. Be a goddamned lady for once. The words the man who raised me often repeated under hushed breaths run through my mind, and I move my hands to my lap as if he's right next to me.

"What's going on?" Dante asks, staring at me.

My mind has frozen, though, caught between the past and the present, trying to figure out how to navigate this.

"I shouldn't be here," I say in a whisper, embarrassment eating at me.

I am not this persona anymore.

I don't fit in here.

That person was all a facade built by a greedy man.

I don't *know* who I am yet, not with all my new knowledge. Not with new goals and a different understanding of how the world works.

But I do know I don't like fancy food.

I don't like waitresses looking down on me because I didn't spend eight hours getting ready.

For some reason, I like the man sitting across from me even though common sense says to *run, run, run.*

I also know I should start trusting my gut more, that I did it tonight by agreeing to trust him, and I did it the day I decided to leave my old life.

But I also know that the new life probably doesn't include this—fancy dinners across from fine-as-hell men.

Before I can stand and run off, though, a hand reaches under the small table, grabbing my own, the skin warm and rough.

The electricity runs through my system, snapping me to attention.

"This is the best idea I've had in four years, *fiorella,*" he says. "You are the first selfish thing I've done in at least two. Please. Be selfish with me. Let's have this."

His words churn something in my gut.

Be selfish with me.

I've felt bogged down by the reminder of how selfish I was since my world turned upside down. It was selfish to let my sister sacrifice so much. I was selfish when I didn't take those journals to heart and dissect them further. Selfish when I never said no to Shane for fear of shaking my safe little bubble.

I've made a promise to live selflessly from here on out, to move without worrying about my own comfort until everything is set right.

And here is a man nearly begging me to do the opposite.

So for some reason, I decide to nod.

I decide to be selfish with the mysterious Dante Romano.

"Yeah. Okay. But . . . can I get a glass of wine?" I ask with a small smile. If I'm going for it, I might as well go full blast.

"Anything you want, Delilah, I'll get for you," he says, but he's not smiling. He's staring at me like he means every single syllable in every single way.

It should scare me, the intensity of his gaze, his words.

But instead, I just smile.

TWELVE

-Lilah-

When we leave the restaurant, a chill has settled, dark rolling in with the night. Across the river, the lights of New York City are blinking in all their glory. Dante holds my hand as we walk, stopping at the railing overlooking the water, both of us looking out before he moves, caging my body between his and the cold metal.

"What now, *fiorella?*"

"*Fiorella?* What is that, like, Thumbelina or something?" I ask, giving him a weird look. It's been bugging me since he first said it.

"No. *Fiorella.* It's Italian for little flower." He says the word with a light lilt, the word coming easy and naturally to him. "It's what my grandfather called my mother."

"*Little flower?*" I ask with what I'm sure is an air of irritation and indigence. I look over my shoulder at him, and he smiles, moving a piece of hair the wind whipped from my bun to behind my ear.

"You remind me of that. Something pretty and delicate. Something to look out for. A daisy or something."

I'm annoyed. I'm so incredibly tired of being pretty and delicate, of being something precious that people want to protect. My entire family fell apart trying to protect me, to protect my innocence.

My father wanted to protect me from being "tainted" in an effort to stop me from being unusable to him anymore.

My mother wanted to protect me from the truth of who I was and the danger that could come with that.

My sister wanted to protect me from the drama and stress that is our family.

But no one *asked* me if I wanted to be protected.

No one asked if I *needed* protection.

And I'm learning I can stand on my own pretty damn well.

"I don't want to be a daisy," I say aloud, staring at the water. "I've been delicate my whole life. I want to be strong. Vicious. I want to be . . . I want to be poison ivy. Touch me and you'll regret it." I look back at him again, and he's smiling at me, something close to pride in his eyes. His hands move, turning me until I face him, my back against the bars. "I want to be covered in it. Pull some away and more will grow in its place."

"Good thing I'm not allergic to poison ivy then, huh?" he asks with that handsome smile.

"I guess so." And then, because I feel good and I had a drink, and for the first time since that hospital room in Ocean View, I feel free, I let myself smile and be silly. Be the girl I was before Johnny Vitale, before I found the journals. "Be careful. You get too close, I might start growing on you, too."

"Baby, I don't think you know what I would give to be covered in you."

I don't have time to register shock or gasp or anything else, because once he speaks, he's kissing me. His lips are on mine, his head tipping down as mine tips up, and I move to my tiptoes to offset the imbalance in our height.

But it doesn't matter.

Because as soon as his lips touch mine, my body lights up like I touched an outlet. My hands move, wrapping around his neck, one of his hands goes to my waist, the other getting lost in my hair as he pulls my face in closer to his, and I know he feels it too.

It's like a puzzle piece that clicks into place, letting you see the bigger picture.

Like the chaos of the world could continue around us, and at the end, we'd still be here in our own little bubble.

His head moves, teeth nipping my lips, and I gasp, opening my mouth. Then, like the all-consuming man I'm learning he is, his tongue enters my mouth, tasting me, and he *groans*.

The sound vibrates through my body, shaking my bones and melting my core.

I move my head, trying to get more, trying to get everything, my hands grasping tighter until a small moan breaks from my body and finally, finally, Dante breaks the kiss. He rests his forehead on mine as we catch our breath, but he dips once more, pressing his lips to mine quickly, like he can't help himself. Like he's a kid who needs one more taste and god, the look on his face is *boyish*.

Elated.

Consumed.

I can only imagine my own reflects that exactly.

Long minutes pass like that as we breathe, exchanging quick pecks and smiling goofily.

"So?" he asks finally.

"So what?" I'm dazed, unsure of what he means, and he knows it.

"What now? What should we do? Your car won't be ready until tomorrow." The hand in my hair moves to my cheek, and the warmth of it feels good against my cold skin. "What do you want to do? You're getting cold."

Something about the question shocks me—the ability to choose, to make the decision for *what next*. I can't remember the last time I was given a choice so upfront. A lifetime of being told when to be where and what to wear when I show up for whatever gala or political fundraiser means that making choices for *me* is kind of . . . new.

And then I take in this man, this relative *stranger* who saved me today. Maybe he could be a white knight—could help me leave my ivory tower for good. Snap the last thread holding me to my past life of being a good girl, obedient, listening, and following the rules that were put in front of me.

"Your place?" I ask, trying to be coy and sexy the way I've seen my friends do after a night out on the town as they choose the men they'll be leaving with.

When Dante smiles, I know I made the right choice.

THIRTEEN

-Lilah-

The home Dante drives us to is gigantic. Even though it's already dark with the mid-fall light leaving early, I don't miss the giant black iron gate we drive through or the winding driveway. I don't miss the way a pathway leads to another smaller home behind the estate. And I surely don't miss the marble foyer and grand chandelier gently lighting the entryway we walk into.

"Uh, wow," I say, looking around and taking in the giant hallway as he leads me up the spiraling staircase.

"It's a home," he says like it's nothing. "A family home."

"A family home? Like you live with—"

"Come," he says, cutting me off and quickly walking down a long hallway. We enter through one door that has a sitting room slash tv area and then through a second hallway before going up another staircase.

The house is a damned mansion.

I stay quiet as Dante drags me through the house until, finally, he pulls me into a room and shuts the door behind us.

"Oh my god, do you live with . . . your parents?" I ask, my eyes wide and confused and, admittedly, a bit alarmed. I pull my hand from his, stepping back into the sitting area and only letting myself get a small glimpse into the huge, gorgeous bedroom.

"Jesus, no. Well, kind of, but not in that way," he says.

I cross my arms on my chest, raising an eyebrow.

Although they always mysteriously stopped calling after a few weeks, I have had boyfriends.

I've had quite a few boyfriends, actually. Boyfriends with money and power and connections.

But also, I've had boyfriends who lived in the same home as their parents and tried to play it off as if they didn't *live with their parents*.

And this man before me is not in his twenties. He's not just out of school, trying to figure things out. He has money and prestige, even if I can't figure out from where. And he . . . lives with his parents?

He steps closer, pulling me into him, and the feeling that fires between us reminds me of why I let things get this far—why I ignored every red flag and kept going.

"My dad lives here. He's older, and I don't trust him living alone. My nephew also lives here, on another wing."

"A wing?"

"A part of the house."

"I know what a wing is, Dante. I'm just saying . . . This house has *wings*?" He smiles like he finds my awe cute.

"Yes, baby. It has wings. Now, can I show you my room, or . . ."

I look around the sitting room, taking in how . . . empty it is. Lifeless.

"Is it as boring as this room?" I ask, using a hand to indicate where we are. The furniture is gorgeous, high-end and seemingly comfortable, the television the newest and biggest version, I'm sure. But the room is empty of anything else.

"Yes," he says with a laugh as he starts to guide me into the bedroom, and he's right. It's vast and gorgeous, a huge four-poster dark-wood bed with a black comforter and sheets that tell me he definitely does not have an angry cat like I do—or any pet for that matter. There's a dresser with a mirror across the bed, a smaller TV in a corner, and a door that I assume leads to a bathroom.

But the room is lifeless, just as lifeless as the entryway.

"Why so boring?" I ask, stepping out of his hold and walking around. "God, this place is like a man cave but not even in the fun way."

He watches my every move, something I feel rather than see.

"It's so . . . gloomy." Dark woods, dark bedding, light-gray walls that remind me of rainy days and overcast skies. No art. No photos. No . . . nothing.

As I'm moving a curtain aside to look out the window at a courtyard, the man in question comes up behind me. He puts a hand on my hip before pressing into me. His breath is hot on my ear when he speaks.

"Maybe I just needed a little bit of sunshine to help me see," he says in a whisper, and the words swirl around me, but just as I start to grasp them, to understand, his hand is moving, a thumb grazing the soft part of my belly that sits atop the waistband of my sweatpants.

"Is that what I am? A little bit of sunshine?"

"You're the whole damned solar system, Lilah," he says, turning me, and the line is cheesy, but his face . . . His face is not.

It's both serious and consumed with heat.

"Dante—" I start, unsure of what to say.

"I found you, and every molecule in my body said I needed you," he says in a whisper against my lips. "I am not this man. I am not impulsive. I sure as fuck never take a woman back here. But here I am spending full days in a goddamned strip club just to get to know you. Finding you and then demanding you let me take you out, bringing you back here. What are you doing to me, Delilah?"

"The same thing you're doing to me," I whisper. "I don't date. I don't trust random men. I surely don't go back to their place," I say.

"Good," he says, and I expect more, but then his lips are on mine and he's devouring me.

It's not soft and sweet, not a lovely kiss to remember like outside the restaurant.

It's a claiming. Dante is staking his claim on me despite no one being around. He's kissing me like he's trying to leave his mark, trying to make it so when the kiss ends, when the night ends, I'll remember this moment.

As if I could forget.

"I need to say something," he says when he finally breaks the kiss, pressing his forehead to mine as I pant, trying to catch my breath. That electricity is flooding my veins, my blood thumping everywhere but my brain, making me feel almost light-headed.

But those words have me falling back to earth.

"What?"

A million and seven things flood through my mind, starting with *he's a murderer* and ending with *he has another woman he's hiding me from.*

"We do this, there's no going back," he says, and the words are almost a whisper through my ears and body, caressing every nerve ending. His hand moves, pushing a piece of hair back. "This. You feel it. Electric."

It's not just me.

"We do this, that's it, *fiorella*."

"What does that mean?" I ask in a whisper.

"You'll be mine." *You'll be mine.* What in the fuck?

"I don't . . . We just met."

"Doesn't matter."

"Dante—"

"Trust me on this. Trust it will be worth it." The words touch something inside me, a familiar voice or words . . . but *trust me* is such an overused phrase. One I heard my father say so many times, so maybe it's flight or fight coming out?

"What?"

"Do you? Trust me."

"I barely know you."

But something about his warmth, about this electricity, it feels . . . easy. Like a thrill but also comfort. Like something new and exciting but safe.

Like home.

"You trust me," he says to himself and then moves to what I assume is his next topic. But first, his lips brush mine once more, that electricity flaring.

"You also have to know, if we do this. I don't do soft and sweet." I move my head back, looking at him and raising an eyebrow.

"What?"

"You're a princess. I bet every man you've ever been with has treated you as such." I open my mouth, ready to confess, to tell him everything about every other man before him, but— "I don't want to know. Actually, from here on out, I don't want another man's name falling from your lips in my presence unless it's you telling me because you want me to beat them to a pulp." My eyes go wide with shock, and he smiles that fucking amazing smile. "Passion, baby." His hand reaches out and flips mine over, fingers grazing where my blood is pounding beneath thin skin. "We've got it. You feel it, I know you do." My tongue pokes out, licking my lips, and he smiles.

"Passion isn't soft and sweet. Passion like this? It's volatile. It's explosive. Electric."

There's that word again.

Electric.

"Oh-okay . . . ," I say, because now I really want to get this going. That electric pulse has moved through me, now throbbing in my clit, dying for something. Anything.

"I will devour your body, make you feel things you've never felt before, but I will not be soft and sweet while I do it."

"O . . . kay?"

"Okay," he says in a whisper then presses his lips to mine again, devouring me. As he kisses me, his hand moves up, under my sweatshirt, to the bare skin of my waist. Those hands continue moving up, up until the sweatshirt is coming with it and he's tugging it over my head. He steps back before sitting on the edge of his bed as I stand in a bra and sweats.

"I want to see you," he says. "Push those down." He tips his chin with his words, indicating the sweatpants I'm wearing, and I bite my lip, my thumbs moving to the edge of them.

Maybe I should just leave. Maybe—

"Now."

His words send a jolt through me, and I do as he asks, like my body is fully under his control. The sweats fall down, pooling at my feet, and I step out of them, leaving me in a bra and a lacy thong.

"Jesus fucking Christ, a dream," he whispers, taking me in.

"You've seen me before," I remind him. The outfits I wore during our private sessions didn't cover much more.

"No, I haven't. This? This is for me alone. That was for the world, baby, for your job. Right now, this is mine." I lick my lips, nervous and hot and eager. "Step forward. Come to me," he says, widening his legs and opening his arms, telling me exactly where he wants me to be.

I step until I'm standing there between his legs, and his hands, starting at the back of my knees, move up gently, thumbs brushing under the curve of my ass, then back down. The feeling is hot, my body going up in flames.

But nothing compares to the way heat pools at my core when he leans forward and presses a soft, sweet, almost reverent kiss to my belly right above the line to my panties.

My breathing is heavy, and I force myself to remember how to drag air into my lungs and let it back out.

His hands move up over my ass and graze my back before undoing my bra clasp. Those fingers drag the straps of my bra down until the entire thing falls to the floor.

Those hands move again, back to my waist, calluses caressing sensitive skin before he cups my breasts. He holds them, a thumb from each hand circling tight and sensitive nipples.

I gasp at the sensation before just barely leaning in to get more.

His eyes move up to me, and although mine are hooded with pleasure, the half-smirk on his lips is still visible.

He doesn't stop staring at me as his head leans forwards, his mouth surrounding one nipple and sucking it into his mouth, this tongue laving the flesh as he does.

I moan low, the feeling incredible, a string that runs straight to my clit pulling tight.

His hand tugs the nipple of the other breast as he sucks, and I whimper, my body instinctively moving closer to get more.

He pulls back and laughs.

He fucking laughs.

"God, you are going to be perfect for me, aren't you?" he asks, rolling the wet nipple between his fingers. The other hand moves back down the curve of my waist, a thumb tucking into my panties and dragging them down. I lift one leg and then the other, and finally, I'm standing in front of this man completely naked, while he stays wholly dressed.

I fucking love it.

I love the power coursing in my veins, the way he's looking at me like I could do no wrong at this moment.

The way he looks at me like he wants to devour, to possess me.

The hand that helped my thong down moves back up, over my knee then to my inner thigh, gentle fingers brushing up as they go.

My breathing escalates as I anticipate what will come next.

The side of his pointer finger moves along me, parting me gently as it does, dragging up.

"God, you're wet," he says, lifting the hand up then putting his finger in his mouth, eyes locked to mine as he tastes me, groaning as he does.

"Hand on my shoulders, baby."

"What?"

"Hands." He takes one of mine, placing it on his shoulder. "On my shoulders." He repeats the move with the other hand.

I'm confused until I need his shoulders to hold myself steady as his hands move to my leg, hitching it up onto the bed.

"That's a good girl." As I steady myself, I look at him, expecting to see him staring at me, smiling at me, but his eyes are on my wet pussy, on the tip of his finger that's slowly circling my clit. "Now I can see you," he says, and I moan loudly, my head moving to look up at the ceiling, my hair tumbling down my back. I'm not sure when he took the ponytail holder out, but the silky hair on my back heightens everything. "No. No, you watch too," he says, and I obey, watching his fingers gently play with me. Teasing touches, gentle slides.

Never giving me pressure, never entering, never anything.

"Dante—"

"Tell me what you need, Delilah."

"Dante, I—"

"I'm happy right here, *fiorella*," he says, that finger moving, grazing my already swollen clit, making my hips jolt. "I could do this all night."

"I need more," I whisper, nervous, the confident siren seeming to sleep while this god is in her presence.

"What do you *need*, Delilah?"

I've never had to do this.

Not that there has been much of *this*.

But I've done this much. Not much more, but this, I've done.

I've never had to walk a man through it, though.

Thankfully, it's then that the siren awakens.

The siren remembers who we are.

We are power.

We are unhinged beauty.

We get whatever the fuck we want.

"I need you to finger me, Dante," I say, and my voice has lost the meek edge to it.

His eyes move to mine, and that *fucking smile* is there.

"There she is," he says, and without moving his eyes from mine, a thick finger slips inside me.

"Oh, fuck," I whimper, rocking my hips to get him deeper. His finger retreats and then slides in again, and I moan, my eyes drifting shut at the pure pleasure coursing through me.

"Watch. Watch me finger you. Watch what my cock will be doing to you." I obey, watching two thick fingers move in me, watching his thumb swipe over my clit.

"It's so good. It's *too* good, Dante. You're gonna make me . . ." My breath and all words leave my body as he adds a third finger, the stretch incredible. Pleasure tinged with just a hint of discomfort.

"That's it," he coos, watching his fingers, watching my body take him. My hands brace on his shoulders. "That's it, baby."

"Oh, god, fuck, Dante—"

"Yeah, you say my name. You say my *fucking name* when I make you come. Do you understand?" His fingers continue their torture, three thick digits fucking me, his thumb starting to rub my clit, pure, unadulterated torture.

"Yes, anything. Please!" I want to come.

I *need to come*.

I need *this man to make me come*.

"When I'm done, when you come saying my fucking name, you get on your knees and return the favor." My pussy clenches at the thought alone and he smiles. "You like that idea, don't you?" The thrust of his fingers gets harder, less gentle, more chaotic, and the swiping of his thumb intensifies.

I'm falling apart.

"Yes," I whisper, and he smiles a devious smile.

"Good. Now come for your man, baby." His thumb presses hard on my clit as his fingers thrust inside me, crooking and hitting a new spot, and that does it.

I come undone.

My fingers dig into his shoulders as I do, and I fight to stay standing. The whole time, his eyes are locked on my face. Watching. Watching like he's seeing the most spectacular show there's ever been as I shake and moan his name, his fingers buried in my cunt.

As the wave of pleasure starts to fade, his fingers leave my body, and I mewl at the loss. His lips tip up, but still, I don't forget his demand.

I move, my foot leaving the bed, and I kneel before him.

Waiting.

"Such a good fucking girl, doing as I said," he coos to me, one hand moving to his belt and the other to my mouth. "Clean these for me." My mouth opens instantly, a slave to his demands, and I take his fingers inside and use my tongue to clean off every last drop of myself from them. His eyes watch me hungrily as I do, his hand moving faster before he pulls out his thick cock and stands from the bed, his cock bobbing before my face.

This could be shameful. Just like dancing on a stage, this could make me feel powerless and less than.

But the look in his eyes tells me everything I need to know. It might seem like he's in control of this, like he has the power, but he doesn't. There's something about kneeling before this man, fully dressed in slacks and a dress shirt, his hand stroking his cock, that feels like power.

Not for him.

For me.

Like I have such fucking power that this man—a man of restraint and control and money—can't even bear to take off his clothes.

The siren smiles at him as I move my hand and take his cock into it, my eyes locked on his. His chest is heaving, moving with deep breaths, his mouth parted as my much smaller hand starts to move, stroking him.

Then I move closer, so close I'm breathing on him. His legs widen, giving me more room to work with. My tongue dips out, the tip swiping where a drop of precum has leaked out of his cock, and a deep moan falls from Dante's lips. I take him and tap the head on my tongue a few times, watching his face as pure lust takes over.

"Jesus fucking Christ, you're dirty, aren't you?" he asks in a low voice, and I smile before moving, slipping the head between my lips and sucking. I moan at the taste and slowly ease him inside, sucking and licking as I do.

The feeling of his eyes on me, of the feral look in them, of him towering over my small body sends a new rush of wet between my legs. As the arousal starts to furl in my belly again, I moan around him, my hand capturing what is left out, and he smiles.

"That's it, suck my cock like a good little girl," he says, his voice low and raspy as I stare up at him, moving my mouth over his cock. "God, such a pretty sight, watching it disappear down your throat." His hand moves to my hair, twisting it and using the new leverage to guide me. My tongue runs along the underside, and he groans deep, urging my face to move quicker along him. I let my jaw go slack, let him use me, let the feeling of this—being so used and overpowered by a man—overtake me.

He doesn't treat me like a precious, breakable thing.

He treats me like a woman he wants to destroy, a woman who can handle it and come back stronger and better.

The feeling is intoxicating as I moan around his cock. My hand moves, dipping down to my wet pussy, and a finger circles my clit, making me moan harder. My hips start to rock against my hand at the rhythm he's fucking my face.

"Jesus Christ," he says, bending, moving his hands to my armpits before lifting me and tossing me onto the big, fluffy bed. I land with a giggle, my emotions and thoughts all over the place, but Dante has no such look on his face.

"You play with that pussy. Get it ready for me," he says, and his eyes are dark, pupils wide with lust, his jaw set tight as he starts to unbutton his shirt. "Now, Delilah," he says, and I acquiesce, running a hand down my body and circling my clit, letting a low moan leave my lips.

"Open your legs so I can see, baby," he says, and I groan but do as he asks, spreading them on his dark sheets.

As I watch inches of tanned flesh come into my line of sight as he undoes buttons unbearably slowly, I give him his own brand of torture. A single finger enters my body, and I moan, my pussy calming down to try and get more, to get anything.

"Fuck," he says, watching the finger leave then return, his own fingers pausing their work.

"Hurry," I whisper.

"*Fuck!*" he says then finishes the buttons, throwing the shirt to the side and stepping out of his pants. His shoes are long gone. And finally, he's crawling up my body.

"Birth control—are you on it?" he asks, and I blush at the words.

It's almost funny if you look at it from the outside. I take my clothes off and dance on a stage for a living. I met this man because he bought my time. Moments earlier, his cock was in my mouth as he fucked my face. But here I am, blushing about *birth control*.

"I have an IUD." His eyes twinkle.

"I was tested recently. Nothing came up," he says. "I would love nothing more than to fill your cunt bare."

His words have a staggering breath leaving my chest.

"I'm... Dante, I've—" I start to explain, to tell him, but he presses his lips to mine, cutting me off.

"You telling me I can fuck you bare, *fiorella?*" The sweet word rolls off his tongue and even here, like this, it melts a part of me.

"Yeah, Dante," I whisper, ignoring the fact that there is so much more we should do, more I should say before this. But I've already made up my mind.

I want Dante Romano.

If only for one night, I want him. I want this. I want to give him this. I want to sever the final tie of being the breakable, protected princess.

He smiles a wicked smile, and then slowly, torturously slowly, the head of his thick cock moves, sliding inside of me like he was made to be there. The stretching is intense, not necessarily painful, but uncomfortable and foreign. But his breath in my ear, the way he's panting there, has my body melting, relaxing to let him in.

"Oh, god," I whisper.

"You're so fucking tight, baby," he says. "Jesus fucking Christ, unbelievable." His words, his *groans* have a new rush of wetness helping him slide in.

"It's too much, Dante," I whisper as he continues to move into me. I don't know if I mean the way he's sliding in, or the pressure, or the pleasure, or maybe all of it combined. He's hovering above me with his forearms planted on either side of my head, his face moving back to look at mine, reading everything there.

"You're tight," he whispers, stopping.

"No, please, more," I say, a total contradiction. My body is on fire, the ache blooming into pleasure. He moves deeper and my face pinches with the stretch.

"You're so fucking tight," he groans, but it's less a groan of satisfaction and more one of torture. "For fuck's sake, Delilah, tell me I'm the only man who's been in this cunt." I don't answer, the shame burning on my cheeks.

I'm a 26-year-old virgin, bound away in my ivory tower, away from all sources of being tainted because my father wanted me untouched for his benefit.

Pristine.

"Fucking look at me," he says, his cock throbbing in me, again that throbbing moving to something more, something better. His hand moves from the bed beside me, grabbing my face and forcing me to look into his fierce, dark eyes. In this light, I almost only see them as black, the dark brown melting into the pupil.

"Were you a virgin?" he asks, and I lick my lips, embarrassed. But that in itself is an answer, I guess. "Fucking hell," he breathes, dipping to kiss me, sinking in just a bit more, and I moan with pleasure against his lips. "Answer me, Delilah. Am I the first man to fuck you?"

I stare at him, unsure of what the correct answer is. Finally, his hand slips to my throat, his cock sliding in until our hips are flush, and I moan out, low and deep and unhinged, because every single moment of this feels *right*.

I'd be lying if, despite putting little to no weight in the act itself in my mind, I told you I never thought about what my first time would be like. Awkward. Painful. Quick. Simple.

I tried over and over to lose this pesky status. Still, the amount of times a friend intercepted or my date straight-up refused is almost humorous.

In recent times, I've wondered which of my friends are on Shane's payroll.

But then Dante's hand tightens, and my eyes refocus on him, my mind stuck on the delicious throbbing between my legs.

"Answer me, Delilah."

His eyes are crazed.

I should be scared.

Any sane human would be terrified.

But still, that thread between us, that thread tying us . . .

"Yes," I say, the word a mere whisper, but the way he tightens that hand, the way his groan is nearly pained, I know he heard.

"Jesus fucking Christ," he says, the moan low and to himself. "Fuck, fuck, fuck."

I panic.

I panic because for one, this obviously should have been disclosed. I'm no expert when it comes to men, but I figured sex was sex, especially for a man like this. That he wouldn't care about some hymen that probably broke ten years ago. But now, I'm thinking I was wrong.

And two, I panic because I'm sure Dante is going to pull out, roll over, and tell me to leave.

Fuck, fuck, fuck.

"Dante, seriously, it's no big—" I start, but then he does the unthinkable.

The hand moves from my throat to the bed next to me and he pulls out before he slams back in.

"Oh!" I shout, a hint of pain coming before heat rolls up my spine. Pure, blissful heat that lands in my belly and starts to curl in on itself, building. "*Oh!*"

"Mine," he growls into my neck. "Fuck, mine. All fucking mine," he says, pulling out again and pounding into me, repeating the word.

The feeling grows, bigger than any orgasm I've given myself, so all-consuming I know I'll leave this room changed in some way.

"No one else's. Never. God, fuck." His words are insane, unhinged, his lips trailing over my neck, nipping and sucking, *worshiping* me. It's almost like he's afraid that if he takes his lips from me, I'll disappear.

I moan as he continues to fuck me, as the feeling builds, as he mumbles incoherent nonsense in my neck.

He's as taken over by this as I am. Somehow, somewhere, I know that. I know that he feels this, that this is bigger than just sex, than losing my virginity. That connection, that fuel that keeps pouring onto the fire isn't typical.

It's us.

And the pressure builds to a point where it's near worrisome, the pleasure taking over. "It's too much, god, Dante."

"Perfect. You can take it, baby. You were made for me," he murmurs, sucking on the spot beneath my neck that has me bucking into him, forcing him even deeper and pulling another deep moan from both of us.

"Yes. I'm yours. God, I'm yours, Dante," I say, and then with one last grind of his hips to mine, I explode, coming around him. The noises that come from my lips are masked only by the unbearable, soul-deep groan from Dante's chest. The feel of it vibrates through me and ratchets up my orgasm as he continues to pound into me relentlessly before he stills, slamming deeper than before and growling into my neck.

"Mine. Fuck, you're mine. God. Mine," he whispers into my skin even as we come down from our high.

And I think in that moment, he truly believes it—that I was made to be his.

FOURTEEN

-Dante-

"You were a virgin," I say, my voice a whisper as I speak the words that have been ricocheting in my mind.

In the last hour, I've cleaned Lilah up, gotten her some water, and now we lie in bed together, nearly silent the entire time. Not an uncomfortable silence, just a new one. Anytime I've ever been with her, she's been talkative and chatty. This is just . . . being. For most of that time, her head has been on my chest, my fingers combing through her long blonde hair that curls at the end as my mind uses her breaths as a calming metronome.

I'm not sure what my expectation was when I said that, but a response . . . wasn't it.

I think I thought she'd pretend to be asleep.

"It's not a big deal."

"You're twenty-six?" I ask, knowing the answer but wanting to hear it anyway. "You waited a long time." She probably wanted rose petals and a hotel room and fancy Champagne. Instead, she got a rough fuck in my bed with a man she, in theory, doesn't even know.

"There were circumstances beyond my control."

"*Circumstances beyond your control?*" I ask, because while I don't feel bad about taking her virginity, I'm confused about what would have a beautiful woman like Delilah holding onto it tightly if she truly didn't care about it.

"I . . . I have an overprotective father. Very overprotective. In the limelight. He chose my boyfriends, set me up on dates, that kind of thing."

My hands move hair from her neck to behind her back as she speaks to my chest, a nervous finger moving up to trace imaginary shapes.

I don't like the words she's saying.

I don't like them at all.

"What does an overprotective father mean, Lilah. You're beautiful. Men . . . I'm sure men were dying to be with you." The thought crushes something inside of me, a will to be kind to anyone who looks sideways at her.

She laughs, but it's self-deprecating.

"I . . . I guess. I don't know. It's . . . It's hard to explain."

"Try." The word comes out nearly angry, a contradiction since I should be elated that she is mine and mine alone.

Especially since understanding that I'm her first has turned my world upside down. Knowing that she gave me something so fucking precious.

"My dad is a politician. He's well-loved in his community, and my mom passed when I was young. I became kind of . . . a part of his image."

"And your virginal status? That was part of the image, too?" She smiles and huffs a laugh, her hand moving to slap my chest like she thinks I'm being an idiot.

I am, of course.

But I'll be an idiot every day and night if it makes that sweet sound come from her when I do.

"I couldn't tell you. It was never in the news that my hymen was potentially intact, and my father never specifically asked about it. Thank god." A small shiver runs through her. "But I *can* say that every boyfriend I ever had didn't try anything beyond . . . basic stuff. Ever." My jaw clenches. "And if we were dating for longer than a few months, as soon as I pushed for more—" My hand tightens in her hair just thinking about other men—*boys*—with her. "—they either ghosted or dumped me." She laughs again, but to herself, like she just figured something out. "You know, I had this friend. We were close, but we met right after I moved out of my dad's house. I am just now wondering if she has some kind of connection to him, too. If I ever tried to hook up with some random guy . . . she was always there."

"A random guy like me?" I ask, my heart pounding in an unfamiliar way.

"I know it sounds insane." She laughs. "I know it sounds very . . . conspiracy theory-ish. But he has power, and he wants to keep it. A lot of things about our home and our family came to light recently, and it has me questioning everything."

"It doesn't sound insane. People in power . . . like to keep it by any means." She hums in agreement but leaves it at that, basic and simple.

Minutes pass, and I watch her hair sift through my fingers. Long minutes where I think she may have fallen asleep, except for that little finger drawing on my skin.

"Is it . . . a turn-off? Knowing I have no . . . experience?" she asks, and I nearly laugh in her face.

A part of me knows that would be the absolute worst response ever, though.

My entire life, I haven't had much that was mine and mine alone. With an older brother, most of my things were handed down. I've always been second best, the last, second thought.

Every achievement, every accomplishment—someone else took at least part of the credit or some kind of ownership whether I wanted that or not. Even my home, despite me being the one to finally pay it down to nothing, despite it being in my name, is the family complex, not *mine*.

Unless I buy it or earn it myself, nothing is mine and mine alone.

Surely nothing given to me has been mine.

Except, maybe this woman lying in bed with me.

Despite her having zero understanding of how big this is, and how big we will be, she is mine.

"Not even close, *fiorella*," I say, moving my hand in her hair until her head tips up to look at me. "Never. I'm honored. Honored to have that privilege."

"It wasn't that bi—"

"Don't. It was. Maybe not for you, but for me." Her eyes go wide, and I smile. "Yeah. So don't take away from it. You're mine now. Yes?" It takes a bit, her staring in my eyes while I try to make her understand. To make her see what this means. What *we* now mean.

"Yeah, Dante," she says with a small smile. I press my lips to her forehead.

But I know right then, she doesn't get it.

She's saying what I want to hear.

Something tells me that's an old habit of hers, one she needs to drop.

But still, she doesn't get that she's mine.

But she will.

Soon.

FIFTEEN

From Libby Turner's journals, written seven years before Lilah was born

Dear Diary,

I saw him again tonight. Arturo. Even his name makes me smile. He was at one of the fundraisers my father dragged me to, his father there with the same intentions as mine. To make connections, to bypass some unseen middleman.

He took me to the kitchen, and we stole a box of cookies, and he brought me to the top of the building, and we ate them. We watched the clouds move and talked for hours. He's like me; he wants more. He hates the wheeling and dealing, hates how it hurts people.

And he likes me.

Can you believe that!?

Actually, he more than likes me. He kissed me! It was beautiful. My first kiss.

One day, I think I'll marry him.

When I snuck back into the party, my father didn't even notice I had been missing for hours.

That's fine.

When I turn 19 next month, my father wants me to consider a marriage proposal more seriously. The right family could greatly help my father's career.

I told Arturo to speak with his father. There may be a connection that could help Daddy.

Then we could all be happy.

Love, Libby

SIXTEEN

-Lilah-

I wake to birds chirping.

That's new, I think. My apartment on the absolute shittiest side of town might as well be a glorified motel, and there's sure as fuck no trees for birds to sing with the sunrise nearby.

But I'm not *in* my apartment.

I'm in Dante's bed.

The near stranger who saved my ass on the side of the road, who took me to a luxurious dinner in sweatpants, and then brought me home and fucked me until my throat was hoarse from screaming his name.

I fight the urge to clear it, to test if it's still a bit raw, because I need to be quiet.

I need to get the fuck out of here. How hard can sneaking out of a man's bed be, really? As easy as pie or something like that.

Except . . . I actually have no idea *how* to bake a pie. That was a skill our mom taught Lola before she got too sick, not me. And when

Lola offered to share those memories with me, my stubborn, asshole teenager kicked in, and I refused.

But whatever. It's fine. Pie is probably more complicated than this, anyway.

The risk of baking pie wrong is getting horrendously sick or burning down your house.

Failing to sneak out of a man's bed, the risk is just humiliation.

I can handle humiliation.

I have absolutely no humility left, anyway.

Looking at the expanse of bed, I estimate there's a good 16 inches between me and the edge. The issue is less about the distance, though, and more about the heavy arm on my waist.

Seems Dante's a cuddler.

Ignore how that feels kind of nice, Delilah, I tell myself.

Cuddling is what you do with a boyfriend.

Cuddling is not what you do with a one-night stand.

Cuddling leads to strings which leads to tangles. And the way my life is being held together by *threads* means I cannot *tangle* with anything whatsoever.

This also means that today when I get into work, I need to tell Marco I'm done with the private dances, period. It might piss off Paulie, but clearly, they're fucking with my mind. I have a mission at Jerzy Girls, and chatting with a wealthy client and then *losing my virginity* to one is absolutely not helpful.

With that ounce of fortitude, I glance at the handsome man and calibrate what I should do. As I take in his arm, the distance from the edge, and where the door is, though, he rolls.

His arm leaves my waist.

He faces away from me.

That has to be God telling me I'm not a total fuckup, giving me the out I need, right? Helping a girl out?

Either way, I use it as my chance to roll, my feet landing soft on the hardwood.

My eyes skim the room, trying to find my sweatpants and sweatshirt. Finally, I find the pants in a corner, pulling them over my ass, not even bothering to look for my undergarments in my panic. I remember my boots are at the door, and I keep looking for my sweatshirt, silently cursing how I didn't even look where he tossed it last night.

I was so lost in him.

Fuck it, I think, grabbing a men's sweatshirt thrown in the corner and claiming it as my own. I ignore the way I shiver at the way it smells, letting it take over my senses, and tell myself it's just a final memento.

Then with one last look at the man in bed, I grab my phone before sneaking out of the house for good.

I wave at the Uber driver, thinking how I'll need to move money around to make sure the charge doesn't bounce, and walk toward my apartment.

And then I stop.

I stop fully in the middle of the parking lot because in the parking space designated for me is my shitty-ass Saturn with four shiny new tires. I stand, staring at the ugly greenish color, before a car honks, the driver screaming at me.

"What the fuck, lady! Are you drunk?! Get out of the road!"

Without responding, I slowly move, walking toward the car, a bit scared that I might actually be insane.

There is no reasonable way my car is sitting in my parking spot less than 12 hours from when I abandoned it with the promise of some tow service bringing it to the local tire shop.

But there it is. I move my hand, hesitating to touch it, but when I do, I find that I'm not hallucinating. It's real, the October cold making the metal hurt my fingers. I move to the front door, shocked and horrified when it opens, the car beeping to let me know the keys have been left in the ignition.

So, not only was this car somehow brought to my apartment, but the keys—which I could have sworn were in my bag—are in the car, and *no one stole it?*

Someone in the spot next to me stares at me, waiting for me to move, to get in, I assume, so they can back out. Confused and delirious, I do just that, moving to sit in my car and slamming the door despite my original destination being my apartment.

I look around.

The tank is full.

The tank of my car has never been full, even when I had a nice car and a well-paying job. I always run it just a little past E before putting in twenty bucks and calling it a day.

What kind of twilight zone am I living in?

But then I look over to the passenger seat and see a note.

Thank you for choosing Mike's Towing Service! If you enjoyed our services, please remember to leave a 5-star review online.

And then scribbled beneath that is a man's messy handwriting.

4 tires
Oil change
Full tank

PAID IN FULL is stamped on the bottom in bright-red ink.

What in the *actual fuck?*

Right now, I'm kind of regretting walking out of Dante's home with absolutely zero intention of seeing the man ever again.

I have *so many questions*.

But it's for the best, right?

I had a good night.

The final tether to my old life was snapped, and in a way, I feel like I'm finally the new person I've been working toward. And even if I had a fantastic time last night, if dinner was fun and sex was excellent, and sleeping was unbelievably restful . . . It's the wrong time.

I am entering a minefield, walking into armed warfare with what feels like a princess wand. I can't have anyone holding me back, anything in my mind keeping me from doing whatever I have to do to get what I want.

And Dante Romano seems like the white-knight type, seeing a woman in what he deems to be distress and wanting to fix it.

He would be a distraction.

So he'll remain just a fond memory.

And with that, I turn off the car, take the keys, slam and lock the door, and head into my apartment to remind myself of my plan and what I'm doing here.

SEVENTEEN

-Dante-

It's cute how she tiptoed out the door, like I didn't take note of the moment her breathing changed, the millisecond when she returned to this world.

I've never been a good sleeper, but something about the way her soft, low breaths sounded like a gentle, constant beat gave me the best sleep I've had in years.

No way in hell am I letting that go. Letting her go.

Two years ago, she saved me, and I lost her.

Six weeks ago, she started working at Jerzy Girls.

Six weeks ago, I demanded a private show.

Six weeks ago, I started the process of trying to convince myself of what a fucking horrible idea this was, ignoring that all the same and starting this obscure game with her.

24 hours ago, I stopped fighting it.

18 hours ago, I took steps to get her into my bed.

12 hours ago, I heard her moan my name for the first time.

But Delilah Turner has been mine since the moment I laid eyes on her.

Not a thing about that woman slips through my notice.

So as the door clicked behind her, as I watched an Uber come to the curb and pick her up, I grabbed my phone and made a call I've been waiting to make for six long weeks.

Longer, if we're being honest.

EIGHTEEN

-Lilah-

When I get into my apartment, my anxiety kicks in, and I do a thorough inspection, checking that everything is the way I remember leaving it. I mean, if they had my keys and knew where to park my car, it wouldn't be too farfetched that they'd come inside, right?

Thankfully, it seems nothing was touched, so I go about my normal routine before my shift, pulling out the note my mom left on top of the box of journals and rereading it.

It's become a reminder of sorts, and folding the note back up carefully and tucking it into the envelope meticulously centers me. It's a reminder of why I'm here and what I'm doing. A reminder to keep going when my body is exhausted and I feel defeated.

And today, it's a reminder of why handsome distractions can't be part of my life.

This little note has become my way to ensure I never lose sight of my true mission.

And the reality is, working at the Carluccio-owned-and-operated gentleman's club has given me the exact in I need to make my plan a reality.

I came to Jerzy Girls looking for the proof needed to take down the Carluccios and take my seat at the Russo table.

What my mom wrote in those journals haunts me daily, the cryptic words making slightly more sense with a fuller picture. The note she left in the box tells me she knew I would find them one day when she wasn't there. She knew that, despite her best intentions, I would need them. I'd need to use the information scrawled in the margins and hidden in lines to unravel my history and find answers to questions that have long since been forgotten.

The day my sister was kidnapped, Johnny Vitale confessed to killing my father. He had known about me since I was born and crafted a complex plan of creating an opening in the Russo family and using his ties to the Carluccios to rule. He planned to make me his unwilling bride, to take me to the Russos and demand he's given what is rightfully mine.

But there is just no fucking universe where the right hand to a powerful Don goes and murders an heir to an opposing family without anyone knowing.

Without repercussions.

Without *approval*.

When Johnny confessed, he made it sound like he was working alone, that he brewed this idea, but I'm not buying it. That family is too intertwined with my own for it to be a coincidence, to be simply a crazed man.

And when I heard the whole story, heard what Johnny confessed, a single passage from the journals that made no sense finally clicked in my mind.

From Libby's journal, weeks after Arturo was killed.

Dear Diary,

My love is gone forever.

Every hope and dream we created together—the plans we had to help me escape this loveless marriage and finally be with my soulmate—have died with him.

And now I am alone.

My daughter will never know her father.

The worst part is, no one knows who did it.

No one knows why.

The family is just accepting what the report says: a random drive-by, wrong place, wrong time. But since when has a mafia heir been murdered accidentally in an unrelated drive-by?

Never.

Coincidences are so rarely ever actually coincidences. They're usually carefully crafted events made to look like there is no need for investigation. The powerful men in this town know the value of leaning on a coincidence. They just think no one will know, no one will look into it.

But I know. I know that Arturo was not killed in a drive-by.

This was intentional.

But even more, I know it surely wasn't just an overzealous henchman nor a jaded potential lover who made that final call.

No, it was bigger than that.

And he needs to pay.

They need to pay.
Until they do, she'll never be safe. Carmine will find her, will finish his plan one way or another.
I need to keep her safe.

The first time I read that entry, nothing made sense.

The third and fourth times didn't either. But two years later, I poured myself over those journals with new knowledge.

And now, I understand . . . to an extent.

The overzealous henchman is Johnny. He admitted to executing the hit put on Arturo.

But who called it?

Now I understand Johnny Vitale didn't kill Arturo Russo on a whim. He didn't do it because he thought there was a chance he could manipulate the families, take me as a bride, and rule the Russo family. That idea? It might have come later. It might have developed over the years as he realized he'd never be number one when there were already two men fighting to be boss. But it wasn't his initial idea.

No, the murder of my father was part of a brutal revenge, I think.

Revenge on the sweet, beautiful politician's daughter who refused to marry the dirty future-mob boss because she was in love with his enemy.

The sweet daughter who got pregnant to avoid a forced marriage. She chose the man she thought was safe. She settled rather than put her lover in further jeopardy by coming between the families who, until then, had a restless understanding. A cease-fire, however uneasy.

But then my mother refused to marry him, and everyone knew the real reason. So Antonio made the call, told his right hand to make the hit, and Arturo Russo was killed in cold blood over a woman.

Over my *mother*.

Because Antonio Carluccio might be able to accept her refusing to marry him, instead settling for safe. Especially as he saw how profitable Turner's greed and addiction could be for the family. But he couldn't accept her going back to Arturo after all those years, taking that risk.

A jealous man-child. If he couldn't have the toy, no one could.

It's what makes sense.

But what was Carmine Carluccio's involvement? What was his plan, and how did he fit into the story? How would he need to fit into my revenge?

Either way, once I understood the hidden meanings, I understood my mission. I have to find the proof that the Carluccio family put the hit out on the family with which there was an amicable cease-fire. An agreement. And to find the motivation.

Once I do that, I can move on with my plan to take them down and make them pay for destroying my family.

NINETEEN

-Lilah-

Walking into work that day, I'm already dreading my shift. My legs (and other parts of me) ache, and even though I feel more well-rested than I have in months, I am dying to crawl into my bed, curl up in a ball, and overthink absolutely everything about the last 24 hours.

But I made a deal, and I have people depending on me, and I have a plan that requires action.

Calling out of work doesn't help with any of those.

So instead, I wave at Marco when I walk in. As expected, he barely tips his chin up at me, those dark sunglasses taking in the room and who knows what else, before I scurry to the dancer's break room.

The noise, the chaos, the chatter, and the gossip—it all helps in its own way, helping to distract me, to keep me from overthinking last night and this morning and get in the zone. Soon, I'm no longer a girl mourning a crush. Instead, I'm a stripper reminding myself to keep my core tight and my back straight when wearing unbearably tall heels.

But when I walk out of the changing room, headed to Marco to talk about declining private dances, I'm stopped.

"Go change," Roddy says, standing in front of me.

"What?" The music is loud as I put in a large hoop earring.

"Go change. You're on the floor today." His dark glasses cover his eyes, and I know from asking him once that they're dark so he can watch all the creeps in the crowd without them knowing.

He has much less of a sense of humor than Marco does, which is really saying something.

"Paulie said I go on at 4." I pull my phone out to check the schedule the sleaze ball texted me earlier this week.

There it is.

Tuesday: 4 pm

"Big Boss says you're a server today," he says, tipping his chin to my outfit. He does it respectfully, like he's just giving me instructions and not eating up the curves on display.

In six weeks, I've learned there are two kinds of bouncers here. One respects women and values their job of keeping them safe and the creeps in line. The second is the kind who uses the job as a flex with his buds and might as well be another patron.

"Paulie said I couldn't be a server," I say, trying to understand the turn of events. When I originally came in and made my attempt to zero out my dad's debts in exchange for working for the club, I offered to be waitress, teetering around the club and letting men pinch my ass while I handed them beers.

It was a no-go, and despite absolutely zero experience and a *ton* of bruises along the way, he put me on the pole.

"Boss man said you're on the floor. No more stage for you," he says, looking at me pointedly. At least, I think he's looking at me. Those glasses make it difficult to tell.

"Roddy, I don't want to get you in trouble. Paulie was very clear—"

"Honey. You listen to me," he says, moving his sunglasses to his head and removing the earpiece before bending a bit to get closer to my face.

Roddy is *tall*.

And *big*.

Everyone knows he's just a huge, grumpy teddy bear, but the look in his eyes right now . . .

"The Big Boss gave me an order. That order was to get you off the fuckin' pole for good. You're working the floor. Put on a pair of shorts, leave the bikini top. Marco will be by later to give you more information, but this will do for now. You're probably going to want better shoes moving forward," he says, eyes moving to the black 6-inch heels. I spent nearly a week in them without stopping when I first got them, practicing how to teeter on them without dying.

I open my mouth to argue, to tell him that Paulie will not be happy, but he speaks before I do. "You know who Big Boss is?" he asks.

I lick my lips, unsure of what the right answer is here.

"The girls have . . . talked." *Junior Carluccio.*

"Girls are usually right with their gossip. Paulie doesn't make the rules here, trust me. You're on the floor."

I stare into his eyes, which are a calming chocolate brown, very much on brand for his teddy bear-ness. And then I nod.

"Okay, on the floor." He nods, and a gentle look of relief comes through him, like he was worried I'd keep fighting him on it.

But really, when I walked in that first day, I was hoping to be a cocktail waitress, smiling and flipping my hair and efficiently serving drinks. I'd done it in college, and while a strip club is miles from a high-end sushi restaurant, I figured I could manage.

But Paulie was very adamant about what he wanted me doing, and that was dancing topless for hundreds of men every night. I wasn't happy, but I still knew it was my in, so I agreed.

But now that I have the opportunity to be a server, I'm going to take it and ask minimal questions. Chances are, Big Boss saw what a shitty dancer I was and decided it was a good business move to get me off the stage.

So I nod instead of arguing with Roddy and head to the bar to learn the ropes.

About three hours later, the crowds are picking up, and a few more girls have come in to start serving too. They're all in the same uniform of hot shorts and a bikini top, but as Roddy implied, the shoes are different than the dancers. Still heeled, but lower, more stable. Less deadly, for sure. I remind myself to grab a pair from my apartment to add to my rotation, unbearably thankful that the 6-inch heels might just be a thing of the past.

Unless, of course, Paulie catches wind of the change and loses his mind, putting me back on the stage.

Which, to be honest, I think is a possibility.

"Hey, princess, come," a familiar voice says from behind me. Marco is there, holding a small pile of clothes and tipping his head for me to follow. I hand over the drink I'm carrying to a man who spent a few seconds too long staring at my boobs before following Marco. He starts walking toward an unmarked door.

"Roddy told you you're serving from now on, yeah?" he asks when the music gets quieter as we walk. I nod. "Weekends, busy nights, you'll be on the floor serving assholes watching the girls. That outfit is fine but find better shoes. You need a pair, you tell me, and I'll order you some." I nod and he continues talking as we stop moving. "But when there's an event in the back, you'll be in uniform and serving."

"Uniform?" I ask, and he hands me a small stack of clothes.

"Your uniform." I take them and stare at him. "Come. You need to change. There's an event."

I lick my lips, so confused by everything. "Marco, why am I moving back here?" I ask, pushing my luck as he leads me to an unmarked door.

"Big Boss says so. Sorry, princess, but you're a shitty dancer," he says with a smile, and I want to be offended, but I'm really not. I *am* a terrible dancer. "But you're gorgeous, and you have a good smile, and you've got the upbringing for this."

"The upbringing?"

"I know who you are, princess. Turner's daughter? I know everything, remember?" My stomach churns at that, and I hate it. I hate hearing *Turner's daughter*, and it's not just because it's now my turn to sacrifice for Shane Turner after Lola was forced to do it for so long.

It's because I'm not *Shane Turner's daughter*. Not really.

And I'm tired of him getting that credit.

"You've been around men with wandering eyes and more money than sense. Know how to charm, the right smile to use." Finally, I think I'm getting it.

"By back room, you mean—" Marco cuts me off.

"This room is the servers' dressing room. There are cubbies for your stuff. This way, you don't have to go into the chaos backstage." I nod, and secretly, I'm happy. I love the girls, chatting and laughing with them and commiserating over shitty circumstances, but it's overwhelming sometimes. "Take those, change. I'll bring you to the back. Explain more." I nod before Marco unlocks the door, and I step in. There are cubbies on one wall with a long, cushioned bench in front of them. In the back are two small rooms, I'm assuming for changing, and in the corner, there is a long, lighted vanity with makeup. I'm guessing it's stocked the same way the makeup, toiletries, and snacks are backstage, and when I wander over, I see I'm right—there's a mini fridge and shelving filled with snacks.

And it's *quiet*.

God, the quiet in this loud place is so damn nice. But Marco is waiting, so I head to the dressing room and shake out the stack of clothes he handed me: a tiny, sleeveless polo with a deep V that looks to be cropped right under where my boobs would be and a tiny pair of hot shorts.

Like a hot golf caddy.

Interesting.

But at least it's more covered than when I'm serving in the tiny bikini top.

It's kind of a relief.

Pulling it on, I find that the fit is perfect, as if someone knew and ordered the exact right size. But I guess when you work at a strip club, you get pretty good at guessing tits and ass sizes. Taking my things, I stuff them into a cubby that's already labeled with my name before walking back out.

"Fits," Marco says, shaking his head with a smile like he's impressed or shocked but he isn't sure why. "He's a psycho," he mumbles under his breath.

"Who is?" I ask.

"No one. Come on, follow me." We walk through another unmarked door I've never noticed, though once we're through, I recognize the small hallway. Straight ahead is where I was brought when I met with Paulie, asking to make my deal. God, that feels like a lifetime ago. There are two doors on either side, and Marco stops before the second on the left. He knocks quickly twice, then waits, then knocks again, waits, then three more. I raise an eyebrow at him, and he smiles.

"Super stealth," I say with a smile. He shakes his head, and I imagine he rolls his eyes beneath those glasses before he starts talking.

"This room is where the games happen." My body tightens, as I know what games mean.

My father got into hundreds of thousands of dollars of debt at these games, playing poker or betting on sports, but I never knew *where* they were. It's not hard to believe the family would have multiple locations, but this makes sense.

Who would assume there was illegal gambling happening in the back of a strip club? There are so many other things to assume, more devious things, but gambling? It's genius, really.

"Okay."

"You speak to the men only to get orders. There's a chair in the corner. They know all you do is *get them drinks.* You understand?" I stare at Marco but give him an honest answer.

"I feel like you're trying to tell me something."

"They touch you, you scream, Lilah. You are not entertainment. You are decoration. Useful decoration, but decoration. You are Carluccio property." I roll my lips together, uneasy. "This world is chaos, babe. I get it. But we're here to keep you safe. You will always have a man in there with you—usually me. I hide in the shadows, but you know I'm there. Sorry to tell you, no phones allowed, no media. You can bring a book, but that's it."

"I haven't read since I was a kid," I say with a laugh, and Marco smiles, but the door opens.

"Might want to start again, babe," he says, leading me in.

I'm shocked that the night flies by, despite having little to nothing to keep me entertained.

Before I know it, the game is over, it's 11, and Marco is telling me to grab my stuff and he'll walk me to my car.

"My shift is until two," I tell him, reminding him I'm supposed to be here until close.

"Your shifts changed. Big Boss rules, remember? You get here tomorrow at two. You'll be home by seven." I widen my eyes, but he just smiles, handing me a stack of cash. "For today. Guys liked you a whole lot, princess."

I don't see how—I barely even did anything. Occasionally, a man sitting at the green-felt table would wave me over, stare at my tits and ask for something to drink, then Marco would walk me out to the bar before walking me back in.

That's it.

It felt . . . surreal.

It felt *fake*.

And holding this stack of cash that I know is way thicker than anything I've brought home dancing in six weeks, I know it's a lot of money.

"Marco, I'm not supposed to take this much home," I say under my breath as Marco pushes the front door open, the cold air shocking my lungs. His brows come together, and he looks at me as I walk past him into the parking lot.

"What?"

"I'm working here. I'm paying off my dad's debts, Marco," I say, manually unlocking my car.

"I don't understand what you're saying, Lilah." He holds the cold metal door open as I stand there next to him, his sunglasses on top of his head. "Paulie takes everything but $20."

Here's the thing: Marco is good at hiding his thoughts.

Very good.

But I see the flash of irritation. Anger, even.

It's terrifying if I'm being honest.

"New job, new rules, babe. In your car. Start it. It's cold." I do as he asks, getting in mechanically, putting the key in the ignition, and cranking the heat. Then he bends his knees until he's face-to-face with me. "Don't worry about that. Those are your tips. Take them."

"Marco, my dad—"

"New job, new rules. I'll talk to the Big Boss, but you're good. Trust me." I lick my lips, unsure. "Drive home, Lilah. Text me when you get there. You don't send me your location in fifteen, I gotta go find you. I really don't want to find you tonight."

"What?"

"New job—"

"New rules. Got it. Are you like, my bodyguard now?" I ask with a laugh.

"No. This is what we do for the girls who work the games. Men in high places think they can get what they want, Lilah. We protect our girls."

That should probably make me feel nervous, but it doesn't.

I feel . . . safe.

And safe is a new feeling for me since I moved here. So I nod, Marco closes my door, and I head home.

And when I get home, I send Marco my location, letting him know I got home okay.

TWENTY

-Lilah-

The next day is just as simple, walking in at two, changing in the quiet, empty break room, and sitting in the corner of one of the poker rooms. Today, it's Roddy walking me out to grab drinks and hovering in the corners, but when I leave, I'm practically skipping. My feet don't kill, I'm not dying of exhaustion, I have a stack of cash I don't have to carefully budget, and I'm out at a *normal human being time.*

I could cry with excitement, with the ease of the day.

And because I have an unexpected extra bit of money, I decide to splurge. I drive myself to the fancy grocery store across town, not caring that I'm in a light-purple sweatpants and sweatshirt set, and start filling a cart with luxuries I haven't had since I changed everything in my life.

Before everything happened, I went to this grocery store almost every night after work, grabbing premade sushi or an expensive salad from the salad bar, not caring what the total was because I knew I was good for it. I lived in a killer high-rise apartment, spending my days overlooking Jersey City while I sent out press releases and chatted with high-end clients. Back then, a $100 bottle of wine on a Tuesday night wasn't extravagant.

But since I started my plan, I've been living in a tiny little apartment, eating ramen and peanut butter and jellies and not even *looking* at the liquor section of a normal store, much less this one.

Today feels like a win after weeks of losses, and once again, it's another heady reminder of what my sister sacrificed for years while I went off and lived my best life.

The guilt makes me lose my appetite, but I still add a pack of sushi to my cart, strolling toward the snacks to stock up on all the things I've missed.

But as I'm pushing my cart, lost in thought, I'm jarred and once again, my world spins as I crash into a man.

"Oh my god! I'm so sorry. I was totally—" I stop my over-the-top apology because I just so happen to know the man my cart slammed into.

He slammed into me not too long ago.

"Dante?" I ask, and when he turns to face me, that sly smile on his lips, I decide then and there that the ability to dematerialize at will would be amazing.

This is my luck. Literally crashing into the man whose bed I snuck out of after letting him fuck my virginity into oblivion, thinking I'd never see him again.

I also just got off work, which means both times this man has seen me outside the club, I've probably smelled of smoke and sweat and had body glitter on my tits.

"What a lovely surprise," he says, that smile stretching. "I was hoping I'd see you around after last time."

"Uh, hi. How are you?" Because that's how you interact with hot older strangers who fucked you hoarse two days ago, right? *Right?*

What the fuck do I know about this kind of thing?

But then he laughs.

The man *laughs*.

Oh god. Swallow me up, ground. Please. I would like to disappear now.

"Much better now," he says, and then my world stops spinning. He walks around my cart, setting his empty handbasket into it, then completely engulfs my personal space. I step back, bumping into the shelf of chips and pretzels, but I don't have time to think about how I'm crunching up someone else's snacks because his hands are on either side of my face, his body pressing into mine, and he's bringing his face down to meet my lips.

And just like that first time, the sound stops.

The universe goes quiet.

All there is are his warm, chafed hands on my jaw, tipping it up until I'm right where he wants me, my heart pounding out of my chest, and the way his lips gently press to my own.

It's like I'm home.

It's like a warm breeze, fresh air entering my tower.

The kind of breeze that would make you want to risk jumping in order to feel it on your skin.

One hand on my jaw moves to the dip in my waist, wrapping me, pulling me tighter, and it's like I'm where I was always meant to be.

This feeling, though . . . regardless of how nice it is, is a reminder.

It's a reminder I'm probably going to ignore, but it's there, nonetheless. A reminder that led me to sneak out of this man's house without a note. A reminder that told me that this feels good—too good—and I don't deserve something that feels this good. I don't have time for something that feels this good. I have hell to wreak, I have debts to pay, and I have rights to wrong.

I don't have time to get lost in my own life.

And I could lose myself in Dante Romano. I could let him be a fucking beautiful distraction.

Before I can act on the unsettling mix of passion and despair churning in my gut, he breaks the kiss, setting his forehead to mine.

"Missed you," he says in a whisper, a genuine set of words that I don't think he means to say, but I smile all the same.

"You don't even know me," I say.

"I know you in all the ways that matter." One of my hands moves to his neck, resting there even if it goes against everything I *should* be doing. "What are you doing?" he asks, his breath warm in my ear.

"I, uh . . . I'm shopping. Getting groceries." I tip my head to the cart, and he laughs.

"Ahh, picky eater fodder?"

"Hey, I got salad stuff, too," I say, scrunching up my nose because there isn't much I'm self-conscious about, all things considered. I work at a strip club to pay off my gambling addict father's debts while trying to take down a mafia family from the inside, so really, stones, glass houses, you know.

He kisses my nose.

"No. No, don't. You're sweet; you're beautiful. You're right."

"I'm right?"

"You know what you want. Why deviate?"

"You know, I've bumped into you twice now, and neither time have I looked decent," I say.

"You're gorgeous. I prefer this to your work outfit."

"Is that right?" I say with a smile, and somehow, it's like I've forgotten we're in a grocery store and not just chatting alone.

Strange how I can feel so easy with this man I barely even know when my whole life I've felt like I have to wear a mask to fit in.

"Unless it's for my eyes only, then yeah. You want to wear one of those outfits off the clock?" A chill runs down my spine. "What are you doing tonight?" he asks, and even though I move to make room for another cart coming down the aisle, he holds me tight, refusing to let go.

I wonder if he feels it, too. The magnetism. The feeling that if I step back and let a gap grow between us, I won't be whole anymore.

That's insane, right?

Insane to feel that?

Is that what happens when you lose your virginity to some hot older man? You become insane and start making up grand gestures and feelings that aren't there?

"Uh, nothing. Celebrating."

"Celebrating?"

"I got a promotion." He continues to stare at me, and I elaborate. "I'm off the stage. I'm a server now," I say with a small smile. "New uniform and everything." He smiles wide.

"Good to hear, *fiorella*. Guess private rooms are off-limits for you now?"

So, Marco didn't talk with him. Does that mean he didn't try to see me again?

"I'm thinking so."

"Good thing I ran into you, then. You forgot to leave your number when you left. I thought I would have to go to your apartment, track you down." This reminds me of the car outside my apartment yesterday morning.

"How did you know where to bring my car?" I ask. "And how did it get there so quick?"

"I told you, a friend owed me a favor. He said your address was on a paper in your car. He called your leasing office to confirm."

"That's a little . . . intrusive, isn't it?" I say, my brows coming together.

"I take care of what's mine," he says. "You get used to it." Then he moves, unpinning me and moving me to the grocery cart before caging me between him and the cart handle. "Let's get food then go to your place, yeah?"

And because I'm either an idiot or a genius, I nod, letting Dante buy me food and take me home.

TWENTY-ONE

-Dante-

"So, this is your place?" I say, looking around Lilah's tiny apartment. It's not quite a studio, but just barely a one-bedroom apartment with the living area and kitchen all in one and the world's tiniest bedroom.

She deserves better.

She deserves luxury and beauty.

Eventually, I tell myself, breathing in deeply. *Eventually*.

"Yup," she says, frantic energy in her eyes as she looks around her place and spots a pile of clothes on the couch. I place the bags from the store on her tiny kitchen table and watch her run there. "Shit, sorry, I wasn't really . . . expecting anyone." She grabs the pile and tosses it into a laundry basket in the corner.

"You have men over often?" I ask with a raised eyebrow, and I can't even start to fight back the rage that begins to boil in my veins.

It seems the flash of jealousy makes her smile her sweet, sassy smile.

"Why? Would it bother you?"

It's clear to me then that she doesn't get it.

She doesn't *see* it.

She will.

She'll understand soon that she's mine. That I don't want a single man to *look* at her sideways. That the thought of her working at Jerzy Girls has me grinding my teeth to dust because she deserves the world, not working to get the world by dancing for tips.

Soon.

I step to her, pulling her into my arms as my hand moves up her back, fisting in her long hair. I fucking love her hair—the feel of it, the look of it, the smell of it. The way her breathing changes just a bit when I tangle my fingers in it and tug just a bit.

Like it is right now.

"Yes. Yes, it would bother me, Delilah. I told you that first night I had you. Mine. You are mine and only mine."

"That doesn't make any sense," she says, her voice low as I wrap an arm around her waist.

"None of this makes sense, Delilah. The way I'm fucking feral for you, the way we met, the way I can't go three damn minutes without thinking about you? But here we are, and I'm not mad about it." My head dips and I press my lips to hers. "None of it makes sense except that somehow in this chaotic life, I found you, and you found me, and there is something to say for how the universe puts people in your path."

"You're saying I was put in your path for a reason, Mr. Romano?" she asks with that sweet smile that screams of innocence and sugary sweetness.

"You were put on this damned earth to be mine, Delilah."

And then, before she can argue, which I'm sure she's going to do because she's Lilah, I kiss her, shutting her up.

I think I love kissing her most of all—the way the world shuts off when her lips touch mine.

The way I can forget who I am and who she is and the mess of what that all means when I'm kissing her makes me never want to stop.

But then I remember what *else* turns off the world.

"Bedroom? Or your couch?" I ask, breaking the kiss, my hands running up smooth skin as I work her sweatshirt up. She lifts her arms like a little kid as I pull it over her head, then I toss it in the corner. I can't resist pressing my lips to her again.

"What?" she asks, her eyes dazed when I break the kiss.

"Where am I going to fuck you, Delilah?" My hand tugs on her hair, her eyes clearing for just a moment as I do.

It's becoming a favorite of mine - bringing her back to earth and watching her realize I'm in front of her, waiting for a response.

"I don't—"

I don't have time for this. I bend, lift her into my arms, and walk to the bedroom. As I kick the door behind us, I smile, noting the blankets are a mess and clothes are strewn around everywhere in a way that is so entirely Delilah.

"Your bed it is." I toss her onto her bed, and she bounces on the soft mattress. "Take off your sweats," I demand, my fingers moving to the buttons on my shirt, wishing I had just put on a tee before heading to the store.

I fight the smile as she eagerly pushes her sweats off, kicking her feet adorably to try and get them off before I give in and help her. Once her feet are free, I toss them in the same pile where my shirt and her sweatshirt are now.

When her hands move to the thin lace at the sides of her underwear, though, I stop her.

"No."

"What?" My hand moves to hers, placing it back on the bed.

"That's my job."

"Your job?" she asks with a smile.

"Yeah," I say, standing straight again and then working on my pants.

"And what do I do?" she asks, leaning back on her elbows. She's wearing a lacy, light-purple bra and panty set that shows off her curves, her lips tipped in a soft smile like she knows what she's doing to me.

Driving me fucking insane with need.

"You lie there and be pretty, wait for your man to take care of you."

Her eyebrow raises, and the thoughts churning in her mind are visible.

The internal battle.

She's spent a long time being a pretty thing, and I think she's over it.

The question is, will she listen and be a good girl?

Or will she do whatever the fuck she wants?

She goes with the latter, just like I expect.

One hand moves, a single red-tipped finger pushing the lacy cup of her bra down until her full breast is out, her dark nipple pebbling both with the cool air and arousal. She licks her lips, keeping her eyes on me as my hands are paused at the buttons of my slacks.

Then she takes two fingers and rolls the nipple between them, her eyes drifting shut as she moans.

Jesus fucking Christ.

A goddess.

A goddess who wants to lead me to ruin.

"Delilah," I warn, my teeth gritted, but for some reason, I don't speed up my undressing.

I don't even move to stop her.

Her eyes open again, and that hand starts to move down her soft belly, fingers playing with the line of her underwear.

"Delilah," I repeat, my voice firmer.

She keeps going, though, dipping below the waistband. Her head tips back, curls tumbling as it does, another low moan falling from her lips. I can't decide where to look, her hand or her face, but when that hand moves, my eyes lock there, and I just *know* she dips a finger inside.

"Dante," she whispers, and that's it.

I move, pushing my pants down as I do, stepping out of them as I lean and put my hands around her ankles, tugging her to the edge.

"You should have listened to me," I say, leaning over her body, the chain of my necklace dangling before her face. She smiles sweetly.

"Or what?" she says, then she moves her head up, taking the St. Christopher medal into her mouth with her tongue.

I feel the move in my cock.

Abruptly, I stand again, not missing the sly smile on her face before quickly flipping her until she's facedown on the bed, her feet planted on the floor. I bend over her once more, moving her hair over her shoulder and taking her ear into my mouth.

"I was going to eat your pussy, make you come on my face and then fuck you sweet. But now, I'm going to smack your ass and fuck you like you want. Because that's what you want, isn't it, Delilah? You don't want roses and sweet nothings. You want me to treat you like you're unbreakable. Unbreakable and completely mine." I can feel her back move as she breathes rapidly on my chest, her warm skin on mine. But I need her response. I need her approval.

"Is that what you want, Lilah?" I ask.

Long moments pass.

I half expect her to say no, to which I would toss her on that bed all over and eat her pussy and fuck her sweet and not regret a single moment.

But then she answers.

"Yes, Dante," she says, and my cock twitches.

"That's my girl," I whisper, standing up and moving her, hand on her hips and lifting until her knees hit the edge of her low bed, her hands moving to the mattress to hold herself up.

Slowly, I use two fingers to dip under the lace and drag down the panties, leaving them at her ankles, before stepping back to take her in. She looks over her shoulder at me, and goddamn.

The sight is beautiful.

"Gorgeous," I whisper, and in her eyes, it's clear she likes that.

Likes that I like the view. "But now I have to make it a pretty shade of pink, yeah?" Her mouth opens a bit, but still, she nods.

She fucking nods.

I step forward, my hand moving to her hair, wrapping it around and tugging gently until she's looking up at the shitty popcorn ceiling.

"When I tell you to stop, Delilah, you fucking stop." No answer. My hand tightens. "Yes?"

"Yes, Dante," she whispers, and I move my free hand out to the side then slap it to her ass, rubbing the spot where it made contact.

A tiny fucking moan comes from her.

Jesus fucking Christ.

"When I tell you not to touch yourself, that it's for me, you don't fucking touch yourself, Delilah. Yeah?"

No answer.

I smile to myself.

Then I smack her ass again.

"God! Yes! I won't!"

Something tells me that's a lie.

Something tells me Lilah will do absolutely anything to get under my skin, to win this game we play, and I really fucking love it.

"Whose are you, Lilah?" I ask then repeat the motion, smacking and rubbing, waiting for her answer.

"Yours," she moans, and I look at her hands, those bright red tips curled into the sheets.

"Good girl," I murmur, then I let go of her hair and step back once more. "Stay there, your man's gonna take care of you now," I say, shucking my boxers and then stepping forward, marveling at how the height is perfect as I rub the head of my cock down her wet slit. "Fuck. Is this from me? Did my spanking your pretty ass get you this wet?"

"Yes," she whispers as if she's now trained to answer any questions I ask instantly.

I know once she comes, that, too, will end.

"Fucking made to be mine," I say, then I slowly start to move into her.

"Oh, fuck, Dante," she moans to the ceiling, clamping down on me as I slowly enter her wet pussy.

Torturously slow.

"God, I wish you could see this, baby," I moan, watching my cock disappear in her, watching her take me. "You take my cock like you were fucking made for it." She moans deep, and my hand glides from her hip to the center of her back, pressing until her upper half collapses, her face pressing into the soft mattress as she moves her hips back to take more of me.

"Fuck yeah, such a good fucking girl you are. My good fucking girl."

"Dante, god, please!"

"What do you need, baby?" I ask, but the words are almost malicious, cruel. I know exactly what she needs. But I want her to tell me.

"Dante, I—" A deep moan comes from her again as she tips her hips, my cock brushing a new spot inside her.

"Use your big girl words, Lilah. Tell your man what you want him to do," I say, and that hand moves up to her neck, twisting in her hair and tugging until she's looking up at the ceiling, the rest of her blonde curls falling in a cascade. The arch in her back has me wishing there were a camera in here, something I could watch over and over on the nights I can't be with her.

"I need more," she says with a whimper.

"What do you *need*, Lilah? I'll give you anything you want," I say, tightening my fingers in her hair, another low moan leaving her lips before she finally gives me what she needs.

"My clit!" she shouts. "I need you to rub my clit and make me come!"

"That's my girl," I say, then I move the other hand on her hip down and in, straight to her wet clit that's already swollen. Once, twice, three times, and then she's gone, clamping down and screaming my name. "Fuck yeah, Lilah. Fuck," I groan, thrusting in deep and then staying there as I fill her before collapsing on top of her, only my forearms keeping me from crushing her. I allow minutes to pass as I kiss her neck lightly, feeling her breathing regulate. When I finally move, her eyes are slowly drooping, exhaustion taking over.

"Oh, no, baby. I'm not done with you." Those pretty blue eyes pop open, and I smile.

"What?" she says

"I'm not done with you. At least two more times before I let you sleep." Her face goes slack with shock, and I laugh, standing and pulling out of her. A small mewl falls from her lips as I do.

"See? You don't even want me to leave you yet. You need more, baby. Let me feed you first, though. Get your energy up," I say, pulling her up and pressing my lips to hers.

"Okay," she says. And then I feed my girl before I fuck her again.

-Lilah-

When I wake, the sun creeps in through the blinds, and I already know before I open my eyes Dante isn't in my bed with me, having snuck out at some point.

I guess I deserve that one.

If there's one thing I've learned in this life, it's that powerful men like to have the scales balanced. If you get something over on them, they want to make sure you get yours in return.

Acknowledging this fact doesn't help ease the disappointment, though.

TWENTY-TWO

-Lilah-

I'm heading home that night when my sister calls again.

She has called me three times today and twice yesterday, not leaving any message, so I'm pretty sure no one's died, but I'm also pretty sure that if I ignore *this* one, she'll come and find me. Except, of course, she won't be able to.

The address she has for me? I no longer live there.

The job I once had? I no longer work there.

The friends I used to spend nights with? I haven't spoken to them since Lola was in the hospital.

And for that reason alone, I answer my phone.

"Jesus, I thought I'd have to call Dad as a last resort. See where you are," my sister says, her voice coming through the speaker.

Speakerphone because I can't handle a ticket today.

It was a long one. I did my new normal, a short four-hour shift in one of the poker rooms, but then Marco asked if I could stay late. One of the servers had the flu, and they needed someone to fill in. Of course, I agreed, staying to help serve the three—yes, *three*—bachelor parties that strolled in before Fancy walked in at nine, saying I could head out.

"How's Libby's?" I ask, ignoring her and any motherly nitpicking I know she's dying to do.

Libby's is the bakery my sister opened after fifteen years of dealing with our father's shit. She finally cut him off—or so she thought—and opened her dream shop named after our mother in our hometown of Ocean View. Conveniently, she works and lives right next door to her tattoo-artist boyfriend, who would do quite literally anything for my sister. That includes knocking out Johnny Vitale and holding him hostage with his own gun while they waited for the cops to come after he tried to kidnap my sister.

The beginning of my end, in a way.

"Lilah! Where the fuck have you been?" she asks, bypassing my question, and it's not irritation in her voice—it's panic and worry.

Shit.

Our mother died when I was 10 and Lola was 15, and she took it upon herself to become the fill-in for her. So even though her own life is chaos—finally the good kind, but still chaos—I know she must have been worried.

"I just talked to you a few days ago! I've been working; I like going out. I'm a busy gal, Lol," I say, stopping at a red light.

"The fuck you are. Called Adrianna, and she said you haven't been out in, like, two months."

Fuck.

I should have known my sister wouldn't let anything go. I heard the disbelief in her voice the last time she called. I should have done more to nip her nosiness.

"I got the flu," I lie, thinking of the illness going around the club. "Plus a promotion."

"A promotion?"

"Yeah. I uh . . . I got a new account. It's keeping me really busy."

God, I hate lying to her. I really do.

But my sister deserves the peace of my taking on this burden. It's my turn.

Lola is quiet for a few long moments as the light turns green, and I start driving again.

The urge to end the silence hits, but I'm not the younger sister for nothing. I can wait out Lola.

"Didn't you just get a new job? At a start-up?"

Fuck. I forgot I told her that.

I need to keep all of my stories straight because they're only going to get messier.

"Yes. And they gave me a new account! Isn't that exciting?" She makes a non-committal *hmm* sound, and I panic that she won't believe me.

I fight the craving to fill in the silence, though.

A lifetime of lies taught me a few skills, I guess.

"You sure you're okay?" she says, and I sigh in relief.

"Yes, Lola. Just getting over being sick and working a ton. Plus, Adrianna only ever wants to go out and party every night. That's why I haven't seen her in a while. I'm getting old."

"Babe, you're 26. Not 50."

"Whatever. How's Ben?" I ask, turning left where I used to turn right, away from the pretty high-rises and toward the crappy apartments.

"He's good. He just got off. I'm waiting for him to be done cleaning. Figured I'd call you."

"He still being a dreamboat knight in shining armor?"

"He doesn't have to be a knight in shining armor anymore, thank god. I don't need him to take care of me anymore," she says, and then there's a deep laugh in the back. "Shut up, you." More deep murmuring, but I'm pretty sure it's of the spicy variety because my sister has to clear her throat before responding. "Benjamin James, I am on the phone with my baby sister!"

"Ooh, what's he saying, what's he saying!" I ask, knowing my sister is a total prude and would never reveal her dirty secrets. I doubt she even *has* any dirty secrets, to be honest.

"Ew, god, shut up, Lilah," she says as predicted, and I laugh, turning into my complex. "You going to come down soon, or do I have to drag Ben up north?" she asks, and I sigh, pulling into my complex.

"I'll come down. Maybe in a couple of weeks, okay?" I ask, but my voice is off, distracted. That's because my eyes are on the light next to my front door.

There's a dark figure standing there.

"Fine, but if you don't, we're coming there."

"Yeah, yeah, I'll be there, Lola. I, uh . . . I gotta go," I say, trying to simultaneously find a parking spot and keep an eye on the figure. Maybe they're walking past, or smoking outside, or . . .

"You good, babe?" she asks.

"I'm good, sissy. I love you. I just got home, and I gotta carry in a bunch of stuff. Need my hands. Talk to you soon?" I ask.

"Yeah, Lilah. See you soon. Love you lots. Please, pick up my calls next time?"

"Got it. Bye, Lol," I say, and then the phone call ends, but my eyes stay on my front door, the panic building now that I don't have to play cool for my sister.

I find a spot, not my normal one right in front of my apartment, though, because, you know, someone is standing *right outside my place*. My eyes stay fixed on the figure. It's a man, a tall man, nearly as tall as the light, which is why I can't quite see him. The way the light hits him, his entire face is in shadow.

But as I turn the key, shutting off my car, he steps forward.

And my body melts, the fear melting with it.

Dante.

Dante is standing outside of my apartment in October.

Dante, who slipped out of my bed before I woke up this morning, who didn't leave a note, who never gave me his number.

That Dante is standing in front of my dingy apartment, waiting for me.

I lean into the passenger seat to grab my bag and gather my thoughts before turning back to the door to let myself out. But in the three seconds it takes, he's standing there, opening the door for me and offering me his hand. I grab it and he tugs, lifting me out of my seat before slamming the door shut once I'm out. And then he's moving, pinning me to the cold metal, hands on either side of my body as his nose runs from the collarbone that's exposed in the slouchy sweatshirt up my neck, stopping to press a kiss below my ear.

"Missed you," he says, the words reminiscent of the grocery store.

I should ask what the fuck he's doing here.

I should ask how long he's been here.

I should ask a million and seven things, including why was he at the grocery store and how did he find me on the side of the road that one time, but instead, I breathe in his scent and my body relaxes.

Goddammit.

And then my vagina—or maybe it's my girly heart, but it's definitely *not* my head—asks him a question.

Again. It's not a good one, not one I *should* be asking.

"Where were you this morning?" I ask in a whisper, the cold air turning my breath into clouds that float in the air between us.

"Had an early meeting." His lips press to where my pulse is already racing, his tongue dipping out to taste. When he pulls back, the cold air attacks that spot, but it flares with heat all the same. "Hated leaving you."

"You could have woken me up," I whisper despite the fact that, again, there are so many other things I freaking *should* be saying.

"Like you did?" he counters, and something twists in me; the thought of him using that as payback hurt. "No, not that. I wasn't getting you back. You just looked sweet. Knew I'd be here tonight, couldn't stay away."

"You knew you'd be here tonight?" I ask, and my body shivers, both from the thought of him planning to be here *yesterday* and the cold of the metal.

"Oh yeah," he says with a smile on his lips, stepping back. "Come on. Let's get you inside. Have you eaten?" he asks, guiding me to my apartment. I dig in my bag to find my key, unlocking the door before opening it, which Dante shuts behind me.

"How did you know where I lived?" I ask, tossing my bag onto the shitty couch and turning to face him.

Once again, he moves to corner me, turning me until my back is to the door.

"You think you could bring me to your place and I wouldn't take notes of where it is? Make it so you couldn't disappear on me again?"

"You disappeared last time," I say in a whisper.

"But I told you, I knew I'd be back." His hand goes to my hip, pulling me into him, and my body can't help but respond, my arms impulsively going around his neck.

It's like I'm a puppet and he's the master, like my body can only respond to accept him, to encourage him.

"But I didn't know that," I say, and I'm embarrassed that the words slip from my lips.

"Oh, *fiorella*. Don't you know?" he asks, the words so damned soft, like he's talking to an injured animal. The hand not on my hip moves until he grabs my chin, tipping it up to meet his face. "You have possessed me. The first time I saw you, I needed to know you." He touches his lips to mine gently, kissing me, my breath halting in my lungs. "The first time I heard your voice, I became a man obsessed. The first time I felt your touch, I knew you'd be mine. Delilah, no matter where you go, I will find you."

His words should terrify me.

They should have me calling the cops.

This man I barely know saying he's obsessed with me, that he'll find me no matter where I go, should have me running for the hills.

But instead, it has me melting into him.

I have always been the pretty, untouchable thing. The china you use when company comes over. The pretty toy you play with on special occasions before placing back in the box. The delicate flower you press between pages, preserving it for another day before it even wilts.

I've been an untouchable princess, fun to look at but never to touch.

Never to possess.

Never to *own*.

My father kept me in the limelight just enough to stir attention, enough to get the men to vote before he'd lock me up, lock me away.

I was meant to be untouchable.

Untouched by men, untouched by drama, untouched by the truth.

Dante is the first person I've ever met who not only treats me like I'm precious, but also like I'm strong enough to withstand his touch and so much more. It's like I'm something he wants to hold and possess and maybe even destroy.

It's intoxicating.

This is what's running through my mind as I lie in my bed with Dante hours later, long after he fed me and then fucked me into a state of calm and ease, his warm body heating me despite the chill of fall.

But still, despite all of this, I know nothing about this man. I don't know anything about who he is or where he came from.

"Who are you?" I ask, an enamored whisper as my eyes grow heavy.

"Yours," he replies, and then he kisses me, taking any questions I might have away with it.

And when I wake, he is gone once again, his side of the bed cold, but the pillow I hold instead of him still smells of him, telling me it wasn't all some kind of elaborate dream.

TWENTY-THREE

An entry from Libby's journals, written six years before Lilah was born.

Dear Diary,

My father won't back down.

He says Tony Carluccio is my only choice and that I have to agree to the arrangement.

I tried talking to him, but he won't budge. He's insistent that I do what's right for the family, but what about what's right for me? I mentioned the Russo family, told him I'd like him to consider Arturo, but he refused.

He said he knew about our private meetings.

He called me a whore.

He told me if I tried to run to him, horrible things

would happen to Arturo. That the Carluccio family is looking for any reason to ignite the fuse of their feud.

So instead, I did something terrible.

I'm going to lose everything because of it, but it's what's best. I have to do it for Arturo in order to keep him safe.

But I will never forgive my father for what he took from me.

Ever.

Libby

TWENTY-FOUR

-Lilah-

The day after Dante stays at my apartment for the second time, I finally hit pay dirt on my quest to find information that can help my cause.

I'm starting to wonder if he isn't a lucky charm. The first time we were together, I got the new position that allowed me inside access to the games where men whisper without worrying about who might hear.

If *I* might hear.

And that's proven to be a useful position.

The thing about being pretty and quiet is that men with big egos who don't value women forget you exist.

Forget that you have ears and a mind instead of just tits and ass.

They speak in front of you without a care in the world, assuming you won't understand.

But I do.

I listen.

I hear.

I know.

That's why this afternoon, I get the first piece of information I need.

I'm sitting in my corner during a game featuring an older, well-known senator and a rumored high-up capo of the Carluccio family.

"So, I hear Vitale is fucked," the white-haired politician says, glancing at the cards in his hands. "What happened there?"

Training tells me to keep loose, to leave my face uninterested.

But my ears—my ears are on high alert.

My mind is taking a recording so I can play it over again and again, dissecting each word they speak in my presence.

"Fuckin' *stunad* tried to kidnap some mayor's daughter in broad fuckin' daylight."

"What the fuck would make him do that?"

"Who knows. You know he's always been a loose cannon. Always running off on ideas and listening to Tony. Both of them are fuckin' unhinged. Neither knows how to play the long game. That's why they're both locked the fuck up," the capo says.

I wonder if he'd be talking like this if not for the fourth whiskey on the rocks he's sipping. I fight the urge for my eyes to drift, to look over at Marco hiding in the shadows. I wonder what he thinks of this, of a soldier spilling secrets.

"That's why Tony is locked up. Played too close to the sun. That anonymous tip to the FBI? Fucked, that shit happened to him." I file that away, wanting to look into it. I haven't focused much on Tony Carluccio, who is already paying with life in prison.

But they're right. Who tipped off the feds? Who hated him enough that they would risk the code of silence to do that? Because word on the street is, if I remember the lore correctly, the call came from inside the house.

"Well, you remember what happened with Russo."

Breath leaves and enters my lungs as normal.

I blink like normal.

My hands stay loose in my lap.

But every part of me is on fire.

"I still can't believe that shit," the capo says. "I don't think Tony would do that, or that Johnny would just listen and carry it out."

"All I know is that at the time, I was in Jersey City, and the Russos were fighting me on a project. They wanted me to approve some fuckin' low-income housing and they were riling up the community for it. But I had a deal with Metro Homes to put in those high-rises. They were giving me a lot of incentive to approve it. Russos kept coming to my house, fuckin' driving me insane, threatening to expose me," the senator says as if he's annoyed that someone had the gall to try and stop his devious doings.

"Never understood those assholes. You could have all the power in the world, could have everything, and you choose to use it against your own fuckin' interests? *Stunads*, all a' 'em."

"So, I go to Tony, say I need help, that the Russos are giving me issues. He tells me he can't step in, his father wouldn't like it, but that I don't have to worry. That soon they'd be *consumed with their own issues*—those are the fuckin' words he said, swear to God—and it would all be forgotten. I asked what he meant; he said don't ask questions. A week later, it was all over the news—Arturo was shot in that drive-by, no suspects. A week after that, I approved the high-rises, bought my boat."

Acid churns in my stomach at the careless words.

My father was murdered, and this man bought a fucking boat with a kickback.

These people are monsters. Absolutely vile.

"But I still don't understand *why*? If he wasn't doing it as a favor to you, why would Tony tell you that it would be handled?" a third man asks, the superintendent of a local school district. Some would be surprised to see someone like him here, but I'm not.

You don't realize how deep the greed goes until you're sitting in hell and see all of the ghosts.

"Who the fuck knows."

"You know, I've heard some theories on that," the man says, moving a card in his hand to the table and grabbing another.

"Are you going to grace us with the honor of your theory, or just fuck around?"

"Fuck off," he says, pushing chips into the middle of the table. "Remember Vin Bianchi? He was working with the Carluccios for *years*, waiting for his daughter to get old enough, marry into the family. She was supposed to hook up with Tony, bring the families together. Vin would get the muscle of the family; Carmine would get the backing of a congressman."

"No shit? Isn't that the daughter who got together with Turner?"

My mother.

"Exactly. Apparently, the Bianchi girl found out about her old man's plan, refused to marry Tony. Went behind his back, fucked his intern, got pregnant." Eyes go wide, and the senator nods, a smile on his lips like he's proud to have the good gossip.

"No shit. Well, that wouldn't look good for his family values platform, would it?" asks the superintendent. Chips move, cards are lifted, and my breathing stays stagnant.

"Yeah, but from what I hear, the girl was fucking Arturo from the start. That's why she didn't wanna get wrapped up with the Carluccios."

"No fuckin' way," a well-known news anchor says, his eyes wide. Clearly, he does not have a poker face. Evident not only with his reaction but the dwindling pile of chips before him. "I don't know if I believe that shit. You're telling me all of this was because of some *puttana*?"

I wonder what he barters in? Cash? Assets? Favors? Kind reporting?

Whatever it is, his number will be up sooner rather than later. Calling my mother a whore gets him on my list of retribution.

"Look, I'm going by what I've heard. And from what I hear, she would do anything not to marry Russo's rival. Tony apparently took it personally, waited a couple years, let it simmer. I guess she was still fuckin' the Russo kid on the side. Tony asked if she was interested in starting something up, but she turned him down. Again."

"You're telling me the hit on Arturo Russo was a bruised fuckin' ego?"

The congressman lifts his hands, an innocent smile on his lips. I'm sure that smile has been used many times.

Maybe on the anchor's prime-time show.

"Just going by what I've heard. I've also heard that Carmine had some bigger plan, planted the seed in his son's ear. You know how the streets love to whisper. But it makes sense, I guess. And now Johnny going down for kidnapping that Turner girl? Don't you think it's all a bit too neat and clean?"

"So what do you think it is? Payback for Tony?"

"No clue. Maybe there's more to the Turner girl that no one knows."

And then I feel it.

Eyes, burning on my skin.

I finally let myself look around the room, trying to see who is staring, but it's not the players.

It's not the dealer.

It's the shadows.

Marco.

And the way that gaze is burning, I wonder if he's staring because I heard something I shouldn't know or if he knows something I don't want him to.

TWENTY-FIVE

-Lilah-

The first time Dante snuck out without saying goodbye, I assumed it was payback for that first morning.

Payback doesn't make for a great fantasy relationship, so I figured that was it. Two extraordinary nights of sex, and then we were even. *I could handle that,* I told myself as I got ready for work that afternoon. I could handle it even though when he was near, it felt like there was pure iron in my blood and he was a magnet.

I told myself that if he somehow magically bumped into me again, I would smile and insist on going home alone.

And then he showed up at my place last night and changed my mind.

Like the first and second time, it was like when he was there, my mind blanked of every single molecule of reason except for the fact that I needed him to breathe.

But then, this morning, I woke up alone again, and I was miserable.

I was miserable because I hated myself for being so damned

stupid, for falling for that shit again. For letting him in, letting my heart start to believe his words about being obsessed and possessed because it's how I have been feeling too. And maybe if we both felt the insanity, we could be committed together.

The whole day I was in a horrible mood, barely putting on my siren's smile in the poker rooms as I took and delivered orders. Thankfully, I was able to pull it together when the gossip went down, but each time I walked through the club, my eyes scanned the room. I remembered those few times he came in, when I danced for him as he asked me silly questions, and I wondered if maybe he'd come by again.

And when the day went normal, when I walk out of the club at 10, another long night but one I could stand given I needed the distraction, I drive home still feeling miserable.

When he isn't standing at my door with apologies and excuses, I'll admit, my stomach churns with disappointment once again.

But as I unlock my front door, thinking I forgot to switch the lights off again, I find Dante Romano sitting at the kitchen table in my apartment, a crystal-cut glass in front of him, one shiny wing-tipped shoe on a knee and his phone in one hand.

He smiles at me, a smile you might give someone you've lived with for years when they walk in the door. A casual thing, a simple smile.

That's when I scream.

I scream and drop my purse, looking around for . . . something to protect myself.

Anything. Anything at all.

"What the fuck are you doing here!?" I shout, backing into a wall, the movement jarring as I do. Dante stands, a curious smile on his lips as he does, like he finds me funny.

"Grabbed your spare before I left."

"You *what?!*"

"It was hanging on your key rack. Better than waiting outside in the cold, yeah?"

"Dante, what the fuck are you *doing here?!*" My pulse starts to calm as I realize he's not cornering me, not trying to murder me in cold blood.

Is he clearly a bit insane? Yes.

But it seems not the murdering brand of insane.

"Waiting for you."

"You're . . . waiting for me."

And then something happens that I don't anticipate.

His brow furrows, and he looks confused. The move makes him look ten years younger, closer to my age. "Do you not want to spend the night together?" he asks.

I think my brain malfunctions. How do I answer that?

How the *fuck* do I answer that without A. sounding insane or B. hurting his feelings? Because for some chaotic reason, I think there's a good chance I could hurt this powerful man's feelings if I say no.

Regardless, my body moves without permission.

One step forward, narrowing the distance between us from four feet to three.

The furrow stays, but what I now realize is concern evaporates.

"It's not that," I admit. "I'm just . . . confused about why you're here. You disappear and then you show up. I have no idea what's going on."

A small, sad smile moves on his face before he closes the gap between us.

"Missed you," he says, arms wrapping around me, and again, I should be screaming, I should be running, I should be finding something to protect myself with, I should be calling the cops . . .

But those words.

They melt into my bones, easing the panic because, for some reason, my body recognizes him, and it feels safe here.

Still, I shake in his arms, my breath heavy as the adrenaline eases.

His hand moves my thick hair over my shoulder, the natural

blonde I got from my mother gleaming in the shitty, dim lighting, before he kisses me in that spot he loves, right under my ear.

It's not sexual, just a thing he seems to do, kissing me there. Like he's reminding himself that I'm here. I'm real.

I get it, after all. Half the time, he doesn't feel real, either.

"Where were you this morning?" I ask in a whisper.

"Had work early. I didn't want to wake you."

I don't like the answer.

But before I can ask any more questions, a black-and-white shape moves near his feet.

"Watch out, she's a bitch," I say, stepping back as my demon spawn of a cat comes our way. She usually hides all day, only noting my existence when she needs me to feed her, at which point she quite literally hunts me around the house. Any other time, I'm basically coexisting and dodging her little paws swiping at me, claws extended.

When I moved out from my home, I wanted something cute and cuddly to keep me company. I found her on Craigslist, thinking she was my new furry BFF.

Instead, I got the feline spawn of Satan.

But again, I'm shocked by this man when he looks down and smiles. And then the bitch starts to fucking *rub her head on his leg.*

"This girl?" he says, bending down, and then I watch in utter horror as he picks her up.

"Dante, I really wouldn't—"

"We were hanging out while I was waiting for you. Weren't we?" this scary giant of a man asks my demon-spawn cat.

And then she starts purring.

Purring.

"What the fuck is going on?" He looks at me, confused, giving the demon spawn scratches behind her ear. She also looks at me like I'm crazy, like this morning she didn't give me a two-inch gash when I wouldn't refill her bowl a third time.

"That cat is evil."

"She seems pretty sweet to me." Then he looks at me with a wide, boyish smile. "But I do have a way of making pussies purr."

I stare at him, not even able to understand what is going on or register his terrible pun. All I know is this man broke into my house, basically told me he is obsessed with me, and now he's petting my cat like they're lifelong pals.

"Are you real, Dante?" He smiles, putting down Molly before pulling me into him again.

"Am I real?"

"None of this adds up. You drop money at a strip club, find me in the wild twice now, slip in and out of my place in the shadow of night . . . What are you hiding? A wife? Kids? Some kind of underground lifestyle?"

"The only person in my life is you."

He doesn't deny the lifestyle.

"Do you trust me?" he asks, and it's not the words but the way he says them that itches something in my memory. Something I can't reach, can't touch, can't quite understand.

Do you trust me?

The memory I can't hold onto slips from my grasp.

But the warmth stays behind.

"Yes," I say. "I think so." The smile he gives me in return is almost boyish, sweet. "Don't make me regret that, Dante. Please," I beg, moving the thick hunk of hair from his head with my fingers. He grabs my wrist and places a soft kiss to my pulse.

"I would die before I let you regret this, *fiorella*. Come. Let me feed you," he says, stepping back and guiding me toward the little table in my kitchen area.

And then Dante Romano pulls out food he brought over and I let him feed me.

"I don't like this place," Dante says hours later as we sit in my bed watching TV. He already fucked me raw once, and I know from my limited experience, a second is coming before he lets me fall asleep on his chest. His eyes move around the small studio apartment. "You deserve luxury. Beauty."

Consider my feathers *ruffled*.

"Luxury does not equate to happiness."

"I know that. I just think you deserve the world, Lilah."

"There was a time when I had the world given to me, and I was the least happy I've ever been."

It's something I've struggled with over the past two months. Knowing that despite the stress, the pressure I've put on myself, and the knowledge of how privileged my life before was, I'm happier than I ever have been.

I'm finally my own person, and knowing this happiness came without the extravagance I once relied on can be confusing.

"You were never given the world, Delilah. You were given the version of the world your father thought you should have. Me? I want you to have the *world*. I want you to have diamonds and luxury but also respect and loyalty. If you want people to hear your name and shake in fear, I'll work to give you that. If you want people to look at you with awe and jealousy, I'll make it happen."

"I want to do things on my own. Earn them."

"I never said I was going give them to you, Delilah. I am going to do whatever I have to to make sure you can grab whatever the fuck you want. I want to mow down anyone who steps in your way or tries to tell you no."

I smile then move, rolling until I'm straddling him, the blanket falling down my naked body. On instinct, I think, his hands move to the dip of my waist, a thumb brushing the skin there.

But fuck if his eyes don't stay right on mine, even if I can feel him getting hard beneath me.

"Is it normal to get turned on when someone tells you they want to kill anyone who gets in the way of what you want?"

His smile widens, and Jesus Christ, I would do some sick shit to see that smile.

"You really are the perfect woman, aren't you?" he asks, his hand sliding up my back until it lands in my hair, gripping and tugging gently. I smile at him, my pretty siren's smile, and then take what I want.

"Are you going to be here in the morning?" I ask, my voice sleepy, my head settling onto his chest. This bed is one of the few things I kept from my old apartment. It's too big for the room, making it so I can barely walk, but with Dante's large body next to mine, I'm happy I brought it. I can hear the deep breath he takes as he processes my question.

"One day, beautiful girl," he says, and his words sound the way I feel. Let down.

"But not tomorrow?" I ask, but I already know the answer.

"Not tomorrow."

"Why not?" I ask, and my eyes close, weights attaching themselves to my lids.

"Because I need to give you everything before that can happen."

And when I wake, his side of the bed is cold, but the pillow I'm holding still smells like him.

TWENTY-SIX

-Lilah-

Two weeks. That's how long this goes on. How long I've been sleeping with Dante in my bed. This mysterious man who comes at night and leaves in the morning. The man who has me sweating in my sheets, moaning his name, writhing, and then cuddling up into his side.

The man who is never there when I wake.

I should be used to it by now, this obscure back and forth. I'm not. I wake up lonely every damn morning, wishing I had the guts to demand he stay. Or at least put an end to it. I need to put on my big-girl panties and listen to my common sense instead of my vagina or, unfortunately, my heart.

But each night, I come home and pray he's there, pray he comes before I go to bed.

There have been a few nights when I went to sleep without him beside me, sure that we were done, only to be woken up with his head between my legs, no time to even question how he got through my deadbolt or how I slept through the sound of him entering my apartment.

In my defense, most nights, as I'm driving home, I'm hyping myself up, ready to tell him this is over.

And then I'm in his presence again, and he's pulling me into him and whispering that he missed me, and the world settles.

That feeling of *home* that I've never truly had settles.

"This is weird, isn't it?" I ask, drawing lines in the hair on his chest. His hand stalls in my hair, and when I tip my head up to look at him, there is confusion on his handsome face.

"Weird?"

"This. Us."

"Us."

"Are we an . . . us?" Oh my god, this might be the most embarrassing moment of my entire fucking life, and I once barfed on a banquet table in front of dozens of high-profile donors when I was twelve. I had a fever, but my dad had a fundraiser, so he dosed me up with cold medicine and dragged me along.

On the bright side, he never questioned an illness again.

The hand in my hair moves, tightening, forcing me to look at him.

"There are a lot of things in this world you can question, *fiorella*. This? This is not one of them." His lips press to mine gently, and the panic settles.

"Why do you only come at night?" I ask long minutes later after wondering if I should even do so, but the words come out before I can stop them.

He sighs, but not in a way that tells me he doesn't want to answer or that he finds me annoying. Instead, it's in a way you sigh when you don't know *how* to answer.

"I have meetings in the mornings." The words feel like a lie. A lie I've been forcing myself to buy, to overlook for two weeks. "I don't want to wake you."

"Sometimes I wake up at six and you're already gone."

"Lilah . . ."

"Are you married?" I ask, the words terrifying as they leave my lips. He responds instantly, a look of shock and frustration clear on his face. Not frustration with me, but with . . . this. The situation, maybe.

"God, fuck, no, Lilah. You. It's you."

"Where do you work? What do you do? What's your family like? You come in the middle of the night and fuck me and fall asleep with me and then leave before the sun rises. What the fuck am I supposed to think?" His thumb moves along my cheekbone, and he watches it move before looking into my eyes.

"I just need you to trust me."

"I don't *know* you!" I say, my voice rising. "God, this is fucking crazy." I try to move, to get up, to put space between us, but that hand in my hair holds tight, not letting me go. Not aggressive, just firm. I give up on my escape, facing this like an adult. My eyes meet his when I ask the next question, ready to decode even the slightest movement. "Am I some kind of secret?"

"No," he says, but again, there's a lie there. I raise an eyebrow, questioning, arguing. "Not the way you're thinking. There's . . . Fuck, baby. There's so much. So much I need to tell you, that we need to talk about. But I'm telling you, once that happens, there's no going back. It won't be easy like this anymore."

"Easy?" *This* is easy? Him sneaking in and out of my apartment with no warning, meeting me while I was working as a stripper, a pile of secrets between us?

"Right now, it's just us. I come as soon as I can, I fuck you, I eat you, and I feed you if it's not too late. It's just us, and you are mine." My mind fixates on that last piece.

"Am I yours? Only yours?"

"Fuck, yes. Please. We have nothing if we don't have trust. If we don't have this foundation, we will collapse when the easy is gone. You have tangled me so deep, you've consumed me. I've never been this lost for a woman. I've never risked everything this way for a woman."

"What are you risking?!" My voice rises with the words, frustration running in my veins.

"I don't want to open that door. Not yet."

"What does that mean, Dante? You're speaking in hidden messages and metaphorical situations. None of it makes sense, and to be completely honest, none of it is very comforting. This isn—" His hand tightens in my hair once more, forcing me to stop talking, and finally, *finally* I see it there.

The honesty.

The fear.

The *panic*.

And something so close to what I've imagined love would look like on his face, that it scares the shit out of me.

"Lilah, one day, it won't be like this. One day it won't be easy and without pressure. While we can, I want this."

I stare at him and don't answer. Every part of me is warring, with different answers and responses running through my mind.

"Please, Delilah," he says, and his eyes say it all. The honesty. The potential, the pleasing. And I know.

I know that even if this man is to be my downfall, I will take this for what it is while I can.

In that moment, I wonder if maybe I really am just like my mother.

The night doesn't get less stressful when a couple hours later, my phone rings, and I look at it quickly. *Dad* is displayed on the screen.

"Little late for calls, isn't it?" Dante asks.

"It's my dad," I say, hitting the button to quiet the screen.

"Shouldn't you answer that?" he asks, and I shake my head. The phone lights up again moments later, the screen showing a missed call.

Four, to be exact.

"Four missed calls, huh?" he asks, smiling at me. I roll my eyes as he moves, lining his body over mine, arms caging in my face.

This is my favorite part about our nights together.

I love—no, seriously, I *love*—when this man fucks me. When my entire body comes alive and for the first time I can remember, I feel like the version of me I was meant to be: beautiful and powerful and *worshiped*. Strange to think a man fucking me is what gives me that feeling for the first time, but that's just who Dante is. Who we are when we're together.

But this part—when we're both sated but not tired, when he rolls over me and we talk?

I could get used to it.

It's like the day in the club when he'd just pester me with little, insignificant questions, learning about me just because he wanted to know more. Except better because his warm skin is usually on mine while he does.

This is the part that makes me hate this stupid arrangement. This arrangement that I'm afraid to question or else have it disappear.

It was the fourth or fifth night of him coming here when I had the realization. He had rolled onto me just like this and started asking me questions—what was my major in school? What do I do for fun? That kind of stuff—and I realized he was listening. He wasn't asking to fill time, wasn't asking as a part of the facade, but because he was genuinely interested in what I had to say.

It was the same when we sat in that private room together, even though I didn't realize it at the time. He was asking me questions to make me feel comfortable, but it was also because he wanted to know me. I think he answered them back because, in a way, he wanted me to know him too.

It was the fifth night of him coming to my place when I admitted I was working at Jerzy Girls to help with a family issue, leaving it at that, but that was enough for him. He didn't put up a fight, tell me that it wasn't right or that I was too good for it. He didn't tell me I needed to quit like the girls have all complained about with men they date outside of work. He just nodded and kept talking.

But after two weeks of this move, of this beloved moment of honesty, I know he's about to dig in.

"You not on good terms with your dad?" he asks, and I hesitate.

There wasn't much my father put on me besides to be pretty, smile, and agree to whatever dates he set me up on. But one of them was to never talk about the family.

Even when I didn't know everything or really, much at all, I knew not to talk about the family. A reporter asked a question? I was to give canned responses or no comment at all. A boyfriend asked about my father? Play dumb.

I remember him saying that when I had a boyfriend ask me about my father's stance on making the Ocean View businesses become more eco-friendly to preserve the ocean it's famed for.

"Play stupid, Delilah. Who fucking cares. Just sit there and be pretty. That's all you have to do."

The memory has me answering more honestly than I would have a few weeks ago, my mind needing to rebel.

"Not really," I say, looking at the grimy ceiling behind his head. A thick hand moves, brushing blond strands back from my face.

"Why?" he asks. The word is simple, not pushy or prodding. Not trying to extract information from me to utilize later. Just a simple question a man asks a woman he's just started to see.

So I answer with a sigh to the best of my ability without giving everything away.

"Things with my dad are . . . complicated." I return the favor, using my acrylic-tipped fingers to comb the lock of hair that always falls onto his forehead. "I'm the baby, and my mom passed when I was ten. I have an older sister who took on a lot of the raising me."

He doesn't say anything, just keeps playing with my hair,

watching me as I try and form thoughts without giving too much away.

"My dad's in . . . politics." I don't elaborate. "And optics are important. My sister became the sweet, devoted daughter at the rallies, kissing babies and keeping the memory of our beloved mother alive."

"And you?"

Another sigh.

"I told you I have an overprotective father. I was the . . . I was supposed to . . . win the male vote. I was the one who would date the sons of families my father needed to get in good with. Date, though—never more," I say quickly when his body tenses, his face getting that deathly glare to it. "It was never anything dastardly. I just . . . I was to stay . . . pretty and clean. That was my part of the image we created. Lola, the strong, smart one, and me, the pretty, sweet one." I lick my lips, embarrassed. "I didn't . . . realize how deep it went until recently. I didn't understand it, how . . . protected I was. Not for my sake, but for his."

There's a long pause as I think about how to proceed and what else to say, but Dante fills it in, pushing me along gently.

"What happened to make you see?"

How much do I tell him?

How much do I reveal of what changed, of my plan?

"I told you I'm at Jerzy Girls for family issues. My dad . . . got in deep with some bad people, and he was having my sister Lola handle it. I didn't know, and she didn't tell me. In her own way, she wanted to protect me, too. I think, to Lola, if one of us got to live free, she'd rather it be me. But we were both so caught in this mess that we didn't know what the other was doing. I didn't know about the debt until something happened and Lola almost got hurt."

"So you took over?" I nod.

It actually feels good to talk about it to someone not involved in this.

"She thinks it's done, settled. I want her to think that, that it's done and she can live without that stress. Without that anger. But I knew that it wouldn't be done and over unless one of us took it . . . further. And honestly? I-I'm mad. I'm angry. There's more to it, stuff with my mom, but I'm . . . It's my turn to take over and let Lola live in peace. She gets the pretty, sweet life now."

"And you?"

"I had that for 26 years. Now I get to make things right. Things happened when I was young, made it so I didn't get to live up to my . . . full potential." I tiptoe around the identity of my father, of the throne he wanted me to sit on. "I want that chance back. I want the people who fucked with my family to pay."

"That's a lot for one woman to do."

"I can. I will," I say, more determined with his all-knowing eyes on me.

"I have no doubt you will," he says softly, lips pressing to mine.

TWENTY-SEVEN

-Lilah-

"Mind if I sit with you?" the thick voice asks the next day while I'm eating my lunch at work, and when I look up, Marco is towering over me where I'm sitting in the back room next to the Big Boss's office. I still haven't seen the man, still haven't even been able to understand if he's even in the building most days, but according to the girls, once in a blue moon, he'll come out and say hi.

But according to the girls, he's also *always watching*.

A shiver runs through my spine every time I think about it—about being surveilled by some all-seeing Big Boss while I work.

I wonder if there are cameras in the private rooms?

Or in the poker rooms.

That seems like messy business, allowing illegal activities and then recording them.

But Marco? I know Marco. I like Marco. He's always kind to the girls who work here but also respectful. He never looks below a shoulder, always asks you how your day is, and genuinely seems like he's here to work—not to check out women as a perk of the job.

Now that I don't work on stage, I find myself eating in the general break room more often, sitting in a corner and scrolling my phone, texting my sister so that she doesn't start asking too many questions again, or typing coded notes in my phone of things I've heard, hunches I need to follow. The back room for the dancers always has a heavy haze of perfume and loud chattering, and in this loud place, I'm always craving some peace.

But today, it seems I have company,

"Yeah, sure," I say, scooting over with my peanut butter and jelly and making room for the brawny man.

"How's your day, princess?" he asks, and something about that always makes me smile, too—the nickname he gave me. If only he knew the history of my being treated like a princess hidden away from danger or the fact that, in a way, *I am* a princess, but to a family who doesn't know I exist.

My Rapunzel existence.

"Can't complain. I've been in the back room on games today. What about you?"

"Been in there with you, girl," he says with a smile.

"Really? But Roddy was taking me to get drinks today, not you," I ask.

"Yup." He pops the p and then unwraps a sandwich from the shop down the road. "Hide in the shadows, and no one asks questions. Boss wants eyes on any girls back there at all times."

"The boss," I say under my breath. "Is that Paulie?" I know the answer, but I came to this club with a plan and haven't done much in the way of making headway. This is as good a time as any to get more insight, I think.

Marco laughs.

A deep laugh, his head tipping back, dark skin gleaming in the fluorescent lighting.

It's the kind of laugh that, if you heard it in public, you'd look around for the sound, trying to figure out who you should be friends with because it sounds like a good time.

When he slows his laughter to low chuckles, a hand moves, and he tweaks the strands of my ponytail like I assume an older brother would do when his sister says something kind of dumb.

"Fuck. That was good."

"So, Paulie isn't the boss, I assume?" I ask, tipping my head to look at him and raising an eyebrow.

"No, Paulie sure as fuck is not the boss. Wishes he were, but he is not."

"When I came in . . . the first time . . . to, uh . . . get a job—" I'm actually not sure how much of my story Marco knows. Is he an employee of the club, or is he part of the . . . family, like some of the girls have mentioned?

"Know about your troubles, princess. Know you're not here because you think the tip money is good and you like the flexible hours."

I blink at him.

I can't quite decide if I should be embarrassed, but I continue on regardless.

"He was who I talked to. To make the deal. Get the job."

"Yeah, I know that," Marco says with a sigh, running a hand over his close-cut hair. "He was playing dress-up. Boss man was out of state on business. Paulie wanted to be a big man, sat in his office. He's the manager of the club, does day-to-day shit. Has the job as a favor to the family." He says *the family* so casually, in a way that I know he knows I know about *the family*, and somehow, I know that if I were anyone else, he'd be speaking more coded, more ambiguously. "Anyway, he technically shouldn't have given you the job, but it's all good now."

There's irritation in his eyes. It's clear as day.

"You don't like him. Paulie."

Marco rolls his head on his neck like he's trying to decide how to answer and move forward with the conversation. Now we're moving into territory that is uncomfortable.

Perfect.

I need intel. Intel is not comfortable. I move a hand to twirl a strand of hair, playing into my siren's role, and Marco laughs again, this time *at* me.

"Princess, you have questions, you just ask. No need to play games. No offense, you're not my type." He tugs my ponytail again and snatches a chip off my plate.

"Hey!"

"Payment. But no, I don't trust Paulie," he admits, but not like it's a burden. Like it's a fact. "And babe, you shouldn't either." A cold chill runs down my spine.

"I shouldn't what?"

"Trust Paulie. He's shifty." He looks at me, and the fun, carefree Marco is gone. His eyes are hard, stern. Like whatever he's telling me, he wants me to take seriously. "Don't go anywhere with him alone. Don't let him corner you."

Corner me?

"You think he would . . ."

"I don't know. But I'd hate to have not given you a warning. I just don't fuckin' trust the man, yeah?" And despite the fact that I barely know Marco, I nod. "If you ever have an issue with him, you tell me right away. Got it?" His eyes are serious, lacking the fun Marco-ness I've come to know and like.

"Got it. Don't trust Paulie. Don't be alone with him." I take another bite of my sandwich, and Marco follows suit until we're eating in silence. Despite the strange conversation and the even more strange setting, I like Marco. I like that he's around, that I feel safe when he's near. And because I feel safe, I ask another question.

"The owner then—the Big Boss?" I ask, playing with crumbs of chips on the paper plate I'm using. "I've never met him. What are your thoughts on him?"

"I'd trust that man with my life, princess," he says, and his words are firm and come quick, with no hesitation. It's like he's speaking of a dear friend, someone who has had a huge impact on his life. "He brought me in when I was a piece of shit, roaming the streets and looking for trouble. Gave me purpose. Gave a friend of mine a job, too. He's good." He stops, thinking, and then smiles a bit. "A bit boring, definitely a bit unhinged, but he's good. When you meet him, you'll know what I mean."

"*When* I meet him?" I ask. There's a smile on Marco's lips that I can't define, almost like he's telling a joke that I don't understand.

"He comes around sometimes. I think he's here today, technically, hidden away in his cave." Interesting. Very interesting. I wonder if that Big Boss would be useful in my grand scheme. But there's one question I can't avoid asking.

"Does he really . . . watch everything? In the club?"

"The club? Yes. He's got CCTV. The poker rooms, yes. He keeps an eye. But there are no cameras in the break room for the girls, in the bathrooms—anywhere private."

"There's not?" I ask, surprised, and Marco laughs.

"The girls talking?" he asks with a laugh, and I nod, confirming that the girls have been, in fact, talking in my ear. "Nah, he doesn't watch the girls. He watches the crowds. The men. It's the men he doesn't trust." He shakes his head with a sigh. "We'll have to have a team meeting again. Remind the girls that there are no cameras back there."

"What about the private rooms? Are there . . . cameras in there?" My mind goes back to my meetings with Dante, spilling insignificant information about myself, but it still feels . . . personal.

Marco sighs.

"Yes, but mostly in case something happens. We need to protect the girls." I nod, understanding, but before I can say anything else, there's a knock on the break room doorframe. We both turn to see Luca, one of the bouncers, standing there.

"Hey, Marco, sorry to interrupt."

"Nope, all good, just finishing," he says, crumbling up his paper. "Need me?"

"Yeah, there was an argument. Men are in the cool-down room."

"Got it. I'll be there in three," Marco says, and Luca nods before walking off. Marco looks at me and smiles, pushing his own bag of chips my way. "Payment."

"Payment?"

"For hanging out with me."

"I like hanging out with you, Marco."

"That's good. Gotta stay on your good side, princess. Here. They're your favorite," he says, then he nods and walks out, tossing the balled-up paper into the garbage. After I watch him close the door behind him, leaving me in a comfortable silence, I notice that he's right—they are my favorite barbecue chips from that fancy grocery store downtown.

But the question remains: how the fuck did he know that?

TWENTY-EIGHT

-Lilah-

Okay, so the secret back room games are a million times better than . . . this.

Back room games might be boring as fuck most days, but this chaos? *No, thank you.*

This chaos being a Friday night at Jerzy Girls, where I'm waitressing because three girls caught the flu and Roddy basically begged Marco to let me serve.

I'm not sure how two weeks of peace and quiet in the back rooms with minimal serving messed with my head so much, but I truly forgot how much I hate a Friday night here.

Men staring at every curve, every bounce of my body as I scoot through what feels like clouds of Axe body spray and sweat and arousal. Trying to hold a tray loaded with beers and the *disgusting comments* that seem to just float in the air.

The poker players are usually so focused on their game, they don't have any energy to spare me other than to request a drink.

But these men?

This is what they came for. Including the especially rowdy group that came in for a bachelor party, the groom already drunk off his ass, and his friends egging him and his bad behavior on.

I've already seen Roddy come over a few times when one of the groomsmen tried to touch a server or yelled at a dancer, but nothing too extreme has happened yet. It's just exhausting, frustrating, and, to be honest, degrading.

But again, the rule of thumb seems to be if something shitty is going to happen, it's going to happen to yours truly.

This is why I should anticipate the worst when I'm walking from the far side of the club back toward the bar and I need to pass by the rowdy bachelor party.

But of course, I'm me, and I don't, so when a hand wraps around my wrist, it's a shock to my system.

"No touching," I say in my sweet customer service voice before my head even turns to the man—the drunk groom—irritation and just a hint of panic settling in.

"Come on, pretty girl. Why don't we go head back and talk?"

"I'm working, and you aren't allowed to touch the employees, sir," I say, my voice getting sterner as I try and pull my wrist away.

He tightens his grip.

Working at a place like Jerzy Girls, you'd think I've had my fair share of close calls, lewd remarks, and uncomfortable experiences. To an extent, you'd be right. But I've only ever been *caressed* in this club by a customer twice, and both times ended quickly with an apology.

I've never had to move, scanning the room to find Roddy or Marco.

"A girl like you doesn't mind," he says, breath reeking of beer.

The bomb inside me starts to tick.

A girl like you. Words I've heard before in a number of ways that play through my mind, building my anger.

What does that even mean anymore?

A girl like you, when spoken by my father's lips, means *a girl like you shouldn't major in politics, shouldn't major in business. Try communication.*

A girl like you, when spoken by a boy I've dated, meant *I'm not going to sleep with a girl like you for fear of your father ruining me.*

A girl like you, when spoken by my sister, meant *a girl like you needs to be protected at all costs, regardless of what you think.*

But a girl like you from a customer here means something different.

A girl like you. A girl with such low morals, a desperate girl, a girl who doesn't deserve my kindness and compassion—that's what so many men have written above their heads when they walk into Jerzy Girls.

And the way he's looking at me, I know what version of *a girl like you* he means.

"Let go of me," I say, my voice firm, my back straightening. I scan the room once more, but Roddy is helping Marco usher out a few customers.

See? Friday nights are chaotic.

"Now, why would I do that?" he asks, his words low and slow, his friends chuckling. "Come on, baby, we could have fun." I tug my hand once again, finally getting it free before I start to move. Still, the man's hand reaches out again, grabbing me, tugging on the waistband of my tight hot shorts, and pulling me into him, where I fall right into his lap. "Much better, yeah?"

"What the fuck!" I shout, and a few heads turn our way.

The world starts to melt as I try and focus on what to do—what next.

The man's hand is touching the bare skin on my hip, hooked under my shorts.

I am in his lap, the smell of alcohol strong.

Roddy and Marco aren't paying attention.

In the back of my mind, I hear Candy on stage calling Marco's name, but I don't have time.

No time.

I move, pulling back, struggling to find my footing, spitting in the man's face and slapping him.

"You fucking bitch!" he shouts, and his friends start to move, trying to tug their friend out of the way, trying to find a solution to the problem they helped to create, but when I feel his hand in my hair, I know it's no use.

The tug sears, and I can almost feel each hair pulling at my scalp. I call out in pain, yelling Marco's name, and I think Candy jumps off the stage, trying to help, but I can't focus on her.

I'm focused on figuring out some kind of plan, a way to get out of this safely.

But before I can formulate that plan, the pain is gone, my hair free from the man's grasp. I'm being pulled into Candy's arms, her naked breasts on me, but I can't focus on that, either.

It's not because I'm dazed.

It's not because I'm in shock from being assaulted.

No, it's because the man who grabbed me is in a choke hold, screaming, his wrist at a strange angle that will probably haunt my dreams for years to come.

Behind him, the crowd is parted like some kind of Red Sea, allowing my rescuer entry.

My rescuer, who I recognize.

I would hope so—he's been in my bed for two weeks.

What the—

"You put your hand on my girl's, I break it," he says as the man continues to scream, his friends standing around, unsure what to do.

A part of me—that badass, unhinged part that's slowly breaking free as I leave my tower—almost finds it funny. Entertaining how a group of men who were so self-assured ten minutes ago are now speechless. Panicked.

It's a pleasure to see, really.

But the rest of me is experiencing my own speechless panic. This is because in front of me, in a white button-down with the sleeves rolled to the elbows, black dress slacks ending in familiar, shiny black dress shoes, is Dante, anger, aggression, and absolute *fury* blazing in his eyes.

"I didn't—"

"The fuck you didn't. We have cameras, dumbass. Heard the girl tell you no politely, heard you giving her shit. You put your fucking hands on her, wouldn't let go. She gave back some of what you gave her, and you decided you needed to go even further. Well, congrats, further is taking you to the *fucking* emergency room." His hand moves, the arm not holding the man in a choke hold moving to his uninjured wrist. "I should fucking break this one, too. Remind you what the fuck happens when you fuck with what the Carluccios own."

What the Carluccios own.

Jesus fucking Christ.

All these weeks.

All these weeks, I had no idea.

All these weeks, I didn't bother to ask.

Does Dante . . . work here?

Is he a *fucking Carluccio?*

No. No. No fucking way.

No fucking way did I somehow get wrapped up in a mystery man while attempting to plan the downfall of his family.

But then my mind remembers he's a Romano.

There is no Dante Romano in the family, not that I know of.

But that falls out of my mind when Dante puts pressure on the man's second hand, a finger being pulled back at an unnatural angle.

"No, man, I swear I'll—"

"DANTE!" I shout, pure instinct coming through as I panic about the repercussions of breaking some bachelor's fingers one by one in a crowded strip club.

It's like a scene from a movie, all fury and zero indiscretion.

My eyes move, somehow my political-daughter instincts kicking in as phones are being pulled out, people recording.

I'm sure there's some kind of plan. Looking back, I'll realize there was no way in hell something like this hadn't happened before, no way there's not a plan in place for it, but I panic all the same.

"Dante, no! Help me!" I say, panic flooding me.

That's all it takes.

Four words before the spell is broken.

Dante's eyes leave the drunk groom, meeting mine and probably seeing a million and seven emotions there.

They shift to the left, and I follow their path, watching Marco jog to us, the crowd parting the same way it did for Dante.

"You were supposed to be *watching her*," Dante booms, his voice sailing over the loud music still blaring. Roddy comes up behind Marco, takes in the scene, and instead of looking nervous, anxious, or even shocked, he looks . . . annoyed.

"Goddammit, Boss man, couldn't have just shoved the kid aside?" he says, and I widen my eyes at the words.

One, shock at the way he's talking to a clearly infuriated, potentially *unhinged* man who just broke another man's wrist for touching me

And two, the words he used.

Boss man.

Boss man.

Oh, Jesus fuck.

Romano.

"Boss?!" I scream. The remaining girls on stage are back to dancing, carrying on like business as usual, and I have to wonder what kind of crazy fucking place am I working at?

"Delilah, not now," Dante says, eyes glancing at me for a second before looking back to Roddy and Marco.

"Not now?! Are you kidding me?"

"Where the *fuck* were you?" he yells to Marco, ignoring me. Somehow, the words are crystal clear over the music.

"There was a drunk. I had to escort him out. His buddies were giving us a hard time. Roddy came with."

"So you leave the girls unattended?" He glances at me, then at the man who is now sitting on the floor in tears, his friends around him. "You leave *her* unattended?" The word her holds a weight that I don't quite understand.

Her.

What does *her* mean?

Obviously, "her" means *me*, but what does it mean in the grand scheme? Who am I to Dante? To Marco and Roddy? Does it just mean Turner's daughter, or something more?

The groomsmen work to help their friend up and eventually succeed when his feet are planted on the ground and steady. His wrist is limp, and I wonder how he's going to explain *that* to his fiancée. If the wedding is soon, I wonder if they'll cancel it. Or maybe she's like my mother, desperate for an escape and willing to take that in any form.

"You. Stay," Dante says, pointing to the men, and they stop moving.

"Man, we just want to—"

"Yeah, well, you're not going to." Dante's eyes move to Marco and Roddy. "Rod, take them to the back room. I'll be there soon."

"Got it, boss," he says, his voice gruff from way too many cigarettes and late nights, but he moves, the crowd parting for a third time as Roddy leads the group to one of the unmarked doors. A new one that I've never been through.

"Candy, you good?" Dante looks at the woman behind me, eyes locked on her face.

Despite the many, *many* cons I'm quickly finding with this man, that's a pro. A sign of respect, a kindness.

"Yeah, Boss man."

"What the fuck is this?" I say, flailing my arms out, ignoring the wince of pain that shoots up from my wrist.

As I should expect by now, Dante doesn't miss it.

"You okay?" he asks, but his words are dark. Angry. Fury bubbles in them like a dark soda, rising to the top and bursting.

"Dante, what in the fuck is going on?!"

"Candy, go backstage and clean up. Marco will be at the door to walk you to your car. I'll pay you out, cover your tips, yeah?" Dante says, ignoring me.

"No need, I'm good."

"I'd feel better if you did, honey," he says, and she stares at him, a small smile on her lips.

Is he fucking Candy, too? I can't help but think, my stomach roiling with the idea.

I feel like my life is once again tipping upside down, and I have no idea what to do with that fact. It's the hospital all over, everything I thought I knew and understood twisting.

Dante's eyes meet mine.

"Get that out of your head. No, Lilah. No."

The other thing I absolutely can't stand about this man is how well he can fucking *read me*.

Maybe I should have called the cops that first time he was outside my apartment instead of romanticizing it.

Or, you know, the third or fourth or fifth time.

God, what a fucking moron I've been.

"Candy, go," Dante says, his eyes moving back to my . . . friend. Yes, friend.

I like that, Candy being a friend.

Candy nods, walking with her back straight and her chin up, the way she taught me to do on my very first day, to the backstage area and then continuing to the dressing room, I'm sure.

"I gotta go deal with that fuckin' *jamook*," Dante says, looking at me, and even though I haven't known him long, I can read what his eyes are telling me.

Please, be good. Please, listen. I will explain.

"Marco. Lilah will follow you into my office. I'll deal with her in a few. Then go wait for Candy, walk her to her car. Have a man follow her and make sure she's home safe."

Marco nods then steps toward me, but I move before he can even touch my arm to guide me *to Dante's office.*

"The *fuck* I will!" I shout, stepping closer to the man who has been sleeping in my bed for two weeks. "The *fuck. I. Will. Dante.*"

"Delilah—"

"Absolutely not! What the fuck is going on here? You'll *deal with me?* I'm not a fucking child that needs to be *dealt with.* I'm a woman, and I'm angry as fuck because—"

Dante grabs my wrist, pulling me close.

I don't miss the way he holds me gently, despite the tug, aware of any soreness.

"Not. Here. Not here, Lilah. It is not safe here. You fuckin' get into my goddamned office like a good fuckin' girl or I'll have Marco carry you kicking and screaming. One way or another, you're going in there, and you're fucking *waiting for me.*"

His eyes are firm, that anger still bubbling, but it's not for me. The anger isn't for me.

Beneath the anger at the situation is pleading.

Please listen to me, Lilah, he's saying.

Unfortunately for Dante, I don't listen to men who don't tell me the truth anymore.

I don't listen to men who deceive me in order to get what they want.

"No." The word is firm, and despite the noise, I know it got to his ears because his face registers the same shock I'm also feeling.

What am I doing?

I am in way too deep.

This is *Junior Carluccio.*

I'm pretty sure of that. I'm pretty sure he's the son of Carmine. He's Paulie's *uncle.*

How the fuck was I so stupid to not see it? Not see the connection. Jesus.

"Don't make me do this, Delilah."

I stand my ground, hands on my hips, staring at the man in front of me.

Is it the right move?

Probably not.

Dante sighs.

"I have shit to handle, Lilah. I'll see you in a few," he says, then he looks to Marco and nods.

And then the large, burly man dips, putting a shoulder to my belly, and stands, taking me kicking and screaming to the unmarked door that leads to the office.

"Marco! Put me down!" I shout, smacking him on the back and trying to hit him with my clunky shoe.

"Sorry, princess. Can't do that. Got orders."

"Fuck your orders! I have free will!"

"Know that. Gotta trust the process." He unlocks the first door, stepping into the quiet hallway as I start to go limp.

What's the point in fighting him here? No one can hear me anyway, the soundproofing top of the line.

"Trust the process? What the fuck is this, a makeup tutorial?" I ask his back.

Another lock clicks, and we walk into a dark, quite room.

"Look, I don't make the rules. Just follow demands," he says, placing me down where I start to pace.

"Who is he?" I ask, and Marco turns toward the door.

"Who is who?"

"Don't play dumb, Marco. Dante? Who is he?"

He stares at me, and there's actually pity there.

"You know the answer to that."

"Do you know who I am?" I ask, and the question holds weight. I'm asking so many questions with just six words. Do you know I'm Delilah Turner? Do you know I'm a Russo? Does *Dante* know I'm a Russo? Do you know Dante's been fucking me for weeks?

"You're sweet, Lilah. Hasn't been a burden working with you," he says, turning toward the door again. "The best part about you is you're fuckin' smart. You know the answers."

And then he walks out, the door clicking and locking behind him ominously, leaving me to stew in my thoughts and wait for Dante.

Or *Junior*.

Jesus Christ. What have I gotten myself into?

TWENTY-NINE

-Dante-
Seven weeks earlier.

"Who's the new girl?" I ask my nephew, watching a blonde attempt to slide down a pole over the CCTV. Curves for days and hair a man wants wrapped around his fist, but she's clumsy. She looks fine on stage, flipping her hair and shaking her ass, but it's clear she hasn't been in the profession for long.

"Told you," my nephew, Paulie, says, kicking his shoes onto my desk and unwrapping a piece of gum. "Mayor down in Ocean View's daughter. Cut a deal with her." *Ah, yes, I remember.* The deal he made while pretending he was the owner of this club instead of just an *employee*, sitting in my office while I was out of town for two fucking days.

My first day back, I added a lock to the door that only my right hand, Marco, and I have a copy of.

Paulie tosses the scrap of paper to the floor, and I stare at it, then back at him.

Fuckin' *gavone.*

"She's not a dancer," I say, moving my eyes back to the black-and-white computer screen.

"The fuck she isn't."

"I mean, she hasn't been doing it long. She's not a stripper by profession."

"I'd fuckin' hope not, politician's sweet, innocent daughter and all. Her father got tied up with Carmine. Tables and horses, owed a fuck ton that he couldn't pay for, put the older daughter on the line for it."

"The drama with Johnny," I say, moving closer to the screen to watch thick hips move across the stage, a sultry smile hypnotizing everyone in the vicinity, including me.

Fuck, she might not have been a dancer for long, but the way she moves, she was born to please a man. Born to intoxicate one, to distract him until he hands over his wallet, his checkbook, the keys to his home, his heart.

"Yeah, the drama with Johnny. Fuckin' idiot, losing his damn mind over some stupid *puttan'*, trying to take her in broad daylight. Have we heard what's going on with that?"

What's going on with *that*, not that my nephew needs to know, is that even if Johnny Vitale gets out of New Jersey state prison in this lifetime, he won't be *leaving state prison in this lifetime.*

Confessing to wacking the sole heir to a rival family in an effort to take over both families will do that to you. My hand hovers over the mouse, moving it until the controls pop up. Marco installed this damn program with way too many buttons and options, but if I ask the asshole for yet another tutorial, he'll make fun of me for being too old to understand it.

As if he's not just two years younger than me.

Ahh, zoom. There. I click the little plus sign and wait.

"The fuck do I know? He's dead to me. Dead to us," I say, moving my eyes back to the dipshit in front of me, scuffed dress shoes still on the mahogany desk as I wait for the screen to load.

I'd like to get a better look at this hypnotist, this siren calling men to their own demise.

"Over some *puttana* who turned him down, we're just tossing him to the side? He's been loyal to grandfather for some time."

I nearly forgot that's the story we spun to the family—that he tried to get payment from Lola Turner, Shane Turner's oldest daughter, in a *non-monetary way,* and when she turned him down, he lost his fucking mind.

Giving the capos the idea that they could build a bridge between the families could cause issues, my father and I decided. And the way Paulie is looking at me, knowing that over the next few years, he and I will be neck and neck in the battle for Don, I decide that was a wise decision. The boy has hunger and greed in his eyes, but not in a way that's admirable. Not in a way that is good for the family. In a way that could take us all down.

Just like his father almost did.

"Paulie, one of the things it would do you well to learn is that what happens out there—" I flip my hand, indicating the general public. "—where the rest of the world exists, impacts us as a whole. The world is getting smaller with social media detectives around every damned corner. Podcast sleuths trying to deconstruct secrets we've kept for decades. If a Carluccio soldier gets caught confessing to multiple fucking crimes while attempting to *kidnap* a well-known mayor's oldest daughter and we don't instantly wash our hand of him, questions will get raised." I look at the screen that's still loading.

Stupid fucking software. Need to talk to Marco about an upgrade to the system once again.

"The last thing we need is to get people on our ass, asking questions, reporters at our doors because some fuckin' *buttagots* decided he couldn't keep his shit straight." My nephew rolls his eyes at my words.

The problem with the younger capos is that they don't quite understand yet. They haven't seen what can happen if someone gets loose, if someone slips up. Paulie's grandmother was killed because my father got too cocky. His own father will be locked up for the rest of his life because he was too greedy.

If you get cocky in this line of work, you end up dead or in prison.

Or, in Johnny Vitale's case, both.

"That's why I'm focusing on the club, Paulie. The clubs and the games are the future. Quiet, secure. Back rooms for private meetings, no ears, no eyes. We control who comes in."

"Both could be so much more, Dante," he says, and I can almost see the fuckin' movie playing over his head like sugarplums dancing. The idealized version of the shows he's watched, the video games he's played. But this is *real fucking life*. It's not some badge of honor to get you pussy.

"I don't want to hear it, Paulie." My eyes move to the screen, I notice it's cleared, and instantly, the blood in my veins turns to fire.

That face.

I know the face.

"Get out."

"What?" my nephew asks.

"Get *out of my office*," I say, repeating myself, but I'm already gone to the world. Lost in the fuzzy black-and-white screen before me.

I know that face.

I didn't know the body was connected to it.

Didn't know there was sheer sex under those kind eyes. That the way she moved would hypnotize a man. But I know that face. It's haunted my dreams, my daytime, my nightmares, and my memories.

It's a face I've spent two long years trying to find, hitting dead end after dead end.

And now that she's here, now that I know who she is, I'll do whatever it takes to make her mine, finally.

And so, my plan starts.

No woman of mine will be dancing for other men. No woman of mine will be wearing skimpy bikinis and showing off her tits for tips.

No woman of mine spends her days paying off debts she didn't earn instead of chasing whatever dreams she has. No woman of mine is in the line of danger, wrapped up with my nephew and his grand scheme that, even though he hasn't told me it yet, I know is brewing.

A woman of mine has no debts.

A woman of mine is safe with me.

A woman of mine chases her passions.

A woman of mine is mine and mine alone.

THIRTY

-Lilah-

The clock over the desk tells me fifteen minutes have passed before I realize I've been in this office before. It's boring and unremarkable, but I remember it.

It's the office I walked into in a tight red dress and offered to make a deal with Paulie Carluccio.

Six weeks later, it seems *his uncle*, fucking *Junior Carluccio* took my *fucking virginity*.

And on top of that, for two weeks, I've been sleeping next to him, letting him crawl into my bed at night and leave before the sun rises.

I don't want to open that door. Not yet.

His words tick in my mind like a metronome keeping time. It won't be easy, he had told me. Once I knew everything, we wouldn't be easy.

Well, no shit.

Jesus fucking Christ.

Maybe my dad was right all along. I'm too weak, too soft, too forgiving to be out on my own. Was all of the babying, the guiding, the using me for his benefit really for my benefit as well? Maybe there was a good reason for me to be protected for so long, protected from the truth, from the world.

Maybe I needed to be protected from myself, too.

I think on this for long minutes, agonizing minutes as I flip from *maybe I'm just an idiot, so sheltered that I can't be trusted in the real world, much less* this *world*, and *no, this is just a really fucked-up circumstance*. The clock read thirty minutes past when Marco locked me in here, and I wonder how much longer it'll be.

And what the fuck Dante—*Junior*—could possibly have to say to keep me from absolutely running in the opposite direction.

Or is it a ploy? All a ruse to get me out of sight before they take me out?

Knowing what I know of the family, I know it's not a *negative* chance, even if a high-profile mayor's daughter going missing while working for the Carluccios after a soldier tried to kidnap his other daughter wouldn't look good for them.

My eyes move to the fancy, high-tech computer on the dark mahogany desk.

Well, just in case I'm not killed in cold blood, might as well try and get something.

Sitting in the big leather chair, I take the mouse and jiggle it a few times.

I fully expect a lock screen.

There is not a lock screen. *So much for super-smart, super-stealth mob boss. God.*

But that's not what has my blood boiling.

It's the black and white CCTV footage that shows the girls dancing on stage in one corner.

The bar at another.

The entrance is the bottom left, and the serving station is another.

I realize now there is no way in hell that Dante has gone nearly two months without knowing who I am.

He's known all along.

Jesus Christ.

How could I have been so stupid?

The rage starts to boil under my skin as I watch Sammi slide down the pole.

For a sweet, pretty thing, I've always had a shit temper.

That why when I stand, I don't even think twice when I throw the mouse against a wall, watching it explode into a million pieces.

It feels *good.*

So I take the keyboard next, toss it as well.

There are papers on the desk that, oops, get tossed all over the floor, the pointy heel of my shoe stabbing a few holes in them.

Looking around, I'm dying for more, more to destroy, more terror to wreak.

The monitor.

Yes. That should go, too.

I tip it over, watching it fall and the tempered glass spiderwebbing out as it hits the carpet.

Oops.

And while I don't feel better or more calm, when I sit back in the leather chair, popping my heels on the desk and surveying my destruction, I'm a little bit appeased to know I made his life more difficult.

Finally, there's a noise from the door, the lock clicking and the knob turning, and I look up, waiting.

It opens silently, and in walks Dante.

The door closes behind him and clicks shut, and then he's standing there, arms on his chest. I stand in turn, walking around the desk I was sitting at as if it were my place, until there are just five feet between us.

"Hello, *fiorella*. Creating trouble again, are we?" he asks with a low laugh, and I want to punch him.

I don't speak.

Even though I spent an hour locked in here, going over what I would say, what I should say, I can't do anything but take in the image of the man in front of me.

He's so fucking handsome, that thick hunk of hair on his forehead from his fingers running through it repeatedly, the rest of the dark waves brushed back neatly. His white shirt has been unbuttoned a few at the top, letting me see the thick chest hair hiding beneath, the gold chain with the Saint Christopher medallion I like to play with when he's lying in my bed at night on display.

The sleeves are rolled up, a single drop of blood on the cuff, and I wonder if that's from whatever errand he was on for the last hour or from the scuffle on the floor.

His eyes move along the room, taking in my mess, and he just laughs.

The asshole laughs.

"You've been watching me for weeks on that stupid fucking monitor, haven't you?" I say. "I took care of it for you. Next time you want to watch me shake my ass, you can sit in the crowd like the rest of the piece of shit men."

"You'll be doing no such thing," he says. "I wanted a new monitoring system anyway. You did me a favor." I grind my teeth because some juvenile, childish part of me wants him mad.

Wants him to feel the rage that is in my veins right now.

Though, that might just be my daddy issues speaking.

"Come here, Delilah," he says, a hand moving out, offering, asking me to take it.

Uh, fuck that.

"Were you ever really a customer?" I ask, the coldness in my words shocking even me.

"Delilah, let—"

"Were you *ever really a customer?*" I repeat, my voice rising.

"Let me—"

"Dante, what the fuck is going on. Or should I call you Junior? That's your name, right? Or maybe Carmine?"

"Stop this shit, Delilah. My name is Dante."

"But you're not a Romano."

"Not by name." I raise an eyebrow. "Fine. My given name is Carmine Dante Romano Carluccio. My mother's maiden name was Romano; it's my middle name. My Confirmation name is Dante. I hate my father's name. No one calls me it."

Seems if I had done some better research, I may have figured that out.

I refuse to back down, though.

"So what, you *work at Jerzy Girls?*" I ask, my voice teetering on the edge of insanity.

"No."

"Oh, you don't? Then what the fuck are you doing here?!" Let's not address the way my mind instantly goes to the fact that he's there to watch other women, and that's what is making my blood boil.

"I own it."

"No, you don't. Paulie does. That's who I spoke with when I came in that first day." My mind is spinning, not wanting to but needing understand, a constant battle. I don't even check my mental notes where Marco confirmed this information just today at lunch.

But then again, Marco is also a damned traitor.

Dante laughs, walking closer to me until we are nearly face-to-face.

That laugh irritates me.

This is *not fucking* funny.

This man is playing with my mind, playing with my life, playing with my *body*.

"Paulie wishes he owned this place. He works here. I was away that week, and he decided to play pretend. Lucky for you, because if it had been me you sat across from, there's no way in hell I would have agreed to you working here. Never in a million fucking years."

His hand moves, pushing hair behind my ear, and I roll my shoulder back, trying to move out of his reach. A smile plays on his lips, but beneath it, I can see the predator there.

How was I so stupid?

"But that's fine. It gave me time, gave me a chance to find you again after all this time. And once I did, I could keep an eye on you, keep you safe when I wasn't around."

The sound in my ears goes static.

My mind goes blank.

My body feels weak, as if I no longer own it.

Dante owns the club.

Moments and fractured seconds of time flash through my mind.

The way Marco never questioned the private dances with *Mr. Romano*.

Roddy telling me the *Big Boss* declared I was to work the floor the day after I spent the night with Dante.

The girls telling me about the cameras.

He's always watching.

Anyone touches you, you tell me. The moment of confusion when Roddy told me that, since everyone knows the men get handsy with the waitresses and no one ever cares. You just tell the men no and move on.

Dante parting the crowd like damned Moses, walking through like he owned the place. Attacking that groom like he had not a single care in the world for the repercussions.

He wouldn't, of course. Because he fucking owns the place.

He couldn't because he's a goddamned Carluccio.

And with that last reminder, the thin thread holding my sanity together snaps. I pull my hand back and slap him straight across the face, loving watching his stupid head turn to the left sharply as I do.

The millisecond after the satisfaction ends, a kernel of fear grows in my belly.

This isn't just some strange, secretive man I met by kismet and who has been slipping into my bed for two weeks like a phantom in the night.

This is the man whose family I am actively plotting to take down. This is the heir of that family.

In essence, he is my enemy.

This is *Dante Carluccio*. This is a man who was born and raised in one of the most notorious mob families in the state, possibly the country.

The man whose family offered and accepted numerous bribes from my own father, who encouraged him to bet until he was so deep, he essentially sold out his own daughter without care.

The man whose brother my mother was supposed to marry in another lifetime.

The man whose family is at constant odds with the family where I am an unwitting heir.

The man whose brother put a hit on my father, his henchman following it through.

The man whose father most likely planted the idea in his son's head.

This is a man who has most definitely given orders for cinderblock swims and mysterious worksite injuries.

And my dumb ass just slapped him.

It was a surprisingly strong slap, I'll give myself that, but it was still a slap from a 5'3" woman in heels given to a 6'0" man who could easily kill me in less than a minute.

His head is still pushed to the side as I process these thoughts, trying to understand what the fuck I did and what the fuck my fate will be when he starts to laugh.

The man starts to laugh.

Okay, he's clearly unhinged and *out of his fucking mind.*

Dear god, I'm probably going to die here.

In a strip club waitress outfit.

What a fucking way to go.

His arms open as his head straightens, a red mark already

growing on his cheek, and I think this is it. He's going to kill me here and now.

Poor Marco will probably have to clean up the mess and explain to the girls that I ran off, unable to handle the pressure of the job.

He steps forward, wrapping his arms around me, and I *know* this is it. I'm going to die in this man's arms while he laughs.

I am so far gone in the hoops I've convinced myself to jump through over the past two weeks that I think that it might not actually be the worst way to go.

But then his hand moves, tangling into the teased blonde curls (again, I'm going to die with *stripper hair*) and he presses my face into his chest gently as he continues to laugh. The sound vibrates through his chest into my cheek and has a strangely calming effect.

The calm eases my panic just enough for me to understand that he's not killing me for the utter disrespect of slapping him.

He's . . . hugging me. And laughing.

What in the fuck is going on here?

"Fucking made for me," he murmurs once his laughing slows, his body rocking my own left to right. "Fucking made for me, baby."

What the fuck is this man on?

I just slapped him across the face hard enough to leave a mark, and he's laughing, telling me I was made for him. I push my hands to his chest and try to free myself, that moment of fear and second-guessing melting as the rage settles back in. "Let go of me, Dante."

"Never," he says, using the hand in my hair to pull my head back and look into my eyes. "I'm never letting you go. You try, I'll chase you. I'll chase you to the ends of the earth and drag you back, kicking and screaming, until you're here where you belong."

For a split second, I melt.

It's strange, a little fucking unhinged, but his words are kind of sweet in a mob boss kind of way.

And then reality kicks in, and even I can understand that train of thought is *undoubtedly un-fucking-hinged*. Reality also reminds me of everything that's happened, and I scoff.

Because I'm remembering how for two weeks, I've been the easy piece of ass he sleeps with at night in secret, the woman he leaves before the sun rises and has working at his *strip club* to *pay off her father's debts.*

Jesus.

I'm an idiot.

"Oh, where I belong is some hidden woman in the corner, your little *gumad,* while you go off and rule? To do what, pray tell? Launder your dirty money through disposal companies and strip clubs and force men to take debts they can't pay back?"

My body stills when I realize I gave myself away. A woman who is made of iron and fire *doesn't care* if she's being fucked well and used. She lets it happen while she plans her grand revenge, allowing it to be the source of her heat. A woman who complains, who lets the disrespect cut deep, is weak. A woman like that can be manipulated and hurt. But either he doesn't notice the slight change in my body or he doesn't care.

Regardless, his next words floor me.

"Where you belong is next to me, ruling alongside me, my daisy queen."

Again, the room quiets, the world spinning just a bit slower with his words.

"What the—"

"I know who you are, Lilah. And I know why you're here." The blood runs cold in my veins, panic setting in.

"I'm here to pay off my father's debts. To blacklist him," I say, my voice going carefree and easy, repeating the story that I told Paulie.

"You're here because your sister was nearly killed by one of my family's men."

Nearly killed.

Not kidnapped.

Not assaulted.

Killed.

"Johnny didn't—" I don't even think about the fact that I'm showing my hand knowing who and what he's talking about.

"You and I both know if your sister's man didn't stop things when they happened, she would be dead or wishing she were." I lick my lips, nausea bubbling at the truth in his words.

I know he's right.

"You want payback on a family who destroyed yours. Who let your father get in too deep when you girls were already hurting from a loss. You want us to pay."

"I just want to balance the scales. To get the debt cleared and make sure it doesn't happen again," I say, my voice low and quiet, nervous.

It seems he ignores me, continuing to talk.

"You're not here to get even. You're here to find a weakness to tip the scale in your favor. Have you found it yet?"

"I don't know what you're talking about," I say in a breathy voice.

"Oh, sweet, beautiful, bright girl. You don't get it, do you? I'm here to help you." The hand in my hair moves, tugging out the hair tie and letting it fall down my back before his arm wraps around the small of my waist.

With his words and the gentle movement, though, he lost me.

I have no understanding of what he means.

"Help me?"

"There's so much you don't know. So much you need to know. But you don't trust me right now. I get that. Let me give you some things you can use against me." His words don't make sense. They don't fit into the puzzle I've created in my mind. "Ammunition. Something to balance our scale."

"What?"

"I know your plans. I could use them, get you killed." A sharp intake of panic. "You don't trust me. And really, why should you? I need to earn that, tit for tat. I'm going to give you some information back. You tell anyone in the family this, it would get me killed,

Delilah. Do you understand?" His hand moves to my jaw, holding it so I have no choice but to look into his eyes and see how serious he is.

"No," I say, because I don't understand.

But I do a moment later.

"Paulie and I are battling for Don. Carmine is old. It was supposed to be Tony, but of course, he's out of commission. My father loves the battle, loves to pit people against each other for his entertainment. He's also easily influenced, letting all the *strunzos* around him sway his decisions and take things too far. This family, it used to be good. Helped the community and bartered with the politicians to get things that could help. Now, it's money. Now, it's dark. It got my brother in prison and my mother killed. The danger of it . . . can be addictive, intoxicating. I could ignore that, move on from it, let it be. But now we're edging toward federal charges. You get caught selling girls, you get the feds. Federal charges mean a future like Tony's. It's too much risk, and the balance is off. It's greed; it's no longer about helping. It's gone beyond making our families comfortable and well-off and moved toward unbearable wealth. And a hunger for more. If Paulie wins, shit will go bad. I don't like where the family is headed. Things need to change. I can do that. You can do that. *We can change it, Lilah.*" His fingers tighten on my chin, but I can barely feel it. I'm utterly floored by his words and what he's revealing.

"I can help you get what you want. I can give you what you need to clean house, get your revenge, then rule with me. We can do it together."

I continue to stare, both afraid to speak and unable to do so.

Words won't form.

Thoughts won't form.

"You hate it, too. Hate the greed, the corruption. I know it. That's why you're here."

How have things changed so quickly? How have my worlds collided? How have I gotten so fucking deep with this man only to realize he's quicksand that could suffocate me without a second glance?

The silence hangs between us as he stares at me and I process.

Clearly, he's waiting for me to respond. It's my turn to add to this insane conversation.

"I just want to settle my father's debts and make sure he can't do more," I lie, my voice a whisper.

"No," he says, that hand on my chin tightening. "You can lie to fucking everyone out there." The hand on my waist moves, motioning to the outside. "You can lie to everyone but me. Never me, Lilah."

That burns.

That stings.

All he's ever *done* is lie to me.

"Oh, like you lied to me?"

"Never lied, Delilah. Tell me one fucking lie I've told you."

"Your *fucking name*," I say, giving the most obvious answer.

"Explained that. It wasn't a lie."

"An omission is still lie, Dante."

"Okay, then I lied. But this? You know I'm not lying about this. Your plans are bigger than this, Lilah. I know that; you know that. But when you started here, I saw you, knew you were mine. Knew who you were, why you were here. That you were here to take down the family. And *I didn't care*. I needed you more. You were mine, and I needed you to know it too. But you'd already made a deal with the devil, a deal with Paulie."

"So? So you, what? You had to fuck around, change my job, fuck me at night, keep me a secret?"

"There is a lot of shit going on in my family right now. Shit I will tell you when it's *safe*."

"I just escaped a lifetime of family secrets, Dante. I can't do more." He sighs.

"I can't tell you everything right now, Lilah."

The safe, protected Lilah starts to fall back, the new, sword-slinging bad bitch pushing her aside.

Funny how I've let the sweet one out more when he's around, willing to let him be the protector. Now I need the stronger version again. That backbone. The hellfire and poison version. The siren who destroys.

"Isn't it strange that you want me to trust you with every fiber of my being, confess my life and my plans to you, and you can't tell me . . . uhm, anything? That you want me to tell you yes, I'm here to tear down your family, but you can't tell me fucking *anything*. You couldn't even tell me your damn *name*. And yet you expect me to just . . . trust in you? Trust in this?"

He pauses, looking my face over, taking his sweet time answering my questions.

As usual, when he does, he surprises me.

"Fucking glorious," he says in a whisper. "Don't lose this, ever. Never fucking back down, Delilah. Be the fucking queen; take no shit from anyone. Surprise them at every turn."

"Don't back down, unless it's a Carluccio heir who wants to fuck me into submission?"

"God, don't you see it?" he says then dips his head, running his nose up my neck. Even in the shorter heels, we're more even in height. "I'm the one that submits to you, Delilah. I'm the one who is a fucking peasant, kneeling at your altar and begging you to give me a fucking chance to fight alongside you. To be a knight in your war."

My breathing comes heavy, and I try to ignore the burn running through me.

"But you won't tell me what your plan is? I have to reveal *mine*, show *my* hand, and hope you won't use it against me?"

He groans, but not the good kind. Not the kind he does in my bed when I ride his cock, the kind he makes when he enters me for the first time of the night, like he's finally home.

It's one of pain and anguish.

"I need you to trust me."

I want to.

God, I want to so bad.

Moments lapse as he looks at me before he whispers words.

"I have what you need."

"What?"

"I have the hit he put out on Arturo Russo. It's coded, but I found it in Johnny's apartment. Other shit was there too, things he was planning to use against us."

Does he know? Know who I am? Who Arturo Russo is to me? Or does he just think that's the evidence I need?

"Are you telling me you have written proof that members in your family told Johnny Vitale to kill Arturo Russo?" I sound like a narc, a wired con man, using full names to catch Dante in the admission of a crime.

He knows it, of course.

I'm sure it's been used against him, wired men trying to ease a sentence with an admission from a higher-up.

But Dante doesn't seem to care.

"Yes. That my brother was to blame. That would clear Tony's position in the family and any of the men loyal to him, probably take down Paulie and his men."

"And your father? You have proof of his role in this?"

And there it is.

A tiny wrinkle in his forehead—confusion.

"My father didn't—" He shakes his head like it doesn't matter, that wrinkle clearing. "I have what you need and more, and I'll give it to you. I'm serious, Delilah. I have a plan. You have your own, but our end goal—it's the same, baby. You need to trust me."

I sigh, unsure of what to do, but my mother's words scrawled in her pretty writing run through my mind.

Sometimes you have to trust who you think is the devil to win your way into heaven.

She'd said it about trusting in Arturo, trusting him to help her find her way out of the marriage with Shane. About trusting the plan he had put together for her to run to him would work, that we could be a family.

It would have worked if it wasn't for Johnny and Carmine. She trusted the right devil. He just got taken down before he could let her into heaven. So I go with my gut, praying that my mother's spirit is pushing me to where I need to be.

"Why didn't you say something from the start? You knew who I was in the beginning. You could have told Paulie, ended this before it even started."

"I told you. Paulie is trouble. And Paulie was interested in you."

"Interested? Like he wanted to fuck me?" He looks at me but doesn't answer. "I'm a big girl, Dante. I can handle myself against fucking *Paulie*." He sighs, exhaustion in the sound.

"I am doing everything in my power to keep you *safe*, Delilah. Do you know what happens when a man like my nephew shows interest in a woman like you?"

"Is it like what happens when a man like *you* shows interest in me? Late, secret nights when you're gone before I wake up? Fucking stalking me, lies upon lies upon lies? Is it blowing out my tire and then bumping into me in a grocery store and then *showing up at my house* for two weeks straight? Never even telling me who you really are? Letting me spill my secrets, tell you about my family, without doing the same? Is that what happens when a man like that shows interest in me?"

Something snaps in his eyes, and he moves me, using the hand in my hair to turn me and press me to the wall of the office. His hand moves to my throat, pressing me against the wall. I can't tell if it's to shut me up or to scare me, but both happen.

"No, Delilah. That is a man obsessed. A man who saw what was made for him and recognized it and is doing what he has to do to secure it as his own. To keep what is his safe."

"I'm not yours."

"The fuck you aren't, Delilah." He tightens his grip on my neck, forcing my eyes to meet his. "You look me in the eyes and tell me that you don't feel it. That pull. You were fucking made to be mine."

There's some kind of truth serum in his touch that, when combined with the way he's looking at me, I can't deny.

So I don't.

But I don't agree either.

Long gone are my days of being the appeasable, friendly blonde daughter of Shane Turner.

That person died in a hospital room in Ocean View.

"What if that pull is because *you* were made for *me*? Why do I have to be the possession?"

"You've possessed me since the day I saw you. You want me to get on my knees and serve my queen right here, I fucking will. You want me to be yours? It's done."

I stare at him, this man who has never had to kneel for a single person in his entire life, a life where for most of it, he knew he would be ruling, or at least close to it.

A prince.

An inevitable king.

"Kneel for me," I whisper, not even recognizing my voice.

My heart is racing.

And then he does.

Not moving his eyes from mine, he slowly lowers to his knees while I lean against the wall, my breathing heavy.

His hands move up my bare thighs, goosebumps following in their wake until they're at the top of my stretchy shorts. Fingers move under the waistband, running along the length of them, over and over, back and forth, as I gasp, trying to catch my breath.

A thumb hooks into the waist, then the other thumb follows before slowly, torturously slowly, he starts to lower them down my hips, to my knees. One hand taps my ankle gently, and I lift. He takes away the shorts, then repeats the process on the other leg until I'm bare from the waist down.

His warm hand moves from the strap of my heel around my ankle, up, up until it hits the underside of my knee where it wraps around and lifts, placing the spiked heel on his shoulder until I'm entirely open to him, my pussy spread in his face.

"God, you're so fucking pretty like this," he says in a low whisper.

"I'd worship you all day if you let me, live between your legs, eating this cunt."

A moan rolls through my chest as I watch him run a single finger through my wet then circle my clit with the tip.

"Finger me, Dante," I whisper, watching him as his chin tips up, eyes meeting mine, a wide smile taking over his lips.

"There's my queen," he says, and I clench, the words alone doing unholy things to my body.

His finger slides in, and I *moan*.

"That's it. Tell me how right it feels. Like this, we can forget the rest, Delilah. Just me and you." He pulls out, slipping in another thick finger, and I move a fraction, dipping my hips, trying to get him in deeper. "More?" he asks, and I nod, my mouth falling open a bit as he adds a third finger, moving them in deeper, harder, rougher.

The man always knows what I need.

His fingers are fucking me, and I look down, watching him, watching his toned arm move as he's kneeling before, but his eyes aren't on my pussy that's wet for him.

They're on me.

"Never fucking question who owns me, Delilah. You. You fucking own me. I can't take a fucking breath without thinking of you. Every moment of every fucking day, my mind is thinking about what I can do for you, how I can find more time to be with you."

A low moan leaves my throat, the intensity in his eyes ratcheting the heat up in my body.

"This fucking pussy is mine, Lilah, but every part of me is yours."

"God, Dante, fuck." I breathe the words out, watching him, my eyes moving from his to where his hand is between my legs.

"What do you need from me, *fiorella*. Anything."

"I need more." I stare at him, and for a split second, shame takes over me.

An then I remember who I am.

I am power.

I am a queen.

I own this man.

"Eat my pussy and make me come on your face, Dante," I demand, and I almost don't recognize my voice, the fierceness there, the power and aggression.

Something about it turns me on even more.

Apparently, Dante agrees because a deep groan falls from his lips. His hands move, thumbs opening me further even though my leg is still on his shoulder, and his mouth moves to me, his tongue taking one long lick from my entrance to my clit before sucking there. I moan out, my hand moving to his hair and holding him there on my swollen clit that's dying for something—anything.

"That's it, just like that, right there," I murmur, watching dark hair as his tongue moves against me, his lips circling my clit and sucking. "Fingers. Add one," I say, and Jesus, my voice is turning *me* on, husky and needy but in control at the same time.

All the while, his eyes stay locked to mine, his mouth on me, tongue licking, finger fucking me.

I need more.

"Another," I breathe. He does as I ask, crooking them, the combination of that and his mouth taking me closer to the edge.

"Oh, god, shit. You're going to make me come," I mumble, my head hitting the wall as my eyes close. But then, to my surprise, his hand moves, slapping the side of my ass until I meet his eyes again.

And then I know: I might be in control right now, and might be the one getting everything, but he has his own demands.

The look in his eyes has the pleasure in my belly curling in on itself, so I'm fine with it.

He moans against my clit, his fingers working harder now, crooking until they're against my G-spot, and then I'm screaming his name.

"Fuck, Dante, I'm going to come. God, please," I say, the words falling from my lips, but he knows.

He knows what I need.

He always seems to.

His teeth gently graze my clit as he sucks harder, a third finger joining, and I grasp his hair, riding his face as I come, moaning his name.

Slowly, I come down from the high, my body grinding on his mouth slower, his tongue continuing to leisurely lick at me. Then, he slowly, torturously takes his hand from me, moving it to my leg on his shoulder and placing it back on the floor. I stand there, leaning against the wall, trying to catch my breath as he moves, grabbing my shorts and easing them up my legs with little to no help from me.

When he's done, he stands, pulling me into him, and kisses me gently.

I taste myself on his lips.

I also feel his hard cock against me.

"What about you?" I ask.

"Later." There's a smile on his lips. "That was for you. To prove my devotion," he says, and I can't help but give him my own lazy smile. He presses his forehead to mine, his lips gently touching my own again.

"Trust me," he says, the words a whisper. "Please, Delilah. That's all I ask. Put trust me in that we're going to do this together."

And despite common sense telling me *to run*, I nod. He smiles and presses his lips to mine, and that smile is the sweetest one I've seen in my life.

"What now?" I ask, confused about how we move forward.

So fucking confused.

It feels like everything I thought I knew has been turned upside down.

"Now you head home, and in an hour or two, I'll meet you at your place and fuck you until you fall asleep," he says.

"Dante—"

"For now, we continue as normal, Delilah. But with nothing between us. No more lies. You know who I am, and I know who you are. Now, we work together toward the same mission," he says, and it sounds lovely.

It sounds like the perfect situation.

Except, he's wrong.

He doesn't know who I am, not really.

And I don't plan on telling him, whether that makes me a shitty person or not.

THIRTY-ONE

-Dante-

The next morning, I wake in Lilah's bed before she does, dreading how I won't see those eyes sleepy and dazed.

I want that.

I want that as badly as I know she does. To wake up with her, to kiss her lips until she's cognizant of the morning. To roll out of bed and tell her to stay, make her a coffee, and watch her drink it while I lie next to her. To fuck her before she even gets out of bed.

But I don't dare tempt myself, tempt fate. Truly, coming here at all is a terrible risk I should never have taken, but that first morning she snuck out of my bed, I knew I needed more.

I tracked her down at the grocery store and spent the night with her at her place.

I told myself that would be it.

I told myself that was the last time until things were settled, were ironed out.

Until she knew who I was, that I was on her side, and we could be a team.

But the next evening, I found myself standing in the cold, waiting for her to come home. Then making a copy of her house key and letting myself in.

I'm sick.

I have an addiction.

The only thing stopping me from throwing everything to the wind is knowing that if I do, I won't be able to give Delilah everything she wants.

One day, I tell myself. *Be patient. You'll have that. You'll have her. And she'll have everything she wants.*

Step one: make sure she's fucking safe as can be and do it without drawing attention to her.

That starts today at the club.

So I kiss her forehead gently, put a pillow where I once lay, watching her wrap around it as if I'm still there before pulling the blanket up and heading home to change, telling myself this two places shit won't be for long.

At four, when Delilah comes in for her shift, she's brought back into my office by Marco. As always, the man has a stern face on, a face that always gets a bit softer when he turns to my girl.

I'll let that slide. She's got a soft spot for my capo as well, and it's easier for her to like the man I've assigned to watch as a friend rather than always question his presence.

"Thanks, Marco. Get me Paulie, yeah?" I say, tipping my chin before he nods and walks back out, the door locking behind him.

Only Marco has the key to my office, a fact that absolutely infuriated my nephew when he realized, but I know if he also had access, his rat ass would either be going through my shit any time I was out or he'd be playing dress-up, pretending to run the place.

Again.

"What's going on, Dante?" Delilah asks, her hands on her hips in those little shorts and the too-small top.

Paulie picked the uniform for the servers, and while it's better than what the dancers wear, I hate seeing it on her. She deserves designer. Velvet and silk and diamonds and gold. That body is a wet dream, but it's *my* wet dream. Not the hungry men of Hudson City.

"Nice to see you too, *fiorella*," I say with a smile.

"What's going on, Dante?" she asks again, the annoyed tick in her brow strangely making my cock twitch. "I thought we weren't *to be seen together?* That no one here could *know* about us? Do you know whose eyebrows raised when Marco pulled me away while I was talking to the girls, said the *Big Boss* wants to talk to me?"

I sigh, knowing she's right, but not for the reasons she thinks.

"We can't be seen together, Delilah. Not yet. Paulie is too damn dangerous."

Instantly, I know my sweet daisy is gone, the feisty queen-to-be in her place.

Good.

That's the one I love the best.

The sweet one saved me. The fiery one will save her.

"What the fuck does that mean? What does *not yet* mean?" She repeats my words in a deep voice I'm assuming is supposed to be mine, and I can't fight my lips from turning up.

That seems to ratchet up her anger as she rolls her eyes and throws up her hands.

"Paulie is dangerous. If he decides I have too much interest in you, he'll get suspicious. He'll start digging and once that happens, you become a target and the plan falls apart."

There's a long silence before he speaks.

"We can't be seen together without a purpose, Delilah." I take a step around my desk, moving to where she's standing in the middle of the room, arms now crossing her chest, pushing her tits up in a way I need to force myself not to hyper-focus on. "I'm working to create that purpose. You need to be patient with me." I slip a finger into the waistband of her shorts when I get close, snapping the elastic against her skin. "I have such a love-hate relationship with these."

She smiles a devilish smile.

She does not like those shorts, that much I can guarantee.

But she sure loves that I hate them.

"They're dress code."

"Not for you, they're not." That little furrow forms in her brow.

"What does that mean?" she says.

"Missed you," I say, ignoring her questions and moving her hair back from her shoulders. Her hair is gorgeous, so damned long, so damned blonde. Her skin is tan, and the combination is breathtaking. "How did you sleep last night?"

Her breathing gets heavier every time I get near her like this, a trait I fucking *love*. The way her body responds to me.

"It would have been better if I woke up with you," she says, and . . . is that a pout? Gone is the angry siren, and in her place is the pouty brat I could devour.

"Soon enough, *fiorella*."

"What does that mean? You keep saying shit like that." She puts her hands on my chest to push me away, angry again, but I don't budge. God, I love how volatile her emotions are, from one extreme to the next in the blink of an eye. I'll never be bored with this woman, that's for sure.

I use my hands to tip her head up, her breasts in that tiny thin top brushing my chest, heaving with each breath.

"Why the fuck should I trust you, Dante? I know nothing about you." She whispers the words, so filled with rage and fire they nearly burn my skin.

"You might not be willing to trust me, but your body does," I say, voice lower, head moving to her ear. "It trusts me to take care of you. To please you."

She lets out a shaky breath.

"That's different. Anyone—"

"Don't you finish that sentence, baby," I say, a hand on her hip pulling her sharply into me, my teeth clamping on her ear, making her yip. I smile as I use my tongue to soothe the pain. "No one controls your body like I do, you know that. I know that. And no one has *ever* controlled my body the way *you* do, Delilah." I know that's important to her, those scales being even, but they aren't.

Not in the least.

If she needed to, if she had to, Delilah could walk away and live her old life or whatever version of her new life she could dream up and never look back.

The same cannot be said for me. If she were to choose to leave, I would crumble. The need, the obsession, the draw to her would win, would take over me. There is no plan B here for me. I shift, moving until my thigh is between her legs, one hand fisted in her curls, the other on her hip.

"You don't understand, Delilah. You fucking own me. I will do whatever I have to do to give you what you want. To help you get even, get your revenge. You want an empire, baby? I'll build it for you, brick by brick, on the backs of those who did you wrong. You want anyone who has hurt you, hurt your family, dead? I'll carve their names into the bullet and hand you the gun." My lips are on hers, kissing, tasting her. Her breathing quickens, and I use the hand on her hip to move her back and forth slowly, showing her how to grind her pussy on me. There are at least two layers of fabric between us, but the heat burns through them easily.

"Dante," she whispers when I break the kiss.

"You don't get it. But I'll show you. You are all I think of. Every move I make on this wicked chessboard is for you. You might not like the moves right now, might not understand them, but one day you'll see." The hand on her hip starts to move her faster, and she pushes down, tipping her hips back until I know her clit is getting the full brunt of the movement.

A low moan falls from her lips, and my head moves to her ear, my own breathing heavy.

"That's it, baby. Use me. Get yourself there. This is what I'll always be. Giving you whatever you need, helping to get anything you want. Fucking *use me*, Delilah," I murmur, but she's already doing just that, using her hands on my shoulders as leverage to continue the movement.

"Dante," she whispers, those nails digging into my shoulders.

"I know, baby," I say before moving to kiss her, lips and tongue and teeth clashing. Her breathing is heavy, and I'm sure she's close, so close to coming on my leg in my office, totally fucking clothed.

A knock comes on the door, and I break the kiss, Lilah still grinding on my leg. She looks gorgeous: her eyes hooded, her lips parted, and her breaths panting. But I should have known.

She's always so damn responsive, a ticking time bomb calibrated just for me.

She's also so damned lost, she doesn't hear Paulie arguing in the hall, telling Marco to just open the damn door.

He won't, of course. He has strict orders at all times, and Marco is nothing if not loyal.

"That's it, beautiful," I whisper to her, using the hand on her hip to aid her movements, to help her grind her clit on my thigh. Those shorts are paper thin, and I can feel a wet spot forming where her pussy is, the idea alone making my cock grow harder. I nip her ear then kiss the skin below it. "That's it, baby. You grind on my thigh, and you get yourself there. You stay quiet for your man, but you come right fucking here, right fucking now." The doorknob moves, an angry gesture, but I don't care.

If Paulie comes in right now, it would be dangerous. He is the boy who always wants what the big kids have and throws a tantrum when he doesn't get his way.

It would be dangerous for Lilah to be seen with me like this. For him to think she means anything at all to me.

Because just like my brother, if I show interest, he wants it. And nothing would be worse than Paulie wanting Lilah, especially if he figures out who she is and the potential power she could claim. The potential power *he* could claim, using her.

But in this moment, I'll risk it. I'll take it.

"Dante," she whispers under her breath, her movements frantic, those sharp nails she files into points biting into my shoulders nearly painfully.

"Come for me, beautiful," I whisper, then I take her mouth with mine as her body tenses and she moans into my mouth. My hand moves to the back of her neck, forcing her mouth to mine harder, making sure not a sound leaves her lips as her hips continue to buck, her body shaking gently with her orgasm. And as her body slowly loosens, I continue to hold her, kissing her slowly as she comes back into the world.

"Oh my god," she whispers, eyes going to the door. "Oh my god!" I let her down gently until her feet are stable before grabbing her face with both hands.

"Mine. You are mine. You know that, I know that. That's all you have to know." I stare into her big, beautiful blue eyes and touch my lips to hers once more. "Do you trust me?"

I wait for her to argue. For her to say no. To fight me as is her way.

She's right: there hasn't been the time needed to build authentic trust. I haven't shared nearly enough with her to have her trust my motives. All there is is the draw, the push and pull between us, the feeling that this is undeniable, a feeling that says she is mine and I am hers, and it was always supposed to be this way.

I wouldn't blame her if she says no. If she says there is no way she could trust me.

But instead, she breaths and nods.

"Yeah," she says quietly.

"Sit in that chair. Don't look at Paulie. Eyes on me, on Marco, or in your lap. That's it."

"Dante—"

"I'll see you tonight."

"What?"

"*Trust me, beautiful,*" I say, leading her to the chair and straightening my clothes. "Just trust me." I stare at her until she nods before I move.

And then I open the door, letting in my right hand and my raging nephew.

THIRTY-TWO

-Dante-

"What the fuck is going on, Dante?" Paulie asks, his voice unnecessarily loud. A child who has never been told no.

That's what my twenty-eight-year-old nephew is.

I am barely twelve years his senior, a smaller gap than my brother and I had growing up, and I think in some ways, it makes him forget that I'm older. Wiser. That I am to be respected and treated as such.

Whatever.

One day he'll learn. I move to sit behind my desk, liking the look of my Lilah across from me, cheeks still flushed and breathing not entirely normal.

"What, were you busy?" I ask, knowing damn well he was anything but. I hired Paulie as a favor to my father, but if I'm being blunt, Paulie is a lazy piece of shit. His workdays include walking around like he owns the places, trying to get laid by the dancers, or drinking my fucking liquor. And when he's not being lazy, he's doing dumb shit that will get him killed or put in prison.

Just like his father.

"Yes, I was. You hired me to manage *your damn club*. So that's what I was doing."

"Let's not play games, now. We all know the girls take care of themselves, and Marco covers the men. What *is* it you do after all?" I ask, looking to my lap and smiling at the wet spot on my navy-blue dress pants. I move that smile over to Lilah, who is blushing. No one can see the wet spot from where I sit at the desk, but she knows.

"Fuck off, Dante."

"And if you're so great at handling my club, where were you last night when a man put his hands on our Delilah here?"

"What, I—"

"In fact, it was me that saw it happen on the cameras, who walked out into the crowd and broke the fucker's wrist, I believe. Is that right, Marco?" I look over to my second-in-command, and he nods stoically.

"Yes, sir," he says, and it takes everything in me not to laugh at *Marco* calling me sir instead of fuckwad or something similar. But when we need to put on the show, he knows how things go. Even Lilah's eyes widen a bit at Marco subservient words.

"So, where were you?" I say, raising an eyebrow. He doesn't answer, stewing in his anger. "Don't worry, you don't have to tell me. Remember, Paulie, there are cameras *everywhere* keeping track of what the fuck you're doing. I have access to those cameras at all times. Fucking Olivia behind the building isn't doing what I *fuckin' pay you to do*."

His face goes red.

"But hey, from what I could tell, you didn't think it would take long anyway, so—"

"What the fuck, Dante?!" he shouts, that rage tipping.

Most won't notice because it's what he's trained for, but from the corner of my eye, Marco very smoothly angles his body to shield Lilah, the hand that was already on his hip moving back to where he keeps his weapon.

"I gave you self-explanatory instructions, did I not?" I ask, my voice moving to anger. "I moved Lilah from the stage—"

"That was bullshi—"

"And to the floor for a *fuckin'* reason," I say, cutting him off. Making Lilah come on my leg eased some of my frustration, but it's creeping in just with the vision of my nephew in front of me, not even to mention how he's trying to defend himself. "And the instruction I gave was that if you could not keep her—the daughter of a fucking *mayor* who you coerced into working here—safe . . ." Lilah flinches with the words, but I continue on. ". . . then I would find other employment for her to pay off any remaining debts, correct?"

"Yes, but—"

"No but. I'm finding new employment for her." Paulie tries to open his mouth, to speak, but I ignore him. "Delilah, from today on, you'll no longer be a server. You'll be my new personal assistant, attending mostly to the girls at the club and any other tasks I require of you in the day to day." I stare at her, running a hand over my polished desk. I hope she understands that *other tasks* will most definitely include taking my cock bent over this very desk. I'm tired of her cunt only being available to me when I sneak into her apartment in the middle of the night.

The apartment has had around-the-clock surveillance when she's home for weeks because the place is an assault waiting to happen.

But that won't matter.

"Your things will be moved from your current apartment to a room in the Carluccio compound. Working closely with the family requires added security measures," I say, and all I can think about is her staying under my roof indefinitely.

Finally.

Lilah's eyes go wide, her mouth dropping open, but I don't have time to hear what kind of argument she'll pose because my bratty nephew is already arguing.

"What the *fuck!?* Dante, no fucking way. You don't have a right—"

"The fuck I don't," I say, cutting him off calmly.

"I hired her. She's working for *me*."

"You might help run this place, but never forget who fucking owns it. Everything in this building? I own. Every*one* in this building? I fucking *own them*. You'll do well to remember that."

"What about my pl—"

"Marco, take Lilah out. Show her where we keep the stuff for the girls' back room so she can keep it stocked," I say of the snacks and toiletries we keep for the dancers and servers. "She can also make sure Martha is still keeping up on cleaning back there." Men are not allowed into the break room for the girls at Jerzy Girls. It's my one rule in a place of utter debauchery. There are also no cameras back there for the same reason.

"Dante—I mean, Mr. Carlucc—" Lilah corrects, blushing at the use of my name.

"Call me Dante, Delilah," I say with a smile. "We'll do dinner tonight to talk about the role, your pay, and expectations, yes?" My eyes lock to hers, telling her that this is not optional, to listen to me for once in her goddamned life and agree.

Thank the lord she does as I'm begging her to.

"Yes, sir, of course." I raise an eyebrow at "sir," and fuck me if that siren smile doesn't come out, making all sorts of thoughts and ideas run through my head. I look to Marco, who nods as Delilah stands then presses a soft but respectful hand to the center of her back, guiding her out the door the furthest route from Paulie.

Marco deserves a raise.

"What the *fuck,* Dante?" Paulie shouts as soon as the door clicks behind him.

I stay seated, not even giving him the courtesy of standing.

Respect is earned.

"Paulie, you had a job. You failed that job."

"She was a good dancer. On stage, no one could touch her. Why not put her back up there?"

"She was a shit dancer, Paulie, even she knows it. I cannot have a mayor's daughter riding a fucking pole and showing the entire city of Hudson her tits."

"Why the fuck not?! She'll bring in the cash. It was already starting to happen!"

"We are not that kind of establishment, Paulie. Period."

"The fuck, Dante. You tell the world we've got Shane Turner's daughter shaking her ass for cash, the customers will come crawling in. The good ones, the ones who can endure an increase in a cover charge. Ones who would pay good money for a lap dance. They'll tip the girls great."

"Is that what you want? The tips? I hear you're collecting them. That shit ends now, Paulie."

His face goes white from knowing he's caught, but he keeps that facade.

"Turner's daughter could make us good money, Dante."

The greed in his eyes, just past the panic, tells me something I don't want to see.

"No, Paulie. It's not what we do here."

"She could have been a test, working off her father's debt."

A rock sinks in my stomach because now I recognize the gleam of greed in his eye.

I've seen it before.

His father once had it.

It got his father locked up for life.

"A test?" I ask.

I've had my suspicions, heard him murmuring to the capos who are loyal to him over the last year. Of ways to build the family, to make more money, have an endless stream of bitches and power and cash.

That once he leads the family, everything will be theirs. No more of this playing-it-safe shit.

The route is dirty and seedy.

For years after my brother was put away, I assumed I would be next in line. I watched the making of the family, watched it grow, watched it take turns I didn't so much like. It veered from earning favors to get around permits, from gaining those favors by having politicians and idiotic men in power play right into our hand, to preying on the innocent. Using our power no longer to get ourselves rich and help the community but to do whatever it takes to be at the top of the food chain.

The Carluccio family was once known as a Robin Hood crew in Hudson City. Take from the rich, from the overly powered, and give to the poor. If a woman became a widow, she'd find a stack of cash in a brown paper bag on her front step in a week. When a team needed funding to go to state or the community center needed a roof, there was an anonymous donation.

Was that money earned above the table?

No.

Was it sometimes tainted by the blood of some *strunzo* who got in too deep?

Possibly.

But we weren't a family to be feared by those who were good.

I remember the days when my grandfather was in power fondly.

But that greed in Paulie's eyes seeped into the family as soon as my grandfather passed. Tony had new ideas, ideas to earn more. Forcing hands and taking the wrong deals. Communicating with the cartel and arms dealers, offering safe passage and transport. Promising protection to small businesses in the community—for a price.

We somehow moved away from the family, away from the community, away from bettering the lives of the people around us, despite it being in shifty ways, to greed.

I wanted to change that. For a while, I thought I could convince Tony to my side and we could go back to the original glory of the family. And then the greed caught him too, so much so, an anonymous tip to the FBI got him locked up on RICO charges for life.

Greed will always get you in the end.

With Tony out of the picture, it comes down to me to take over the family. I need to prove to my father my path is the right one so when it's time, I can take the reins and run it how it should have always been run.

This club is my point of proof—a club with beautiful women who we take care of and don't exploit. A high-class place for men to come to do business. Secret back rooms for games, liquor, and a cash system to easily clean money and keep us above board. Our connections could help us expand, make acquiring permits and liquor licenses easier, the same way we've done with Carluccio's Disposal for decades. The framework is already set. It's just a matter of convincing the family to try it—to bet on a long-term investment, a slight hit up front in exchange for a sure-fire thing. For a safer option for all of us.

And the best part is it's expandable. Jerzy Girls is already an attraction of sorts for local high-powered businessmen. Large deals have been made while watching a beautiful woman shake her ass or, in the back room, being served scotches by gorgeous servers over a game of poker.

Golf might seem like the gold standard for business deals regarding high-powered men. Decisions that impact millions happen on the manicured greens of the course, by why not the felted green of a poker table?

We can change things.

We can change things and make ourselves unbearably rich by doing so while also making my grandfather proud of the legacy he left.

In those years after Tony was locked away and written off by the family to avoid further digging, I knew I needed to start planning. To be smart enough to earn my father's trust, to earn that power transfer, but also set a Renaissance into motion.

I want to go back to the glory of the old days, when there wasn't a constant fear of the FBI knocking down your door with RICO charges, when we weren't constantly worrying about another family fighting us for power or territory.

The made men who rose with me, the men I brought on who answer to me, they see my vision. We've talked in quiet corners. They've raised their concerns and worries and told me they think we're straying too far. Things are getting too dangerous; innocents are getting pulled into the mess. They have families. They have children and wives. People they don't want to leave. They see a community afraid of us who used to rely on us, a community that struggles without the aid of our power.

But then Paulie turned twenty, and things got . . . confusing.

My father started making comments. Small at first, comments about Paulie following his father's footsteps, asking how he would handle things. If he were to choose Paulie, what would he do? How did *Paulie* handle situations? Where did he see the future of the family?

Soon, Paulie brought on his own men into the family, his own capos, all of who were undeniably loyal to him, and it became clear: my father was pitting us against each other, looking for us to fight to prove who is worthy of the title of boss. He's enjoying the battle, watching any hope of a relationship between us disintegrate slowly.

And that would be fine—with the greed bubbling in Paulie's eyes, I could say fuck it, lose that relationship with my nephew, kiss my father's ass and play the game until I get the nod of approval, the right to run the family the way I know is right. The way my mother would have wanted. The way my grandfather would have wanted.

Except Paulie is planning. He's planting men in positions that will cause me trouble in the long run, planting seeds in the minds of capos to the point that I think when I do take over, there will be a mutiny. He's making it so that even if I win in the end, I'll lose.

That's why this plan—one I've been working on for two years—is vital. And when Lilah fell into my lap, taking every sense of self I had with her, the vision became clearer.

But Paulie . . . He's going to need to be dealt with.

This all being said, when Paulie says that Lilah could be a *test*, the blood in my veins turns to ice, chilling me to the bone.

"A test?" I repeat when he doesn't say anything, eyes narrowing on the man who is my blood.

Paulie doesn't respond, and the debate is evident in his eyes.

Does he want to reveal his plan, his ideas for a business that isn't even his? Or does he want to keep his hand close and let it play out in his own little way?

Then it's my turn to debate: do I push him to explain or wait him out.

Normally, the answer would be obvious. Wait. I could wait out Paulie for a century, wait for his dumb ass to slip up and then handle it when the time comes.

But when it comes to Lilah, his plans matter. They matter a fuckuva lot, regardless of the fact that no matter what, any plans that involve Lilah and Paulie will absolutely not play out.

If Paulie were smart, if he knew how to play the game, he'd wait me out as well. Wait for me to ask. But the boy is so young, so green. He doesn't understand how the game works, sitting in his entitled chair and never down in the trenches, learning how to play.

So he spills, of course.

"She could be the trial, Dante. Can't you see it? I already have a few inquiries, questions about her." His words make me sick, but I keep my face bored and irritated.

"Stop playing games, Paulie." He rolls his eyes and huffs, further proving what a fucking child he is.

"Selling pussy, Dante. But not just pussy. *Expensive pussy*." I don't speak, that ice crackling further, running into my heart, stopping my breathing.

On the outside, though, the face is neutral.

The body is loose.

That's the key to success in this world. No matter what is going on around you, what people are saying, you play it cool. Even if you're three seconds away from pulling out a gun and shooting them between their eyes, *you never show your hand.*

Lilah knows the game.

She plays it well.

One of many things I fucking love about the woman.

"Turner's daughter—she's hot. She's a fucking wet dream, always smiling for the cameras but never enough. Men are . . . interested." I let him dig the hole. I need to know everything, get the ammunition I need. Knowledge is power, after all. "We sell her to the highest bidder, Dante. Use the stage as a way to display her, let her dance for a month, then hold a silent auction. The winner goes home with her."

"So you're telling me you want to prostitute her? To prostitute a well-known mayor's *daughter?* A daughter who has been in the limelight her entire life? A daughter whose sister was just nearly kidnapped by a Carluccio soldier?"

How does he not see how fucking messy that would be? How many fingers would be pointed our way?

It would take one wrong person hearing about this "auction" to get an all-out investigation running.

"No. Not really. Just the once. I don't give a fuck what happens after." I look at my watch, making it seem like I don't have time for his shit, like I have other, better things to do, but I'm really looking at my watch to see how long it's been since Lilah left, how far she could have gotten from this sick fuck. "She's just the beginning," he says, and I think this time my heart stops.

Not for Lilah.

For this fucking family.

For my nephew.

For the understanding that my brother's child can't be involved in this family. He's too dangerous. Too greedy. Too *fucking stupid.*

"The beginning?"

"A test, I told you." He's smiling now, eager to tell me his plan. "We start with the politicians, the dumb ones, other big names. Get them in deep to where they can't pay. Hold their daughters, their wives, whatever, as collateral." His words make me sick. Holding *human beings* as collateral for dirty bets they didn't make as if they are some kind of property. "When we sell them, they're even, and we can start the process all over again."

"We do not sell pussy," I say firmly.

"Not yet," he says with a smile.

"This is my club, Paulie. I'm telling you, we do not sell fucking pussy here."

"We'll see what grandfather says about that. It's a great plan, *Zio Dante*. Would bring in a new audience to the family, new streams of revenue."

And that's when I know.

This is his plan to secure Don.

The fucked-up asshole has been planning this.

The sick smile on the bastard's face says it all.

"Johnny almost fucked it up, of course, going for the sister, making a big scene . . . But fuck if we didn't get lucky when she walked right into my office."

"*My office*," I remind him. "That day is also why there's now a lock that you can't fuckin touch on this door. Because that day, you were a child stepping into the shoes of a grown man, toddling around because they were too fucking big for you." He cringes but doesn't let it show much that the strike hit true.

"What you don't seem to be able to get through your thick fuckin' skull is that sex trafficking is a *federal crime*. None of this greasing local judges' palms to get out unscathed shit." His chin ticks.

I can't tell if he genuinely thought that this would be a good idea I'd be on board with and he's disappointed or if he's irritated that he hadn't thought of a federal charge and the trouble that would make.

"You only get hit with a federal charge if you get caught."

"You truly are a fuckin' moron. Too fucking young and ignorant to understand how the real world works."

"I'm not young—" I cut him off, over this conversation. Over this kid.

"Then act like it. I've been hit with local and state charges five times, Paulie."

"What—"

"Marco has three." Paulie licks his lips. "Carmine? Seven. But local charges, they get dropped. Federal charges, they don't go anywhere. They get publicized, get used as a lesson, a feather in a fuckin' cap. The men who nail that charge get the promotion and the corner office. The shit we do here? That's fine. The disposal company, the politicians? We can work our way out of that, got enough people in our pocket, enough shit on enough people to be safe. Even the games, we can get around that shit. But you start prostituting fucking *politicians' children*, Paulie, you're begging for a fuckin' fed to come knocking. Don't be stupid. Sit back, watch, *learn*."

"I've learned enough. Grandfather thinks—"

"Jesus Christ, kid. Get over yourself. *Listen to yourself!* Grandfather this. Carmine Carluccio doesn't give a shit. He's using you because he wants to fuck with me, the same way he did with your father. He wanted us to take his side, but we took your fuckin' grandmother's. Holds that shit against us. You were too young; you didn't take sides. He sees that, likes that."

"I don't think—" Finally I stand, and Paulie stops speaking as I walk around my desk to him, grabbing him at the collar of his shirt and pulling him close to me.

"Listen to me," I say. "Listen. To. Me. You could be great, Paulie. You've got men loyal to you, I know that. I'm not stupid. Know you set them up so if things don't go your way, it's gonna make my life difficult. I get it. Whatever. But what you don't get is we can *help each other*. We can both win."

He crosses his arms like a child. "I don't believe you. You want to be Don."

"I don't," I say, and it's not a lie. He might not know the truth, but he can have *that* truth.

Over the years, I've learned that you can bend the truth to fit the mold of who you're talking to. The closer you start to truthful statements, the easier to gain the trust and change their minds.

If this is going to work, I need to change Paulie's.

Even if only for a short time, until I get the title passed.

I need him to trust me and watch as he either decides to go safe or let greed win.

The greed wins, I put him down.

His common sense wins, and he can be an asset.

But I need time.

"Give me three weeks. Three weeks, and I'll come to you with new information. An offer."

"Why the fuck should I believe you?"

"Because I have something you'll want, but I need to make it stick first. You wait, Paulie, and I'll make you a fucking king."

He stares at me, licking his lips.

"This is bigger than our family, Paulie. So much bigger."

He continues to stare, making his decision, and I continue to hold his shirt tight.

"Fine," he says finally. "Three weeks. Three weeks or I'm taking the mayor's daughter."

I release his shirt, pushing him toward the door.

"Get the fuck outta my office. Go work. Stop fucking the girls."

And then he leaves, and I'm left to figure out how this new piece of the puzzle can fit in.

THIRTY-THREE

-Lilah-

"This is your new room," Dante says when we walk into the Carluccio mansion that I've been to one other time for what I thought would be a one-night stand and the loss of my virginity.

The last strand holding me to my old life.

Funny how I thought it was a sign to get it over with, but it was truly just a sign to keep going.

Or maybe turn away and run. I'm still not quite sure.

"My new room?" I ask, looking around, but it only takes a few moments to recognize the things in this room—some of them are mine: frames with photos of my family, my old friends who dropped me as soon as I became less cool, tchotchkes that I've collected over the years, the black trunk I found thrifting with Lola once where I tossed all of my stripper shoes and clothes so I don't have to stare at them when I'm not working. The bed isn't mine. It's a massive four-poster with elegant white sheets and a comforter, a light, white gauze hanging to create a pretty canopy. A vanity in the same dark wood sits in the corner, and I just know somehow, the closet holds all of my clothes.

"This is my stuff," I say, moving around the room, touching things I recognize, afraid to touch those I don't. When I turn back to Dante, he's facing me, arms crossing his chest.

To the rest of the world, he looks like a tough mafioso, heir to one of the most infamous families on the East Coast. The glare, the lift of his eyebrow, the permanent lines of frowning and judgement etched into his face—it's all there. The tee shirt—shockingly casual for the typically well-dressed man—shows his tattoo on the inner arm on his bicep.

I asked him once why he would put a tattoo on such a strange spot, not understanding the meaning of it - the well kept secret of the Carluccio family insignia.

Closest to my heart, he'd said. *But not on my heart.*

But me?

I see him differently. Not tough and uncaring.

He's *nervous*.

He's nervous because he has no idea how I'm going to act, respond, and the man—as crazy as he is—wants me to like this.

"My apartment?" I ask, mimicking his stance.

"In two weeks, you'll have your full deposit and months paid out returned to you, including the rent for the two months you stayed in that shit hole."

"I'm sorry?" I ask because that makes no sense.

"You should be sorry, living there. It's a piece of shit apartment, not safe. Had soldiers there nightly, patrolling, keeping an eye on your front door."

"I'm sorry *what*?" I ask again, this time because this is alarming news.

"Please, *fiorella*. Not now. For the love of fuck." The look shifts again, and again, I don't think the average person would see it, see the change.

He's exhausted.

"Honey," I say in a whisper, and he looks over his shoulder at the door and then back to me before moving to the door and closing it, turning the lock, and swiping the chain over it.

"That place was shit. Here, I get to you quicker. Here, I leave later. Here, I know where you are at all times."

"For my safety?" I ask with an eye roll, but he's moving, and I'm moving back until I hit a wall where he cages me.

"Yes, Delilah. For your safety. But also for my peace of mind. Things are about to go off the fucking rails, and I need to know where you are. I need you under my watch. I *need that*. Do you hear me? Do you understand?"

"I don't, Dante. I *don't understand*."

"Paulie's going to have questions about me going insane over you, breaking a man's wrist in my fuckin' club, taking you off the stage, making you my assistant. I explained it away, but as much as I hate to admit it, he's not a complete fuckin' idiot."

"So, what? You shuttle me to your house, and now I'm some kept woman?"

"Never. You're here because I need you as close to me as possible. This is partly selfish. I want you here. Need you here. Anyone who works for the family this close has a detail, someone watching them. This isn't too far off. It's still going with the plan, Delilah."

"What plan, Dante? I know nothing about this fucking plan you keep talking about except that every time I get a single bite of the story, it seems to explode even bigger."

"You will. You'll get it soon. I'm going to get you what you want, anything you want. What you deserve. You'll get retribution for your family, baby." His hand moves, brushing long hair back, his thumb running along the collarbone he loves to kiss when it's late and we're alone and I'm sleepy. "You're going to rule, *fiorella*. You're going to get your revenge, and you're going to be fucking magnificent. But we need to be smart. We need to be safe." He leans in, pressing to my lips to his gently, and I know that this is bigger. So much bigger than I could ever have imagined.

When I walked into Paulie's—*Dante's*—office to make that deal, priority one was getting Lola free, two was stepping into the role I was born for, and three was to get retribution on the family who killed my father and ruined my mother.

We could have been free, all four of us. Lola would have been loved by Arturo—he said so in his letters. And a sick, twisted part of me thinks that if he hadn't died, if my mother hadn't felt that guilt in his wake, she'd still be here.

A part of me thinks it wasn't cancer that ate her insides and rotted her away until she was gone—it was losing the love of her life.

Did a part of her start dying the second she realized she was falling for a man with power, a man with a gun constantly pointed at the back of his skull?

I consider this because I wonder how long it will take for that infinitesimal part of myself to consume me, the desire and tenderness I feel for the man in front of me to eat me alive.

"Lose the look, Delilah. You and me. All that matters."

"You'll still be sneaking in at night?" I ask, exhaustion that matches his own in my voice.

"Lilah . . ."

"And leaving in the morning?" Another sigh. "Like a fuckin' *goumad*, a whore you fuck for the night before going back to your fancy life?" The fire in my backbone burns, reminding me of who I am.

I am Rapunzel, taking her future into her own hands.

I am a siren, forcing men to shred their boats at my shores so that I can gain the power I so desire.

I am not a hidden secret, something to enjoy in the dark of night.

"Delilah, you know that's not true."

"Do I? Because that's what this is. I'm your dirty little secret, and you're essentially my enemy, Dante."

"I'm not your enemy, you know that."

"*Do I?*" I repeat. "Do I? Because I want to take your family down for what it did to mine, and whatever this is between us won't change that."

"I know that, Lilah. I also know I'll do anything to give you that."

"What about your father?" I ask, my mind moving to the way his face changed in his office.

"What about him?"

"He's part of the problem, Dante."

"It's Paulie. It's Tony. It's the men they recruited. Not my father. He's good. He just... He's gone astray."

It's funny to think that just a few months ago, I was Dante. Despite being nearly 15 years younger than him, I was just like him. Cautiously optimistic about my father. I knew he wasn't great, but I thought he wasn't terrible. That he had something—*anything*—redeemable about him.

"He hasn't, Dante. He's the heart of it."

"You don't know him, Lilah."

"I don't have to. I know the men at the club. I hear the whispers. I know my father. I know my mother. I know it wasn't a fluke that Johnny went after my sister."

"I know you're caught up in it, Lilah, but—"

"If I prove it. If I prove your father is poison, will I change your mind?" I ask, panic rising.

For a moment, I convinced myself that we could work together toward the same cause. That he saw the world—this world—the way I did. That when the chips fell, when the war was over, we'd rule together. The Russos and the Carluccios bound together to bring back the golden age of what these families could have been. *Should* have been.

But maybe I was wrong. When I see the warring in his eyes, him trying to decide if he should agree or fight it, I think I must have been wrong.

But then it shifts.

And clear as day, I see it without him even speaking it aloud.

For some reason, I win. For some reason, in his internal scales of trying to balance his family, his duty, his morality, and his goals, I come out on top.

"I don't think you will, but if you do, yes. I'll help you take him down, too," he says, and his words are solemn. Sad, even.

I know the feeling. It comes right before you accept that the people you idolized were nothing but a facade.

I want to take that look away, change it. So I step closer, putting my hands on his chest.

"So, where's your room?" I ask, smiling as I play with the lapel of his suit jacket. "I don't quite remember the way. The last time I was here, I was kind of distracted."

He gives me a wide smile in return, and *goddammit*.

It's moments like this I wish more than anything that this is our normal.

That I'm just a girl falling for a man. That I'm not caught in some tangled web that I didn't choose to be born into, that I don't need proof or revenge.

And it's when I wish that Dante is just *Dante*. A normal man, not some potential future heir. That we aren't working to fix a mess other people made; that we aren't risking everything every step of the way.

"If I tell you, you'll cause trouble," he says, smiling and kissing my nose.

"Me? Trouble?" I'm nearly intoxicated by this, by us.

By the ease of us.

Everything is burning down to embers, the chaos winning, the uncertainty taking over, but something about being in his home, there being so much *less* hiding between us? It's giving me hope.

Hope that this could maybe work at the end of everything.

That we could work.

That somehow, I'll get everything I want: the title, the revenge, and the man.

Famous last words, I suppose.

THIRTY-FOUR

-Lilah-

Weeks pass.

I work in the back of Jerzy Girls, filing papers and making calls, processing paychecks, getting new girls on the books. It's strange to think that this place actually has some kind of system to keep it in business.

And each night, I find myself tangled up with Dante in my bed. Each night, I drive to the giant mansion alone and crawl into the giant bed in the room I've been given. And each night, I'm awakened by soft kisses—up my thighs, across my belly, right on my pussy.

Every night, he whispers I'm perfect, beautiful, worthy. He tells me he's obsessed with me, that I'm an illness infecting his every thought. That I'm his and his alone forever and always.

And each morning, I wake up alone, the man already having slipped away into the dusk.

And each morning, I die just a little, knowing I can't see his face in the sunlight, that one tiny glimpse of it being when I snuck out that first time.

I wish I had known. I would have taken a photo of it and captured it for the mornings.

I wish I had stayed that first morning, let him wake up with me and we could have seen where it would have taken us. Sometimes I wonder if I had chosen differently that first morning, if things would be different right now.

But today, I don't wish that.

That's because Dante didn't make his way into my bed late last night, satisfying my need to feel that connection, to validate my feelings, to feed my own addiction.

I wake unrested, groggy, and panicked.

It's strange, falling for a mafia man who can't be seen with me, who has some kind of unknown plan he needs to see out before we can be together, before we can take over the world. Every moment that I'm not with him, I find myself craving him, and in the moments I'm not craving him, dying to be in his space, I'm worried for him.

He is not a doctor.

He is not a tattoo artist.

He isn't even just a strip club owner.

He is next in line to be the Don of the Carluccio crime family, with people nipping at his heels to take the spot from him.

I roll over to my bedside table, looking for my burner phone and praying there's a note.

But it's not there.

Swiping the phone from the table, I tap the screen several times, checking my messages.

Nothing new.

I check the email he set up for me.

Nothing.

Then the panic begins.

Sitting in the bed, I force myself to take a deep breath, to let the air reach deep, deep down until I can feel it hit the bottom of my lungs, and slowly breath out.

If something had happened, I would know.

The club would call me.
Paulie would call me.
Marco would call me.
Someone in the house would knock on my door and tell me.
Right?

Right, I tell myself, because it's the only thing keeping my anxiety out of worst-case scenarios. Walking over to the closet, I type out a text to him.

> Hey, everything okay?

I'm sliding a pair of jeans up my ass, still panicking as I reach for a long-sleeve Henley. My new uniform as assistant to Dante *fucking* Carluccio is not so much a uniform as a "wear whatever you want but cover your tits and ass because those are for me and me alone" rule. I don't mind it because being covered up means I blend into the chaos. Men don't have as much to look at, and thus, they don't pay attention to me.

The last two weeks have been by far the easiest since starting at Jerzy Girls.

As I'm about to pull my shirt on, my phone chimes with a new text, and I almost trip trying to get it, to see what he says.

To get that reassurance that all is well.

> Yes. Long night. See you at work.

Relief washes through my veins, but frustration quickly follows it.

A long night. He couldn't even bother to text me, to tell me he wasn't going to come over? To let me know he's safe, that nothing horrible happened?

If I even so much as *thought* to disappear for a night, to not be exactly where he expected me to be, he would tear down the entire city to get to me, to drag me back where he wanted me.

But this dipshit gets to just *have a long night?* And then what, not say a goddamned thing?

Fuck that, I think to myself, tossing the light-grey long-sleeve shirt to the ground and grabbing a tight lace-up corset top.

He had a long night?

I'm here to make it even longer.

Once I'm dressed, I walk down the stairs and out the front door where Roddy is standing, leaning against a blacked-out car, smoking a cigarette.

Roddy drives me to work now.

Roddy isn't just a bouncer, it seems.

Interesting to know that the girls don't have *all* the dirt.

He stands there, and I move around him, opening the door and letting myself in. He holds the door open as I try to close it, popping his head in as he squats to look at me.

"You gonna change?" he says, staring at me.

"Fuck off, Roddy."

"Big Boss isn't going to like that, babe."

"Well, Big Boss can go fuck himself," I say. "Drive me to work, please."

I expect an argument.

I expect some kind of strong-arming, telling the little lady to get back in the house and dress appropriately.

But instead, Roddy laughs, a deep, hearty laugh. He then stands, slams the door, and gets in on the driver's side.

"He's got his hands full with you, doesn't he?" he says, cluing me in to the fact that, like Marco, Roddy knows about us beyond just me working for Dante.

"Drive, Roddy," I say, taking the sunglasses off my head and placing them on my nose, then I try to zone out as Roddy and his laughter drive me to work.

The anger and irritation simmer all day but boil over when I'm in the girls' break room restocking snacks and I hear two of them talking.

"Who knew Big Boss was so fine," Sammi says, and my guard is instantly up.

"Seriously! How come he never comes in here looking like that? Always walking around pouting and shit."

I'm sorry, what?

I tip my head over, smiling at my friends, and Marty smiles back. "Have you seen this? Your boss and Angela Sigano out last night?"

Your boss and Angela Sigano out last night?

The words vibrate in my mind.

The girls don't know that the man the rest of the world knows as Junior Carluccio is *Mr. Romano*, the secretive man who spent weeks paying for my time, having me dance for him for hours on end.

They don't know that the owner who insisted I move to start working as his assistant isn't just a kind man who realized the stripper was a shitty dancer and offered her a different job she was much better at—the story I spun for them.

They sure as fuck don't know that he comes into my room each night and fucks me sideways. They don't know I'm a Russo or that, in some way, Dante thinks he's going to help me take his family down without tearing down the house of cards we're standing on.

"Let me see," I say with an easy, practiced smile, trying not to tip into psycho-girlfriend territory.

And that's the fuck of it, isn't it?

I feel this possessive control over a man, and the rest of the world doesn't even know he looks my way other than to tell me to add snacks to the break room.

Is Dante my boyfriend?

Am I his girlfriend?

It shouldn't be this hard, this confusing, the voice in my head whispers, telling me to run.

But instead, I take Marty's phone and stare at it.

Acid crawls up my throat.

There stands Dante—my Dante, the handsome man who has me questioning everything—in a black suit with a black button-down, ever the dark prince. His hair is combed back, that hunk that falls out meticulously secured with some kind of hair product, I'm sure.

He's staring directly into the camera, eyes dark, no smile.

He looks like a god.

He takes my breath away.

But that isn't what has me sick to my stomach.

She's touching him.

There's a hand on his shoulder, the other on his abs, her smile tipping up to his face like they're some kind of happy couple that has been together for decades.

And then the caption tips me into the lava of anger flowing around me.

Junior Carluccio and Angela Sigano attended the heart foundation gala last night. Rumor has it that Carluccio was seen at a jewelry store shopping recently. Are wedding bells in the future for this gorgeous couple?

I want to vomit.

"Cute!" I say happily before Marty takes her phone back to examine the photo again. Conversation continues, but I can't hear a single word through the buzzing in my ears, the fire burning in my veins.

I need to be calm, I tell myself as I finish stocking snacks.

I need to be reasonable, I think as I wipe down a mirror.

I need to refocus on my mission, I remind myself as my jaw aches from clenching.

And then that photo pops into my mind again.

Then his text flashes across my eyes.

And then I remember his plea to let him do what he needs to do before I start my retribution.

Fuck that.

Fuck. That.

And fuck being shy, fuck being quiet, fuck letting this relationship run under the radar for a while.

If he gets to be psychotically possessive over me, telling me to stop dancing and to change my outfits and to stop flirting with his men, I should be able to do the same right back.

Decision made, I walk. I start for the back office, zigzagging through customers and waitresses with speed, my heels clicking as I do.

"Lilah!" I hear from behind me, but I ignore it and keep walking, my eye on the door that says *Private*.

"Lilah!" the voice bellows again and again, I *ignore it*.

"Lilah! Stop!" A hand is around my elbow, and I spin, coming face-to-face with Marco. His hand instantly drops, probably not wanting to have his hand on his boss' girl for more than a few moments.

But what does it matter when you're one of many, right? What right would Dante even *have* to be annoyed with him or me?

"What?" I spit at him, venom that shouldn't be directed at him spewing.

He doesn't even flinch.

"Saw your face. Sure you heard about Angela, girls have big fuckin' mouths. Know about . . . you two." I scrunch my nose, trying to fight the stark laugh that tries to fly out at how uncomfortable Marco looks. "It's not what it looks like."

"God, all of you assholes are the same, living by the same fucking bro code. But heads up, Marco. I'm not a *bro*. I live by my own code." He sighs.

"There's no code, princess. See your face. Know you're mad. Trying to save *myself* the headache of you two fuckin' going at it."

I ignore him, as he deserves.

"Is Paulie in today?" I ask pointedly.

Marco looks to the ceiling, probably bartering with God to help him handle yet another crazy woman.

I wonder if Angela Sigano *is another crazy woman he has to deal with.* She's probably sweet and docile, smiles when she's told, and sits quietly in the corner.

She definitely doesn't plan revenge.

"No," he says under his breath, as if he knows that's the only thing that could hold me back and he wishes the man were in today, even though he doesn't like him much.

"Good," I say, a cat-like smile on my lips as I turn back the way I was going.

"Jesus, fuck. Lilah! He's in a meeti—"

I twist the knob on the door leading to Dante's cushy office and surprise even myself when it's unlocked, but I push it open anyway.

"So you see—" a balding man starts to say, but Dante's eyes are already moving from the man sitting across from his giant mahogany desk, his fortress, and moving to my own.

I find joy in the fact I can read the emotions flashing in his eyes, the man of ice that it seems I can thaw temporarily.

Frustration, intrigue, joy, confusion, and then settling on something I can't pinpoint, not exactly. Admiration, maybe. A hint of entertainment.

"I have to talk to you," I say, crossing my arms on my chest.

"I'm in a meeting, Delilah."

"I don't fucking care, *Dante*," I say in the same tone.

The man turns to me, eyes wide at my clear disrespect in using this powerful man's Christian name.

Names hold power.

If you use them right, *you* hold the power.

"I tried to stop her, Dante. I swear—"

"It's fine, Marco. I know how unpredictable our Delilah can be." His eyes are filled with entertainment, like he's living for this moment.

Like he was waiting for it.

I refuse to look into the way that makes me clench a bit.

His eyes stay locked on mine as I stare at him, my tongue sliding between my front teeth and lips in irritation. "Richard, we don't need legal counsel. Thank you for the offer, but there are many other attorneys much more qualified to take on our complex businesses."

"Excuse me—"

"Now leave." His eyes graze the jeans, tight, low-cut top, and the sliver of belly that's revealed, and heat is added to the feelings in his gaze.

"Just because some bitch—"

Marco's arm wraps around my waist, pushing me into the office from where I stand in the doorway and against the wall, stepping in front of me as Dante's chair scrapes against the floor, slamming into the wall behind him. The man stops talking, his face going pale as he understands where he went wrong. If you ask me, I'd say he went wrong when he tried a combover to hide thinning hair, but that's just me.

Dante's tanned hand grabs the collar of the ill-fitting shirt the man is wearing, dragging him up and out of the chair. I tip my head to the side, trying to look around the big man guarding me to get a better view. Marco looks over his shoulder and shakes his head, rolling his eyes.

"Made for this shit," he murmurs low, and I just smile.

A compliment from Marco? I'll take it.

"You came to me for help because you can't find a single client in the tristate area willing to work with you and your shitty track record. I will not be helping you because you're an entitled piece of shit. I do my research before I take a meeting, Richard. I know about you. You deserve what came to you. Pack up, leave the tristate, and start over somewhere else. I'll be contacting my associates to make sure they don't offer their business to you, either. Now about you calling our Delilah here a bitch."

"I didn't—"

"But you did." His head turns to Marco, and his eyes catch me peeking out behind his shoulder to watch. Just like his right hand, he shakes his head, exasperated by me. "Marco, please escort our friend here out. You know the drill." I don't catch Marco's face, just the nod of his head as he grabs the back of the man's collar, moving toward the door.

I'm assuming "the drill" is not just giving the man directions to the turnpike.

"And lock the door on your way out, yes?" Dante says, and again, Marco nods.

"That's not necessary," I say as Marco leaves, ignoring me and letting the door click and lock behind him. "I won't be here long. I just have a few things to say to you, and then I'm out of here."

"Oh, my sweet Delilah. That's not how this works."

"I'm serious, Dante—"

"I see that fire in your eyes, baby. Gonna let you get it out, do your yelling and screaming at me, and when that's enough, I'm going to fuck some sense into you, bring you back to earth. Calm you down." I blink at him, at the smile on his face as I stand there, hands on my hips and *raging*.

"Excuse me?!"

"You heard me, baby. Now let me have it. What has you so riled up?" he asks, rolling his sleeves to the elbow as he walks around his desk, leaning against it and crossing his feet at the ankle.

He is not the hottest thing that has ever graced my presence.

Nope.

Now, if I could just convince my body to believe that.

"Come on, Lilah. I didn't have you last night. Let's get this part over with so I can fuck you on my desk." My mouth drops open at his words, at the fucking *gall* of this man, but this time, I don't let that stop me from speaking.

"Angela Sigano?" I say the words like a question, but they're really a statement. "That's what kept you from coming to me last night? Your *long night? Angela fucking Sigano?*" I cross my arms under my boobs and don't miss how his eyes move there.

"What the fuck are you wearing?"

"Don't change the subject."

He doesn't listen. "I told you, cover your tits."

"From the looks of the photos the girls showed me, Angela's tits were out and proud last night. Didn't seem to bother you." His lips tip up, the irritation at my outfit leaving almost as quickly as it came.

"Ah, the gossip mill has started. Good."

"Good? Jesus Christ. I swear to fucking god, Dante. This game of yours? I don't want to be playing it. I don't want to be a part of it." I turn, done with everything in this room, but his hand catches my wrist, stopping my retreat.

"Game?"

"This game where you tell me you have some plan, some kind of grand scheme to keep me quiet and amiable, then try to use my emotions against me. Yes, the girls are gossiping about how fucking perfect you two looked last night on some red carpet. Last night while I was sleeping in the fucking guest room of your house like a kept woman because I'm not allowed to go home. The guest room you've snuck into every night for weeks because you're *so obsessed with me* and *I'm meant to be your*s." I wiggle the fingers of my free hand to show him just how much I think of his bullshit. "But here you are, off fucking some bitch."

"Aww, baby, did you miss me last night?" he says, smiling.

"Don't treat me like a child, Dante. This isn't funny! You're a fucking asshole, making this all a game. That's what this is, isn't it? Some fucking game to you? Another power play, fuel for your big fucking ego. And here I am, a piece of convenient pussy to entertain you unless you have something better to fuck? Someone more interesting, someone with better standing?" I try and twist my wrist from his grasp, ignoring his darkening face, and surprisingly, he lets go. "I'm done with this. I'm done with the secrets and the games and the mind fucks."

"You're not done with me."

"Or maybe I'll even the playing field," I say, hands on my hips, fury burning in my veins. "Maybe I'll go fuck Marco or Roddy. I'll—"

He moves, his body herding mine backwards, barely touching me until I bump into the wall.

When my back is pinned there, his hand moves, starting at my belly, moving between my breasts, a thumb grazing my decolletage until his hand is at my throat, positioning my face until I'm staring into his angry eyes. It's then that I'm reminded that this man is *insane*. He's unhinged. He could kill me right here, and he has an entire crew of men that would help him clean up the mess without question.

"I'm saying this once and only once, Delilah. You are mine. Your mind, your body—your goddamned *soul*. They belong to me. Do not play fucking games; do not make jokes about fucking my men." His head dips, and he runs his nose up my neck and over my jaw until his mouth is at my ear. "But it works. We work. Those scales are balanced, baby. I am yours. My mind. My body. My soul. Only yours. You need to trust that, know that to your soul." A chill runs down my spine.

"How am I supposed to know that if you tell me *fucking nothing*, Dante? I'm in the dark! All I know is you didn't come to me last night and you went out with some woman whose father, word on the street says, is very interested in building ties with your family."

"My father wants me to marry Angela Sigano." The blood stops in my veins. "He thinks it would create ties, yes. Strengthen families. But the reason I agreed to go last night, listening to her drone on about purses and manicures instead of eating your sweet pussy, is because the connection was suggested to him by Paulie."

My body freezes.

I can't quite decide why, can't figure out which part of his little speech has my emotions stringing me tight.

"Paulie?"

"I told you, *fiorella*. He wants to prove his worthiness. He needs to be resourceful and he needs a way to take me out of the running for don. I marry a Sigano, I work for them. It's an easy out for Paulie." He breathes heavily in my ear, and it's like his breaths have a direct line to my pussy, an electric shock going through me as each hits my ear. "I needed to go with her. I needed to show her a good time. It would have been too suspicious if I declined. Paulie's already too interested in you, in your connection to me. He's angry that you're working for me, not on the stage."

"For this to work, we have to be equals. You can't know more than me. You can't be sacrificing for me and letting me sit in the corner, no idea what's happening. Seeing those photos? Being blindsided by that? Fucking *killed* me, Dante. I hate that. I hate that you're so deep in me that it felt like a betrayal. You had chances to tell me you wouldn't come to me, that you had to go to some dinner."

"Would you have let me?" he asks, and the question stops me. "Would you have been okay with me going out with another woman, making it seem like we were an item. With me leading her on, flirting with her, letting her think there's a chance?"

Having a better understanding of how the night had gone makes me sick.

"If I understood why, then yes," I say, and I can't tell if it's a lie or not. "But I needed to know that. Otherwise, it feels like a cruel move an arrogant man makes because he doesn't have to listen to the whims of the woman in his life." His face looks sad when he answers.

The look is new for him, the sadness, the regret.

"Oh, my sweet Delilah. I can't tell you. I wish I could. You know I'm crazy for you, would die for you—" I stop him.

I might be angry.

I might be sad.

I might be frustrated and confused.

But I don't ever want that.

"I hope the fuck not." He ignores my words, and panic slowly starts to creep into me.

"I want you to have what you want. You want to control those who hurt you, hurt your sister, your mother. I get it, baby. I want that for you. I want to give you the world. But I can't do it if you won't help me." His hands move to my hips until he's lifting me, turning, and placing my ass on his desk.

The fire in me begins to simmer.

I hate the effect he has on me.

I also kind of love it.

"Let me help you," I say, my hands running up his chest, looping around his neck. "I spent my whole life being pretty and quiet and protected. I want to be loud and ugly. I'm not delicate."

"I know that. You're also mine."

"What about Angela? Did you tell her she's yours? Did you kiss her? Did you sleep with her?" I ask, taunting, the acid burning in my stomach all the same. His hand goes to my hair, tugging, holding me in place in front of him.

"Drop this shit right fucking now, Delilah. Fuck Angela. I don't give two shits about her. It's you who keeps *me* happy. And it's my job to keep *you* happy," he says, then his nose runs down my throat and back up, his tongue tasting the skin behind my ear. "Let me make you happy, baby," he says, his words a coo, and despite all common sense, despite any and all frustrations boiling under my skin, my legs widen just a hair.

"That's my good girl," he says, and my eyes start to drift just with those words alone and what they do to my body.

Goddammit.

His hand goes to my knee, gently moving up, up until he hits the center of my jeans, his thumb pressing there. I bite my lip, determined not to moan.

He knows.

He knows what he's doing to me.

He knows he's about to win.

I can't find it in me to care, though.

"Dante," I whisper.

"I know, baby," he says, stepping back and moving to his knees before deft fingers work at the strap around my ankle.

His eyes stay on me all the while, watching me watch him, watching my tits move in the tiny corset as my breathing picks up.

From the man removing my shoes.

Jesus Christ.

I had no chance, did I?

He stands when the shoes are in a tidy pile, moving back between my legs and working on the button and zip of my jeans. "Up," he says, and I obey, lifting onto my hands so he can tug down my jeans, kneeling once again when he brings them down with my panties, pulling them over my ankles, and tossing them on top of my shoes.

And then he stays down there, hands running up my legs as I sit on his desk, moving up, up, up until a thumb runs over my clit and down to my entrance.

"Already fucking wet for me, yeah?" he asks, and I don't answer.

His eyes are no longer on mine.

Instead, he's fixated on my pussy, where his thumbs open me for him to look at. I move, leaning on my hands as I watch him before me, then he runs a single thick finger up and down.

"Dante," I whisper.

Again, he doesn't look at me, but I can see the smile on his lips as he slowly, torturously slowly, slides one finger into me. "Ahh," I breathe.

He slides the finger in and then out, repeating the delicious torture until I'm squirming.

"I need more, honey," I say. "I need you."

"And you'll have me." His eyes finally meet mine. They're devilish with a small smile hidden there. "Eventually."

And then his mouth is on me, sucking my clit as his tongue laps at me, two fingers now fucking me.

"Shit!" I shout, my hips moving to try and get more from him, to demand more. But I don't tip my head back, despite the overwhelming pleasure.

I don't close my eyes.

Because while he fingers me, while he eats me, his eyes are locked to mine.

"Dante, I'm going to come," I whisper moments later, even though it hasn't been long at all.

I can feel the smile on my pussy.

See it in his eyes.

He stops, sitting back on his heels as he wipes his mouth on his forearm.

"Dante!" I say, frustrated in more ways than one. "I was close!"

He stands, moving to me and lifting me off the desk by my hips, turning me so we're back to front as a hand moves my hair over one shoulder. His face moves to my ear when he speaks there.

"You'll be coming on my cock, *fiorella*."

Everything in me melts, especially when he presses between my shoulder blades, forcing me to bend over his desk. I lie there, the sealed wood cold through the fabric of the corset he hasn't taken off me, and hear his hands moving, undoing a belt.

And then the head of his cock is running along my slit, the head popping into my entrance before he repeats the move again. Up, down, in. I try to move my hips back to get more, but his hand moves to my hair, fisting it and tugging until I'm staring at the ceiling.

"Remember that I am yours, Delilah. I exist on this planet to please you," he says before slamming into me, drawing a loud cry from me as he does.

He pulls out, slamming into me again, and I moan his name.

"That's it. Say my name."

"Please, Dante. Please!" He moves to bend over me.

"Who do I belong to, Delilah?" he says in my ear, his back lining mine as he continues to pound into me, my hips hitting the mahogany with the force. "Tell me. You fucking know whose I am."

His demand is hot in my ear, his breathing heavy, but it also reminds me that I'm still fucking angry. That bitter jealousy still stirs in me, not yet appeased by an orgasm.

"Do I, Dante? Do I know that?" I say through gritted teeth, trying not to moan the words. He groans a sound that has me tightening around him before he pulls out and stands up. I look behind me, baffled, as he steps back, his pants not even fully down, just pushed enough to get his cock out. "Dante, What the fuc— Oh!"

His hands move to my waist, turning me before he picks me up and places my bare ass on his desk, then he places his hands on my thighs and widens my legs so much, it's almost painful. But any pinch is overtaken by him slamming back in.

"You want to question whose I am, fine. But you'll do it looking in my goddamned eyes while I fuck you, telling you who the fuck you are to me."

"Dante," I moan, his hand going into my hair and tugging until I'm forced to look into his eyes.

"You are mine. I've never had anything that is mine until you, and I do not fucking plan on losing that. But more importantly, Delilah—" He pulls out and slams back in, and my eyes drift shut at the deliciousness of it. His hand tightens in my hair again until I open my eyes. "Most importantly, I am fucking yours. Yours and only yours." Again, he pulls out and thrusts in brutally. "Do—" *Thrust.* "You—" *Thrust.* "Fucking—" *Thrust.* "Understand me?" he says, then he continues his assault on my body, the pleasure ratcheting up, his face moving to my neck, licking and biting. Leaving a mark, I'm sure. "I am so fucking crazy for you. I would tear down my entire family, burn it to the ground if you asked me to, Lilah. You don't get it." His hand releases my hair and the arm wraps around my waist as the other drifts to my hip, moving in until his thumb gently lands on my clit, and I moan.

"You don't get it. I can't breathe. I can't function. Every move I make is on your chess board. You are my queen." The pressure on my clit increases, and the pleasure in my belly starts to curl in on itself as I move, wrapping my legs around him because I need him closer. My hand slides up to his neck, wrapping around the back, holding him, and something changes in me.

The anger and frustration melts as I look into his eyes because gone is the joking. Gone is the teasing and the smiles.

It's panic. It's all-consuming regret. It's so much more than fucking your secret lover on a desk to appease her because she's mad she couldn't be the one on your arm last night.

In there is a man desperate to make me understand how much I mean to him. In all sincerity, I see clearly how much his secret kills him, and how honest the words he's speaking are.

He can't breathe or function without me.

He is crazy for me.

He would burn his world down and let me use the ashes to make diamonds for my crown.

"Dante," I whisper, but that's all I need to say.

"Yeah, baby," he says back, and then his lips are on mine, and his thumb presses down, and I come, my arms and legs tightening as I do, his groan muffled by my lips, dragging another jolt from me as he follows me over the edge.

And just like that, we're on the same page.

"What's gonna happen with that guy?" I ask, kicking my legs on his desk. Dante has cleaned me up, redressed me, and then came back with a drink. He told me I wasn't allowed to leave his office until I lost the smile "that you always get when I fuck you good," but I like to think he just wanted to steal some extra time with me.

Not that I'm complaining.

"What guy?"

"The one in here before. Bad combover?"

"Marco handled him. I would have, but you had that look in your eyes like you wanted to set me on fire, and you needed me more." I pause, waiting a long moment and trying to decide if I should tell him what flitted in my mind just now, remembering the look on his face.

"That was hot, you know."

"What?"

"You defending my honor. Making a grown man shit his pants because he called me a nasty name."

"That's my job, Delilah."

"Yeah, I know. Big bad mafia boss in training, gotta keep everyone in line." He smiles and shakes his head, walking over to me and stepping between my legs.

"No, my job is to defend you. But also, meant to talk to you about that. When shit is going down, Lilah, you do not peek around Marco's fucking shoulder to watch when he's covering you, for the love of God."

"I was fine. Nothing was going to happen," I say, my hand moving the hunk of hair from his forehead. His hands go to my cheeks, pulling me in and pressing a soft kiss to my lips.

"You'll put me in an early grave, yeah? Please. Things ever get crazy, I need to know you're safe."

"I'm safe, Dante."

"Do you know how to protect yourself if something goes down?" I open my mouth, and he cuts me off. "For real. Against real people trying to hurt you. I'm not talking about that shield you have up, Lilah. Not talking about your sharp tongue. If someone were to come for you, do you know how to defend yourself?" I scrunch my nose, knowing he won't like the answer I have.

"I'll take a kickboxing class or something."

"Do you know how to shoot a gun?"

"My dad hates guns," I say, and Dante laughs out loud. "What? He does. It was one of the platforms he ran on."

"Your father got himself so deep in illegal betting that he tried to sell out his daughter." I blink a few times, unable to answer because he's not wrong.

Then I laugh because, again, he's not wrong.

"I'll take you to a range."

"A date?" I say, and I can't fight the smile on my face. *A date with Dante.*

He smiles, but the look doesn't reach his eyes.

"A quiet one," he says. "Just us." A hint of the excitement drops out. "Soon, Lilah. Soon I'll stand in front of everyone and anyone and tell them that you're mine, that if they even look at you sideways, I'm coming for them."

"And if someone looks at *you* sideways, I'll come for *them*," I say, and he smiles.

"I don't doubt it, *fiorella*. But until then . . . "

His words trail off, but he doesn't have to finish them.

Until then, we love in secrecy.

And I fucking hate it.

THIRTY-FIVE

-Lilah-

Early the next morning, there's a knock on my bedroom door.

It wakes me, and instantly, I turn to what I've decided is Dante's side of the bed, only to see it empty, that body pillow I always wake up with still smelling like his cologne.

"Princess, you up?" Marco asks, and my brows furrow in confusion. Rolling out of bed, I grab my robe as I check the time, confused to see it's 7 am.

Tying the robe, I undo the locks and open the door to see Marco standing there, hands in his pockets.

When we're at the compound, he doesn't wear the glasses.

Marco has lovely, kind eyes.

"What's wrong?" I ask, panicked.

There's no reason for Marco to be waking me up at seven on a Sunday.

"Get dressed. Going out."

"Going out?" I ask, confused.

"Errands. Get dressed. Something warm."

"Warm?"

"How does Dante do it?" he mumbles, and I can't help but smile despite my grogginess.

"I'm usually caffeinated, which helps."

"Get going quick, and we'll stop for coffee." I smile and nod.

"On it. Quick. Dress warm." Marco nods, and then I get ready for . . . an adventure.

Less than an hour later, coffee in hand, Marco pulls up to a cabin after driving through windy roads.

"What are we doing here?" I ask, looking out the window.

But before Marco can answer, a figure walks out of the little cabin door, a smile on his face.

Dante.

Our date.

The doors click, unlocking, and my hand is fumbling with the handle almost instantly, opening it, and then I run, meeting Dante halfway where he catches me and spins me as his lips press to mine.

You'd think I haven't seen the man in months, rather than hours.

"You're good, Marco," Dante says over my shoulder as my legs loop around his hips, and I can see it from where I am, even so close to his face. His head goes into my neck, warmth blooming there as he murmurs, "Missed you."

He has the world's biggest smile. He feels it too. That inexplicable joy when we're together without the eyes, without the hiding.

"Three hours?" I hear Marco's deep voice ask, and then Dante's head nods before he presses his lips to my forehead and turns, walking us away from him. I wave at the big man with a goofy smile on my face, and he shakes his head, giving me a wave before getting into the blacked-out car and driving off.

"What are we doing here?" I ask, his hands moving to my ass to extricate me from him, planting my feet on the ground and grabbing my face before kissing me like he missed me more than air itself. When he breaks the kiss, I smile at him dazedly. Finally, he takes my hand, leading me around the cabin to the back. "Working on your protection."

"What?"

But then I see it—behind the cabin is a small shooting range.

"My protection?"

"You know how to shoot a gun?" he asks, and I shake my head "no."

"Don't I need like, a license for that or something?" I ask as we approach the area. He looks at me with a smile.

"Baby, I think sometimes you forget who I am." On top of a wooden shelf is a handgun.

"Got it. No licenses." He takes a pair of earmuffs and puts them on my head, then puts a set on his.

"No way to track a bullet back to who purchased it," he says, lifting the gun. His words travel through some unseen microphone right to my ears, and I widen my eyes but decide not to ask any more questions. He proceeds to show me the gun, where the bullets go, how to turn on the safety, how to know it's loaded, and finally, how to shoot it. About ten feet before us is a paper man target thingy that Dante aims at before shooting, hitting the man right between the eyes.

"Impressive," I say with a smile, and he smiles back. "Why do I need to learn if I've got you?"

"Want you safe. Don't worry, you'll get there, *fiorella*," he says, then he moves so my back lines up with his front, his hands grabbing mine until we're both holding the heavy metal gun.

"It's a lot heavier than I would have thought," I say.

"That's why we're practicing. If you need to grab a gun and protect yourself, I don't want you surprised by little things."

Having the weapon in my hands reminds me how crazy this all is.

"Are you sure I need to be doing this?" I ask as he positions my fingers where they need to be.

"You want to rule by my side?" he asks, pressing his lips to the spot under my ear that gives me chills. I don't answer, unsure of *how* to answer. "Then I need to know you know how to protect yourself." His tongue moves, flicking out to lick my skin there, the cool air an erotic chaser to the hot move.

"Hand here, finger there," he says as he finishes positioning my hands. "Then look down the barrel and aim. When you pull the trigger, there will be some kickback. I'll help counter it, but know without me, it's more," he says.

"Got it."

"Now aim and pull the trigger, baby," he says, and I do, shocking myself with the way it vibrates my cold hands. "That's it, great job."

"I didn't even hit the paper, Dante," I say with a laugh.

"You're learning. Try again." His hands move to my hips, letting me aim on my own without him, and this time, I actually nick the edge of it.

"Good girl," he says in my ear, the sound reverberating through my body. "Again."

I do as he asks, my body on high alert with his voice, and this time, I get a shoulder.

"Again. Look down the gun, and aim it exactly where you want to hit," he says and I do, pulling the trigger and watching the paper man shake a bit.

"Gut shot. You hit a man there, not a great shot of him making it without a hospital trip." His lips press to my neck, right under where the bulky earmuffs stop. "Again."

I get a knee and he laughs.

"Definitely a mob princess, going for the knee caps. You hit there, they can't come after you, but they can still shoot. Gotta decide if you want to run or finish the job." He says it with such ease, like *finishing the job* is nothing more than a simple fact.

I guess in this world, it is.

"Again, Lilah."

This goes on for nearly fifteen minutes before Dante stops, changing out the paper man riddled with holes with a fresh one before coming back, taking his place behind me once again.

"Again," he says, his hands sliding up my hips.

"Dante, what are you doing?" I ask as his hand moves up the thermal shirt I'm wearing. Calluses grip my skin, scraping as he dips under my soft bra until his hand is cupping my breast. His back is pressed to mine, his breath in my ear.

"Distracting you." His thumb and forefinger twist my nipple, and a bolt of heat runs through me. I start to lower the gun, unable to even steady my hands. "No, no, stop. Aim and shoot, *fiorella*."

"Dante, that's—"

"Shoot the gun, Delilah." With the earmuffs, his voice is right in my ears, a hidden microphone carrying words to me, the only thing I can hear, all-consuming. "Now." His finger tightens on my nipple as I pull the trigger, attempting uselessly to hit the center, and I miss terribly.

He tsks me, the sound patronizing but also somehow seductive.

His other hand moves down my belly, down, down until his thumb settles under the waistband, his hand pressing until my hips move to align with his where his cock is hard.

"Dante—" I breathe. "What are you doing?"

"Distracting you. Now aim and shoot. Don't miss this time, yeah?"

"Why are you distracting me? I have a fucking gun in my hand."

"Because when you have a gun in your hand, you have to be able to aim no matter what's happening around you." The hand moves, fully dipping under my sweats and underwear until he's cupping my sex. "Or to you, in this case."

"Dante—"

"Hit the target and you get a reward, baby. Shoot."

Okay, well, that sounds like a fair reward system. His hands are just resting on my body now, unmoving, so I focus on the gun, the target, and shoot.

It hits the little paper guy's leg.

"Better," he coos, rubbing my nipple again, a single finger running up my center and gathering the wet that's already there. "Getting better. Again." He circles my clit, and my hips jolt back into his, a soft moan falling from my lips.

His finger pauses, not moving, just hovering on my clit.

He wants me to shoot.

I stare down the barrel, not thinking about his hand in my pants or the one clamping on my nipple and aim before pulling the trigger.

A shoulder.

"Good girl," he whispers, the mic picking up the words and bringing them to my ears. It's unbearably erotic like this, trying to focus on one thing and having his words so concentrated and direct in my ear. A finger moves now, entering me, and my knees go weak at the simple touch. His breath gets heavier, the sound fully surrounding me. "Uh uh. Stand strong, baby. You've got this. God, you're wet for me, aren't you?" I lick my lips, trying to force my eyes to open fully. He slowly fucks me with one thick finger, his thumb swiping methodically on my clit as his other hand cups my breast entirely. Need is consuming me, flames licking my skin. "Again."

His finger doesn't stop.

My mind won't think about anything but that finger slowly working me, gently pressing forward to graze my G-spot, slowly building a fire in my belly.

"Again, *fiorella*." He doesn't stop, and I realize this is his game. Tease me, play with me, make me squirm. "As soon as you get the center, you come on my hand, yeah?" he asks as if he knows my thoughts.

God, at this point, he probably does.

What I would give to know his, the twist and turns.

"Dante—" I breathe, bucking my hips to get more of . . . anything.

"Shoot, baby," he says and doesn't stop like I expect. Instead, he pulls out and inserts a second finger. I moan loud now and pray that when he said the place was empty, he meant it. "Now," he says then slams his fingers near violently.

"Shit!" I shout, the feeling pulsing through me but still, I obey, aiming and shooting.

The other shoulder gets a hole.

"Focus, baby. Be my good girl. Show me you can handle this," he says, his fingers continuing their hard thrusts as he rolls my nipple harder. He's upping the stakes. "You said you can protect yourself. I believe you. But I also want to equip you. If something ever happened to you, I'd burn down the world. I need to know that while I'm setting it ablaze, you can take care of yourself."

Something about that snaps something in me, makes me want to do this, to get that bullseye, that kill.

Not for me, but for him.

So I shut the mental door between my focus and my pleasure, and I aim.

And right before I pull the trigger, he slams in a third finger.

"Fuck!" I scream, grinding down and trying to come, but those fingers are stagnant, unmoving.

"Uh uh. You missed, baby. You need to concentrate."

"You cheated!" I whine, bucking my hips, but he doesn't budge.

"There is nothing fair about the war we're about to fight, Delilah. No one will care about the rules or cheating or playing nice." His fingers slowly move out and then in. "Now be my fucking queen and kill him for me. Then scream my name," he says in a growl, and though I can't see him, I know his teeth are gritted. "Once you come, you put that gun down, you get on your knees, and you suck my cock." I moan again at the mental image, at the promise in his words.

It's never been my thing, but with him?

I aim.

I look down the barrel, trying to ignore my swollen pussy, the way his palm is now grinding on my clit, the way I'm inadvertently riding his thick fingers, the way he's breathing in surround sound.

My finger holds the trigger, and I breathe in deep, eyes on my target.

And then I pull.

"Hold it steady while your man makes you come," he says in a proud whisper, and I see the single hole in the forehead of the paper man. His fingers drive up, hand grinding on my clit, my hips bucking, but I do as he asks, continuing to aim.

"You're so fucking beautiful. My beautiful killer. So fucking strong. An honor to have you by my side, to have you with me as we tear this world apart and rebuild it to our liking." I moan, clamping down. "That's it, baby, you come for me. Come on my fingers," he says, and I do, screaming out his name one more time, my head tipping back and my finger pulling the trigger once more as I come.

And come.

And *come*.

My body starts to quake, shaking against him, my knees weak.

"Fucking gorgeous, That's it, take what you need, baby," he says, and I ride his fingers to another orgasm, his hand on my breast wreaking havoc as it roughly pinches and pulls my nipple.

I feel strong.

I feel beautiful.

I feel unbreakable.

And in a way, I feel protected—not from something, but by something.

Myself.

Protected by me. And this man gave me the ability, the chance to take my safety and protection into my own hands for the first time in my life, to wield it like a strength rather than a curse.

And as I come down, I hear him in the headphones, my eyes still closed as the pleasure moves in waves through my body, pulsing.

"Holy fuck, you hit the heart," he says, and I think for a second he means him. I've hit the heart of him.

But as my eyes open, as light filters in and I start to see, I look at the paper range guy moving gently with the wind and see it.

Dead center.

A hole in his heart.

Bullseye.

THIRTY-SIX

-Lilah-

A week later I'm in the girls' break room before the next shift swaps in, filling snacks and adding toiletries, when there's another presence behind me.

"Hey, sorry, just refilling—" I start, thinking it's one of the girls, but instead, Paulie is standing against the wall, arms crossed on his chest.

He's wearing an outfit similar to what Dante wears, the seeming uniform of the Carluccio men and their soldiers: a solid button-down shirt with the top few buttons undone, a thin gold chain with some kind of pendant hiding right beneath. The sleeves are rolled up, making the business slacks and elegant, shining shoes seem almost casual.

But there's nothing casual about the way Paulie is staring at me.

There's nothing casual about the way he's in the girls' dressing room, where no men are allowed.

"Paulie," I say, trying to get my thoughts to work, my mind to work. "What are you doing in here?" I put the box filled with individually packaged snacks down on the counter and turn to face him.

I refuse to show fear.

Refuse to let him see past the stone walls of my fortress.

The fortress I was put in for my own safety is now the one I stay behind to hide from the world.

Stone walls are coated in diamonds created by pressure.

He looks at his nails, inspecting them as if he doesn't get them buffed and trimmed weekly by a manicurist. But then his eyes move up, zeroing in on me, and there is *venom* there.

The man is sick. He is greedy and hungry, and I have to wonder if he knows that I'm somehow in the way of him getting what he wants.

"You're spending a lot of time with my uncle," he says, and then his eyes, those venomous, hate-filled eyes, roam my body in a way that makes my skin feel dirty.

In a way that makes me want to vomit.

"He's really fucking up my plan," he continues.

"I don't know what you're talking about," I say, every moment of training snapping into place. Moments of being the pretty, quiet daughter, the one who smiles and lets my sister or my father talk. The one who is to look gorgeous and shut up, not draw too much attention for fear of the world finding out who I really am.

What I really am.

"But you really shouldn't be in here, Paulie. It's the girls' safe space, and Dante wants us to keep it that way."

Mistake number one: mentioning his uncle.

Though lately, I've been wondering if mistake number one was walking into this club in that red dress that spoke volumes and making that deal with the devil.

With the name, the fire flares in Paulie's eyes, and he pushes off the wall he was leaning against, taking one step toward me. The corridor is narrow, with barely enough room for two people to walk side by side, so the single step closes the gap between us quickly.

I step back, trying to avoid him, but my ass bumps into the counter where we keep the snacks.

"I don't give a fuck about what my uncle wants. His fucking morals, stupid fucking safe spaces." He glances down the hall and then the other way, like he's looking to see if anyone will catch him in the act.

But in the act of what? I think, my pulse racing.

It's then, I understand.

Paulie Carluccio is dangerous. Not the kind of dangerous you might expect, where he's in an organized crime family happily and is willing to do whatever it takes to uphold that standard.

But in the way that he'll do whatever it takes to get what he wants.

And right now, I worry that *what he wants* is me.

"Fucking Dante, fucking up my plan," he says under his breath, and that fire has shifted, changed, and now the look in his eyes is *unhinged*. Crazy. "Always getting in the way. It can't be him, Lilah. In the end, it will be me. It would do you well to remember that." The blood in my veins goes cold.

He doesn't know who you are, fiorella.

Dante's words are a small condolence, a comfort, but truly, nothing about where I am right now is *comfortable*.

His hand moves, tipping my chin up with a finger in a move so similar to what his uncle loves to do, but it feels so incredibly different. The hand is too smooth, too cold, and makes me nauseous.

"We could be good, you and I."

"Paulie—"

"What's going on with you two? You and my uncle?"

"Nothing," I blurt quickly. *Too fucking quickly.* I continue to talk to cover myself. "Nothing, Paulie. I'm working for him. Taking care of the girls. Paying off my dad's debts. You know the deal," I say, trying to remind him of why I got here in the first place.

Bad move.

His eyes go cold.

"You know, when you first came here, I had plans. Plans to use you to prove myself. You're a pretty thing, Lilah, got the sex appeal and that body, but you're a terrible stripper. But I knew if I waited, got the word out quietly, men would come. The right men." The finger moves hair behind my ear, and the trailing sensation of his touch is like that feeling when you think a spider is crawling on you. I fight the urge to swat at it, letting the feeling seep into my bones.

"Paulie, I don't think—"

"There are men who would pay a pretty penny to fuck a mayor's daughter, Delilah Turner."

I stop breathing.

The words ricochet in my head, piercing me as they do, tiny pinpricks of pain.

There are men who would pay a pretty penny to fuck a mayor's daughter, Delilah Turner.

Either he doesn't notice my shock or he doesn't care because he keeps speaking.

"Do you know my uncle and I are in a quiet battle, vying to be next in line? It was supposed to be my father, but he didn't make it that far. My grandfather loves it, us giving him new ideas to grow the family business, to bring in more money, more notoriety. You were my bargaining chip. I was going to use you as a proof of concept, seal my fate as Don when the old man passes."

He doesn't have to explain further for me to understand. The hints Dante has told me, the parts of his plan he refuses to share—the puzzle isn't complete, but it's making more sense.

Dante told me that Paulie couldn't get too interested in me. That it would be dangerous.

It makes sense now.

"Dante fucked that plan, took you off the pole, then off the floor, took you as his own." He's so close to me now, I can feel his breaths against my face.

They're laced with the smell of liquor.

He's drunk.

That's why he's so brave, why he's spilling everything.

"He promised me more in exchange, told me to wait. Said he had a plan we'd both be happy with." His hand moves down my bare arm, and it takes everything in me not to cringe.

This man could hurt me.

This man *would* hurt me, no questions asked.

I need to play it smart, drag out the time until one of the girls walks in and interrupts. They can go get someone, or maybe the spell will be broken.

"The problem is, I'm getting impatient. Seeing you walking around every day in those heels, those curves that should have been mine. I would have had a test drive before renting you out, of course." He licks his lips, and my stomach roils. "Maybe I should take my chance now, taste you. Let my uncle know I'm getting bored waiting."

"Paulie, I—" I start, trying anything I can to stop him, to stop this before it starts, but it's no use. His hand goes to the back of my neck, and he pulls me in, pressing his lips to mine harshly.

It's not the mix of pleasure and pain I feel when Dante kisses me like this, like he can't wait for another second, like he wants to devour me. Instead, it's just pain and sour and horror. His hand moves into my hair, and he groans, grinding himself into me.

And when I feel he's hard, that's when the panic takes over.

But as I'm lifting my arms to push, I hit air.

Paulie is gone.

He's held against a wall by Marco, Roddy right behind him.

"Come the fuck on!" Paulie shouts. "I just wanted a taste, see what my uncle is hiding away from me."

"You know you can't touch her, Paulie. You have a deal," Marco says.

"A deal?" I ask, but I know no one is listening to me. It's like I'm not even here.

"He's not fucking her, so one of us might as well be. So busy with Angela, thanks to *me*, by the way." He's nearly spitting in Marco's face.

"None of my business, none of yours. Right now, you're in his business, touching his property."

His property.

"I'm not—" I start because, despite the panic that was taking over me moments ago, anger boils at the thoughts of being someone's *property*. But all words stop in my throat as Marco's normally kind, joking eyes dart toward mine and shoot daggers.

I stop.

"She *was my* property."

"You brought her into his business. Makes her his." Paulie laughs a viscous, evil laugh.

"God, you're all such fucking losers. I can't wait until I'm in charge and you all have to fucking lick my boots the way you do his. Get fucking ready, boys, because when Carmine falls, I'll be standing at the top."

Marco just shakes his head.

"You need to go home, man. Sleep it off. I'll be talking to Dante—"

"Does he have you on bodyguard duty, keeping her precious little cunt pure?" Paulie asks, cutting off Marco, and again, the world stops.

Marco is not my bodyguard.

I don't *need* a bodyguard.

Marco and I are friends. We joke together, we eat meals together, and we—

Marco looks my way, and instead of the kindness, instead of daggers, there's an apology there.

"God, he did, didn't he? What a fucking idiot, protecting snatch like it's made of gold."

"Roddy, get him to his driver, make sure he gets *in the fucking car*," Marco says, pushing Paulie to his coworker. He reaches into his pocket, sending a text to someone. "Tino will be right outside and waiting to help."

"Got it," Roddy says in his gruff, no-nonsense tone, leading Paulie out.

"Fuck you guys. This is bullshit."

"Talk to Dante about it, Paulie, not me, not Lilah," Marco says, moving toward me. As Roddy opens the door with Paulie in tow, there's a scuffle, but then I hear Tino's voice, and they must have it covered because the door slams behind them, and Marco doesn't look back.

"Are you okay?" he asks, looking me over, standing a respectable distance from me. I'm still pressed with my ass to the counter near painfully, as I continued to try and move back to get away from Paulie, but I'm frozen, unable to move. "Did he touch you?" he asks, but he knows that answer. He walked in on it, so he changes his question. "Did he hurt you?" I shake my head.

The worry clears a fraction.

"Let's get you out of here," he says, gently touching my elbow and leading me away.

"The snacks—"

"Martha's got it." I nod because Martha can handle refilling snacks and hair products, of course.

"I have to call Dante, have to—"

"No," I say, my voice strong. "No. Don't call him."

"Lilah, I have—"

"Are you my bodyguard?"

Marco's face freezes out any sort of emotion or tell, and his body stills.

"You are, aren't you. Dante assigned you?" No response, just that blank face.

It's strange seeing him, seeing who I thought was a friend just because we worked alongside each other, not because he was assigned to fake it, have this blank, mafia-man face on.

He's just like the others.

"When?" I ask.

"Let's get you to Dante."

"Oh, I'll be talking to him. Right now, I'm talking to you, Marco," I say, my voice firm, my shoulders moving back.

In that moment, I remember who I am.

I remember my goals.

I remember my mission.

I am not Shane Turner's daughter, victim of gambling addictions and poor choices.

I'm not Dante Carluccio's woman who needs protecting.

I am Delilah Turner, daughter of Arturo Russo. The man my mother secretly loved with all her heart.

I was born out of determination and true love.

I was born to rule, to be a queen, not a beautiful jewel to be kept safe.

I will take my place at the head of the Russo family when the time is right and when I do, I will demolish the Carluccio family as it's known now, whether Dante wants to help or not.

I am not a princess to be hidden in an ivory tower.

I am a queen in a fortress, aiming, waiting until my target comes close enough.

"Your first day."

My first day.

"My first day working for Dante?" I ask, staring at Marco and pretending to believe that is the case. Pretending I don't understand what he means.

My own version of protecting myself.

But his eyes say everything.

"Your first day at Jerzy Girls."

I roll my lips together at the betrayal, my single tell, before I nod and stand tall.

"Take me to Dante," I say, and Marco nods, reaching for his phone. "Take me to Dante, Marco. Do not call him. Take me to him," I say, and Marco sighs.

"Lilah—"

There are no cameras in the girls' room. I remember Dante telling me this, that the entire building is wired and monitored, but here isn't.

That means no ears.

"You know who I am. You know what I am to him. You know what the plan is. That means you know who I am to you." The power weaves through my words. Power I didn't realize I was already ready to wield.

Aching to wield.

The look in Marco's eyes tells me everything I need to know.

It shocks him too.

But I'm right—he knows it.

And just when I think he'll argue, that he'll tell me he works for and answers to Dante and Dante alone, he sighs, slipping his phone back in his pocket and moving a hand to the spot between my shoulder blades.

"Let's go, princess," he says, and it takes everything in me not to let the cat smile reach my lips.

THIRTY-SEVEN

-Lilah-

I don't have to worry about hiding that smile as we pull up in front of the Carluccio complex, the blacked-out windows of the town car making the gigantic home look Gothic and daunting. The entirety of the ten-minute drive was spent thinking about the thousands of times I told Dante I didn't need protecting and the thousands of times he agreed.

The times I told him how shitty my family keeping secrets from me had made me feel, the times I told him I was tired of hiding away, protected from reality.

And the *millions* of times he'd mention his plan without elaborating.

Paulie wanted to sell me to the highest bidder, my mind tells me, unscrambling the drunken words he'd said in that hallway.

The car stops at the front, and I know Marco wants me to wait.

He wants to open the door for me, to walk me up the front stairs, to probably follow me to wherever the fuck Dante is and make sure I don't rip his head off.

He probably feels guilty, since he thinks I'm most mad that he is not my friend but my bodyguard.

And yeah, that part stings, knowing I felt like I had one person who liked me in this crazy fucking family, one person who saw me as a human being instead of an asset or a puzzle piece.

Until a few hours ago, I thought Dante felt that way, that he saw me as an equal, that we were working toward the same end goal—no matter how secretively. But more and more, it seems like I'm in the same protective state I fled months ago, just with a different handler.

So instead of waiting, I open the door and walk up the stairs.

"Jesus, Lilah!" Marco yells, standing beside the car, clearly unsure what to do.

"Go away, Marco. Go make sure Roddy and the girls are good," I say, giving orders as if it's my place.

"I gotta ask Dante, princess, you know that." I'm looking over my shoulder at him, reaching for the front door when his eyes go wide, and even though I'm not looking, I know.

I know he's there right in front of me, that electricity snapping in the air between us.

I look at him, and his eyes are on the man behind me.

My fucking bodyguard.

"You're good, Marco. Go," he says, and then a door slams, and Marco drives off.

Then I'm looking up at Dante, hands on my hips, fuming as his eyes watch the car leave. Standing in the entryway, he's an extra six inches taller than me, and I feel small.

I *hate* feeling small.

Small makes you feel like there's a reason people are protecting you.

Fuck that.

I walk past him into the house.

"You're home early," he says, and the door shuts behind me, the lock snicking in a way that feels final.

"A bodyguard?" I ask, venom in my words.

I could elaborate.

I almost do.

But there's a moment—a millisecond—where Dante's eyes register shock.

It's gone before I can even decide if it's real.

"Marco is not your bodyguard, Delilah."

"Don't lie. He told me. I know."

"Not in the sense you think," he continues as if I didn't even speak. "Marco was to keep you as his main priority while at the club. You're beautiful, Lilah. Any man sees you, he's drawn to you, but you're mine. I don't want anyone to touch what's mine."

"I don't need a bodyguard."

And then something clicks in his mind. It happens and I realize instantly I lost the edge in this argument. Any high ground I had starting out is gone as Dante realizes that I wouldn't know I *had* a bodyguard if there wasn't a reason for me to find out.

"What happened?" he asks, his eyes boring into mine.

Now I'm at a crux.

I could admit what happened and that I needed Marco.

Or I could deny it, and he'll find out what happened anyway because Marco is nothing if not loyal to Dante.

So instead, I use the information I acquired to try and get more.

"Paulie wanted to sell me?"

Wrong choice.

Wrong *fucking choice*.

"Paulie?" he asks, and I don't answer. "What did Paulie say?" His voice is dangerous, and the way it sounds, I sure as fuck wouldn't want to be Paulie right now.

But honestly, I wouldn't want to be *Dante* right now when this anger is burning in me.

"Not much because my *bodyguard* stepped in."

"Well, it's a good thing you had one, isn't it?" he says, crossing his arms on his chest. There's a small smile on his face, a smirk, but it doesn't hide the fury and anger burning underneath.

Good.

Because I'm fucking furious as well.

I stand, staring at him, trying to decide how or if to respond, how not to scream at him and scratch his eyeballs out, which is what I really want to do right now.

"Obviously, there was a good reason to give you a bodyguard, Delilah."

"You could have talked to me about it."

"And what, had you pissed off at me and trying to find ways to sneak around it just to prove a point?" I kind of hate that he's not wrong.

"It doesn't matter! I should have known! You could have told me what Paulie was planning, that there was something—"

"I know who you are, Delilah Turner," he says, and something about his words makes me stop. They mean . . . more. I poke my tongue out, licking my lips. "I know who you are and not because my dumb-as-nails nephew told me a mayor's daughter was working at the club." He steps closer to me, forcing me to tip my chin up to look at him.

What does he know?

How much does he know?

We both live in this chaotic web of lies and half-truths, and now we're trying to figure out which threads will strangle us.

He knows I'm Shane's daughter. Knows I came not just to settle a debt, but to try and take down his family for what they did to my sister. He's on board, allegedly, and working his own mission alongside me.

His mission to clean up the family and beat Paulie to the head.

But he doesn't know . . .

His hand goes up into my hair, holding me there so I can't break his gaze. "You are the granddaughter of Alfredo Russo. Turner shouldn't be your last name, but that doesn't matter. We'll be changing that soon enough."

I open my mouth to speak, but nothing comes out. His hand

tightens in my hair, strangely bringing me back down to earth, adding some surety to my footing.

"*I know who you are*, Delilah Russo." Blood drains from my face.

I play it off, of course.

I was trained for this moment, raised for it, to combat any bad press with a sweet smile. I keep my face neutral, my body already knowing how to control my breaths, but that facade can't last long, not when he's looking at me like this, spilling secrets and revealing everything.

"Paulie, he doesn't know. He's too stupid to keep his ears open, keep his eyes open. He's so fucking lost on trying to win over Carmine, trying to beat me, that he can't see what's in front of him. A woman who isn't here to settle debts. A woman who is here to tear him down." My pulse races, my stomach sick. I want to step back, to run, anything, but that hand in my hair holds tight, keeping my face staring at his, which is dark and serious.

Maybe I was right.

Maybe he's going to kill me.

"Drop that look, baby."

"What do you want from me?" I ask with a whisper.

"I want that scared look off your face. I want my sweet, strong girl." I don't respond.

I stare into his eyes, hard and soft at the same time, the brown that I could stare at for days no longer just that sweet, comforting shade.

"You're here to take us down. And you're doing it not just to get revenge, but so you can head your own family."

The words spin in my mind, circling around me.

I don't dare open my mouth, gnawing on the inside of my lip.

My mind reels as I try to think of a way to spin this, how to save myself, save my mission.

But Dante already knows what he wants to say.

"You told me in your apartment you want to take your throne. You want to become head of the Russos?" I lick my lips. "But you need to prove yourself first, yeah?" The fingers in my hair loosen then gently scrape against my scalp, a slow, pleasurable movement that you do to someone you're just lying in bed with. A comfort, a casual, easy move when there's nothing crazy happening.

Not something you do to someone you've been fucking, knowing they want to take down your family and are the enemy.

"Johnny killed your father. Tony made the call, told him to do it. Fucking idiot, so caught up in his own shit, his ego too big, wanted your mother too bad. Years later, my family let your father get in deep and then went after your sister. You want revenge."

Breathing is impossible.

"Your mother wasn't able to follow her heart. She couldn't marry Arturo because she was supposed to marry my brother."

How does he know so fucking much?

"You didn't know until recently. Until that *strunzo* Johnny Vitale tried to kidnap your sister, make you his bride, rise to power."

"How do you—"

"You'll learn soon, *fiorella*, that if you ask the right people, pay the right people, there is not a single piece of information on this earth that can't be yours. You just have to know who to ask and what they need in exchange to give it."

I don't speak.

Dante doesn't speak.

So many sentences start and stop in my mind. Conversations, roads to take, denials.

But what's the point? Eventually, the truth will come out.

But why now?

And why hasn't he exposed me sooner?

"Okay, so you know who I am. Why haven't you told Paulie?"

"Because if Paulie finds out who you are, he'll want you for himself. And if Paulie knows who you are, my plan will be useless."

He runs a single, thick finger down my chin, pressing at the spot where it meets my neck, where a small nick could kill me in mere moments.

He thrills me.

Strangely, this terrifying man absolutely *thrills* me.

"I told you I'd make you queen—you thought I meant just at my side." The air freezes as I understand every hidden meaning he's ever said. "You'll be a queen in your own right. We'll change the world together, my love." My pulse pounds in my ears. "Paulie can't know who you are—if he does, he'll be too interested. He'll see the potential you have, the power you hold. He'll go batshit, just like Johnny did."

"So, what? You're playing some secret kind of game on my behalf? But never once told me the full story?"

"I have a plan to give you what you want."

"What do you know about what I want, Dante? All you do is go off and make decisions for me, keep me out of things, play complex games, and refuse to even tell me the rules."

"You want to rule the Russos." I open my mouth to argue but his hand tightens in my hair, silencing me. "I can read you better than you know. I'm going to give you everything you want, everything you could ever dream of. We're going to do it side by side, but you need to trust me."

"I barely know you! All I know is lies and plans and secrets."

"But you can trust me. You know that. This? It's bigger than your father and my family. It's about us. There is something here, Delilah. There has been since the beginning. But since the beginning, there has been danger at your goddamn tail, nipping at your heels." His hand moves to my face and brushes a lock of hair behind my ear so tenderly, I nearly give in. "That's why you have Marco, Lilah. You walked in, and I knew who you were. I knew you were fucking trouble, but the kind of trouble I like a fuckuva lot. But I also know my nephew. He's power-hungry. Paulie . . . Carmine and I decided it would be best not to clue him in."

"Carmine knows who I am?"

"Carmine knows all, same as me."

"So *he* knows your plans?" Dante sighs.

"His only weakness is me. I'm his blind spot. The son who

never lived up to his potential. The consolation prize when my mother was killed, and runner-up once his first choice for heir was gone."

"So Carmine knows about me, but not your plan? Paulie would want to use me to strengthen ties. You said Carmine is just as power-hungry. Why isn't he trying to use me?" He doesn't say anything and I scoff. "Let me guess, you still think he's all rainbows and butterflies, don't you?"

I pause, but I can see it in his eyes. The regret. God. I hate this. I hate that these selfish assholes have put us into this position. Put their pasts, their misdeeds, their *greed* between us and made it our job to unravel.

"Delilah . . ."

"I have the proof, Dante." His face goes blank, that hand in my hair loosening. "I have the proof you need."

"Delilah—"

"You said if I had the proof your father was just as poisonous as the rest of them, you'd take him down, too."

"Baby—"

"Johnny Vitale sent me a letter from prison." Silence hangs in the air with my words before he speaks, a mix of shock and outrage.

"*What!?*"

"Johnny Vitale sent me a letter from prison. Man has nothing else to lose. I figure he just wanted to clear his conscience. Or maybe take everyone down with him. We all know that even if he doesn't get life, your father will make sure he gets *life*."

"What the *fuck,* Lilah?"

"Your father told your brother to put the hit on Arturo." The room goes silent. "Let the world think it was a bruised ego, but he saw the potential of me, Dante." I put a hand to his face and look in his eyes, trying to tell him everything I know down to my soul is true. "He conspired with Shane Turner."

The universe shakes as I admit what I haven't said out loud.

"Seems Shane wasn't too keen on my mother leaving him for a

mafioso. Wasn't excited to tell the world that his youngest daughter wasn't his at all."

"Delilah, I know you want to make all of this make sense, want it to line up, but—" Despite the argument, there's a battle in his eyes. For some unknown reason, he feels loyalty to that man, but the image is cracking. It's becoming hard to justify the way he acts.

"In what world would I want my sister—who has sacrificed enough—to have no parents the way I do. In what world would I want to craft some kind of chaotic story in my mind where I need to tear him down and make her an orphan like me, because Dante—Shane's going down, too. Your father. Paulie sure as fuck is. I'm taking them all down, whether you help me or not. They need to pay."

"This isn't—"

"You're right. It isn't. It isn't a time for kid gloves anymore. It isn't time for plans and secrets. It's time to take action. They need to *pay, Dante*. For what they did. What they took from me. For what they *plan* to take. Your brother is an idiot who was greedy and had a big fuckin' ego, but he wasn't smart enough to come up with the idea himself."

"So what, Johnny Vitale spins some story and you believe it? About what? My father making marriage plans for a fucking newborn?" I stare at him and honest to God, I feel pity for the man.

I don't think a single soul in this universe has ever felt pity for Dante Carluccio, but here we are.

"Is it really that crazy? Set me up with Paulie, and you merge the families. Or maybe Johnny, like he thought, and then he'd have good standing with the family. Think about it, Dante. It makes sense. Fuck, they were willing to do it with a congressman. Imagine the power if they had a politician and the rival family who has turf they want?"

He doesn't speak for long moments that stretch for a lifetime.

He's either going to believe me or not.

He's either on my side or he's not.

"How can you believe him, Delilah? He tried to kill your sister.

He wanted to kidnap *you*."

"What does Johnny have to lose, Dante?" No answer. "He says there's proof. In your brother's things. Gave me all the details where to find it."

"In Tony's things? Those are all boxed up."

"Who has access to them, Dante?" I ask, but I know the answer.

I know the answer because Johnny told me, but it's confirmed on his face.

"Me." I raise an eyebrow. "And my father." His face looks resigned.

"They're going down whether you want it or not. This is bigger than you, bigger than us."

"Nothing is bigger than us, Lilah." I sigh, wanting so badly to believe him, but it's just not . . . true.

"We don't work," I say in a whisper, knowing *that is* the truth.

"The fuck we don't. We work in all the ways that matter, Lilah."

"It's bigger than that, and you know it. The world . . . is more than that."

"You love me, yeah?"

I stare at him in disbelief.

I can't believe he's pushing this now, of all times.

"Don't do this, Dante."

I have waited for weeks for this conversation. Some kind of confirmation that he feels the way I do, that the draw isn't just mental and physical but goes deeper. That what we are is more than obsession and sex.

And now, when the world I thought I understood is crumbling beneath me, he wants to do this.

"I am so fucking tied up in you that I won't let you go easy."

"There are things you don't know."

"Then tell me."

"I can't, Dante."

"Tell me. You want revenge, but there are other ways to get it. We both know that. What made you walk into Jerzy Girls and sell your soul to me? It wasn't just what happened with your sister. Help me understand."

How much do I tell him? I think to myself, the scales tipping tumultuously.

How do I explain to him it wasn't just Johnny?

That the deception, greed, and hunger go so much deeper?

How do I explain how I feel like it's my job to get retribution for *my entire family*? Some I've never even met. Some I didn't even know *existed* until two years ago.

"What made you come here?" he asks, hand to my throat. Gently, no pressure, but his eyes are begging me to tell him the truth. To drop the fabricated lies and admit it all.

Once and for all, to let it all out into the open.

"My sister. My mother. My father. Me."

"Explain. I need to know," he says, pressing into me more. His eyes are volatile, like he's on edge.

Like he knows that in the same way what happened with Paulie and then Marco changed how I saw things, what I'm about to tell him will change him.

"Dante, you're scaring me," I start, staring up at his black eyes demanding an answer.

Instantly, he moves his hand to my hair, the touch soft, and his face dips until he's nose to nose with me.

"You never fear me, Delilah. Ever. You fear the lives of anyone who puts their hands on you. You fear for the lives of anyone who gets in the way of what you want because I will cut them at their knees for even thinking it. But you never, ever fear me."

Somehow, I know he means that. I know it's the truth.

"Now, tell me everything," he says. But still...

"No." The word vibrates in the room.

"What?"

"I can't just tell you everything. I *won't*."

"Delilah, this isn't a game—"

"I can't give you more when you give me *absolutely nothing*." I stand straighter. "You want me to give you everything, lay it at your feet. You expect me to just say, *Yes Dante,* and do whatever you ask. You keep telling me to trust you." I lick my lips which feel inexplicably dry all of a sudden. "Tell me why? Why should I trust you when you tell me *nothing?*"

He stares at me, and it seems like time stops.

I wonder for a moment if this is it, if he'll say no. If the spell will be broken and we'll both see that this won't work. This could be the end.

Because I understand now, in my own way, that we're at an impasse. I need something to keep the scales balanced.

But then he speaks, and it changes everything.

"I almost gave up," he says, and my breathing stops. He's looking at me, but it's almost as if he's not *seeing* me. He's somewhere else, lost in some far off memory. "At some point, I realized he wasn't good. I'd spent... god. I've spent my entire life trying to see the good in him. My mom wanted that—for Tony and me to have a good father. *He's a good man, Dante.* She told me that a lot. I was young, but I remember that." His hand moves to my cheek, thumb brushing the skin there like a metronome.

In time with the rapid breaths I'm taking.

"In some way, it felt like if I saw the truth, if I admitted even to myself that he was bad, that things had gone too far and Carmine needed to be stopped, I was destroying her memory. It's stupid, but. . ."

I cut him off.

"No. It makes sense. I did the same. I saw the best in Shane because it's what my mom wanted." He gives me a small, sad smile.

"Two years ago, I was sitting outside a police station in Jersey City, ready to end it all." The world stops. "I had everything I needed. Recordings and notes and receipts. Names. Locations where bodies are buried. It was the only way I could think to stop the fucking poison that my family had become. The greed and the ambition started to hurt innocents. It wasn't . . . it wasn't what the family was supposed to be about. I was done." My hand moves, brushing the hunk of hair that falls onto his forehead back, and his face moves into my touch, like he needs it for comfort.

"I wasn't looking for WITSEC. I wasn't looking for immunity. I was willing to pay whatever I had to. I also know . . . once things started rolling, once things were brought to court, I probably would . . . I wouldn't be around long."

A suicide mission.

"I was okay with that."

He was willing to die to set things right.

Jesus Christ,

"Dante. . ." I say in a whisper, but he keeps speaking.

"So, I'm sitting on this bench, trying to get the courage to move my feet. I've got my head in my hands, elbows to my knees, and this little thing comes over and starts talking to me. Chatting my ear off." His hand moves to my hair, brushing it behind my shoulder and staring there, like he's seeing it differently. "You had these little flowers tied in your hair. *Fiorella.*"

The world stops spinning.

I stop breathing as it all comes back to me.

"Pretty sure you were drunk, but you just sat there and talked to me."

"It was Halloween," I whisper. "My friends and I were all dressed like princesses. I was Rapunzel." The man sitting there. He was wearing this black hoodie so I never got a good look at his face. And he's right. I sat there and just started babbling.

"I think somehow you knew," he says, ignoring how my world is exploding. "You knew what I needed even then. You said, 'Life is beautiful if you let it be, you know? Trust me on this. Trust me that it will be worth it.'"

"Dante-"

"I think you were sent to me. A promise. If I worked to fix it, to make things right, I'd get something as beautiful as you." His words are a whisper.

"Honey-"

"Two years. I spent two years looking for you. Your friend came over, you ran off with her. Do you know how many early 20s blondes there are in New Jersey?"

"A lot," I whisper.

Finally, he smiles.

"There's a lot. Marco thought I lost my damn mind. But then you just... fell into my lap." He leans forward and presses his lips to my cheek, and it's only then I realize I started crying at some point. "That's how you can trust me. Because I've been working for you for two years, before I even know who you were, what we were. I've been searching for you and trying to earn the reward that was you."

All this time, I have been terrified to trust this between us.

And never once did Dante.

Because all along, he knew.

"Then one day, Paulie is going on about the blonde he hired - a mayor's daughter. I was ready to tell him no, to just call it even with the shit from Johnny and then... and then I saw you in the footage. I fell in love with you in black and white and you brought color to my world. I paid to spend time with you because I needed to know if it was you. If you were everything my mind had dreamed up over two years."

I laugh a bit, knowing there is no way I did with my rebellion and constant frustration.

He grabs my chin and forces me to look at him. "You were. And so much fucking more. Never think anything less. Now, what made you come to Paulie, Lilah?"

And then I finally tell him everything, confident in what we are. Who we are. Who we've always been, apparently.

"My sister. My sister, because she did the heavy lifting for fifteen years and spent most of them breaking her back to keep me safe from a danger I was too up my own ass to know existed. I should have known. Should have seen it. But I ignored the signs and lived my life while she struggled. I came because I knew that even if Johnny was out of the picture, Shane wouldn't stop, Lola would still be on the line, and she deserves a beautiful life. So it was my turn to step in."

He looks at me as I stop breathing, gives a sharp, concise nod, then continues.

"I knew that already. Your mother?"

This gets trickier.

"Two years before the shit went down with Johnny, I found her journals." I've talked about this aloud one time and one time only, in a hospital room when my sister was being seen after nearly being kidnapped. Despite Lola asking me, despite the missed calls piling up from Shane, I never spoke about it again. Except for now.

"They went all the way back to when she was a teenager. She fell in love with Arturo Russo when she was 18. Wanted him more than anything. They snuck around and had an affair. When my grandfather found out, he threatened to ship her to boarding school for college. He had plans for her." I laugh an ugly laugh, not missing the parallels between my life and my mother's. "Her father wanted to build ties with the Carluccio family. She was to marry your brother."

I don't miss the slight widening of Dante's eyes and I wonder if he's just now seeing how similar our stories are. How history seems to be repeating itself in some kind of fucked up way.

"She didn't want to. He was in a rival family, after all." A small smile plays on my lips as I raise a brow to him, and he mimics the slight tilt of his lips with a tiny shake of his head.

Again. The parallels.

"So she got involved with Shane, betraying Arturo but knowing it was also her only way to save him and avoid marrying your brother. He was a political science intern at Rutgers, working for my grandfather. She got pregnant by him, and my grandfather forced them to marry to avoid the bad press it could cause, and that was that. Arturo was furious, but he saw why she needed to do it."

That passage is seared in my mind.

"What does that have to do with you selling yourself?" Dante asks, interrupting my trip into my memories. I cringe at his words.

"I didn't—"

"You know what I mean, Lilah. You weren't there because you like to dance. You didn't come with cash in hand. You came with your body, willing to dance to pay off a debt."

I stare off beyond his head, trying to explain the story that is so twisted and confusing.

"My mom loved my dad . . . Shane . . . in her own way. I saw it in her journals. Watching him become a father to Lola, watching him become passionate about politics, about his town, she thought . . . She thought she succeeded in getting out of the darkness that was her father."

"And then Shane went dark."

"And then Shane went dark. And my mom supported him through it regardless. Helped him. She became consumed by him. He became her life's purpose; keeping him out of trouble became her everything. I think that was her biggest weakness. She loved too easy, too deep."

"Where do you come in? If she was happy with your father, why would she go to Arturo? How were you brought in?"

"She wanted him to stop getting deeper and deeper. He was meeting with your father, just like my grandfather had. My mom knew from her own father where it could lead, and not only did she not want that for herself, she didn't want that for Lola—a father who was in too deep, who had greed in his mind. Shane didn't like that, her getting into his business. Didn't like how she was giving her opinion. Their marriage started to fall apart. He became manipulative, verbally abusive in his own way, but she stayed all the same." I sigh. "There was a big fight, and she ran off for the night. She wanted to blow off some steam and, along the way, called her ex. She disappeared for two weeks, holed up with Arturo, wishing she had made the right decision back then." I shake my head.

"Your sister? She just abandoned her for two weeks?" I cringe and nod.

No one in this story is a saint.

"I don't think Lola knows this part. She was four, too young to remember. But from what I can see in the journals, yeah. She left her with Shane and ran off to fuck her ex."

"So your mother had an affair, and you were born." I nod and stare at Dante, praying this is the right call. That my gut is right and I can let him my fortress, and he won't pillage the town. "She was going to leave Shane. Spent the pregnancy planning it out, knew that once I was born and looked nothing like him, it would be obvious, at least to him. She had money set aside and was trying to figure out how to leave with Lola, take her with her. She wanted me to be out of the newborn stage, safe and healthy, before she did. But then . . ." I pause, my mind wondering what my life could have been.

"Arturo was killed," he says.

"My birth father was killed. No one knew why. The case was cold until Johnny confessed. But I think my mom knew all along."

"Your mom knew?"

"She left clues for me in her journals. There was a note on top; she wanted me to find them. There were clues, and I didn't understand most of them until Lola was taken. Then things became clear. I know who made the call." Another sigh leaves my lips, and I wonder if he knows this part or if what I'm about to admit will tear up his world. "My mom deserved more. Your family . . ."

"Johnny. It was Johnny, Lilah. He admitted it when he took Lola."

"It was, but it wasn't, Dante. Johnny was your father's number one." He doesn't have an argument for that. "Johnny killed Arturo, but it wasn't on a whim. Tony put out the hit, and Carmine told him to do it. It wasn't just a random, chaotic thing."

"No, Lilah. Johnny wanted to clear the way to you. Tony planted that seed."

I wonder what kind of bad blood is between the two brothers. What makes him instantly blame his brother rather than his corrupt father. "Your brother put out the hit, Dante, yeah. But it wasn't just him." His face screws up with disbelief.

"Yeah, he was mad. Mad that my mother refused to marry him because she didn't want to be entwined in the family but then went and fell for Arturo. Mad that she risked everything and went back to him, got pregnant, was planning to run off with him. Not sure how he found out that part, but it doesn't matter. But your father . . . Your father had a plan for me."

"Delilah, I know that all of this hurts, that you want to believe there is some bigger reason, want to be able to plan a grand revenge, but—"

"Three months after Arturo was killed, your father came to my mother."

Dante goes silent.

"Gave her an offer. Come to him. Leave my father, stay with the family. Consider getting with Tony."

"By then he was married, and Paulie was already born."

"He was going to leave his wife." His face goes white with understanding. "He was going to leave his wife, take on my mother, Lola, and me. Your father would have a pulse on me, his link to the Russos. His in to take over." Dante licks his lips.

"It was your father who told Johnny about me. He didn't know why he was carrying out the hit. Once your brother was in prison, Johnny rose to Carmine's right hand, and Carmine saw a way to still get his in with the Russos," I say, and the room goes quiet. The air goes static.

"Carmine agreed that Johnny was unhinged, that we needed to keep what happened under wraps because it would give the capos ideas."

"The only person giving Johnny ideas was your father. Your father sent Johnny after me."

"I don't understand—"

"You have your people; I have mine. I have my own connections, my own sources, Dante. You need the proof, and I've got it. The Russos have been your family's rivals since the dawn of time. Your father saw an opportunity. He couldn't take me on—that would be too dark, even for him, and people would talk. But he knew Johnny wanted power, was greedy for it. He knew if Johnny had control over the Russos, he could maintain control of Johnny. He wanted to give Johnny the Russos, Dante."

"There's no way. You were a *baby*. My family is poisoned by power, but—"

"You were, what, 15 when it happened? You might think you know everything, but you were left outside the truth, too."

"And you were a newborn baby, Lilah. How do you know any better than I do?"

"I have my mom's journals."

"Lilah—" There is pity in his eyes, like he feels bad for me for believing some crazy conspiracy.

"Ask your father." My words are firm, and the room goes cold. "He'll know, Dante. Tony couldn't just put a hit on an heir on his own. Just think about it. It makes no sense. Only the Don could do something like that. Wouldn't that need approval?"

"There's no way. The families—they would rebel. It would be utter chaos."

"The Russos don't know, not for sure at least. A drive-by, remember? I've looked at the police reports. They had no idea who it was until recently."

In Dante's eyes, the pieces are coming together, the math is adding up, and I'm watching his world fall apart.

"So what, you're going to tell the Russos and let them destroy us?" He looks at me with near shock in his eyes.

"I don't know, Dante! I jumped into this without looking. And then I got tangled with you, and you made it so much more complicated. I feel like I'm reliving the past, like we're star-crossed lovers with a fucking sea of lies and deceit and blood between us. And yes, I want revenge. I want to make things right. I am *mad*. I am *furious*." I step away from him, waving my hands around.

"This world is sick. It needs to stop. Who knows what else could happen? Marriage proposals for little girls, men being killed because of egos." I start pacing in the entryway of the mansion, my mind reeling. "My sister, my sweet sister who has never wanted anything in this world other than to make everyone around her happy, was being tormented by *your family* for months. Years, even! And that ended in her almost being *kidnapped*. If Ben wasn't there—" My words cut off, that lump coming into my throat the way it does every time I think of this. "We both had trusts. Mine went to school and setting me up for adulthood. Lola's went to your family. Paying for my dad's gambling debts." His eye twitches.

"I'm not blaming you. But I *am* to blame. I know that. I spent ten years in denial of Shane's shady behavior, of Lola's dedication and suffering. Of her sacrifice. I was protected because I was too delicate. Because the world was too dangerous for me. Because I couldn't know the truth. And the worst part is Shane used that against Lola."

I cringe, my stomach nauseous at the memories. "Lola went through that and I lived my life. It's my turn. So yeah, I came here to make things even, to end the debts and make Shane unable to dig the hole again. But I also came because I lost something before I even knew it existed. This world?" I wave my arm around, not indicating the luxury or the glamor, but the *family*. The history and tradition. "I was meant to be here. To grow here. To reign here."

"Your father. You said you were doing it for your father?"

I lick my lips.

The last secret.

The last secret that Lola doesn't know.

My dad doesn't know.

My mom may have known, but it died with her.

"He left me a letter," I whisper. I've read it a million times, tracing the words with my fingers and trying to find some kind of connection to the man who made up half of me. Staring at the photo taken in secrecy of a young man completely overjoyed, holding a tiny baby in his arms.

Me.

It's me.

The man loved me more than life itself. You can see it clear as day in his eyes.

"My father loved me. He said that he couldn't wait for me to make a choice— and a change. The family is all men, he said. That's not right. *Not for my principessa.* He hoped I'd get the chance to rule if I wanted. Hoped the world wouldn't be so dramatic, so violent by then. Hoped it would be safe for me to lead his family into the next generation."

"You want to take over the Russos, and you're going to take down my family to prove you're worthy?" he asks, and I bite my lip. His eyes are locked on mine and that truth serum is flooding from him into me, so I answer in a dangerous way.

"What are you going to do if I say yes?" I ask in a whisper.

He doesn't answer, and I panic.

"Are you going to kill me?" His eyes go soft, so soft I'm reminded of late nights in bed with him when I'm just Lilah and he's just Dante and there are no conversations about blood.

No conversations about betrayal and hits and complicated family ties.

No bodyguards and heirs and fights for thrones and power.

It's just us.

And I feel safe.

"No, Delilah. I would never hurt you. It's you and me. This is it. It's just complicated as fuck now. But in the end, it will be us."

It's honestly not the comfort I was hoping for.

I sigh, giving him a dose of reality.

"We won't work, Dante. You want to beat Paulie, head up your family. I want to make your family pay. And when I'm done, I'm taking my rightful spot. The rightful spot where I'm your *enemy. We won't work.*"

"What if we can?"

"How?"

"Give me time, Delilah. I need time to put things in order and keep you safe." I sigh and try to push off him, but of course, he doesn't let me go.

"I'm tired of being some princess locked away for safekeeping."

"You're a queen." His words run a chill down my spine, but that irritation is still flaring.

"Queens don't hide away. Queens aren't kept women. Their kings don't come to them in the middle of the night to eat their pussy and then run when the morning comes."

"I'm not a king."

"Fine, a prince."

"No, you don't understand, *fiorella*. I'm a knight. I serve you and you alone."

"One of us will rule one day, Dante," I say in a whisper. Because now that this is all out in the open, it's the truth. In all likelihood, if I succeed, there won't be much of a family for Dante to rule. If I fail . . . ... well, there might not be a me to be a ruler.

He stays quiet for long moments, and I wonder if I went too far.

But then he responds.

"You're right," he says then steps back.

"What?"

"You're right. Stay here," he says and then disappears through the hallway

"Let's go," he says when he returns, a small suitcase in one hand and an overnight bag in the other.

"Go where?" I ask, even though I am still burning with rage and anger and confusion and a need to know *what the fuck is going on*.

"I can't talk to you here. I'm not comfortable."

"It's your home."

"*Lilah*." I continue to stare. "You want to talk; you want answers? Come with me." I cross my arms on my chest, the feeling of wanting to know wrestling with the need to stay angry. "Please, Lilah. Come." His voice is lower, his words softer, and he has a genuine plea in his eyes.

And I decide to trust him.

THIRTY-EIGHT

A passage from Libby Turner's journals, written 7 months before Lola was born.

I called Arturo yesterday and told him I was to marry Shane. I'm pregnant with his child, my plan to escape my father's wishes complete.

His fury broke my heart.

He's done with me.

I don't blame him, but I wish he knew I did it for him. If I married Tony Carluccio, I would always be the sharp edge between the future heirs. It would put Arturo in danger forever.

I've done nothing but cry ever since.

I'm sure Shane will be a great, attentive father, and we'll have a beautiful life together. I'm sure I'll learn to love him, that I won't feel this unending pain over time, but I'm destroyed right now.

The thing that hurts the most, though, is the guilt.

In some sick way, I feel relieved, knowing I won't be tied to the Russos or the Carluccios. That potential avenue is forever shut down.

The truth is, I don't think I could have handled living that life if I somehow could be with Arturo. This is the first time I'm admitting that to myself. I think the constant worrying if something would happen to him, if he'd get caught up in the greed and the filth, would destroy me. Knowing my child would be inheriting whatever mess he left behind, would be expected to head the family if he's a boy, that would kill a part of me.

I want more for my children. More than dirty politics and secret deals. More than cash-lined handshakes and the constant worry if their daddy will be at the dinner table or in prison or the morgue.

And more, I can't stand the idea of furthering my own father's corruption by tying myself to the Carluccios. Tony is absolutely barbaric. I've heard the stories—everyone has. Marrying him would be a death sentence at best.

And though I know I've made the best choice for myself and for my family, I still can't help but feel like I've lost a part of me I'll never get back.

Every night since, I've gone to bed crying, wondering what I have done.

THIRTY-NINE

-Lilah-

I don't speak for some time, sitting with my arms crossed for the first hour of our drive, waiting for Dante to start talking. We loop and turn and repeat the same circle along streets both familiar and foreign to me more than once before we slip onto 87, heading out of state.

Watching for a tail.

Or losing one, more likely. *Now, why would Dante have a tail?* I think to myself.

But then again . . . why *wouldn't* he?

One of four phones in the center console rings, and Dante looks, flipping the old phone open and pressing it to his ear.

"Yeah?" he asks the caller, eyes to the road. The highway lights are starting to flick on, dusk setting in. "No, I won't be in until Tuesday. Yes, the dinner is Monday. Yes. Yes, Lilah will be with me." A longer pause. "She's sick. Tell him that she's scared to come to work, and she's taking a few days off." "Him" must be Paulie. I wonder which of his henchman Dante is giving directions to. "No, that's all.

Watch the girls. Have Bianca take over, yeah?" And then he snaps the phone shut.

"Marco," he says, and I run my tongue over my teeth, fighting the urge to speak. "He said he's sorry."

I battle with that, with Marco feeling guilty. It's his job. I should understand more. But also, he gained my trust and friendship. Now, I'm forced to question it.

"Are you going to talk to me at all this drive, or will we sit in silence for four hours?" he asks, and I wrack my mind through all destinations four hours from here, trying to understand where we could be headed.

I don't talk, though.

"Got it. Silence it is." Finally, I snap.

"You're the one who says you have things to tell me. Plans you'll finally unveil to the silly little girl you've been stringing along for weeks," I say, the words creeping from my lips without permission. I don't look at him, continuing to watch the lights haphazardly come on, some blinking a few times, some missing the memo altogether.

"I need to keep you safe, Delilah," he says, his eyes on the road, and despite the dark, despite my anger, I hear the plea in his voice. A plea that I know is on his face as well. "I want to tell you everything. Do you think I want there to be secrets and plans between us?"

"How would I know? Every moment of our relationship started with lies."

"That's not true."

"Oh, really, *Mr. Romano?*" Even in the dark, I can see his lips tip up, and god, I hate that I want to smile too. "What about my flat? Did you do that too?" I ask the question that's been bugging me for weeks. This time, he turns his head to face me for a moment, and his smile is big.

"I don't leave things to fate, Delilah," he says, answering my question without answering it.

"Jesus Christ," I mumble, but in my own way, I fight a tiny smile because it's just *so fucking Dante.*

"In my line of work, you learn that if you put a nail in a tire just right, you've only got three, four miles before it's too flat to drive on."

"Jesus. So, I'm right? There's nothing but lies and secrets in this relationship."

"How I feel about you is not a lie, Lilah. I'm crazy for you. I'm risking everything every damned night just to get minutes of your time."

"So crazy for me, yet you don't even let me in on any of your bullshit."

"God, Lilah." He sighs, a hand moving from the wheel as he runs it through his hair. "I wish I could tell you everything, tell you the plan. Our plan. It's all for you, baby. I need you to know that. But once you know, you're in danger. You didn't grow up in this life, not really. In this life . . . knowledge is dangerous. I want to protect you with every fiber of my being. I can't do that if you know everything. I just can't."

"But it's not just this terrible plan hanging over us like a cloud of death that you're keeping from me, Dante. It's everything. I know *nothing*. Nothing about you, about your family. About *who you are*. You know everything about me, whether I've told you or not. You know things about me and my life that my own *sister* doesn't know. But here I am, living off scraps, trying to paint a picture without all of the colors."

"You know I love you."

"Do I?" I say, looking at his profile. He glances at me, answering with his eyes.

But it's not enough. "A man who loves me wouldn't keep me as a dirty secret." The words come from my lips without thought, seeping into the air like a poisonous gas.

The truth of them makes me unable to breathe.

"You're not a dirty secret."

"The fuck I'm not, Dante. The *fuck* I'm not. This whole thing—" I turn in my seat to face him, moving a hand between us to indicate our relationship. "—has been a mess of dirty secrets. My job, you owning the club. Who I really am. Who *you* are. The way we met." His lips tip up with the words and god, it takes everything in me not to smile too. But this is too important. "You can't tell me your plan," I say, the words solemn and sad.

"I can't." He doesn't even sound apologetic.

"I want to accept that, Dante. I do. I want to take that and run with it and live in my own little world until whatever you're doing sorts itself out. I *want that*. But I can't. We don't live in that kind of world right now. I can't when your nephew is cornering me in the girls' break room, and I'm living off scraps of your attention. When I get secret kisses in hallways, and I get your nights but never your mornings. I want everything. My mom accepted the scraps. She took that from Arturo and from my dad, and look where it got her? Six feet under with secrets weighing her down. So no. I can't just accept some obtuse promise of a plan and sit back and wait. Not when I have *nothing else* to hold on to."

Silence lingers between us as I wait for his response.

I don't know what I'm going to do if he doesn't give just a little.

If he sticks to his secrecy, what are my choices?

Will I ask him to take me home? To let me finish paying off my debts and then let me go? Will I give up on my own revenge plans and try to move on with my life? Start over?

Or will I be like my mother, surviving on scraps and half-truths until it kills me?

My heartbeat fills the car, and I wonder if he can hear it. I watch the clock as the illuminated numbers on the radio screen flip from 7:28 to 7:29 to 7:30.

I fight the urge to break up the silence, though. He needs to make a choice once and for all.

And then, finally, he speaks.

"My father did not protect my mother," he says, his voice low as he stares out the windshield. "I watched him mourn her. Watched the man cry and repent. Do you know what it's like to see a man who, to you, is larger than God cry like that? We went to church every

Sunday until I was 18, and he lit a candle for her. In my eyes, he was a good fucking man. A flawed man but good. My grandfather had raised him well, teaching him about the family, about the importance of community. I thought he was the same." He switches lanes, forgoing his blinker.

"But then it happened again when he let my brother take the fall. Both of their names were on the documents the feds had tying them to that pump and dump scheme, and Tony went down for it. He didn't even try to save his own son. Washed his hands of him and kept going. Maybe that was when I should have stopped believing in him. Believing he was a good man."

"Dante," I whisper, because I think at this moment, during this car ride, in the last hour, he's come to some kind of life-altering realization. It's like I'm watching his childhood crash down around him, that moment when you realize someone you looked up to might not be that great.

And I'm the catalyst.

"But then it was just Paulie and me. When Tony went away, I knew that we—the family—were going down a bad path. An attempt to break into the drugs went awry, and, thankfully, my father backed off, pushing further into the things he knew: gambling, protection, schemes, loans . . . whatever it took to make more money, to feed the greed.

"The family . . . I don't like where it's going, Delilah. I knew for a while, but when everything happened with your sister, when I realized we were allowing political figures to use their children as fucking collateral . . . It's not who we are. Not who we were meant to be. I'm not going to lie and say that the Carluccios are shining members of society. We're not. But that? No. No fucking way. I thought after what happened with Tony . . ." He sighs again.

"The club was my way to offer an avenue of legitimacy. Give my father an example of what we could do. I couldn't take over and insist we back out of the worst of the shady shit instantly. It would be fucking mutiny. The men are used to making certain money and having a certain level of power. I needed a proof of concept that a safer way of life could still give them what they wanted. We could funnel some of our efforts into creating a luxury brand of clubs where not only men come, but women wanted to as well. It might be profitable enough to ease us into the light. We'd treat the girls right and keep them safe. We'll never be fully out of the bread and butter—the gambling and the loans and the schemes—but we'll just be . . . something more." He turns his head to me, the overhead lights on the highway flickering on his face, and in the dim lighting, I can see it. The remorse. The shame. The fear.

"I want kids, and I want to be around to see them. I don't want them visiting me in prison, adding money to a card to call me on Christmas."

He stops speaking like that's enough, like that's all he's going to say.

And really, it's more than I knew before.

But still . . . I want more. I want it all. If this is going forward, I can't keep getting scraps.

"Where do I fit in with this?"

"You're everywhere, Delilah," he says, and I stare at his profile as he drives.

"Explain."

"I heard you were working for me, that Paulie gave you a deal and you were paying off your father's debts, and I knew two things. One, my dumb fucking nephew was blinded by beauty, had no idea who you were other than a mayor's daughter, and definitely had no clue what you truly wanted. Two, he had bigger plans for you." The drunken conversation comes to mind. "Yes, beautiful. You were to be a proof of concept. We're in battle, Paulie and me. My father . . . Up until recently, I believed he was good, started with my grandfather's influence, helping the community, but got sidetracked. I thought . . . I don't know. He's my father."

"I get that, Dante," I say, knowing that my image of Shane has been greatly skewed in the last year.

"I should have seen it," he says, staring at the highway. "Seen him turn sour. God, he's spent the last five years pitting Paulie and me against each other, trying to make us prove we're the best choice as heir to the family."

"Do you want that? To be the Don?" I ask, even though I don't want to interrupt story time. I feel like this, though . . . This I need to know.

"No. Yes. Fuck, I don't know, Lilah. Not for power or for money. But because it's . . . God, it's my right. It's my family. There are people that rely on us, good men. The community." He sighs. It's strangely a relief having him driving while we have this conversation —a distraction from his searing gaze granting me the ability to think straight. "But lately, I've been seeing it differently."

"Different how?"

"I don't want to rule—not alone, at least." I don't respond. "You and I . . . we could change everything, Delilah. The Russos and the Carluccios working together, ruling together?"

"I don't want to be some kind of pretty trophy to sit on a throne with you."

"If you need me to be the trophy, I will be," he says instantly. "You want me to sit back and watch you be fucking gorgeous and all-consuming, it's done. But I was thinking we could be a team."

"Merge the families."

Silence takes over the car when I can't figure out how to respond, and I watch Dante. I watch his face move through emotions and thoughts and plans as he tries to figure out what to say.

"Why didn't you take this to your grandfather?" he asks, finally breaking the silence.

I don't expect the question.

"What?"

"This information Johnny gave you. You could have taken it, walked right into their compound, and told him that my father was planning to take over the Russos since day one and wanted to use you to do it. They're not powerless. They could have done something. Started a war."

A war of my own starts in my mind as I try to bring my thoughts to words.

To tell Dante the truth.

Because the truth will give him all the ammo he needs against me; the power will shift to his hands. The truth will reveal just how much he means to me.

"Because it put you at risk," I admit, and now it's my time to distract myself with the streetlights, watching as they speed past us.

Dante doesn't answer, but his eyes burn on me intermittently.

Finally, I look over at him and catch him glancing at me before looking forward again.

"If my family decided a war was necessary with the information I gave them, you could have been hurt. You'd be the obvious person to retaliate with. The obvious first hit. I need . . . I need a better plan. I need more information. I need . . ." I need a million things.

"You didn't tell them because you wanted to keep me safe," he says, and it's not quite a statement, but also not exactly a question.

Neither of us talks.

I watch four minutes pass on the digital clock in silence before I finally answer.

"I guess so," I say.

"That's how I know," he says in a whisper that I almost don't hear over the quiet hum of the engine.

"What?"

"That's how I know we'll be okay." I stare at his handsome profile but don't respond. He hits the blinker, pulling over, slowing the car onto the shoulder before he slams the car into park and turns to me, cupping my face in his hands.

"That's how I know we'll make it through this. You sacrificed your revenge to keep me safe. You have what you need to take them down. Proof that the club has illegal games, that there's been at least some talk of prostitution. You know your father is deep in debt. Find the right FBI agent, give the information to your family, all the dominos would collapse and you'd be standing there, free and clear and smiling. But you let it sit. You let it eat at you, burn a hole in your pocket because using any of that will bring me down too. I'm not clear, Delilah. I might not be toxic filth, but I'm far from clean. I'm far from good. I broke a man's wrist for *touching* you. I've done worse—much, much worse. And you know that. But you feel it." His nose rubs mine, and my eyes sting as he says the things I haven't admitted to myself.

"I will sacrifice *everything* to keep you safe. I will tear my own father down for even thinking of hurting you. I will make everyone pay, Delilah. I will put you on your fucking throne. This will work because, for some fucked-up reason, the world put you in my life and everything changed. You changed everything for me. And in a way, I know I did the same for you."

My throat closes up, tears lining it.

"It's going to be hard. I won't bullshit you. Change isn't easy, and this kind of change with these kinds of men? It's not just difficult; it's dangerous. I can't just fight, force the takeover. As much of an ass as he is, Paulie has pull with the capos he brought on and the soldiers loyal to Tony. We need to be smart. Strategic."

"Your plan?"

"It's changing, but it's still there." I sigh. I hate this. I hate it so damned much. "I need to reassess. I need to keep you safe. Keep us safe. Give us a fucking future. I don't want a future where you don't have what you need and I'm constantly worried I'll be sent off to prison, where I can't see you every day. But change like that—it takes *time*."

Time.

I don't want it to take time anymore.

"I'm tired, Dante." A single tear drops. "I'm tired of hiding. I'm tired of being kept in the shadows. I want to be me. I want to be me with *you*."

"I know, baby. We'll have that beautiful life, I promise. I'm going to give you the world."

"You can't even give me your mornings, Dante." The look that flashes in his eyes tells me that my words hit, and they hurt.

He is a man who has everything and probably has never been unable to give everything to a woman in his life—and here he is, unable to give me something so fucking simple.

"Play pretend. For a weekend."

"What?"

"We're going away, you and me. No one will know us there. We'll be free to be us."

"Really?" I say, my voice telling even my own ears that I don't believe him. He smiles.

"Vacation. Two days. Just us, no eyes, no ears. Us being together without the rest of the complications the world brings." I continue to stare at him as he sits across from me. "'It means mornings. It means going to breakfast at some place on the lake. It means curling up with you for a fuckin' *rips*."

"A *riposo?*" I say with a smile.

My heart is suddenly unbearably full, my mind distracted by the simple promise of *Dante*. Of being with him like normal. Of him being my *boyfriend*, for lack of a better word, without the insanity.

"Recharge after a mid-day fuckfest." I snort out an unladylike laugh and it feels good. It feels light after the incredibly heavy shit that's going on inside his car.

His hands move to my face again, pulling me across the console until our noses are touching.

"I can't give you everything I want you to have right this second. I can't give you the crown, the title, not yet. I can't give you all my mornings or smile in front of the cameras with you on my arm. I want you to have that—*I want to have that*—but I can't give it to you yet. I want you to have the plan, want you to know everything, but I *can't give that to you yet*. You have nothing from me yet, Delilah. I've given you fucking *nothing*, while you've given me *life*. Do you know what that feels like? To find someone like you, trick you into falling for me, and not be able to give you the world? To not be able to fully prove that choosing me, stooping down to my level when you could have the moon, was worth the risk? How the fuck can I win you, keep you, if I don't have that? I want you to have everything, but the time isn't right. I can't do it yet. So I'm *begging* you. Please. Give me this. Give me this chance to prove myself to you. To give you something to believe in."

"I want to say no," I say in a whisper. My mind is fighting my heart—the common sense telling me to force him to turn the car around.

But my heart wants to give him that. Wants him to have that chance.

So, because I'm stupid when it comes to him, I nod. "Okay."

He kisses me again, the console digging into my rib cage, but I don't care.

Because through his kiss, I taste a single salty tear.

I don't have it in me to ask if it was from him or me when he finally breaks the kiss and drives off into the dark.

FORTY

-Lilah-

Hours later, Dante parks in front of a small cabin.

I can't get the smile off my face as he jogs around the car to open the door, a new, goofy smile I've never seen on his.

"Where are we?" I ask, the wind whipping my hair around. It's dark now, but there's a light on at the front of the house that seems to be on a lake.

"Lake George," Dante says, opening the mailbox and grabbing a key.

Favorite childhood vacation?

The question hits me, and I remember it's one of the many he asked during those first few days at the club before we were anything at all.

"Lake George," I whisper, and in the glow of the front light, his lips tip up further.

"Whose house is this?" I ask, slowly following him as he unlocks the front door to the small house, opening it and flicking on the lights.

"It's mine. Ours. I bought it."

"Ours?" I mimic like an idiot. "You bought it?"

"Yes, baby. Right after you told me about coming here. Figured one day we could bring our kids here, make it a tradition."

"Our kids?"

"Two, at least," he says with a smile.

Then he bends, scooping me up before walking me over the threshold, kicking the door closed behind us.

Locking out the rest of the world.

"Why are we here?" I ask as he sets me down on the hardwood floors.

"You said your favorite vacation as a kid was here. Close enough to drive to, far enough to hide away."

"So those days in the club, you pestering me with questions—were you always planning this? Planning to buy me a house in Lake George and whatnot?"

He smiles, and it's funny how much more at ease he looks here, away from it all.

"No. I actually started those meetings to make sure you weren't trying to tear my family down." I snort out a laugh, and he follows suit, pulling me close and pressing his face into my neck as he does.

"You're a shitty detective then," I say, running my fingers through his longish hair.

"I'm a great detective. I knew that first day why you were there. But I'm also a wise man in that I found the woman I wanted and needed to convince her to spend time with me."

"So you bought my time and grilled me while I wore lingerie?" He licks the skin of my neck, sending a shiver down my spine, before lifting his head and looking at me.

"The lingerie was a perk."

"I'm sure." I roll my eyes.

"Marco suggested I give you the option of wearing street clothes."

"That's because Marco's a decent man."

"Marco is the best man. I obviously vetoed that option."

"Obviously." He smiles, and it's like being this far from home has made him ten years younger. The smile is boyish and sweet and makes me wonder what he'd be like without all the pressure and drama.

"We're here because I want to be normal for two days. You gave me your trust, gave me everything," he says, looking into my eyes. "I want to give you a taste of how beautiful our life will be," he says, answering my previous question.

"Are you ever going to tell me what's going to happen when we get back into the real world?" He holds my hands in his like a plea, kissing my ring finger before brushing his nose against mine.

"Delilah. You want to rule, and I'm going to make you a queen. You want to burn this thing down to the ground, I'll find the kindling. I have a plan, baby. I have a plan to get you everything you want, to get us everything we want. To get Paulie out of the way, to deal with my father, to make you more than a political pawn. But in order to do that, I need to keep you safe. I want to tell you, baby. Want to tell you everything. But there's more to it. And it's not safe for you to know it all now."

"Dante—"

"My mother was killed because she knew too much."

I stop.

I stop breathing.

I stop moving.

"It's not like the movies, Delilah. Not like in the shows where the women are protected and safe. Where they live life blissfully unaware. My mother knew everything. She knew who my father was in business with, his enemies, and his co-conspirators. My father loved her like crazy, despite his flaws. He lost his mind when she died. But she died because she knew too fucking much and he didn't do a thing to keep her safe."

"Who is going to know what I do and don't know, Dante?"

"My mom would have liked you. You're a lot like her, Delilah.

You have passion, and you're eager. You want the world to be good and want to help people even if you're in danger when you do it. If you know my plan, you'll get in the way."

"I'd only want to get in the way if the plan was fucking dangerous, Dante. If you were in danger."

"Every plan is dangerous. In what universe is changing the mind of every man that supports my father, that supports Paulie, that supported Tony going to be safe and easy?"

"I can *help*."

"I know. You will. We just need time." I stare at him, and he sighs, pressing his lips to mine.

"Two days. Two days to be us. Give me that. Let me show you how beautiful life will be when we don't have to hide, when I don't have to worry about you, when we don't have to plan and meddle."

"I don't—"

And then the man who has had everything he's ever wanted in this life moves down to his knees.

I'm standing in the foyer of a small, quaint home on Lake George, staring down at a man fifteen years older than me, the man who, at one point, I thought would be just another barrier to tearing down this family that tormented my own. A man who bought this house just because I told him I have fond memories of being here.

And he is now on his knees, his eyes wide with pleading.

"I am begging you, Delilah. Please. Give me this. Give us this. This is my life—my mess. Before you, I was planning to go down." The world stops moving.

"Before you walked into my life, I knew a change needed to happen. I knew if it didn't, it would hurt everyone around me. People I cared about. People who didn't deserve to get dragged into this shit. Delilah, I was going to take it down from the inside and take them with me."

"Dante—"

"I didn't know if it would mean death or prison, but I was fine with it either way. My family . . . they've created a mess. I thought it was all Tony, his greed decaying away what was once good, but with what you've told me . . . It doesn't matter. What matters is I was ready to take whatever came in order to make things right."

"Your plan . . ."

"You walked into my life, and that plan changed. I had something to live for. Someone to live for. I had a reason to make this world better and give it to you whole. I had a reason to find a new way."

"Dante—"

"Please. Give us this. Give me this. Two days of us. Two days of knowing what is waiting for us at the other end." I count my breaths as he waits for an answer.

One.

Two.

Three.

When I hit ten, he's still silent, still waiting for me to speak.

On eleven, I answer.

"Okay. Okay, Dante."

And then stands, kisses me, and reminds me that I made the right choice.

FORTY-ONE

-Lilah-

I wake up with the sun.

Something is different.

It's not the bed.

It's not the bedding, though the crisp white sheets aren't mine.

It's the body mine is lying on.

The steady heartbeat under my ear, the hand running through my hair. The warm skin my hand is resting on.

It's Dante.

It's morning, and Dante is in bed with me.

I spend long, long moments breathing in, trying to hold in the embarrassing emotion that flows through me as my throat gets tight.

A simple moment, something that most would take for granted.

Waking up next to the man you love.

But it's something I've never truly had other than that very first time.

And I realize now it's something I thought I'd never get.

"Good morning, *fiorella*," the low, croaky voice says.

Morning voice.

Dante has a morning voice.

That's what makes me lose it, what has me bursting into tears.

"Baby, what?" he says, his voice full of concern as his hands move under my arms, dragging me to him.

I continue to cry, mourning what I knew I missed but not realizing how much I did. How badly I wanted this.

"Baby, no. What's wrong? Are you okay?" His hand moves smoothly through my hair as I lie on top of him, my face buried in his neck. "Lilah, you're scaring me. What's wrong?"

I sniff a few times, forcing myself to get it together before popping my head up and looking at him. He's so damned handsome, his eyes concerned but still a bit dazed with sleep, a single line on his cheek from the pillow.

"You have a morning voice," I say because it's the only thing I can think of. His hand moves, pushing my hair back, and he stares at me as he tries to decode my words.

He's so damned good at that, hearing what I say and understanding what I mean, even if I don't fully grasp it. His face goes soft when he gets it, his eyes holding just a hair of sadness.

"Good morning, Delilah," he says, then he uses the hands on my head to pull my face to him, to press his lips to mine.

A good morning kiss.

I force myself not to cry through this, too. To enjoy how his lips feel on mine first thing in the morning, the grogginess of sleep still in my veins as his lips move softly over mine. When the kiss ends, he pulls back and looks at me, his thumb moving to brush a tear aside before pressing his lips there.

Like he's taking away any sadness and replacing it with pure, unadulterated love.

When he pulls back, he's smiling at me.

"Morning sex or coffee first?" he says.

I smile.

And even though I barely function without a first thing in the morning jolt of caffeine, I roll on top of him, kissing him instead of answering his question.

FORTY-TWO

-Lilah-

We spend the morning in bed, but around noon, we finally make it out of the cabin to a little downtown area, where we grab a table at the cutest little sandwich shop.

Nothing is like I remember, but I was a kid when I came here, and I pretty much only remember jumping in the lake with Lola and making s'mores and feeling like I had a place in the world, my mom still there to hold our family together.

Funny how things come full circle. As we walk around, hand in hand and out in the sunshine, though bundled up because it's fall in upstate New York, I feel like I'm whole.

I feel like I'm finally becoming the person I was supposed to be. Not that Dante makes me that person, but like he helped to dig her out, if that makes sense.

We keep walking and then stop, Dante looking down at me with a smile.

"What?" I say, looking up and smiling back.

"Like this." He turns until he's facing me, putting a hand on my waist to pull me close. "Being with you like this. Easy."

"Me too, Dante," I whisper, looking up at him. We're in the middle of the sidewalk, and though there isn't heavy traffic either way, it's clear he wouldn't care if there were.

"You know I'd do absolutely anything for you, yeah?"

"I know that, baby," I say, combing back that chunk of hair. "I'd do the same."

"Never want that." I smile because I knew he'd say something like that. "I never want you to do that. You've given up enough for my family's shit. Now we're gonna be our own little family, and you're not giving up a single thing ever again."

"Dante—" I start, ready to tell him that's not how things work. That's not how I want us to work.

"Come," he says, cutting me off and stepping back. He grabs my hand, tugging me into the store we stopped in front of.

"Why are we going in here?" I ask as we enter the fine jewelers. "Dante."

"I need to pick something up."

"Dante."

"Hello, Mr. Romano," the man at the desk says with a big smile.

He knows Dante.

Or a version of him, at least. I try not to smile at the use of his "other" name.

"Hey, Julius, how's it going?"

"Better now that you've walked in, I assume," he says, and I laugh out loud. "Is this her?" he asks, and I look up at my man, wondering how on earth he has such a repertoire with a jeweler out in Lake George. Dante looks down at me with that boyish smile and taps my nose.

"I've been stocking up for you," he says.

"Dante!"

But he doesn't answer.

Instead, he walks over to a case of thin gold chains.

"This one. Can I see it?" he asks, pointing to a particularly delicate one. Julius walks over and takes it out, laying it on a velvet tray and going over the details, but Dante isn't listening.

Instead, his hands are at his neck, undoing his own gold chain.

Then he's removing it, slipping the St. Christopher off into his hand.

Then he's slipping the flat, gold medallion onto the more delicate chain before he moves behind me, fastening it to me.

My hand goes to it, and before I can even say anything, Julius has a mirror before me.

I should have my eye on the expensive, thin chain.

I should be looking at the medallion.

But I'm looking at Dante standing right behind me, his mouth to my ear.

"St. Christopher. My mother was very Catholic, old school. It's for protection from sudden death. She gave me this."

"Dante—"

"I want you to have it."

"Dante—"

"She would have wanted you to have it, Lilah." That stops me. "She would have loved you, baby."

I take in a deep, shaky breath, looking into his eyes.

They're begging me to accept.

Then I look at the chain, the St. Christopher that would sit perfectly against my skin if I didn't have a turtleneck on.

And then I nod.

But because I can't be easy . . .

"Julius. Do you have any St. Christopher medals on hand? Ideally, the biggest one possible? This guy needs it," I say, and though Julius laughs big and nods, off to find a new medal, I'm watching Dante in the mirror.

He's smiling.

"That's my girl," he says, and then he kisses my cheek before stepping back and meeting with Julius to pick out his own.

FORTY-THREE

-Dante-

Monday morning, the dread starts to creep in before I'm even awake.

It's time to go.

Our days of paradise, of being us in the open without having to worry about stealthy eyes catching us and exposing our secret, are over. We must head back to Jersey, to secrets and plans that I can't share with my girl. To the world of payback and retribution and trying to scorch the earth as we know it to build anew.

She wakes slowly, too early for her night-owl tendencies, I'm sure, the sun barely dipping into the room. My fingers are playing with her hair, and she moans lightly at the feeling. She's like a cat, moving her head toward my hand, eager for more.

A low chuckle rolls through my chest, and her head tips up to look at me, and god. She's gorgeous. Her eyes blink open, and slowly, an easy, sweet smile takes over her face. Just like myself, she got color over the weekend, and she looks even more delicious and beautiful than ever. Like this, she just looks like . . . mine.

God, what I'd give for that.

What I'd give for this every morning.

Every morning I leave her before she wakes kills me just a bit, but I can't bear to wake her, to see this face and hear her voice and be tempted to stay. Seeing her like this, I know I made the right choice in the past.

"Hi," she murmurs, her voice soft and craggy with sleep. I smile at her as a hand brushes hair from her face, tucking it back behind her ear.

What on earth did I do right to convince this woman to give me the fucking time of day?

"I've been waiting months for that," I say in a quiet whisper. Her face moves through confusion, the look mixing with her sleepiness in the most adorable way. "What you'd sound like when you wake up. The look you'd give me. Blew all of my expectations away." My chest tightens, seeing the look on her face, the small, shy smile. Yesterday, she had her own moment of awe at having a morning together. I guess this is mine. "There's nothing I hate more each morning than leaving you there asleep. A fucking angel sent to me from heaven. I think it every time I see you sleeping so damned peacefully. It kills me to leave you."

"Why do you?" she asks, and I think she shocks herself by asking it aloud.

"Too many eyes." The eyes. The ears. They're everywhere but here.

I hate them.

I want this. I want us. I want easy and normal.

But we have a battle to fight first.

"I hate it."

"Me too, *fiorella*. Soon, we'll have this every single morning." I roll on top of her naked body, my cock already hard. "Let me show you what we'll do when we have that."

She smiles her gorgeous, unguarded smile she saves for me for times like these when there's no one around and nothing between us.

"You ready this early, old man?" she says with a laugh, a hand on my cheek that needs a shave.

"I'll show you how ready I am," I say, then I use one hand to guide my cock to her, slamming in to the hilt.

"Fuck!" she moans, but her arms and legs wrap around me, her already wet pussy clamping down like it, too, doesn't want to let me go.

"God, you're always ready for me, aren't you?" I say, looking down at her, her eyes hooded, her mouth slightly open.

Fucking gorgeous.

I can't wait to give this woman the world and for the world to know how mine she is.

"Yes," she moans, but her eyes stare into mine, telling me she means more than just ready for me to fuck her.

She's ready to face the world with me.

Ready to take it on.

Her face is telling me she trusts me. She loves me. That whatever comes, she's ready, as long as I'm there.

"God. Jesus. I love you, Delilah Antonia," I say, pressing my forehead to hers. "I'm so fucking lost in you."

"Dante," she moans in a whisper, like she's worried that if she speaks too loudly, she'll break the spell.

"I know, baby." Her hand moves, curling around my neck, fingers diving into my hair. "I know."

"I need you so much." I know she doesn't mean that she needs me to help her come, that she needs my body or my cock.

I know because I need her just as terribly. That hole in my fucking gut never fills unless she's in my arms, unless I'm breathing her air.

"Dante," she says again, and as she does, she clamps down on me.

"That's it, baby. Come for me, right now," I say, pressing my lips to her as she moans, and I plant myself into her, grinding on her clit and filling her as we come together.

I stay there, holding my weight on my forearms for long minutes as we kiss, smile, and delay the inevitable before she speaks.

"Let's stay here," she whispers almost frantically. "Let's stay here and start over."

"What?"

"Let's stay here. Change our names, get normal jobs, and be normal people. Start over." Her eyes are going wide, excited, like she's convinced herself already. "It could be just us. No families or retribution or rise to power or takeovers." I sigh. I want that and I hate that I need to bring her back down to earth.

"You'd never be safe, baby. I need to make you safe."

"I'm tired of being safe. I'm tired of following some stupid plan, of trying to make up for shit I didn't do."

"I know." Silence fills the room, and I watch her, thoughts flowing over her eyes as she tries to decide if she wants to let them run free.

"I don't want to relive history, Dante."

"What?"

"My mom. Arturo. They thought . . . They thought they could change things. They thought they could be together. They were a secret, and he ended up dead."

"Never. That will never be us, Delilah," I say, my hand on her chin. "Ever."

"You don't know that."

"I know I will move heaven and earth to give you whatever you want."

"I want you. I want us."

"As do I. But I also know it would eat at you, baby. Not having that closure. That revenge." The battle in her eyes continues until it settles, and I know which side won.

"Come. Let's get dressed. We have a long drive ahead of us." She opens her mouth, but before she can even argue, my phone rings from across the room.

My burner.

There are only a few people who have that number, and really, none would be calling me right now.

"I need to get that," I say, pressing my lips to her hair before rolling off the bed and padding to the dresser.

And the name on the display makes me wonder if maybe I should have just agreed to her plan of getting lost and changing our names.

FORTY-FOUR

-Lilah-

When we arrive back at the Carluccio compound, Marco is on the steps waiting. He walks down them, and seeing him has the dread curling in my belly.

We aren't a couple touring Lake George anymore.

We are back to Romeo and Juliet, star-crossed lovers on opposite sides, praying it doesn't end in tragedy. We're back to secrets, stolen kisses, and trying to undo a lifetime of wrongdoings.

"No one's here, boss man," Marco says through the window Dante rolled down.

"Great, thanks. Can you park this so I can take Lilah to her room before everyone shows up?" Marco nods before Dante puts the car in park and opens his door.

I don't move.

Not because I'm trained to stay in a car until someone opens the door for me, but because I don't want to leave this car.

When I leave this car, it's done.

When I leave this car, we're back to secrets and hiding.

Dante opens the door, holding his hand out for me. I stare at it.

"We'll go back soon," he says, voice low, always knowing.

How does the man do it? Always knowing what I'm thinking like we're on the same wavelength.

"For a weekend?" I ask, and he must know I don't mean New York. That I'm asking if we'll go back to that freedom again, and if it will just be for stolen, secret weekends.

"Forever, my love," he says, and his lips tilt in the smallest smile. "Just need some time."

I sigh, taking his hand and letting him lead me into the lion's den before he locks me back in my tower.

At least this time, I go willingly.

"You're meeting my father tonight," he says when he walks into my room, the door locking behind us in a way that feels ominous.

Fitting with the way my blood freezes in my veins.

"What?"

"Family dinner tonight. You're attending."

"But I'm just . . . I'm just your assistant." I would quite literally do and say anything to get out of this dinner.

"You've never been just my assistant, Delilah." I roll my eyes. "But also, you live in my home. You work for the family. It's a family dinner."

A family dinner.

A family dinner.

God.

"Who's all going?"

The look in his eyes tells me I don't want the answer.

"Lots of people, the capos, their wives. Paulie's mother." That I find to be of interest. I've read in the journals about Teresa Carluccio, the woman who is still protected by the family despite her husband being in prison for life. "But you should also know Angela will be there." My nose wrinkles, and the fire that's been kept at bay for a day or two flares.

"Oh, your date will be there, and I'll just be the sweet little assistant you fuck on the nights you're not with her?"

"Delilah, this dinner is important. It—"

"So I have to go to some big fucking dinner that, let me guess, is all a part of your big plan?"

"This dinner is important, Lilah."

"Of course it is—to you. But to me, it's just a misery I'll have to endure, trying to figure out how to keep the look of horror off my face while she's on your arm."

"Don't act like you don't know how to play the game, like you won't put on your siren's smile and make every single man in that room fall for you."

"Oh, is that my job tonight? Is that my task? Is that what this is? Tonight, am I the lovely distraction for the men while you put on some dastardly plan? Is that what all this is? I'm just a ploy, something to further your own plans?" He's mad. I can see that.

Good.

So am I.

"Maybe I'll go off, play the part perfectly. Take Tino or Roddy into a coat closet, suck his—"

"Don't play this fuckin' game with me," he says, pinning me to the back of the door we walked through.

"What's the game, Dante? I can't play if I don't know the rules. All cloak and fucking dagger, every day. You have some master plan that you keep telling me to wait for, that it will help, that it will all work out, that I'll get what I want—but all I know is I work in a strip club, I was cornered by your scumbag nephew who wanted to prostitute me, and that you're fighting tooth and nail to be the next man in power. In power of a family that destroyed mine." My chest is heaving, panic rising as the words I've been fighting down come out. "You don't even believe me when I say your father is the problem, do you? You think there's something you'll find that will prove me wrong, save his soul, save him from what he deserves. We should be enemies, Dante. I'm a Russo. I've sent a note out to Johnny already—"

"You what?!" Dante bellows, and I smile.

"You've got your plans, baby, and I've got mine," the siren inside of me says, despite his hand on my throat.

"How?" He looks at me, trying to scan my face to detect lies, to decide if I'm telling him the truth. "Are you an idiot? You sent a fucking letter? Just a nice little greeting card saying what? Hey, got your letter and I'd love to set up a time to chat about any other trade secrets you'd like to share?"

"I'm not dumb, Dante. I went through the correct channels and sent a note with zero tracking. There's a payphone in Newark. I'm going on Thursday at four. If it rings, I answer."

"And what if someone else is on the line, Delilah! This is not fucking Chutes and Ladders! This is real life. This is not some mob TV show you can turn off at the end of the night!"

"You think I don't know this is real, Dante?" I ask, ducking under the arm braced on the wall and pacing the room. "My sister. My mother. Shane. Arturo. I know it's not a game! But it's my turn to make shit right! There is no other Russo to head the family. If I do it, if I prove myself and take over, I can run that family. I know it. I can run it for my father, for my mother. Arturo . . . He left me a letter. That's what he wanted. He wanted me to do this. He wanted me to have this, to run it right, center the family and the community. Go back to helping people instead of fucking them over."

"This isn't *Robin Hood*, baby."

"Why the fuck not? It could be. I know you know that. You see it too! This family—" My arm moves to encapsulate the Carluccio estate. "This family could be more. It could save this town. You want that. I'm going to make it happen." He stalks my way, moving until his hands are under my armpits and tossing me onto the plush, perfect bed.

"I should put you over my knee, turn your ass red for this shit. Are you insane? This twisted plan of yours. Did you think that maybe one of Paulie's men watched you send that note? Intercepted it? Would follow your trail?"

I didn't.

"I was safe."

"I've been doing this a lot longer than you. You're never safe enough, especially if you don't have backup. If you think you're safe, you're the most exposed you've ever been. If that did happen—if his soldier followed you, if they have your letter . . . What did it say?"

I lick my lips but smile. "Nothing that they would understand. There was a line in his letter to me. I pulled from it. It wouldn't make sense, but to the right person . . ." There is a flash of pride in Dante's eyes that gets swallowed quickly.

"If Paulie—"

"What will he do, Dante? Tell me. Tell me everything." My mind is burning with the potential of knowing, the potential of being a team instead of being stuck in the dark.

Dante opens his mouth, though, and I know before he even speaks.

I know he won't tell me anything.

"This plan . . ."

"The fucking plan," I say with a sigh, the shine of our trip already fading.

"Soon, Lilah. Soon."

"I'll know?"

"Yes." His eyes go dark, and something about them makes me want to recoil, makes me wish we had never gone back to Jersey to face the real world. Like his plan is dark and devious and everything we should be avoiding. Then he's on top of me, balancing on his hands and hovering above me.

"Dante, I—"

"Do you trust me?" he asks, and it doesn't take longer than a single millisecond for the answer to come to my lips.

"With my life," I say, and I expect a smile, a kiss. Something.

I get neither. I get another fierce question.

"Do you know I love you?"

"Of course, honey," I say, my voice going soft because I do. In our own fucked-up, unhinged way, this man loves me, and despite all signs pointing to run the fuck away, I love him just as crazy.

"Do you know that I would never—" He grabs my chin, forcing me to look him in the eyes and see what's there: honesty and fear and longing and regret. "—never fucking put you in danger? That everything I do is for you? That every fucking move I make is to keep you safe and to give you the goddamned world?"

"Dante, this—" His grip tightens, and he speaks through gritted teeth.

"Do you fucking understand that, Delilah?"

"Yeah, Dante. Yes."

"I need you to trust me tonight. No matter what. You put on your siren's smile, and you sit pretty and pretend you're not deadly. Got me?"

"Dante, you're scaring me."

"I will find you tonight. I will explain." His phone rings from where he left it on the vanity across the room, and he curses under his breath. His fingers dig into my chin harder, and he looks at me.

His eyes are frantic.

He needs this.

I can give him this peace, this knowledge that I understand, that I know he loves me, that I trust him. That no matter what chaos happens tonight, I'll be waiting for him after.

"I trust you, Dante. I love you. I know you would never hurt me; you only want to keep me safe. Now please, god, tell me—"

"I can't. You can't know, not yet. It has to be real, *fiorella*. It has to be real."

It has to be real. What? The love? The . . . fear?

"I'm doing this for you, baby. Just trust that. I'm fucking insane over you."

I take a deep breath as his phone stops ringing and then starts again.

"Okay, Dante. Okay."

"Good. I have to go. That's Paulie calling."

"Paulie?" I ask, a foreboding chill running down my spine as I remember the last time I saw the man, drunk and pinning me to the counter before Marco came in, saving me.

"Paulie."

"Why is Paulie calling you?"

"You trust me?" he asks again, and again, that cold creeps over my skin.

I don't like this.

I don't like the look in his eyes, the panic, the unease.

The fact that Paulie is somehow involved in this grand plan of Dante's is worrying. Paulie is poison, that much I know. His idea for how to move forward with the family is toxic. Greedy.

But still, I answer.

I answer even though I know somewhere deep that if I had to, I'd take down this man before me to get what I need. I know that if he teamed up with Paulie, if this whole thing was a charade, I would do it. I would find a way to use my siren's song, the song of my body, my lips, my words to crash his boat against my rocks until he was no more.

"Yes, Dante," I say, and he smiles like he knew I'd answer that way. "But don't mistake my trust for weakness." I stiffen my chin as I stare at him, and the man just smiles that proud smile.

"Never. Your fortress is made of diamonds, my queen. Anyone who could look at you and see you as weak isn't seeing you at all."

That answer is a good one, so I leave it there. He presses his lips to mine, hard, bruising, before standing up, lifting me, and walking me over to the closet. "Come, you have to get ready."

And then Dante shows me a gorgeous gown I'm sure he picked out himself before he leaves me standing in the guest room, fully and utterly panicked about what is to come tonight.

FORTY-FIVE

-Lilah-

The two days of peace and happiness are gone, stripped from him, and back is the man that's tired and worried.

At three-thirty in the afternoon, there is a knock on the guest-room door. My door, I suppose.

The Carluccio compound, I've learned, houses every one of blood who is unmarried or unattached and a few others. One of the others is Marco.

When I open the door, I leave the chain on, opening it just enough to see who is there before smiling at the familiar face.

"Smart, princess. Don't open doors for just anyone." I close the door, undo the chain, and open it again.

"Marco, your heel to that door would be more than enough for you to knock it down," I say with a laugh, but he doesn't even smile.

He stares at me instead.

"You'd lock the deadbolt, hit the panic button, and call Dante."

"What?" I ask, my voice going low at the seriousness of his words.

"You see someone in the doorway you don't want to see, you close it, deadbolt it, hit the panic button, and call Dante, yes?"

"Panic button?" I ask, confused.

"Here," he says, stepping in and walking to the vanity to the right of the door. He pulls out the third tiny drawer, and there's a small red button. A panic button. "It was added while you were away, after what happened backstage. You hit this, I get buzzed. Then you call Dante. He took you shooting, yes?" he asks. And I nod, my breath going more shallow. He opens the fourth drawer, and there's a gun. "Don't be stupid—this is loaded."

"Isn't that, like, dangerous or something?" I ask, my pulse pounding.

"Yes. So don't be stupid," Marco says, and he's smiling.

It takes a moment to realize this is all normal to him.

What kind of life am I living now?

"This is not normal to me, Marco," I say. "I did not live a life of panic buttons and guns in my vanity."

It's then that Marco looks at me, and I know that when Dante says he's his right hand, his number two, he means it.

Marco *knows*.

Marco knows who I am, what I am, and why I'm here.

"If your life had gone another way, it would have," he says, his voice low. "You would have been a princess, but a safe princess." He clears his throat, lowering his voice. "I know your grandfather."

The words ricochet through me like a ping-pong ball.

"He's a good man. He would have made you safe, if you were raised with that family. Not safe because you were locked up, but safe because you knew how to act around dangerous men. You've got some of it in your blood, from your father or from your mother, I don't know. But you've got the sense, can handle the soldiers who step out of line, handle Dante better than I've ever seen." I force myself not to smile. "But in another life, you'd know how to protect yourself."

I keep staring and wonder what this means. What it means for me, for Dante, for the plan, that Marco knows everything. I'm assuming he knows from his boss, but . . .

"Dante knew the day he saw you who you were. You've been my priority since then." Again, the breath stops, answers to questions I've forgotten to ask Dante coming to light. "Never intrusive, just keeping an eye, princess. He worries. There's danger out there, danger you couldn't dream of. And the goals you have, the plans you both have . . . an extra set of eyes is good. Don't hold that against him."

I could argue.

I could yell.

Instead, I nod. Some of this is news to me, but some of it is things I've come to understand myself.

"But next time you need to deliver a fuckin' piece of mail to someone trying to spill family secrets, please, for the love of fuckin' God, don't do it yourself. Jesus." My eyes go wide, breath stopping. "It got to him, princess. But not because you did your job right. Because I found it and delivered it."

I stare at the big man in front of me.

"Dante didn't know about my note until this morning, Marco," I say, my voice whisper soft.

"I don't work for Dante, Lilah," he says, and the world stops.

"What?"

"I don't work for Dante. Love Dante like a brother, listen to him when I have to, do a lot of work on his behalf, even *with* him. But I do not work for Dante."

"I don't—"

"You do. If you think about, you understand. You really think that family would just ignore your existence all these years?" Before I can say anything else, his phone rings, and he glances at the screen.

"We have to go."

And then Marco wraps his thick fingers around my elbow and leads me out to the dining room, where my entire world falls apart.

FORTY-SIX

-Lilah-

Carmine Carluccio is both everything I thought he would be and absolutely *nothing* like what I thought he would be. He's got that air of old money, like he has no understanding of what it's like to be without it, but he also has a second side that makes it feel like he's an underdog.

Dante takes me to meet him almost as soon as I'm escorted to dinner.

Marco stands close to my back, and to me, that is incredibly telling.

"Father, this is Delilah. My assistant." Dante waves his hand between us, and I put a hand out to shake the Don of the Carluccio family's hand.

My enemy number one.

The man who planted the seed to have my father murdered.

The man who crafted a plan to marry me off when I was just a baby.

Funny that now I'm in bed with his least favorite son.

"Ah, of course! The pretty blonde. Turner's daughter, yes?" he says, and before I can nod, his hands are on my cheeks, pulling me in, a kiss to each cheek. "Great to meet you, little lady."

I need a shower, I think to myself.

On the outside, the siren takes over as I smile.

"I've heard so much about you, Mr. Carluccio."

None of it good.

"And I you, Delilah. Carmine. Call me Carmine. We're practically family, after all," he says, and the look in his eyes . . . I've seen it.

In Dante's, when a part of his plan is clicking into place.

My stomach churns.

"With you working for Dante and all," he says, clarifying, but not convincingly.

"Yes. Of course." I force a smile to my red lips, and a hand appears on Carmine's shoulder, a taller man leaning down to whisper in his ear.

"Sure," he murmurs to the man, then he turns his attention back to me. "We'll catch up soon, yes? There's a matter I must see to."

I nod, and Dante says something I can't process before the man walks off.

"You did great," he whispers in my ear before standing straight.

"Dante, who is this?" a sugary sweet voice asks, and when I look, there she is.

Angela *fucking* Sigano, her fingers wrapping around *my man's* elbow like she fucking owns him.

She is everything I will never be in a million years.

Tall and lithe, a Kate Moss-style model. Her hair is long and dark, and her dress is a perfect light-blue color that compliments her skin perfectly.

I want to tear it off her.

Marco, the saving grace he is, takes my balled-up hand and places it on his own elbow. I don't look up at him the way I want to, don't give him a smile, but I do tighten my hand just a hair in thanks.

"This is my assistant Delilah. Lilah, this is Angela Sigano." His eyes are on mine, never looking at the woman next to him, and I don't miss the way he steps to the left just a smidge—just enough to move her hand off him as he puts his in his pockets.

It's then I notice his tie is a deep green, the exact color of my dress. Not a perfect, fair blue.

I smile at him, not the siren smile, not intending to wreck his boat on my shores, but the sweet princess. The one he protects.

My hand moves out to take hers. "Lovely to meet you, Angela. I've heard all about you," I say, and my eyes tell her exactly what those words mean in a way that only a woman can translate.

A small noise comes from Marco's throat, but I just smile.

The bitch stares at my hand and nearly sneers at it.

I raise an eyebrow.

"Funny. I've never heard about you. Lily, was it?"

"Yes, well, Dante and I do spend quite a bit of time together," I say, playing the game, and I watch with pleasure as her face turns a light pink that clashes with her dress. "More time to dish, you know?"

She hasn't learned how this game works, clearly. Hasn't figured out how to hide when the punches hit, how to predict the next move. She's standing in front of me, refusing to shake my hand, and we both know it's not me who looks silly.

Her lips purse just a fraction before she puts her hand out limply, giving me a half-assed shake.

"Dante, can you come with me? I have someone I'd like to introduce you to."

"Maybe later, Angela," he says, and then he has his own nonverbal conversation with the bitch.

Leave. Now, his eyes say.

She sucks her teeth but looks at me, thinking we're still in some kind of battle.

The poor thing.

"I'll see you at dinner, Marco. Nice to meet you, Danielle," she says, and Marco actually uses a foot on my exposed toe to keep me from laughing.

"She seems delightful," I say low when it's just us three in the corner, no one within 10 feet of us.

"Delilah," Dante warns, and Marco finally lets out a small laugh.

"Just saying. You could have picked a better cover. A nicer one, maybe," I say.

"*Delilah*," he repeats.

"Nice tie, by the way. Is that ivy on it?" I ask, taking the time now to see the nearly invisible pattern of leaves on it.

"Covered in you, *fiorella*," he whispers, and a chill runs down my spine at the memory of our conversation, about my wanting to be deadly like poison ivy instead of a delicate flower. Such a small moment so long ago that he clearly remembers.

"Good thing you're not allergic," I whisper in return. He smiles, and suddenly, although a chill in the air tells me the night is only going to get worse, my belly warms.

Everything is going to be okay because this man wants to be covered in me and me alone.

"You should mingle, boss man," Marco murmurs, looking around the room. "Don't want to attract any whispers."

"Got it," Dante says and then looks at me. "Tonight, I'll be by. No matter what fucking happens, Delilah, you wait for me in your room."

"What?"

"Yes?"

"Dante—"

"Agree, Delilah."

The look in his eyes is panicked.

I've never seen it before.

It's *terrifying*.

Regardless, I nod.

"Yes, Dante. Yes."

"Good," he says, relief crossing those eyes. "Stay near her, yeah? You don't have to be on top of her, but near, yes?"

"Got it," Marco says, and then Dante nods and asks off, leaving me more confused than ever.

About ten minutes later, a woman walks up to me in my corner where I'm trying to avoid the party, and even if I hadn't done my research, I would know who she is.

Teresa Carluccio.

The woman who married Tony when my mother refused.

Paulie's mother.

She's gorgeous, of course. She has tan skin and dark hair that stops at her shoulders, a long, deep purple dress on, her makeup so perfect, I just know she had it done professionally. She barely looks 35, much less in her fifties.

"Delilah," she says, a small smile on her lips.

"Mrs. Carluccio," I say, and she raises an impressed eyebrow at me. "I'm well-trained." I smile, and she laughs. "But even if I wasn't, your son is your spitting image."

"Ah, you've met my Paulie, that's right. You're working with Dante?"

"Yes, I am, over at Jerzy Girls. I started as a dancer, but now I'm his assistant."

The key to lying really sits in telling the truth. You can convince people of a lot more if you weave the lies in with the honesty. Bonus if it brings your own status down, if it makes you just a bit more human.

"Dante's done great things over there. Treats the girls great from what I hear."

Interesting.

I wouldn't think Mrs. Carluccio would do much more than plan dinners and go shopping with dirty money she didn't earn.

But instead, it seems she keeps her ear to the ground.

"You look like your mother, you know," she says, and that has me pausing.

How do I play this?

I don't have time to make a move, though, because she keeps talking.

"But even more like your father."

"My sister is the one who looks like my dad," I say, the same line we've always used. Lola looks like Dad, and I look like Mom.

"Not Shane, darling," she says. "Arturo."

My tongue comes out to lick lips that suddenly feel so very dry.

"No need to stress, my girl. I knew your mother. She was a good friend to me in a time of need."

"I'm . . . I'm glad to hear that."

"Yes, well, I just wanted to stop by before dinner and say hello. Let you know that if you ever need me, I'm here. My son—he's a real shit sometimes. Gets that from his fucking father." I blink, unsure of how to respond, and she laughs, a tinkling, rich sound.

"Anyway. Us girls need to stay together, Delilah." Her words have my mind reeling, a memory I can't quite grab firing to life, but before I have time to answer, she's smiling and raising her hand, looking somewhere in the crowded room. "It was a delight to meet you. Let's do lunch soon, yes?" she asks, and before I can answer, she's off, and I'm left shaken.

When dinner is called, we're given assigned seating. Marco is to my left, and Angela Sigano is sitting across from me.

The woman is gorgeous, if not a bit brain-dead, and any man would be an absolute moron not to fall head over heels for her—or at least the promise of her.

Dante leans over to whisper in Angela's ear, and I bite the inside of my lip, using my fork to move around the fancy dinner on my plate. I hear her laugh, the sound tinkling and sweet and perfectly appropriate for the setting.

"Ignore it," Marco says in my ear.

"I'm trying," I say through gritted teeth.

"You know, he has good intentions."

"You know, the reason I got involved with him is because you vouched for him, said he wasn't a creep."

"I said that?" he asks, and I smile. "I was definitely lying then. Man is for sure a creep. Just a creep who is crazy for you." I laugh out loud, and Marco smiles, white teeth against dark skin so handsome, I can't fathom why he's single. "Uh oh," he says, and I look across the way to see Angela smiling and Dante absolutely *glaring* at me.

The look is part like he wants to bend me over the table and spank me and part like he wants to bend me over the table and fuck me so everyone knows I'm off limits.

He does neither.

I smile at him, and he rolls his eyes at me.

The dish is taken away, and I'm that much closer to going to my room to wait for Dante.

Another course and a dessert later, though, and that smile is long gone from my face when there is a tinkling of metal on glass.

Dante is standing across the table in front of me, holding his rocks glass in one hand and looking over the long table.

Over his family.

Every sinew in my body feels wrong as his eyes skip over mine and he looks at everyone.

He skips mine like he doesn't want to see me, doesn't want to know what he might find there.

Then he begins to speak.

"First and foremost, I want to thank you all for coming. We used to do these more often, and I fully plan on getting back into that habit. Having you all here has been an honor." There's a cheer, glasses raising before the room settles to listen to Dante again.

"This morning, I had a long conversation with my nephew Paulie about how the family will be moving forward."

Paulie called him this morning when we were still in Lake George.

God, that feels like an eternity ago.

Paulie also called him when he was in my room. "The Carluccios have always been a strong family and a huge fixture in the Hudson City community. Carmine has done a wonder at growing this family, at making sure we all prosper. But eventually, the torch must be passed." Carmine does a strange chuckle that seems like he both hates Dante's words and enjoys them. "We all know my beloved older brother is not with us, but his only son is. Paulie has been like a son to me over the years, and it's been an honor to watch him grow."

Paulie tips his chin to his uncle like he appreciates his words, like they aren't mortal enemies fighting for the same position.

Like he didn't just get his ass handed to him by that uncle for cornering his assistant in a dressing room and threatening her with prostitution.

My skin crawls.

"And eventually, he'll honor his father in the best way possible—by taking Carmine's place."

The air in my lungs seizes.

He'll what?!

Dante continues to speak, his eyes moving across the room, but not a single word registers. A lifetime of training tells me to keep my face neutral, relax my jaw, straighten my shoulders, and regulate my breathing, but all the while, my head is spinning.

Is he handing off the family to Paulie?

Trust his plan. What the fuck kind of plan is this?

Paulie wants to drive the greed deeper, not clean out the wound.

If Paulie takes the head of the family, it won't be enough to just take down the worst of them—to destroy Paulie and Carmine and anyone who is too loyal to them—I'll have to take them all down. I look around, seeing men I recognize from the club. Men I thought were bouncers or employees who must be soldiers. Men I like, men I laugh and joke with every goddamned day.

Men I know have wives, have children, and have people relying on them. Men who have become my friends.

This web is becoming so much more tangled than I ever anticipated.

For the first time ever, I question my plan to infiltrate this family, to create relationships and bonds with the men here.

Bonds I'll have to break.

But then Dante's eyes land on me, and the comfort, that electricity, that feeling of home accompanies it.

The waves of panic begin to recede.

His face doesn't change, neither does his tone, but I can hear his words circling my mind.

Do you trust me?

Do I?

Do I trust this man who, in the past 24 hours, has been nothing but confusion and surprises? The past three months, really. This man who keeps me hidden away, who tells me it's for my own good, that he's keeping me safe? Who says he wants to help my mission? Who could potentially head the family I want to destroy?

". . . and everything is going to plan," he says at the end of a sentence, and the room laughs, but I don't.

I watch his face, his face that doesn't leave mine, and I know that those words were for me. That was off script.

The plan is going the way he wants it to, and he wants me to know it.

With those words, I have my answer. I trust him.

Turns out, I'll need to for what happens next.

"And even more so when our Lilah fell into our laps." *Our Lilah.* Ours? I'm theirs?

His, yes.

A Russo? Yes.

Theirs? The Carluccios'? *The fuck I am.*

"When Delilah fell into our laps, it wasn't for the best reasons, but thankfully, we're all beyond that now. Delilah Russo has been an asset to the family over the past three months, working with Paulie and me on the business and being a joy to be around."

Russo.

Gasps fill the room all around me, and an easy smile comes to my face.

But inside, I'm screaming.

He just revealed who I am to this entire fucking room. What happened to *if they knew who you are . . . ?*

"Some of you may know Delilah is the daughter of Arturo Russo, who we lost years ago. As we all know, it was a rouge family member who created the rift between our families, a family member who is no longer with us." *Created the rift* as if it hadn't been there for decades prior, growing as his father went down dark roads and my grandfather wanted to maintain the peace.

Everyone around us is whispering and talking, but Dante's voice gets louder as he speaks his next words.

They ring in my mind as if no other noise is in the room.

"And now, I'm happy to announce that Delilah has agreed to marry Paulie, connecting our families forever to end a decades-long feud and grow together."

And the world drops out from under me.

ACKNOWLEDGMENTS

Acknowledgments are weird to me because I'm an anxious girlie which means I undoubtedly assume I'll forget someone.

But over the last year and change, I've built a team of the most amazing, kind, loyal humans I could ever ask for. As someone who has always had a hard time making friends, it's crazy what happens when you put your passion and interest first and find people who align with that.

I'd be remiss to not thank them all.

First and foremost, thank you Alex. Every book I write, I say its for you and that you're all the inspiration I need. You're a real life book boyfriend who deals with my crying jags, self-doubt, and emotional roller coaster not only with kindness and love, but with ease. I don't know how I would do this all without you and I really hope you never make me find out.

Next: Ryan, Owen, and Ella. Please never read this or any of my books, but if you do, let's never ever speak of it. But thanks for letting me be your mom and for being awesome.

Thank you Lindsey, the world's best PA. I'm so fucking proud of what you've already done and I can't wait to see how you grow. Thank you for doing all the stuff that stresses me out and being my favorite cheerleader. I love you to pieces.

Thank you Emily. Thank you for letting me brain dump my ideas to you. Next year is going to be the most amazing year for you and I cannot wait.

Thank you Norma Gambini for taking my mess and making it

readable, for telling me when the girlies are going to love something, and letting me know when the ADHD was ADHDing too hard.

Thank you Madi from Madicantstopreading for the most GORGEOUS cover, for keeping us on track during coworking calls, and for giving me more ideas than I could ever use in a million years. Get ready for Barnes and Noble, babe.

Thank you Steph from stephlivesinpages. Thank you for yelling at me when the imposter syndrome is kicking in too hard, for being the kindest human, and for whining about mom issues and kids with me. 2023 is going to be your YEAR and I can't wait to watch you flourish.

Thank you to my beta ARC's who receive this story and catch the last minute typos and hype me up.

Thank you to my ARC team, the true stars of any hint of success this book will receive. You accept my crazy stories, read them, and share them with the world. I can't thank you enough.

Thank you to Booktok - yes, the whole damn thing - because without you, this would all be something I dream about but never do. Thank you for enduring my cringeworthy videos, finding gems, liking and sharing and reading my books. It makes me cry if I think too long about how much you have changed my life.

But most of all: thank YOU, sweet, beautiful reader. I've loved books for as long as I can remember and when I wrote my first book, I published it thinking there was no way people would enjoy it. You all laughed in my face and demanded I give you more. Being able to share these people and stories with you all has been life changing.

So, thank you from the absolute bottom of my heart.

I love you all.

WHAT NEXT?

Diamond Fortress is coming soon - but not soon enough. So what should you read next?

If you haven't read it yet, Bittersweet is Lilah's sister Lola's story, and a prequel of sorts. It's on Kindle Unlimited here!

Most life changes start with a wake up call.

Lola Turner's wake up call came in the form of saving her politician father one too many times.

Now she's determined to be 'New Lola' - the version of herself that has always been hiding beneath duty, guilt, promises, and secrets since her mother passed away when she was 15.

But the problem with a wake up call is you're the only one to get it. So even though she's moving on, starting her own bakery on the Ocean View boardwalk, the mess that her father always seems to get himself into still is finding its way to her.

Ben Coleman left his hometown and the family business that should have been his to pursue his true passion: art and tattooing. Coleman Ink has become his world, and he's tailored the business to fit his life the way he wants it, rather than the life that was originally laid out for him.

Until early one morning he's woken up by what he thinks is an intruder only to find it's just his new neighbor. His new neighbor, who has no regard for her own safety, wakes up way too early, and seems to have made it her job to tempt him.

But what happens when the grumpy neighbor decides that it's his job to keep her safe, even if she drives him insane? Will Lola open up and share her burden with someone else? Will she be able to keep her family's secrets without getting hurt?

Bittersweet is a contemporary grumpy sunshine, enemies to lovers romance. It is book three in the Ocean View series, but can be read as a standalone.

It is a full-length romance with a Happily Ever After that features sexually explicit material and profanity. This book is intended for 18+

WANT THE CHANCE TO WIN KINDLE STICKERS AND SIGNED COPIES?

Leave an honest review on Amazon or Goodreads and send the link to reviewteam@authormorganelizabeth.com and you'll be entered to win a signed copy of one of Morgan Elizabeth's books and a pack of bookish stickers!

Each email is an entry (you can send one email with your Goodreads review and another with your Kindle review for two entries per book) and two winners will be chosen at the beginning of each month!

ALSO BY MORGAN ELIZABETH

The Springbrook Hills Series
The Distraction
The Protector
The Substitution
The Connection
The Playlist

Holiday Standalone, interconnected with SBH:
Tis the Season for Revenge

The Ocean View Series
The Ex Files
Walking Red Flag
Bittersweet

The Mastermind Duet
Ivory Tower
Diamond Fortress, coming Jan 2023

ABOUT THE AUTHOR

Morgan is a born and raised Jersey girl, living there with her two boys, toddler daughter, and mechanic husband. She's addicted to iced espresso, barbecue chips, and Starburst jellybeans. She usually has headphones on, listening to some spicy audiobook or Taylor Swift. There is rarely an in between.

Writing has been her calling for as long as she can remember. There's a framed 'page one' of a book she wrote at seven hanging in her childhood home to prove the point. Her entire life she's crafted stories in her mind, begging to be released but it wasn't until recently she finally gave them the reigns.

I'm so grateful you've agreed to take this journey with me.

Stay up to date via TikTok and Instagram

Stay up to date with future stories, get sneak peeks and bonus chapters by joining the Reader Group on Facebook!

Milton Keynes UK
Ingram Content Group UK Ltd.
UKHW021315161023
430705UK00021B/762